SINS OF HER FATHER

KATHLEEN MIX

Entangled Publishing, LLC
2614 South Timberline Road
Suite 109
Fort Collins, CO 80525
Visit our website at www.entangledpublishing.com.

Select Suspense is an imprint of Entangled Publishing, LLC.

Edited by Alethea Spiridon Hopson
Cover design by Fiona Jayde
Cover art by iStock

Manufactured in the United States of America

First Edition September 2015

To my husband, three sons, late father, and late father-in-law, and to all the other men who do their best to be good fathers. Every one of you is a hero.

Chapter One

Step one: Lay her body in a casket.

Step two: Bury the casket in the ground.

Step three: Pack her belongings in boxes.

Faith chewed her bottom lip. What about step four? What happened after the boxes were dropped at Goodwill and the last physical remnants of a life disappeared? What more could be taken away?

Early April rain pelted the bedroom window, and she envisioned cold drops turning the fresh dirt of her mother's grave into mud. Her heart squeezed painfully. She shivered inside her gray hoodie and wrapped her arms around her chest.

Finish packing her things. Keep going. Deal with one step at a time.

She dragged a cardboard box to the closet, removed an olive-colored uniform from its hanger, and folded it lovingly. The fabric was threadbare from countless nights of manual labor, but it was a symbol of a single-mother's struggle to support her baby daughter after her firefighter fiancé died a hero.

They're probably together now. Her difficult days are over. Maybe she can finally be happy, standing for eternity beside the love of her life.

Faith removed and folded another uniform. When the box was full, taped shut, and labeled, she filled another box with Mom's huge stockpile of light bulbs. Four cartons on the closet shelf remained to be sorted.

She pulled in a deep breath and tossed her tight braid back over her shoulder. Soon she'd be able to shut the bedroom door, walk away from the drafty tenement where she'd grown up, and go back to the security of her orderly apartment and her exacting job helping to design the next generation of space probes. But would she ever get used to the idea that Mom would never hug her again?

On tiptoes, she stretched up and slipped the first box from the closet shelf. She brushed off a layer of dust and removed the lid. A faded photograph of Grandma cuddling a blonde baby, probably her. Another showing Grandpa when he'd had a full head of hair. A smile tugged at her lips. The box held dozens more to linger over later.

The second box was heavier, the air that escaped musty. A first-place ribbon from a spelling bee. A bracelet of multicolored beads. A young girl's diary.

A diary. Faith blinked, paused, and wiped her soiled palms down the sides of her baggy gray sweats. Fingers shaking, she picked up the fat book and opened the cover.

This diary belongs to: Suzanne Marie Rochambeau

My life from: September 1989 Through: August 1990

Her pulse jumped. This worn volume Mom had cared to keep all these years could supply the answers she'd given up ever knowing. The time span was right. The pages could hold the story of how her parents met. Or a description of her father. Or her mother's thoughts when she was born.

Faith swallowed and moistened her lips. Maybe the pages held the words of pride and love she'd always hungered to hear. Nerves singing with curiosity and anticipation, but stretched taut by a jumble of guilt and fear, she flipped to the first page.

September 15, 1989

Dear Diary, I'm a cheerleader!!! Coach posted the list of who made the squad at lunchtime. Mom says I can stay after school for practices as long as I keep up my grades and get home before dark. Hip Hip Hooray!

Faith turned more pages, picturing her Mom at a lamp-lit desk recording her innermost thoughts. The innocent teenager's happy words warmed her aching heart.

September 19, 1989

Dear Diary, I haven't written much lately because I had to study for an algebra test (98!). Cheer practice is long and lots of hard work but really great! We got measured for uniforms today. They have these really, really cool pleated skirts.

Faith hastened from page to page. The rain-dimmed afternoon decayed into a leaden dusk and the inked words grew indistinct. She switched on the overhead light and stood alone in the silent room, the diary open in her hands.

She turned a page and frowned at the messy script, the ink blurred as if by tears.

I want to die! I don't know what to do…

Faith's fingers turned to ice. Her hands trembled as her eyes sped from line to line. The words slashed through her heart. Sour bile rose in her throat, and she slumped onto the ancient, creaky bed, knees too weak to support her body. She slammed the diary closed, crushed it to her chest, and squeezed her eyelids shut to block out the horrid images.

Oh. My. God.

• • •

Maybe losing her identity was the key to finding *him*, confronting *him*, and banishing the images and questions from her head.

With a spark of hope, Faith dragged her luggage to apartment ten and knocked.

"I need your help!" she blurted as her cousin Josie swung open the door.

Josie blinked, then eyes wide, opened her arms in invitation. "For heaven's sake, what's wrong? Come in, tell me what I can do."

Bending over the baby bulge at Josie's middle, Faith dove into the embrace. She soaked in the free-flowing love and clung to the person who'd always been there for her, the one person who might understand her pain when she revealed her terrible truth.

Josie stepped back and searched her face. "I've been meaning to stop by your place ever since the funeral. You look pale. Are you okay? What's with the luggage?"

"It's a long, unpleasant story."

Josie patted her midsection. "I have seven weeks to listen. What help do you need?"

Faith rolled the bulky black suitcases into the foyer, closed the door, then pulled in a fortifying breath. "I want to borrow your identity until after the twins are born."

Saying the words made the plan real. A jolt of fear accelerated her heartbeat.

A frown wrinkled Josie's forehead. "Why?"

"I went through my mother's things. There was this old diary." Faith squeezed her eyes shut, fighting back the wave of shame gushing through her bloodstream. She stared at the floor and struggled to still her quivering chin. "That story I finally badgered out of my mother, the one about my father, how he died a hero. It was a lie. My mother and father were never engaged. My father didn't die saving six people from a house fire." Acid rose in her throat, and a tight knot formed in her stomach. Could she spit out the ugly truth and let it poison the air? Was she wrong to come here? Wrong to burden Josie so late in her pregnancy? Wrong to share her dirty secret? Wrong to think she could right a wrong?

She gulped a lungful of air. Josie would understand, and she desperately needed someone, because she couldn't face this alone. "My father is a rapist. He brutally raped my mother, stole her virginity, left her by the roadside bleeding, traumatized, and pregnant."

Josie gasped, her fingers flying to cover her mouth. She blinked, stared, blinked again. "Oh my God. Do you know his name?"

Faith wet her lips and forced herself to measure out the syllables. "Victor Telemann. It was in the diary. She recognized him from school."

"Was there a trial? Did he go to jail?"

"No. He threatened her, told her if she ever said a word to anyone he'd find her and do something worse. She was terrified and never told a soul."

"But how did she explain her pregnancy to Grandma and Grandpa?"

Faith pictured the tear stained pages in the diary, and her heart knocked once, hard. "She hid it for as long as she could. When she started to show and had to admit I existed, she let them think she had a boyfriend but refused to tell them his name."

"Oh, Faith." Josie pulled her into another tight hug and rubbed circles on her back. "The strict curfews, the super-conservative clothes, her panic when we wanted to live off campus, the way she messed up your mind with the strange ideas about men and sex so badly that you're still a virgin, it all makes sense now. No wonder she was so paranoid."

"I want to forget what she wrote about that night, but I can't. Her words keep haunting me. They'll probably give me nightmares for the rest of my life." She blew out a long slow breath and summoned up a sliver of courage. "What he did disgusts me. I have to do something about it."

Josie leaned backward and cocked her head to the side. Her eyes clouded with concern. "What exactly are you planning?"

Faith stepped away, wrapped her arms over her chest, and resisted the impulse to pace. "I'm going to find him and see he's brought to justice."

"Whoa. Finding all this out while the pain of your mom's death is still raw must be hell. But come on. It's not like you to be rash. Slow down, think this through."

"I have. I need to see his face." *I need to know I'm not like him.*

For the hundredth time in the last fifteen hours, her mind's eye saw a textbook illustration of how both the mother and father contribute genes and chromosomes to a fetus. She shuddered. Could she ever stop wondering which of her genes came from the animal who'd raped her mother? In what and how many ways she was his daughter? If she'd inherited evil in her bloodline?

She looked up, waiting for Josie to reassure her she was a good person, needing to hear logical arguments from someone else. But Josie's lips were pressed tightly together, contemplating her plan to find *him*, seeing only the surface of her anguish.

Faith stared into near space and fought her inner demons.

"Do you know where to look or anything about him?" Josie finally asked.

"He wasn't in the local phone book, but I looked through an online directory and found he has an older brother who still lives in town. I called the brother and told him I was helping my mother plan a high school reunion. He gave me a current address in Palm Beach, Florida." She motioned toward her luggage. "I'm on my way to the airport."

Josie's frown deepened. Maneuvering her big belly with

care, she sank onto one end of the lilac leather couch. "I'm not sure that's a good idea. What are you going to do? What can you do?"

"For a start, I can apply for a job at his company, watch and listen, dig into his past, and examine his life under a microscope. If I find out everything there is to know about him, I can identify his Achilles' heel. I've already Googled him and dug through some of the results. The Victor Telemann who lives in Palm Beach is married to a rich widow, runs a chain of exclusive stores named Emmeline's, and has a penthouse office at the corporate headquarters." She perched on the other end of the couch and fisted her hands in her lap. "It's not fair. Mom had to drop out of high school and spend her life as a penniless cleaning lady. Yet her rapist is living in luxury."

"Does he know about you?"

"I don't think so. Nothing in her diary indicates she ever saw him or talked to him again."

Josie's warm hand squeezed Faith's forearm. "I don't like this. You don't know what you'll be getting into. If you accuse him of being a rapist, he could become dangerous."

Faith stiffened her spine and gathered her confidence. "If I borrow your identity, he won't recognize my last name and suspect I know about his past. I'll be able to stay under his radar while I size up the situation, explore my options, and hopefully, collect evidence. People have always thought we were sisters. I can pass for you."

"If I let you do this, you'll be miles out of your element," Josie said. She gathered steam. "Have you ever even *seen* a real criminal? Why not leave it to the police?"

"All I have is Mom's diary, and she never even reported

a crime. He'd just claim the sex was consensual. I called a lawyer friend who works for the Commonwealth's Attorney and asked her opinion. She said the only way to put this creep behind bars without a victim's testimony is a confession."

"Even if he did confess, it's been twenty-six years. Wasn't the crime too long ago?"

"Virginia doesn't have a statute of limitations on felony rape." She clenched her jaw. "I have to do this. I'll never have peace of mind until he's punished. I considered doing nothing, taking the safe and easy path, but then I'd be giving in to fear, admitting I'm weak, acting as badly as people who walk away when they see a crime in progress. I don't want to be that kind of person. How could I live the rest of my life knowing I'm a quitter and a coward?"

"Revenge can be an ugly goal."

"I know, and I know some people won't approve of what I'm doing. But if I crawl away from this, it will haunt me forever."

"Look at this objectively and give it up," Josie said. "He probably won't confess."

Disappointment pressed on Faith's shoulders. Josie was blind to the crevasse the shameful truth of her parentage had carved in her soul. No one else could understand her hunger for inner peace.

"If he won't confess, I'll see justice done some other way. I'm terrified, but I'm not going to let my fear stop me. I'm going down there. With or without help."

Josie met her gaze, hesitated, then cleared her throat. "I don't like you putting yourself in danger. So much could go wrong." She crossed her arms over her chest. "Okay. If it's that important to you, you can use my identity, but only under two conditions."

Faith's heart did a somersault. Relief or fear? "Thank you. What conditions?"

Josie's chest rose as she sucked in a long breath. "First, you have to agree to think carefully about everything you do. You can't let this get out of hand." Her hands slid lower and caressed her baby bulge. "And I mean that from a selfish angle, too. I don't want any trouble with the babies coming. Protecting them has to be my first priority."

"I could never endanger you or them. I promise not to do anything stupid, and I'll accept full responsibility for every move I make. What's the other condition?"

"You have to totally be me. You have to take my clothes, my makeup, my shoes, and even act like me." Josie fingered Faith's gray slacks then her tailored, white blouse. "Knowing you, those suitcases contain six outfits in shades of gray and another six in navy. To convince people you're me, you'll need bold colors, prints, and stripes."

"Hopefully, no one there has ever met you."

"Hope isn't a good enough strategy. The slightest glitch could give you away. What if someone checks an employment reference? One of my former employers could make an offhand comment or relate an anecdote that reveals you're an imposter. Plus there's always the chance someone where you're working could be within my six degrees of separation. Or yours. Some of our Tech classmates were from that part of the country." She smiled like an understanding sister, and her gaze softened. "Who knows, wearing my things could even be good for you, get you out of your shell."

"You tried dressing me in bright, sexy clothes in college, remember?"

"That didn't work because you were still Faith in every other way. Now you'll be me. Anything you do will reflect on me, not you. That'll be liberating."

"What if I embarrass you?"

"Have you ever known me to be embarrassed?"

A slide show of memories tugged Faith's lips upward at the edges. All her life, she'd sat on the sidelines and secretly envied Josie's ability to mix with people and have fun. "Now that you mention it…"

"Good, then it's settled. You take my pre-preg wardrobe, and just to be sure you don't back out and wear something conservative or mousy, you leave all your stuff here."

Faith shook her head. "I doubt the masquerade is necessary."

"Maybe not, but you can't be sure. You don't know anything about the situation there or what this man might do if he figures out who you are. You'll be safer if you become me 100 percent. Of course, if you'd rather not use my identity…"

"Hard ass."

"You have to promise you'll give an Oscar winning performance." Josie held up her right hand.

The man who'd ruined her mother's life had strolled away, become rich, and was leading the good life. Somehow, she had to bring him to justice, and somehow she had to untangle the mystery of her DNA. Until she knew whether her genes were stained by black, remorseless evil or just one gray, guilt-laden mistake, how could she not worry about who she was deep inside?

Faith raised her hand. "Okay, I swear. Acting like you should be a slam dunk compared to getting a criminal who is walking around free to admit to rape."

. . .

Faith breathed deeply of the aromatic steam and sipped chamomile tea from her mug. The penetrating heat soothed her taut nerves. She glanced at the clock on Josie's nightstand. "Yikes, my flight leaves in less than three hours." Feeling a jolt of panic, she went back to emptying her suitcase. "We'd better hustle if I'm going to make it."

Josie folded a crimson mini-dress and said, "I hate to see you chop off your beautiful, long hair. But you definitely have to dye it. As a blonde, you resemble your Mom more than me. That similarity could spark a memory and give you away."

"I know. I'll get it cut and dyed when I get to Florida. I bought tinted contact lenses so my eye color will match yours. But the plane tickets are in my name, so I need to use my own ID to go through airport security."

"I'll have to keep my driver's license, but you can take my passport and birth certificate for later," Josie said, pinching her chin. "You should take my social security card and a copy of my résumé for when you apply for a job."

"Using your résumé probably wouldn't work if we hadn't both majored in Computer Science, but hopefully I can pass for a database specialist."

"Speaking of jobs, what about your job in Norfolk?"

"I called my boss and told him I'm taking my three weeks vacation plus another three weeks leave without pay. If this takes me longer than that, I'll have to quit."

Outrage flashed in Josie's eyes. She planted her hands firmly on her hips. "Don't you dare even think that. You worked too hard to get where you are. You've dreamed of having a part in space exploration for as long as I can remember."

Faith forced nonchalance into her voice. "I'll have to do whatever's necessary." Her mind ran through the list of everything else at risk: the self-esteem she'd scraped together since college, her reputation and the respect of coworkers if it became known her father was a felon, and if there was the slightest legal repercussion, the future that depended on her secret-level security clearance.

She pushed away her worries. She would approach this problem systematically and deal with it quickly, smoothly, and discreetly. In six weeks, she'd be back home, in her familiar office, going on with her career and her life.

First steps: Finish packing, call a cab, twenty-five minutes to the airport, fifteen minutes in line to check her bags, security screening, a rental car reserved…

"I almost forgot," she said. "I may be forced to get a driver's license in your name once I change my appearance. Is that okay with you?"

"Go ahead and sign my name if it's necessary." Josie huffed out a breath and gave her a smile laden with love. "You and Cal are the only two people in the world I trust enough to say that to." She reached over, grabbed her purse from the closet, and pulled out a wallet. "Here, you'll need a credit card."

Tears of affection and gratitude blurred the plastic card as she pushed Josie's hand away. "I can't take that."

"You have to. If you use your own card, you could blow your cover." She smiled. "Wow, I've never said *blow your cover* before. This is a little exciting."

A chill rippled down Faith's spine. "Terrifying is more apropos."

Josie banged the heel of her hand against her forehead. "Sorry. For a minute there, I forgot this isn't about my little cousin setting off on an adventure. It's a search for a scumbag and some justice."

"I hope so." Faith flipped open her purse. "I'll leave you some cash to pay the credit card bills until I get an address where you can forward them."

"Wow, where did you get that wad?"

"My mother was paranoid about men, and men run most banks, so she never trusted banks. I found cash hidden under rugs and her mattress and taped to the backs of drawers. She had five thousand in the refrigerator in a plastic bag. Altogether, she stashed almost thirteen thousand. It seems fitting that I use part of it to finance my trip to find her rapist."

Josie sighed. "Poor Auntie. That man really messed up her life and her mind."

Faith nodded and sank onto the bed next to the suitcase. "Reading about what she went through broke my heart. Her diary entries from before the rape were written by a normal teenager. She was excited your mom was pregnant with you and anxious to become an aunt. But afterwards…."

The lump forming in her throat made breathing difficult. "Grandma and Grandpa put her through hell, dragging her to mass every day and making her sit through counseling sessions with a priest. They shamed her for having premarital sex and browbeat her with the idea she'd been brought up respectably. The quote in the diary was 'You should have followed your sister's example of proper behavior.'"

She stole a glance at Josie's swollen middle. Their

grandparents had cut Josie out of their lives when she'd moved in with Cal without being married. Now that Cal had been deployed to Afghanistan and the twins would be born before next June's wedding, they no longer spoke Josie's name.

Maybe she, of all people, can understand what Mom went through.

Faith pulled her focus back to her mother and the events described in the diary.

Josie moistened her lips. "The more I hear about the terrible things that happened back then, the more worried I get about what you're planning. This man is evil, Faith. You need to be careful. He could hurt you and ruin your life too."

Her heart went stone cold. "He did that years ago. Every second of my life, he's been like a black cloud hanging over my head. Every time my mother looked at me, she had to be reminded of the horror of that night. Every time I misbehaved, she had to wonder if I had his evil tainting my blood. I was a weapon he tortured her with right up until the day she died." Hot tears flooded and stung her eyes.

Josie rushed over, sat beside her, and squeezed her hand. "Your Mom loved you."

"She tried. Really tried. And I loved her more than she'll ever know. But her love was poisoned by uncertainty. It was probably not conscious, but she always made me feel like I was fundamentally flawed. Do you remember when I was nine she accused me of taking money from her change jar? I lost my bike for a month. And after the shortage turned out to be a mistake, the jar was hidden away to remove a source of temptation. I felt the distrust and believed it must be deserved, but never knew why."

Faith strained, but couldn't get her voice to rise above a whisper. "Mom always had doubt and worry in her eyes. I understand it now. She wrote that she couldn't be sure how I'd turn out, whether I'd be a product of nature or nurture."

Josie rested a hand on the bulge at her middle. "No parent can be sure of their child's future. Worrying you'd inherit your father's dubious character must have been hell."

Faith hesitated, wanting to divulge how tortured she was by those concerns. Wanting to reveal that, just last year, she'd shown dubious character by cooperating with the CIA when they'd asked her team to adapt a long-range radio signal detection system so agents could eavesdrop on Americans overseas who were suspected of consorting with terrorists. At the time, she'd rationalized invading someone's privacy as justified for national security. Too late, she'd realized the project randomly spied on innocent tourists and exchange students.

Since reading the diary, that moral lapse had acquired a disturbing new dimension.

Guilt and her oath of secrecy caged the confessions inside. "He caused those doubts, did that to her. To our relationship. I'm not going to rest until he's held accountable for all his crimes."

She dropped her gaze. She'd been telling herself to approach this problem the same way she'd build a complex software program, one simple step at a time. But logic and her old coping mechanisms were failing. Everything kept coming back to raw, bleeding emotion.

She had to know: Who was this man who'd fathered her? Were her mom's worries justified?

Chapter Two

Five hours after leaving Josie's apartment, Faith stuffed her luggage in the rental Toyota's trunk and drove away from the West Palm Beach airport. The air conditioner fought a valiant battle against the April afternoon's heat. She squinted into the blinding sunshine. Palm trees lined the six-lane highway, each one a silent reminder she'd entered a foreign world.

A jumbo jet lifted from a runway and roared overhead. It banked and headed north, and she longed to be flying home to Williamsburg, her mission accomplished.

She jerked her eyes back to the road. She had to attack the next few weeks one day at a time, and the current day's remaining challenge was to get to her hotel.

It was a Sunday, but her home streets had never seen this much traffic, even on a weekday at rush hour. Speeding cars and trucks recklessly cut from lane to lane. Entrance ramps merged, right and left lanes were exit only, the python-like highway curved and branched. How was she supposed to both drive an unfamiliar car and navigate? She chastised herself for letting her nerves get the better of her. She should have had the presence of mind to input her destination into the car's GPS before she'd left the airport.

Squeezing the steering wheel and worrying her bottom lip between her teeth, she hugged the right hand lane and kept pace with the traffic to avoid posing a hazard. Sign after sign sped by, announcing unfamiliar roads and places. After twenty grueling minutes, she spotted exit thirty-nine, took the turn, and braked at the end of the ramp. Her foot poised to pounce on the accelerator, she flipped on her left turn signal and waited for a gap in the passing traffic.

Someone blasted a horn. She glanced in the rear view mirror and cringed at the disdainful scowl of the driver in the car behind. Gritting her teeth and tuning out his noisy protests, she focused on the traffic whizzing by in a solid line. The Marriott sign and driveway came into view just past the next intersection. With a sigh of relief, she turned in and parked in the only empty spot, four rows away from the five-story building.

Dressed in Josie's scarlet scoop-neck tee, skinny jeans, and half-size-too-large, strappy stilettos, Faith rolled her carry-on across the oven-like parking lot and into the crowded lobby. Men in dark suits stood talking in small groups. Had she stumbled into a convention?

Every man she passed seemed to stare. The unfamiliar attention plucked at her already stretched nerves. If only she had access to stealth-paint technology that would make her invisible.

She queued up at the end of a mile-long registration line.

Her brain swirled with thoughts of long-ago rape and recent death, finding her way in a strange city, and confronting a criminal named Victor Telemann. Her father. She pictured a faceless man cackling like the Wicked Witch of the West when she demanded a confession.

Josie's words echoed in the vault of her memory: *If you accuse him of being a rapist, he could become dangerous.* Was that true and was involving Josie a mistake? Suppose somehow her ruse put the people she loved in harm's way? Guilt crawled up her spine and sat down heavy on her shoulders. Maybe she was being selfish and should risk using her own name. She shuffled closer to the desk.

Look at this logically, the voice of common sense whispered in her ear. *Josie will be safe in Virginia, a thousand miles from West Palm Beach.* Her pounding heart slowly calmed. Not to worry. She wouldn't let her plan go awry.

Of course, it would help if she actually had a solid plan.

She'd spent most of her flight trying to work out the details of a plan and had gained little more than a splitting headache. Everything hinged on the situation as she found it. Trying to draw up a detailed plan without more information was like attempting to solve a differential equation with a million and one variables. Next to impossible. As much as she'd love to have a waypoint-by-waypoint roadmap to follow, the most she could hope for right now was the ability to see a few steps ahead.

The key to everything was to get close to Victor Telemann without being noticed. Then with some luck, some social engineering, and a lot of electronic snooping she might be able to determine if he was involved in any criminal activity. As soon as she found something significant, she would go to the police and convince them to open an investigation. They could get permission to bug his office, search his trash, analyze financial records.

With his arrest and exposure as a criminal as her goal, her best course of action was to pursue Plan A—get a job at his company. But that could be a dead end. Or she could fail to find evidence he was breaking the law. In either of those cases, she could try Plan B, which was to confront him while wearing a recorder and try to get him to admit rape. Since success with that scenario was a long shot, she needed a Plan C. Which, right now, she didn't have.

She rolled her carry-on two feet forward and noticed a middle-aged man obviously staring at her chest. She angled her back toward him, and her cheeks heated in mortification. Why had she ever agreed to dress as Josie? She stole a quick glance back at the man to see if he'd looked away. A smirk twisted his lips. His prying eyes seemed to be mentally undressing her, violating her privacy. A chill crawled across the back of her neck. Did her father give women the creeps too?

Disgust flared in her chest. The creeps of the world shouldn't be allowed to win.

Be Josie. React like Josie would react.

Faith straightened her spine and glared at the man until his eyes skittered to her left.

A tiny thrill of victory tickled her soul, and she turned her attention back to the line. She was next. The clerk met her gaze, smiled, and nodded.

She stepped toward the registration desk. Once she signed Josie's name, the die would be cast. She would start the lies and deceit.

"May I help you?"

Faith squared her shoulders. "Yes, I'm Josie Ashland. I have a reservation."

. . .

Persistent ringing jarred Kent Telemann from a deep sleep. *The phone.* He groaned and rolled toward the bedside table, reached out, and blindly felt for the receiver.

Finding the smooth surface and distinctive shape, he dragged it to his ear and mumbled, "Hello."

"Good morning, dear."

"Hi, Mom." He sighed and opened his eyes. His eyelids were heavy as lead, and he rubbed his fingertips across them and blinked. "What's happening? I hope after twenty-nine years you're not still trying to change my habits and teach me to get up early."

She laughed. "You know me too well."

Kent sat up as the blonde who'd spent the night in his bed walked out of the bathroom fully dressed. Memories returned. The sex had been great, but she'd kept him awake for an hour with her attempts to cuddle and spoon. He rubbed his scratchy eyes again. Why did she have to be a snuggler? It was always hell lying there wondering how soon he could break away without hurting a woman's feelings. Why couldn't they just roll over and give him space or, better still, go home?

"Hang on a second, will you, Mom?"

The blonde smiled broadly, strutted to the bedside, then leaned over and placed a soft kiss on his brow. "I'm starved. Are we going for breakfast?"

Kent stared at the cleavage conveniently positioned only inches from his face, but resisted the temptation to fondle her offering. "Sorry, sweetheart, I have a lot of work to do. Why don't you go home, and I'll try to call you later."

The woman stuck out her lower lip in a pout. "I could come back to bed instead."

Kent shook his head, took her hand, and kissed her fingertips. "I'd love to, but I don't have time today."

The woman picked up her purse and pantyhose, gave him a fluttery-fingered wave, and strode toward the door, strutting her stuff. The sway of her hips rang a bell. A beauty pageant runway. Was she Miss Arizona? Miss Alaska? Arkansas? Kent realized he didn't remember her name, or even her state, and wouldn't be able to call. He shrugged off the disturbing thought, stood, and walked naked toward the drapes drawn to obscure the wall of windows.

"Are you still there, Mom?"

"Yes, dear. Do you have a woman there with you again?"

He pulled the cord and opened the drapes to reveal the four-million dollar view of Jupiter Island's beach and the Atlantic Ocean. "Yes, Mother, I had a woman here. But she's on her way out the door."

He heard a sigh on the line. "Do I know her?"

"No." *I don't even know her.*

"I don't suppose you want my lecture about destructive, shallow relationships and how much I wish you'd gone through with your marriage to Angela."

The front door clicked shut behind Miss Some-state-beginning-with-A. He vaguely remembered she'd followed him home in her own car sometime after three, so she didn't need a ride.

"No thanks. Other than my sex life, what's on your mind this morning?"

"I want you to plan on coming to the house for dinner Friday night after you get back from your trip."

Kent strenuously avoided any event where he'd have to be near his stepfather. He pictured sitting down to dinner with her and Victor, and the thought of watching Victor pretend to be a faithful, loving husband ignited a slow burn in his stomach. If only she would stop refusing to see the truth and finally demand a divorce.

"Listen, I'm going to be really bushed that night, Mom, you know, jet lag and all. Can I beg off and see you after you get back from Paris?"

"I'm not going to Paris."

"What? Why not?" he asked, suddenly wide awake.

"Victor's going alone. He thinks having me there will be too much of a distraction from work. We decided to plan another trip later when we can just take a vacation."

Kent squeezed the phone receiver and gritted his teeth, wishing he could ring that bastard's neck. He'd lay odds the work excuse was a crock of pure bullshit. Victor had probably decided to take along his mistress.

He set his jaw in determination. Next time he met with Victor, he would be adding a new topic to the meeting agenda. Unlike his acquiescent mother, he didn't intend to stand idly by and let Victor get away with this sleazy trick.

"You should insist he take you anyway," he said. "If I know you, you've been looking forward to a couple days of serious shopping."

"I was, and I'm disappointed I won't be able to visit my college roommate before she and her husband move to

Hong Kong. But the shopping can wait, and I'll see Renee next year at our reunion."

Her voice seemed overly cheerful, like she was hiding her hurt. Or maybe something else was going on beneath the surface. Kent hoped she suspected Victor would be cheating on her. She always pooh-poohed the idea when he'd suggested his stepfather had a roving eye. Maybe she was ready to accept the truth.

"I could arrange for a detective to keep an eye, and a camera, on Victor," he said.

She chuckled, but there was no amusement in her voice. "Don't be silly, dear. I'm not worried about Victor. You're the one I worry about. You need a home with a wife and children, not endless parties and meaningless sex night after night."

Kent blew out his breath, not wanting to go there. He suspected she'd switched the topic back to his sex life to avoid the subject of Victor's infidelity.

To both his pride and frustration, his mother was a classic southern lady. Emmeline Morris Telemann had attended an exclusive finishing school, was always perfectly dressed and coifed, and was unable to act counter to social decorum. Accusing her husband of whoring would be crossing a line and admitting her life wasn't impeccable and proper. In her mind, confrontation just wasn't done. Marriage to a man like Victor required a stiff upper lip.

Kent wanted to give Victor a fat lip and send him packing.

"I like to date beautiful women, Mom. There's nothing wrong with that. Besides, it's your fault I need to shop around. You spoiled me as a child and set the high standard for all my dates to meet."

She laughed. "I did spoil you, but it was because you were so charming. Anyway, stop trying to change the subject. When are you going to get serious about a woman?"

"I don't know any women I'd want to be serious about. I have all the companionship I need, and I'm happy. "

"Did you ever call Sarah Davis after I gave you her number?"

"No." Out on the beach, his new neighbor settled her two young children and their buckets and shovels at the water's edge, then she stretched out in a lounge chair. He wondered if this Sarah was looking for that sort of quiet, family life.

He ran his hand through his rumpled hair. More likely she was someone who could make his life a living hell. His mother's marriage to Victor had shown him how disastrous a bad marriage could be. Better to spend his life with a parade of empty-headed bimbos than let down his guard and put his neck on that chopping block.

"But, dear, Sarah's a very nice girl. A talented lawyer, I believe."

The better to squeeze a huge divorce settlement from the schmuck who marries her.

"The only serious date I want is with my mother. How about meeting me for brunch at Andres' before my flight? The deal should go smoothly. Emmeline's two major stock-holders should be able to celebrate a little early."

"A champagne brunch sounds wonderful. Shall I bring Sarah?"

Kent laughed. "If you do, I'll stand you up."

He disconnected the call and snorted at the irony of the situation. His goal in life was to see his mother divorced. Her goal was to see him married.

. . .

After a restless night, Faith waited her turn at the hair salon recommended by the beautifully-coifed woman at the hotel's reception desk. She ground her teeth and breathed in the choking odors of perm solution, hair spray, and dyes. She hated the idea of putting chemicals on her hair, but a wig would be too hot. Dye was the only answer.

A stylist named Margie directed her to a chair. Faith squeezed her hands between her knees and squelched the urge to run.

The stylist frowned as she ran her fingers from Faith's crown to the hair tips that brushed her waist. "I have clients who would kill for this hair, Sweety. You sure?"

"Positive. Give me the style and color in the photo."

Faith shut her eyes, waiting for the first slash of Margie's scissors. The comb pulled and parted. The scissors clicked. She choked back tears. Ever since she was a little girl hungry for her mother's approval, her hair had been a source of pride. The silky locks had brought her attention. She'd clutched every compliment to her heart like a stash of ammunition to use against her insecurities.

What would she do without her hair?

Her head became lighter and lighter, and with every click of the scissors, she felt more exposed to the world. She clutched the armrest. Her hair had added a tiny bit of flair to her personality. She'd hidden behind a flip of the ends or a head-shake to whip it back off her shoulder. Without those crutches, she'd be naked.

She held her breath. The makeover would keep her identity secret and was only temporary. The part of herself she was losing could be regained when all this was over.

. . .

Faith left the hair salon and sat for a minute in the parking lot. She flipped down the car's vanity mirror and inserted a blue-tinted contact lens over one gold-flecked brown eye, then shifted her head and inserted the other. She drew back and stared at her image. Wavy chestnut brown hair and almond-shaped blue eyes. Once she applied Josie's lipstick, eyeshadow, and mascara, she'd be able to fool most people unless she and Josie were standing side by side.

She blinked and pulled in a shuddering breath. The old Faith was gone, hidden under the strange, new person in the mirror. Right or wrong, phase one was complete.

Time for phase two.

She pulled her address book from her purse and input the location of Emmeline's corporate headquarters into the car's GPS. Nerves jumping and mouth dry, she started the engine and followed the computer's directions toward Victor Telemann's office.

When the digitized voice announced she'd reached her destination, Faith pulled to the curb and stared at the six-story building. At the street level, one display window glittered with jewelry and oozed luxurious furs, and in the other, a mannequin wore six hundred-dollar shoes and a designer dress that probably cost more than the average store employee earned in a year. The doorman on duty by a tasteful, goldleaf-gilded sign spoke volumes about the clientele the store's management hoped to attract.

Recalling the building layout from a magazine profile she found on the Internet, she shifted her gaze upward, past the royal blue awning over the entry, the shimmering windows of the retail section on the three lower floors, and the offices of the company headquarters on floors four and five. She focused on the top row of windows. The penthouse. The location of the executive offices. Somewhere behind the expanse of tinted glass, in a big office, sitting at a polished desk and luxuriating in power and prestige, was the man who'd ruined her mother's life.

The sixth floor was the domain of Victor Telemann, rapist and scum of the earth.

Goose bumps erupted on her skin. What was he like? In the years since he'd raped her mother, had he been a model citizen or committed other crimes?

She sucked in her breath. The chances of him being a model citizen were probably zip. Anyone who could rape a defenseless girl was lower than whale shit and would always be lower than whale shit. A predator stayed a predator, and a beast wasn't likely to change his ways until someone stopped him. She squeezed her shaking hands into fists. No one else had done the dirty job, so she'd have to be the one to chain him in a cage.

A rumbling truck pulled up beside her car, momentarily blocked her view, then roared away belching diesel fumes. She stared back at the store entrance as the doorman tipped his cap and ushered two shoppers inside.

What would Victor Telemann's exclusive clientele think if they knew he was a rapist? Would they shun his stores and cause him to go bankrupt? She gritted her teeth and squeezed the ribbed surface of the steering wheel until her knuckles were white and her finger muscles cramped. She swallowed several times, fighting the urge to get out of the car and stand in the middle of the street screaming the truth to the world. After a minute, the pounding in her temples decreased, and reason won out over blind emotion. She couldn't publicly accuse him.

Yet.

Faith pulled back into traffic and drove away, watching the building in her rear view mirror until the blue awning was lost in the jumble of storefronts. She corralled her outrage. Time to focus on essentials.

She scanned the signs and storefronts. Four blocks down the road, she spotted the real estate company specializing in short term rentals that she'd searched for and found online. Easing the car to the curb, she parked, and went inside.

. . .

The unfurnished tenth floor studio apartment was tiny, but it included a balcony overlooking the Intracoastal Waterway and was within walking distance of Emmeline's. An hour after stopping at the real estate office, Faith signed Josie's name to the lease, paid the security deposit and advance rent, and arranged for the entry door to be strengthened by the installation of a barricade lock anchored with a sturdy steel rod.

Buoyed by a sense of accomplishment, she collected the key to her mailbox in the lobby. With an address, she could get another cell phone and a driver's license, then she'd be able to apply for a job at Emmeline's and infiltrate Victor

Telemann's empire.

Faith called Josie to alert her to the reference check by the real estate agency.

"Are you sure you're okay?" Josie asked. Her tone said she knew the answer but expected Faith to put up a brave front and conceal the truth.

Faith's stomach was full of madly flapping butterflies. She missed Josie and wished she were home waking up in her own bed and realizing this was all a bad dream. But she raised her chin and said, "I'm fine. There's absolutely no reason to worry."

After she hung up, she stopped at a furniture store and bought a dinette set, a convertible couch to sleep on, a bookcase, a chest of drawers, and three lamps to keep away the darkness. Back outside, the sun was low in the sky, and her stomach rumbled at the tantalizing aroma of fresh bread emanating from a nearby restaurant. She ducked into a sandwich shop, and ordered a six-inch seafood salad sub, a bag of chips, and a soda.

A dark-haired man seated nearby looked her up and down. "Care to share my table?"

Faith blinked and remembered she was wearing another of Josie's form-fitting outfits. She gave the man a cool, but polite, smile. "No thank you."

She shifted her weight from foot to foot and stared at an ad on the wall while she waited for her food. When it was ready, she grabbed the bag, rushed back to her hotel, and locked herself into her room an hour before sunset.

She stripped off Josie's clothes, took a quick shower, bundled in a robe, and stretched out on the bed. She'd spent last night tossing and turning, too tense to sleep, and expected to do the same tonight, but a few minutes later, exhaustion slammed her eyelids shut and tugged her toward oblivion.

Faith dozed. A thump overhead jolted her awake. Deathly quiet. She listened for a full minute then closed her eyes again. Jovial male voices echoed in the hallway. She sighed and sat up to eat her sandwich. Sleep wasn't going to happen.

She turned on the TV to smother the unfamiliar noises plucking at her nerves. Night fell, and she switched on all the lights. Her mother had feared the darkness and never allowed it to invade their apartment. As a child, Faith had learned to share her mother's fear. Now, especially, she had no desire to break her lifelong sleeping-with-the-lights-on habit. Light was safety. Under the cover of darkness, monsters came out. And some of them committed rape.

• • •

Two days later, with her new Florida driver's license in her purse, Faith drove the route to Emmeline's again. She pulled into a parking spot on the opposite side of Worth Avenue and sat staring at the building for several long minutes. Job interviews were like descending into hell, and facing an interrogation about her skills when she wasn't even applying as herself was bound to be a nightmare. Filling out the online application had been easy and had won her a screening interview. Now came the hard part.

The voice of doubt chattered inside her head. Her conscience whispered that lying was a sin. She pictured the tear-stained pages in her mom's diary. She had to stay. Getting a job in the beast's company was the only way to get close to him and see justice done. God would have to understand.

Faith pulled in a deep breath, released it slowly, and calmed her strumming nerves by focusing on positive thoughts. She gathered the portfolio holding the copy of Josie's résumé and dodged two lanes of traffic to cross the street. The doorman said "Good morning," and tipped his cap as she went inside. She checked the building directory and rode the elevator to the fifth floor.

Her throat was so dry she didn't think she'd be able to talk. She ducked into the ladies room to gather her courage, glanced into the mirror, and gasped. Dark hair and blue eyes. She stared at her image. Was this for real? A month ago, she'd been living in her tiny apartment, slipping unnoticed through a drab, worker-bee life. Now she was navigating a strange, intimidating world. How could any of this be happening?

Squaring her shoulders and standing tall, she put on her game face, marched from the ladies room, pushed into the human resources office, and announced to the only person in sight, "Good morning, I'm here for a ten-thirty screening interview. Josie Ashland."

The woman behind the lone desk had a smile on her lips and boredom in her eyes as she accepted a copy of Josie's résumé. She glanced at the paper for less than five seconds then looked up and gave Faith a once-over. "Are you new to town?"

"Yes, I arrived a few days ago."

"Are you planning to stay or just here temporarily?"

"If I can find a good position, I plan to stay."

The woman pursed her lips then said matter-of-factly,

"Well, your qualifications are impressive, but right now, I don't have any positions that require your expertise."

Disappointment squeezed at Faith's chest. "I have experience in a wide variety of computer-related jobs. I can work in any department at any level."

"We don't have any openings."

"Would you keep my résumé in case something opens up?"

The woman shook her head. "We keep applications and résumés on file just in case, but I'm sure nothing will open up. We're not hiring now and probably won't be in the future." Her tone left no doubt she'd recited the words hundreds of times before.

A crushing weight pressed on Faith's shoulders, and she tried to keep them from sagging. Her head spun as if she'd been slammed against a stone wall. Without an excuse to be in this building, her effort to bring the beast to justice oozed life like roadkill on the highway to failure.

The woman motioned toward the door. "We'll call if we have interest. Good day."

Chapter Three

Faith left the human resources office feeling as if her body had turned to stone. She crossed the corridor and stood with a group of two women and a man waiting for the elevator. She chewed her lip, remembered the words in the diary, and slid deeper into despair. No job. No building or computer system access. No hope for Plan A.

When the elevator doors slid open, she hung back while the three other people swarmed aboard, then she stepped into the car and shuffled to the nearest corner. Her brain searched a maze of mediocre possibilities hoping to discover a new plan.

"What a great piece of jewelry," the man said, inching closer and staring at her chest.

Jolted out of her conjuring, she leaned farther into the corner, raised her hand, and touched Josie's hammered silver pendant. "Thank you."

The man nodded his head of dark, wavy hair and

motioned toward the pendant. "Very unique. Would you mind if I examine it closer?"

Faith flinched.

The older-looking, redheaded woman volunteered, "You don't have to worry about him, honey. Ronnie isn't attracted to girls."

He smiled. "I'm not trying to hit on you. I have a friend I haven't been able to visit for several months. A pendant like that would be a great gift to send and say *I miss you.* Where did you get it?"

To avoid having him invade her personal space, Faith slipped the pendant off over her head and handed it to him for inspection. "I'm sorry, but you won't be able to buy one like it. My cousin made it. In her spare time she designs unique pieces for her friends and relatives."

"Just my luck. I love the colors and textures." He ran a fingertip over the inset red stone and the hammered surface. Nodding approval, he turned the piece over and examined the delicate solder line. "The workmanship is remarkable."

Josie would be beaming with pride. Faith had an idea and was certain Josie would concur. "Why don't you take it then? My cousin can make me another."

"Are you serious? How much do you want for it?"

"No money. Just your appreciation of its beauty."

The elevator stopped at the fourth floor. The women waved to Ronnie and got off.

After the door closed again, he grinned at Faith and said, "Thank you. My friend will love this. Can I repay you by giving you a hint?"

"Sure, I guess. What kind of hint?"

"I assume you're looking for a job." When Faith nodded

he continued. "The personnel office here is just a front. The store manager does retail hiring. All the corporate office hiring is handled by the Richford Agency over on B Street. Openings are kept quiet and usually filled by word of mouth. So your best bet is to go dazzle Richford's with your qualifications."

The door opened at the ground floor and they both stepped off. Optimism seeped back into Faith's soul.

"Thank you," she said, smiling wide. "You've just made my day."

Ronnie shook her hand and dangled the pendant from the other. "You've just made my day, too." His expression became more serious. "Don't get your hopes up too far. Emmeline's is a hard nut to crack, but as they say in the acting world, break a leg."

· · ·

Faith left Emmeline's and rushed straight to the Richford Agency.

"I'm impressed," the employment counselor at Richford's remarked. "And I'm sure I can find you something quickly. In fact…" She rummaged through one of the mile-high stacks of papers on her desk, "I've just gotten in a request for a Software Project Leader from Parrott International. They're designing a new patient data storage application for hospitals. They'll probably snap you up in a heartbeat."

Faith smiled politely, squeezed her hands together in her lap, and said, "No thank you. I want to work for Emmeline's corporate headquarters."

"Parrott is a prestigious company. They pay well and offer excellent benefits. Their campus is gorgeous, and they have a young workforce full of well-educated, single men. I can get you an interview this afternoon, and you'll be working by Monday."

"I'd really rather work for Emmeline's."

The woman sighed, shook her head, and suspended her search. "They don't have any openings for database specialists. The only position available there is for a website designer. And even that is temporary."

"I'll take that."

"You're optimism is admirable, but it's not that easy. You don't have any qualifications in that area."

Faith bit on the inside of her cheek and scrambled for a reasonable argument. Before switching her major concentration to Electronic Communications Systems Studies in her senior year at Virginia Tech, she'd worked every weekend and three summers doing online marketing and website design. But the résumé she'd offered stressed Josie's experience with databases. How could she convince this woman she was qualified to do something not even mentioned on the résumé?

"I moonlighted as a website designer to pay my college tuition, and I spent three summers as an intern at Websoft. I just didn't bother listing everything on my résumé."

"Do you have a reference at Websoft?"

Wanting to keep the story as simple as possible, Faith seized on the first rational answer. "My supervisor quit the company, and I lost track of him." She hit on an idea that could dig her out of this pit, and excitement accelerated her words. "But I can do better than a reference. I'll show you.

Does your agency have a website?"

The woman slipped off her reading glasses, stuck one earpiece between her teeth, and leaned back in her chair. "Well, yes, of course."

"Would you like it updated?"

"What are you proposing?"

"Let me redesign your website for you. If you like what I do, then you can vouch for me at Emmeline's." She tried not to sound like she was pleading.

The woman frowned. "Why do you want to work for them so badly? I could get you a much better permanent position."

Faith raised her chin. She'd anticipated the question and had a ready answer. It didn't quite fit anymore, so she quickly edited her mental cue cards. "I had to work my way through college with a second part-time job as a salesclerk. I used to see the ads for Emmeline's and dream of someday selling high-class merchandise using my brain and computer skills instead of my aching feet. Working for them became my personal symbol of success. It may seem silly to you, but to me it's a milestone, something I've always strived for."

The woman gave a *whatever* shrug. "To each her own." She picked up Josie's résumé, put on her glasses, and studied it again. "Sorry, but we contract with a company that maintains our website. They wouldn't like you touching it. I really need a reference."

"What if I do a mock-up of a home page for Emmeline's? You know, a page or two that says something great is coming soon?"

Suspicion walked through the woman's eyes. Faith wondered if she'd pushed too hard and was about to be booted out the door. She racked her brain for anything in Josie's experience she could use to bolster her website qualifications. Her pulse raced.

"Nothing great was ever achieved without enthusiasm," she blurted, quoting from Ralph Waldo Emerson. "I could take a job someplace else, but I'd rather be eager to go in every morning and enjoy what I'm doing."

The woman tapped her pen on her desktop for several heartbeats. "Are you sure you don't want the position at Parrott?"

"Positive."

The employment counselor twisted her mouth, deep in thought.

Faith fisted her hands to dissipate the tension building in her frame and keep herself from squirming in her seat. She hoped the woman was thinking about the placement fee she'd get from Emmeline's and devising a way to add it to her income.

"I can't keep the job at Emmeline's open for very long. How long will it take you to do a mock-up?"

• • •

Faith started her job at Emmeline's the following Monday.

"You come very highly recommended," her superior, Gladys Pooson, said.

Faith stapled on a smile and tried to keep her expression professional, but her heart was thumping like a bass drum. Soon she'd have access to Emmeline's computer system, and be able to start studying Victor Telemann and his world.

"Thank you. And thank you for the opportunity to work

for Emmeline's. I'll do my best to design a fabulous virtual store and website for you. Building an online presence for such a distinguished company will be a challenge and an honor."

Gladys gave her an incredulous look and stood. "Come with me, and I'll show you to your office. You'll be on the fourth floor."

Faith decided she'd overdone the enthusiasm. She fell in alongside Gladys, and as they walked to the elevators, she shifted to a more pertinent subject. "How is the computer system set up? Is there a separate systems administrator or does each developer control their own files?"

"We don't have a very sophisticated system, and you'll be the lone developer. We just have a local network for the administrative office personnel. There's a separate financial network for the stores."

"What about online security?"

"The security department is focused on physical security. I'm not sure the guy who sits down in the security office staring at monitors knows anything about protecting a computer system. We contract with a software firm to check for bugs once in a while."

"Do they handle creating new accounts? I'll need administrative level access."

They boarded the elevator and Gladys hit the *four* button. "The rep was here yesterday and set you up. He comes in on a monthly basis unless we have a problem."

Faith caught her smile before it fell and struggled to keep worry from causing a waver in her voice. A knowledgeable computer tech could interfere with her plan to snoop in the company system. "Does he monitor the system remotely on a daily basis or just do maintenance checks from inside when he's here?"

"He's just our backup. You know, when things crash or a virus infects somebody's machine. You'll be responsible for everything to do with expanding the store system. Whatever security the website needs, you'll have to design it in. Can you do all that?"

"Absolutely."

The elevator dinged and stopped. The doors slid open. Faith followed Gladys into a hallway and suppressed a Cheshire-cat grin. So far, so good. She needed to find out everything she could about Victor, and lax security would work in her favor. Until the contract support company rep came back in a month, she could wander around in the company files at her leisure. If evidence of other crimes Victor had committed existed, she'd be free to search for it. Even if she found nothing, she'd know more about how his mind worked and be closer to figuring out a way to get a confession for prosecutors.

"Here we are," Gladys said. She stopped by a wood-grained door with an empty nameplate slot and pushed it open.

Faith peered into the tiny, windowless office, shuddered at the semi-darkness, and felt for a wall switch to turn on the lights. When the overhead fluorescent fixtures blazed to life, she pursed her lips and frowned. The desk faced the far wall, and the computer monitor was positioned in such a way that the display would be visible to anyone looking in the doorway. First thing, she'd have to rearrange the furniture so passersby wouldn't see what files she was browsing.

She stepped inside and wrinkled her nose at the foul

odor of ancient coffee. A brown stained mug with mummified grounds stuck on the bottom appeared to be the culprit.

Gladys walked to the desk and placed a hand on a two-inch-high stack of papers and leaflets. "This should be enough information to get you started."

"Does something there include the name of your hosting company, username, and the account password?"

Gladys tilted her head to one side and flipped through a few pages on the top of the pile. "It should. We had a college intern a couple summers ago, and I had him reserve our domain name. Okay, here it is." She picked up a dog-eared sheet and handed it to Faith. "We've been paying for the domain and the server space ever since."

"I'm surprised a major company like this didn't develop a site years ago. Why did you wait so long?"

"I don't make the decisions, they come from the top. Plus, you'd be surprised at how many of the most exclusive stores and top designers don't feel the need for a website. Forty percent of high-end brands don't sell online. They believe customers want the physical store ambiance and experience. Maybe Mr. Telemann thinks a website makes the store more common." She shrugged. "I do know that some of the younger executives have been encouraging him to modernize for years, but until recently, he's resisted."

"What made him change his mind now?"

Gladys got the look of a stern high school teacher. "I don't question Mr. Telemann's decisions. And if you want to be here for very long, you won't either."

. . .

On her lunch hour Tuesday, Faith pursued the next step in her plan: hire a private investigator.

Rain rapped on the car roof, and the wipers slapped fat drops from the windshield. She followed the directions from the rental's GPS and turned left, her nerves stretching tighter by the minute. The neighborhood had been deteriorating for the last several blocks and the litter and decay on this street was even worse than on the last. She double-checked to be sure her doors were locked and had second thoughts about her choice of investigators. She'd expected his office to be modest but hadn't expected to feel frightened just to get out of the car.

Her GPS said, "Turn right to your destination." 2219 Federal Avenue was a gray concrete building and cheerless under the weeping clouds. Rainwater tumbling from the broken gutter made clean streaks on the dirty facade.

She slowed and parked. When she swung open her door, the smell of oily, wet streets and stale humanity rushed in. Clutching the canister of pepper spray in her pocket, she stepped over the crushed cigarette pack floating in a puddle on the sidewalk and ducked inside the building.

The interior was well-lit and reasonably clean. Her heartbeat leveled off at slightly above normal as she paused and reviewed the decision that had brought her this far.

Faith pictured the three listings she'd found in the yellow pages. Zurich Investigations' quarter-page, block ad had been biggest. But the deciding factor had been the claim that Steve Zurich had been born in town and lived here his whole life. The other two listings had been for satellite offices of companies based in Miami. If she hired one of them, the people they sent to work her case might stand out as strangers and cause suspicion. She wanted to deal with someone local who knew the city intimately and had a good network of connections. Low rent location or not.

Reaffirming her initial decision, she squared her shoulders and walked deeper into the lobby. A tall, muscle-bound man chewing on a toothpick stood, thumbs hooked in empty belt loops, waiting by the elevator doors.

Reluctant to be trapped alone with him, she pretended to read the building directory until after the elevator arrived, he got on, and the door closed. Then she advanced to the doors, pushed the up arrow, and waited. On the next cycle, she hustled aboard.

Third floor. Suite 305. Zurich Investigations.

A buzzer sounded as she stepped into a room with six fake-leather chairs arranged facing a bow-legged coffee table. Through the open door to an adjoining office, a deep voice called, "I'll be right out."

Faith noticed the odors of whiskey and maybe pastrami. She considered the worn carpet and dog-eared magazines and decided business at Zurich Investigations wasn't booming. A minute later, the bear of a man she'd seen board the elevator walked from the adjoining office and stuck out his big paw. "Miss Ashland? Steve Zurich. Come on in."

As she shook his hand, her cheeks warmed with embarrassment. If he'd seen her avoid riding the elevator with him, he might have been insulted.

"I noticed you downstairs, stalling so you could catch the next elevator," he said. "You're smart to be cautious. You never can tell what's gonna happen when you let yourself be closed in alone with a strange man."

She smiled and relaxed. "I'm glad you understand. It

wasn't anything personal."

"Nah. In my business, I'm suspicious of everyone. I've seen all kinds. I know it never pays to drop your guard and leave yourself vulnerable."

She was starting to like this man. He seemed observant and savvy. He looked only a few years older than her, but his eyes were tough, like he'd survived more than she wanted to know and could hold his own against the world's evils. "Well, Mr. Zurich, shall we discuss some business then?"

He motioned at a chair. "Call me Steve. My father is seventy-two, he's Mr. Zurich."

She sat near his desk. "Then please call me Josie."

His chair groaned as his bulk filled it. He leaned back and laced his fingers behind his head. "So what do you need, Josie? Pictures of a cheating husband with his girlfriend? Proof of child abuse for a custody case? Background check on a fiancé?"

"I want you to investigate the background of a man who committed a crime almost twenty-six years ago and got away with it. He can't be charged unless I can convince him to confess, but I want to find out everything I can about him so I know how to proceed."

"What did he do?"

Her throat closed and she croaked out, "Rape."

His hands came down to grip the arms of his chair. "Why are you coming after him now? Were you the victim, as a kid?"

"No. He raped my mother."

Steve blew out his breath, leaned forward, and picked up a pen. "What's his name?"

"Victor Telemann. He's the CEO of Emmeline's, the

upscale department store chain. Their headquarters are on Worth Avenue."

Steve looked up. "Have you met Telemann?" His expression was puzzling.

His reaction to the name made her original unease return. "I haven't met him yet, but I just started working at Emmeline's, so I'm sure I'll meet him soon."

The compressor in the window air conditioner clicked on, and the machine's hum increased to a growl.

"Telemann's a powerful guy, and he's in tight with a lot of shady characters. As far as I know, he only sees them socially. But this might not be a place for a pretty young lady to stick her nose. You could be opening a real can of worms. You got any proof he raped your mom?"

"She wrote a complete description of that night in her diary. But she died of cancer last month, so she can't testify against him."

Steve shook his head. "Telemann would have to be crazy to turn himself in or confess to something now."

She shook off his discouraging words. "One of the other things I'd like you to do is find me a small recorder I can conceal. The confession doesn't have to be a formal document, just enough to convince a prosecutor to press charges and for a jury to believe he did it."

"You want to wear a wire and trick him, you mean?"

The room seemed cold enough to induce frostbite, and she wrapped her arms around her middle. "Something like that."

"I can get you the equipment, but I doubt you'll get your confession. And even if you do, a judge might not allow it as evidence."

"If not, I'll be able to testify he confessed to me. And a recording will convince the prosecutors I'm telling the truth. If it's admissible, it might provide leverage to convince him to make a deal."

"Suit yourself. I'm just saying I don't recommend you try to match wits with Telemann. When it comes to dirty tricks, he's probably way out of your league."

She shivered, unsure if the lack of circulation in her extremities was due to the room temperature or her anxiety. "I don't expect any of this to be easy, but I'm still going to try." She pulled in a deep, fortifying breath. "Do you think you can handle a background check? I want to know if he's tried anything with other women, been in trouble with the law, or been suspected of shady dealings. I want a complete portrait of the man. If I can't make the rape charge stick, maybe I can find evidence he's done something else."

"Sure. I can get a friend in the Palm Beach PD to check for a local or state rap sheet. And I can sniff around on the street to see if I can find any dirt. But it'll cost you. Not just my fee, but I'll need some green for informants."

She pictured him ducking into an alleyway with shifty-eyed man and then huddled in a dark, smoke-filled bar with a half-naked hostess. He could go places she would never go and talk to people who she'd never approach. "I can pay."

He tapped his lips with his pen. "You want family info too, or just Telemann?"

"Just Victor."

"You want any sensitive info? I don't do it personally, but I know a hacker."

"No, I want to keep everything legal," she said, hiding half the truth. She did want to stay within the law, but if hacking became absolutely necessary, she'd do the digging herself. Paying someone else with unproven skills could leave a trail and be risky.

After a three-lip-tap pause, he said, "I'll need seven hundred up front. That'll cover a background check and some time on the pavement digging for underworld connections."

Faith opened her purse and pulled out the new check-book she'd acquired when she put her cash in a bank account and her mother's diary in a safety deposit box. If he could uncover even one crumb of valuable information, hiring him would be well worth the cost. She needed live intelligence and, other than some money, what did she have to lose?

. . .

As Victor Telemann turned his calendar page to Thursday at nine in the morning, he got a call on his private line. When he answered, Brody's whiney voice announced, "Word on the street is that the cops are trying to infiltrate the organization."

Victor sat up straighter in his plush swivel chair. "You got details?"

"One of the beat cops we own passed on the tip," Brody said. "That's all he heard."

"We got anybody new positioned at a store?"

"Nada."

Victor adjusted the position of his black silk eye patch. "Keep your ears open. Tell that cop to dig deeper."

"Sure, boss."

He hung up on Brody, hit the button on his intercom, and switched to a more reserved but authoritative tone. "Peg, have we hired anyone recently?"

A couple seconds of silence, then his secretary answered, "A young woman named Josie Ashland started a few days ago."

The time frame fit. He tapped his fingernails on the desktop. "Who did we hire before that?"

"A man named Ronnie Carmona, at least three months ago."

"Is that the gay guy?"

Victor pictured the man he thought of as *the fag* and snorted in disgust. If he'd known the guy was gay, he would have made sure he wasn't hired. But now the company was stuck with him thanks to the bleeding hearts and increasingly spineless Congress. Who were they to decree who could be fired and on what grounds? They were taking away his freedoms, giving his employees a million reasons to file discrimination suits, sticking the government's nose where it didn't belong. He shook his head. What a pain in the ass. If it wasn't for the media scrutiny a campaign would bring, he had half a mind to run for the senate and pass a few employer-friendly laws for a change.

Peg hesitated. "I believe there are office rumors to that effect."

"What does he do?"

"Inter-departmental liaison and contact person for stores with problems."

The fag wasn't likely to be a cop. He'd learned many lessons growing up with a cop father, and one of them was that the boys in blue hated limp-handed cocksuckers as much as he did. Plus, if there was a mole it was probably someone more recent. "What's this new girl's job?"

"She's developing the website."

He shook his head and rolled his eyes. The damn website he'd had to agree to in order to get his prick of a stepson off his back. Another burr in his butt. "I want to meet her. Get her up here right now."

"Yes, Mr. Telemann."

He removed a fat, Cuban cigar from the mahogany humidor on his desk and clipped off the end, wondering if he should fire this bitch on the spot. The operation had run smoothly for fifteen years. He didn't plan to let the frickin' website ever be operational anyway. Maybe he should kill the project now before he had to kill an undercover cop.

But how could he cancel the project this soon? He'd resisted the pressure to modernize for as long as he could pull it off without raising suspicion. Later on, he could hire a geek to hack and sabotage the website, and claim online sales were a failure. But for a while he wanted to appear to be embracing technology. Keeping the project would placate the top executives and his troublemaker stepson who thought cash transactions and brick and mortar stores were fast becoming relics.

He clenched his teeth. Right now, the problem wasn't website business sucking away his profits. It was a spy.

The intercom buzzed and interrupted his thoughts. "Yes."

"Miss Ashland is here."

"Have her wait. I'll buzz when I'm ready for you to send her in."

Ten minutes cooling her heels should be enough to assert his dominance. He chuckled. Getting her in his office could be fun. It wasn't every day he got to jerk on a cop's chain.

Deciding to postpone the cigar and use it as a prop, he turned his attention back to the spreadsheet he'd been about to review before Brody's call. Keeping a running total in his head, he quickly checked each tidy column of numbers. Things were going along on an even keel, and his profits were mounting. He should be able to chuck this setup and retire to the good life soon. An image of a pristine beach in Grand Cayman helped improve his mood.

Fifteen minutes later he looked up and checked his watch. He tucked the spreadsheet and his ledger away in the hidden compartment of his safe. He was smiling and deciding which of his healthy foreign bank accounts to pad with another two-hundred-grand deposit when he buzzed Peg and picked up his cigar.

. . .

Victor flicked his lighter as the door opened and a young woman walked into his office. Nice looking broad. A good rack, but too small for his tastes. He focused on her emotion-filled blue eyes. Was that alarm, mortification, or hate?

"Have a seat."

He puffed on his cigar until the end lit and glowed red, using the time to study her. Stiff. Uncomfortable. A bad actress. Could be she was just nervous about being called to his office. But the eyes said much more. Cold. Calculating. Suspicious. If she wasn't a cop, he'd eat his chair.

"I'm Victor Telemann," he said, blowing smoke toward her face. "I like to meet all our new employees, Miss…?"

"Ashland. Josie Ashland." Her delivery was almost a stammer.

"How are you getting along? Finding everything you need?"

She moistened her lips and he noticed she had a nice, full mouth. How far would she go to get dirt on him? Could he have some fun while he strung her along? Probably not.

"Yes," she said in a small, shaky voice. "Everything is fine."

"Are you married, Josie?"

"No."

"Boyfriend?"

"No." Her expression was wary. "Is that relevant to my job?"

He pasted on a fatherly smile. "Of course not. I just like to know a little bit about the people we employ. We're one big happy family here."

Victor stood, forcing her to look up at him, and walked around his desk. He always enjoyed looking down on people as a way to intimidate, and he especially liked touching women to establish his superiority. Only a few feminist bitches dared object. The rest knew their place.

He walked behind Josie and rested his fingertips on her shoulder.

She flinched and drew in a sharp breath.

He savored her reaction. As an undercover cop trying to blend in, she'd bite her tongue rather than make a scene. Having her trapped spiced his pleasure.

"I hope you'll be happy working for Emmeline's. Is there anything I can do to make you more comfortable?"

She rotated her shoulder in a meager attempt to shake off his touch. "No." She muttered something that sounded like *thank you* but seemed to be an afterthought.

Mission accomplished. He lifted his hand and intentionally brushed her hair as he drew it away.

Her back stiffened.

He chuckled to himself and decided to let her stay. He'd allow her to snoop and ask questions for a while, because she was easy to read, and he'd be in control of the game. He could get rid of her at any time, but when he did, the cops would try to slip in someone else at another level. Better to deal with her here where he could watch her than risk them sneaking in someone else who'd pose a real threat.

"Well then, get back to work," he said. "I'm not paying you to sit in here throwing yourself at me."

She whirled around and looked at him wide-eyed, then jumped up and turned tail like a spooked rabbit.

He puffed on his Havana and walked to his chair, ignoring her as she rushed from the room. After the door clicked shut behind her, he leaned back and enjoyed a belly laugh. The cops were pretty desperate if they thought a sexy body was enough to distract him from business and bring him down. He'd learned how to survive in a jungle before he was old enough to shave, and he was smart enough not to be taken in by some wet-behind-the-ears bitch.

He squelched his laughter and sighed. He'd have to deal with her, of course. Figure out the right approach. He stared into space and puffed thoughtfully on the cigar. His best bet was to send her off on a wild goose chase.

He smiled. Distraction was a good ploy and could work two ways. Why not distract her by feeding her someone who she'd assume was a player but actually knew nothing? He'd get both of them off his back, and she'd end up circling an empty carcass.

He nodded, liking the idea more and more. It was genius, proof that he was still sharp after all these years behind a desk. He'd throw her that bastard Kent to chew on for a while and take care of two hyenas with one bone.

Chapter Four

Arms clutched tightly around her middle, Faith rode the private penthouse elevator down to the fifth floor. Where could she run to escape that awful man? Where could she hide?

She slipped through the open crack as soon as the elevator doors slid apart, then rushed into the nearby ladies room and fell to her knees in the end stall, gulping air and fighting back tears. Her stomach rolled viciously, and she fought the urge to vomit. The spot on her shoulder where Victor had rested his fingers burned as if seared by a branding iron.

Her ragged breathing echoed in the pink-tiled room. The chemical smell of pine deodorant didn't quite mask the odor of stale urine. But she tilted her head back, sucked restroom air in through her nostrils, and found it preferable to the stench of cigar smoke clinging to her clothes.

The words in her mother's diary swirled in her head. *Wouldn't let me go…cried and begged… hurt so bad…*

The man she'd just met had dragged her mother to the ground, forced his knees between her thighs, violated her body in the worst way possible. Left his sperm. Fathered a child.

My father.

Her skin crawled. After all these years, she'd met her father.

She pulled in a breath and smelled cigar smoke. Visions of a fireman carrying a limp woman and fighting his way through smoke and flames to bring her out of a burning building swam before Faith's eyes. The heroic fantasy she'd been fed as a child seemed laughable when overlaid with the scene that had just taken place upstairs. For more than twenty years, she'd fallen asleep at night believing her daddy was selfless and courageous. Yet in truth he was a self-important coward who'd run from his crimes.

She'd loved her fantasy father. All she could feel for the real man was revulsion.

He'd saved no one but himself. He hid behind the smoke of an expensive cigar.

The smell of smoke had always held positive associations in her mind, always been linked with her heroic father. Now the scent made her want to gag.

She pictured her real father's smug face in the midst of the acrid cloud. The black patch he'd worn over his right eye sparked a memory of more words from the diary. *I scratched at his eyes…* Was the patch the result of a twenty-six year old wound? Had her mother succeeded in causing her attacker a small bit of pain?

The possibility enfolded her like a blanket of calm. An eye for an eye…or a rape. If her mother had injured him, then he'd never forgotten the girl he'd raped. He'd had to live with a reminder of that night too.

Faith slumped against the wall, rested her forehead on the cool, hard tiles, and squeezed her eyes shut. She wanted to run away, go home, forget she'd ever met him. Her chin quivered, and to keep from crying, she concentrated on how satisfying it would be to sit in a courtroom and hear him sentenced to prison for his crime.

Her conscience tried to interrupt, whispered her grand-parents would be mortified if they knew why she'd come here. They'd tell her she was making a wrong choice, that she should do the Christian thing and practice forgiveness. She clenched her teeth. They were good people who'd al-ways preached the word of God to her mother and their granddaughter, but they didn't know of the evil a rapist had imposed on their daughter.

She pulled in a series of deep breaths, blowing air out slowly in-between. After a few minutes, her heartbeat decel-erated to normal, and her legs felt strong enough to support her body. She stood, left the stall, hung her head over a sink, and splashed cold water onto her face. After dripping over the basin for several seconds, she ripped off a paper towel and patted her skin dry.

Her reflection in the mirror grabbed her by the throat. The ruthless look in her eyes was an exact match to the look she'd seen in Victor Telemann's. His genes were polluting her body like a cancer out of control, polluting everything she'd always believed about herself.

She clenched her hands and lifted her chin. His genes were proof of his paternity and proof a crime had been committed. She'd come to West Palm Beach to find out what kind of man he was and gather enough evidence to make him pay for ruining her mother's life. The man who had summoned her to drop everything and rush to his big office so she could be treated like a peon was far from sweet or repentant. He didn't deserve her forgiveness or compassion. He deserved jail.

Determination surged in her veins. He had the position of power now, but she was going to gather information, and information would give her power too. She had to march back out there and, when necessary, face him again.

Justice needed to be done, and the scales wouldn't be balanced until she saw him behind bars.

• • •

Kent hid behind a mischievous smile as he pulled the bouquet of lilies from behind his back and presented them to Victor's secretary. "For my favorite girl. Happy Friday."

Peg blushed to the roots of her swept-back gray hair as she fixed him with a schoolmarm glare. "Don't you try to charm me, young man. You were supposed to be here half an hour ago."

He spread his hand over his heart. "But I couldn't. I had to stop for flowers."

"Enough of your line. I know the truth. Jack called about your flight delay. That's what happens when you fly commercial. I just hope the jet is repaired before he,"—she tilted her head toward Victor's door—"needs it. And I'm thankful you have a responsible personal assistant who keeps me informed."

Kent chuckled. "You know I love you, and neither Jack

nor I would let you get in trouble." He inclined his head toward Victor's office door. "Are they waiting?"

"Yes." She took the flowers, raised them to her face and breathed deeply, then smiled ear to ear. "Thank you. They're beautiful."

Kent lifted her free hand and kissed her fingers. "So are you. Seriously, thanks for covering for me. You're a gem he doesn't deserve."

"Then hustle on in there before I get fired. You know how furious he gets when anybody makes him wait."

"Yes, ma'am." His mood sobered. "I really don't care if he gets furious, but don't ever worry about being fired, Peg. I'd hire you back with a huge raise and in a better position before he could turn around twice."

He smoothed down his silk Hermes tie, pushed open Victor's office door, and strode inside, ready to squint against the blinding sunlight that usually streamed in through the huge window behind Victor's desk. The aura of light behind the desk chair, and the long walk across the massive room, were design tricks meant to emphasize Victor's divine power. But to the contrary, the vibrations of self-importance saturating the air always made Kent want to laugh out loud at Victor's bloated ego.

Today, the blinds were closed against the glare, and Victor sat behind his huge desk, eye patch removed in the dim light and cigar smoke swirling around his head. Ever since he'd been a boy, Kent had secretly liked the idea that Victor's damaged eye was so sensitive to bright sunlight that he was often forced to retreat to the shadows like a mole or bat. Associating Victor with a rodent had always seemed fitting.

Victor wasn't alone. Ben Kipfer, thin-lipped and

hollow-cheeked, sat ramrod rigid on a straight-backed chair balancing a pile of paperwork on his knees. Ben was speaking in his nasally, singsong voice. Victor held up a hand to interrupt him, glared at Kent, and said in a churlish tone, "It's about time."

"I'm sure Peg explained about my flight being delayed."

He swung his briefcase onto the corner of Victor's desk, because he knew the action violated Victor's precious territory and would irritate him all to hell. Three years ago, Victor had recognized Kent as a threat to his power. Ever since then, Kent had relished every opportunity to poke at the man's temper, and the two of them had been circling each other like boxers looking for the chance to land a punch.

Blithely ignoring the scowl Victor aimed at him, he turned toward Ben, and extended his hand in greeting. "How are you, Ben?"

"Good, Kent. You?" They shook hands. "How was your trip?"

"Successful." Memories of the tense meetings twisted the muscles in his neck. He kept his posture and expression nonchalant. "The contracts are all signed."

Ben rushed to take the sheaf of papers Kent removed from his briefcase and held out in his direction. "Wonderful. Wonderful. You had us worried for a while."

Victor blew smoke in their direction. "What in the hell was going on out there?"

"Somebody else beat us to the punch and bid up the price."

"Who?"

"I have no idea."

"You damn well better find out. Next time it could cost

us even more."

Kent's blood heated at his stepfather's superior tone, but as a skilled negotiator, he'd learned to control his emotions. He managed to force his sneer into the shape of a stiff smile. "Don't try to order me around. In case you've forgotten, I own forty-nine percent of this company and the money we're discussing is half mine."

When Victor glared at him, he got back to the subject at hand. "I might be able to pry a name out of Gardener later, after he's done licking his wounds. But for now, he's pretty upset about the flood driving the company into the ground and forcing him to sell out."

Ben waved the contract in the air. "This was a great deal, even up six mil from our estimate. The location is a gold mine. Tremendous potential. Tremendous. Gardener could have held out for a lot more."

Victor pointed his cigar at Ben. "Go ahead back to your office, Ben. I want to discuss something about this with Kent in private."

Ben deflated like a leaking birthday balloon. "Yes, sir, Mr. Telemann. Right away, sir." He gathered his papers into a ragged pile.

While Ben made his exit, Kent settled into the loveseat on the far side of the office and ran his fingertips over the bronze model of Victor's thoroughbred racehorse. He kept his demeanor casual, but distrust had his insides on high alert. Ever since he'd decided to protect the value of the chunk of stock he'd been left in his father's will by getting more involved in the business, he'd suspected something in the organization wasn't right and Victor knew all about it. He intended to find out what was going on. If it was something serious or illegal, Victor needed to be stopped. Plus, if he could gather proof, he might be able to convince his mother to protect her controlling interest in Emmeline's by taking back her proxy and dumping her cheating husband. So, as he watched Ben leave, he pondered Victor's strange meeting interruption and decided any topic that couldn't be discussed in front of the CFO was potentially interesting.

When Kent heard the door click shut behind Ben, he said, "What's up?"

"I've got a suspicion about how we got stabbed in the back."

Interest piqued, Kent leaned forward and dangled his hands between his knees. "Yeah? How?"

"We have a new girl on the payroll who's asking too many questions. I'm betting she's a corporate spy."

"So fire her."

"I don't want to. At least not yet. I want to know who's paying her."

"Ask her. You seem to believe money can buy anything. Pay her to come clean."

"I have a better idea." Victor licked his lips. "I want you to use your boyish charm to get close to her. Women fall at your feet. So use it to our advantage. Get her head over heels, put her under your spell. Then get her into bed and pump her for everything she knows."

Kent snorted. Business by sex and deception. Typically Victor. "Go to hell."

"Don't you want to find out who's trying to screw us over? You're the one getting blindsided in the negotiations."

"I don't play that kind of dirty game. Emmeline's is a respected company."

"Bullshit. This is war. We need to play as dirty as the enemy. You're a smooth operator. Any woman will tell you whatever you need to know if you make her believe you're falling in love."

Kent had heard enough. Blood heating rapidly, he stood and walked back toward Victor's desk. He prided himself on honesty in his relationships. His dates always knew they were temporary. Pretending something more for the sake of information was just plain slimy. "I sleep with women for pleasure, not business."

"What's the difference? It's all pussy. You screw strange babes all the time. Just once you could do it for the good of the company. I'd do it myself, but I'm a married man."

Right. And a goddamned cheater.

Planting both palms on the desk, Kent leaned across to glare into his stepfather's eyes. "Speaking of which, what's this crap about not taking Mom to Paris?"

Victor puffed on his cigar, using the stalling tactic Kent had seen at least thirty million times before. After a minute, he blew out a stream of smoke. "She'd be a distraction."

"Don't give me that bullshit. You're taking somebody else."

"Please watch where you say things like that. Your mother is a very sensitive woman. We don't want to upset her with that kind of talk."

Sharp teeth showed in Victor's grin, and his fake concern held an underlying threat. He could choose to be a mean bastard and taunt his wife with his affairs.

Kent understood the subtext, but his blood was bubbling like red-hot lava and he wasn't about to back down. "Tell her you changed your mind and take her with you."

Victor leaned back in his chair and rolled his cigar between his fingers. "I'll tell you what I'll do. You agree to cozy up to the spy, and I'll take my wife to Paris."

Resisting the urge to flatly refuse, Kent snapped a tight cap on his anger. He made himself consider Victor's suspicions as he straightened, shut his briefcase, and slid it from the desk. Was there a spy or was the screwed-up deal the statistical one-in-a-million fluke any negotiator should expect? Did sensitive information get leaked to a competitor, or did he simply make a mistake?

He tried not to think with his pride, jump at Victor's explanation of a corporate spy, and shift the blame for his near failure. But the memory of how Gardener's sudden stubbornness had caught him off-guard and left him scrambling to negotiate a new deal jumped out and nipped at his gut. Damn it, he was going to examine every angle and determine what had gone wrong. He was going to enter his next negotiation with a clear view of the playing field and prevent a repeat of this past week's close call.

He clenched his teeth. He had to be sure no stone was left unturned, and the possibility of a spy was a huge, jagged-edged boulder. He pondered the possibilities. If the woman knew who he was, the plan wouldn't work. So he'd have to fly under the radar. Seducing her was out of the question, but it wouldn't hurt to have a couple conversations, buy her a dinner or two, and determine if she was on the up-and-up. If he accepted Victor's deal, he could eliminate the spy scenario plus repeal Victor's free pass to cheat on his mother. Unless the woman smelled like a dead rat or looked like a warthog, he probably couldn't lose.

Shaking off the bulk of his distaste, he said, "Okay, you

call and tell Mom to start packing. I'll lay some charm on your suspected spy and see what I can find out."

. . .

Kent pondered the best approach to checking out the possible spy for the rest of the morning and called his assistant, Jack, into his office just after two. "What kind of car would you want if you needed to buy one right away?"

With less than a second of hesitation, Jack answered, "I've had my eye on a loaded Mustang GT convertible with wire wheels, deluxe sound system, spoiler, five-speed on the floor, and a sunroof."

"Color?"

Jack's dark eyes sparkled in his café-au-lait face. "Candy Apple red, of course."

"Okay, here's the deal. I'll buy you one as a bonus for your help on the last deal, but I'd like to borrow it for a few days. Do you mind if I drive it before you get a chance?"

A huge smile spread over Jack's face. "Hell, no. Thanks."

"You deserve something for saving my ass, but if you don't want a car, I'll rent something, and you can have a cash bonus instead."

"A car's great. But what's up? What happened to your Carrera?"

"I want to take a woman out to dinner without giving away who I am. I can't drive a top-of-the-line Porsche and look like a mid-level employee. So I thought I'd buy you something you'd like, then you could use my car for a few days while I drive the new one. Once this charade is over, I'll have the new car detailed, and then it's yours."

"Do I want to know what you're up to?"

"Victor thinks a new employee is a corporate spy, that she's the reason our last deal went sour. I'm going to check her out."

"How?"

"Turn on the old charm and see if I can get her to say something incriminating. I'll have to meet her, talk to her, spend some time with her, see if I can figure out who she knows or reports to. The object is to get her to relax and hope she drops her guard."

Jack shook his head. "You'll need more than a low-profile car to fool any woman with half a brain. As soon as she hears your name, she'll clam up."

"I know, but everyone here calls me by my first name. They know I hate *Mr. Telemann*. I'll just neglect to mention my last name. If she asks, I'll use *Morris*."

He liked the idea of using his birth name. He'd wanted to remain Kent Morris after being adopted by Victor, but had no choice as a child. Going back to his real name now would be easy. Plus he'd be less likely to choke on a lie if it held a grain of truth.

"What if someone else tells her who you are?"

"All I'll need is a couple conversations, one date, two at the absolute max. To be doubly cautious, I'll approach her late in the day after most of the employees go home. That way the halls should be empty. You can scout her out to be sure she's alone and give me the all-clear before I make my entrance."

Nodding slowly, Jack asked, "You figure Victor's right about her being a spy?"

"How else would someone know to bid against us?"

Jack pursed his lips and arched one eyebrow. "A spy would explain a lot."

"Yeah, but I plan to move slowly and carefully. If Victor will lie and cheat on my mother, he'll twist the truth about other things when it suits his purpose. And the more I study his management methods, the more I see him playing people against each other for his own benefit. I don't want to end up a pawn in one of his nasty power-grabbing games or set myself up for getting slapped with a sexual harassment suit."

Jack snorted. "You know how I feel about him."

Kent met his eyes and gave him a look that communicated *yeah, and you know I hate him even more.*

Jack had been in and out of trouble as a teenager, and when he was caught cheating and lost his football scholarship, he'd had to drop out of college. But when he realized he was stupidly sabotaging his future, he finished college in night school and straightened out his life. Kent and he had become friends after sharing the top honors in a darts tournament, and Kent had insisted on giving Jack a chance to make good. He'd hired him as his assistant, over Victor's strenuous objections.

Victor hated Jack because he was a symbol of the power struggle between him and Kent that he'd lost. He resented Jack's presence and never missed an opportunity to treat Jack like an inferior or show his disdain. Jack pretended indifference to Victor's face, but Kent knew Victor's constant hostility gnawed at Jack's gut.

"Anyway, you want the car then?"

"Sounds good to me. We can really use a second car, and I'm not going to balk at a few miles on the odometer." Jack shook his head. "But as much as I'd love to get my hands on your ride, I don't dare street park a Carrera in my neighbor-hood until they catch the guys who've been midnight shop-ping for the last couple months. I'll keep driving Carrie's clunker."

Kent tapped his fingertips on his desktop. "Why don't you and Carrie and the baby move into my guesthouse for a while? You can drive my car, she can spend the days on the beach and enjoy the maid service. You can have meals delivered so she won't have to cook. We can arrange a tem-porary baby nurse to change diapers or whatever. Call it a new-mom's vacation."

"I'm sure she'd love that. After walking the floor all those nights when Christian had that fever, she could use a little bit of a break."

Kent saw the softening in Jack's eyes when he talked about Carrie and marveled at how love, marriage, and fatherhood had mellowed him. A mere two years ago, Jack had been able to drink Kent under the table, juggle a lady on each arm, and close every dance club in town. He missed Jack's easy companionship now that his old friend was out of circulation. But he loved Carrie like a sister and sometimes secretly wished he'd met the vivacious ex-schoolteacher first.

"Then it's settled. I'll call the Ford dealer on Broad Street and tell him you'll be in to pick out a Mustang convertible. Write him a check from my personal account and line up the installation of the best security system they can find for when you take it home. Insist he have it ready for delivery Monday morning. Then take the rest of the afternoon off and get Carrie and my godson moved into the guest cottage."

Jack grinned. "She's going to flip out. We haven't had a vacation since she quit work to stay home with Christian."

Kent walked over and slapped his friend on the back. "Tell her that after my business is done we'll get together and do the town. Oh, and you're welcome to come along too."

Jack punched his shoulder and went into a boxer's stance. "No stealing my woman, man."

Kent raised his fists and they sparred for a couple minutes. After a jab to his middle landed hard, forcing him to suck in his breath, Kent held up his hands in surrender. "Okay, she's yours for now. I'll wait and steal her later when your hairline starts receding and you're popping Viagra."

Jack faked a sucker punch. "I wish you'd go find your own woman and stop ogling mine."

Kent laughed and straightened his tie. "You got the last good one. What's a guy supposed to do?"

Chapter Five

Faith read her printout of Steve Zurich's preliminary report while she drank her Monday morning coffee. When she'd finished the last of the four pages, she put the report down, sighed, and flipped through the scanned newspaper clippings.

Most of the information duplicated what she'd already read in online company profiles and news feeds. Victor was married to a woman named Emmeline who was born into a society family. She was the company's namesake and wealthy widow of the company's founder. One gossip column mentioned they lived in a stately mansion, owned a condo in Vail and a fifteen-room "cottage" in Maine, and a few years ago, Victor had purchased a half interest in a thoroughbred race-horse. From the society page copies, she concluded he and his wife attended every gala event in Palm Beach.

She stared at one of the photos. Victor's chest was puffed out, and he stood like a reigning king. The caption said he'd declined repeated requests to run for an open congressional seat, but pledged financial support to the nominee of the party.

Her blood heated. He didn't deserve to be happy and successful. He didn't deserve accolades, didn't deserve respect. He was a common criminal, even though he had no police record. Somehow she had to reveal his true colors to the world.

She shoved the useless report into her desk drawer, logged back onto the Internet, and continued with her own investigation. Her fingers flew over the familiar rows of plastic keys, each with its neat block letter and slightly concave upper face. The clicking of the keys soothed her nerves. Working alone on a computer, she was comfortable and in control. Unlike people, the machine didn't care about personalities, or money, or manners, just precise commands, proper logic, and established procedures.

If only the problems in life could be solved like a computing problem.

An hour later, she had an unsolvable computing problem. The error message read:

The information you have requested is not available online.

Please visit our office for access to the pertinent microfiche records.

Her search of the marriage records in New York City had hit another dead end.

In previous searches, she'd uncovered an obscure reference to Victor's address in his maternal grandmother's obituary and deduced that shortly after he raped her mother he'd left Williamsburg and gone to New York. About a year after she was born, when he was twenty-two, he'd applied for a marriage license with a Ruby Swain. This morning, she'd hoped to dig up some information about that marriage. She'd tracked down the likely location of the records, but they were too old to be online.

She made a mental note to find and contact a detective in New York who could search the archives, then turned her attention to the computer system at Emmeline's.

The Unix operating system was full of security holes, and the source code was readily available for anyone to modify. The email system should be easy to hack.

Faith smiled sadly, remembering Richard, the computer lab partner who had taught her advanced hacking skills her sophomore year of college. His genius IQ and insatiable curiosity had drawn her to him, and for a while, she'd had a crush on him, or more correctly, his exceptional brain. Being a socially stunted geek and hanging around with other geeks like Richard, she'd learned many skills outside the realm of a normal engineering curriculum.

For a while, she'd enjoyed the thrill of sitting by Richard's side, helping him circumvent corporate security firewalls and probe system loopholes, plant messages for security personnel informing them they'd been outsmarted, and triumphantly back out leaving everything intact. But Richard lost his hero status when he devised a plan to break the law and hack a military database simply to prove it could be done. Fearful of the ramifications of being caught, she'd told Richard to count her out. He'd been scornful of her reluctance, belittling her capabilities and inflaming her insecurities.

The hurt was still there, sending out poisonous messages whenever she had thoughts of the future and someday meeting another interesting man. The little negative voice never failed to warn her to protect her heart and not even think about a serious relationship. She'd seen Richard's behavior as proof of her mother's warnings: Men couldn't be trusted to do the right thing, and love was stupid. Trusting would make her vulnerable to getting her heart bruised again. She'd heeded her mother's advice and avoided men, that way she'd never have to face the pain of loss.

There's no time for emotion or analysis of the past or future now.

She pushed the disturbing memories away and concentrated on remembering the wealth of skills she'd learned from Richard, one of which would prove useful today. That skill could get past Emmeline's pathetic system defenses and give her access to copies of all Victor Telemann's new and archived emails.

A ripple of anticipation and excitement raced down her spine, followed quickly by a reprimand from her conscience. She was eating a forbidden fruit and excitement was a bad sign. It might be revealing she had bad genes passed on by her father.

Chewing her lip, she told herself violating Victor's privacy was a necessary evil that would bring a criminal to justice and reading a few emails was nowhere near as invasive as the communication monitoring in the system she'd helped design for the government. She logged onto the Unix network server, typed two lines of code at the prompt, and then stretched her finger toward *enter*.

Gladys Pooson stepped through the doorway.

Faith's heart skipped a beat, and her fingers froze. Trying to act casual, she reached for the *end* key. *Hit it.* It activated a pre-programmed macro. She held her breath as the window on her monitor cleared then flashed up a block of code for a data entry form.

She aimed a smile at Gladys. "Hi, is there something I can do for you?"

Behind her friendly mask, her pulse pounded madly in her throat. The thick carpeting in the hallway made hearing people approach almost impossible. She needed to be more aware, stay alert and on guard. Keeping her job and access to the computer system was priority one. No one could discover her snooping.

Especially anyone who might report her to Victor.

• • •

Four forty-five. Time to make his move and find out if Emmeline's was harboring a corporate spy.

Kent ducked into the small private restroom attached to his office, checked his appearance in the mirror, and smoothed down his lucky silk tie. Jack passed him the keys to the new car, and he stashed them in his pocket, then walking beside Jack, he headed for the elevator. When they stepped out onto the fourth floor, he saw the door to Josie Ashland's office was open and nodded to Jack.

Jack strolled down the empty hallway, glanced in the proper doorway, continued a few paces, then turned and came back. He flashed Kent a grin and a thumbs-up, she's-in-there-and-alone, before boarding the elevator for home.

Wondering what prompted Jack's grin, Kent launched his approach. He'd braced himself for a warthog face by the time he stopped at the doorway to size up his target.

Relief washed over him. The woman's eyes were trained on her computer monitor and her fingers poised over the keyboard, but he saw enough to know she was pleasant to look at. Shiny brown hair, cute little chin, slightly pursed, red lips that looked absolutely luscious. He usually preferred blondes, but in this case he wasn't choosing. And if he had to spend time with a potential spy, at least this one would be easy on the eyes.

Rapid clicks and clacks flowed from the room as she worked. He made a quick scan of the tiny office. Not a picture, or plant, or personal item in sight. No cartoons thumbtacked to a corkboard. No clues to her interests or personality unless the lack of feminine nesting paraphernalia meant she was prepared for a quick departure in the case her true reason for being there was exposed.

He cleared his throat.

She started and glanced up.

Gorgeous blue eyes. "Hi, are you Josie Ashland?"

She tapped a single key on her keyboard then gave him a stiff little smile. "Yes. Can I do something for you?"

"I hope so." He strolled into the office and extended his hand. "I'm Kent. I work over in the financial department."

The windowless room was filled with harsh artificial light and the scent of synthetic cinnamon air freshener. He thought of the phrase *a rose cloistered in a broom closet* as she took his hand.

He shook her hand gently, prolonging the contact for a few seconds more than necessary. Her skin was soft and warm, and he had a ridiculous fantasy of her fingertips roaming over his bare back.

She drew her hand away. "Hi, Kent. What do you need?"

The greeting held a note of apprehension.

He pulled his mind back to the reason for his visit. "I understand you're a computer wiz, and I was hoping to steal you away from Gladys after you're finished with the website. We need someone in financials on a permanent basis, and I wanted to put a good word in for us early so you'd keep us in mind."

"Well, I'm flattered, but I really haven't given any thought to where I'll work next. This could be a several-month project."

Not if you're working for the competition. Your ass will be out that door so quick, you'll be dizzy.

"I understand the timeframe is fluid," he said with a shrug. "We just ask that you keep us in mind. When this assignment starts winding down, come over and see what we're offering."

"Okay, I'll do that. Thanks." Her tone indicated a desire to put a period at the end of their conversation.

"Have you been working around town long?"

"No. My last job was in Norfolk, Virginia."

"Oh. How are you finding your way around?"

"Good."

He slid the keys to the new Mustang out of his pocket and moved closer to her desk. "I've lived here all my life and know the area pretty well. If you need help finding anything or getting settled, I'd be glad to help."

"Thanks."

Her one-word answers gave up little information, and her reticence added to his suspicion. He didn't want her to babble. In fact, babbling women drove him crazy. But why wasn't she making any attempt to engage in polite conversation?

He stood where the monitor would block her view of his hand and casually placed his keys on the desk. "The furniture in here is arranged kind of weird. I can shift things around for you if you'd rather have the desk face a wall."

"No thanks, I like it this way."

She moistened her lips in a nervous little gesture. He noticed the seductive motion of her tongue, and his blood pressure responded with an odd sudden spike.

He nodded and pretended nonchalance. "Okay then. I'm heading out. Nice to meet you. I'll be in touch."

She smiled again, but he had the impression her good will was forced. "Thanks for stopping by."

He gave her a small salute and left. *Phase one complete.*

· · ·

Kent paced the lobby and checked his watch for the umpteenth time. Half an hour had passed since he'd positioned the keys and set up his intercept scenario, and Josie still hadn't come down the elevator. What exactly was she doing up there after most everyone else had gone home? Was this the time of day she'd chosen to riffle through papers left out on executive's desks?

Deciding to investigate, or maybe catch her in the act, he reached for the elevator call button. Before his fingertip made contact, the button *dinged* and the *down* arrow lit up. He tapped his foot and watched the ornate bronze indicator arrow over the elevator doors sweep in an arc to the left. It passed over the two and then continued toward the one.

Another *ding*. The doors opened. Josie stood inside,

a contemplative expression on her face. He made a quick downward scan and got his first view of her shapely hips, smooth-skinned legs, and peek-a-boo, open-toed shoes. A smile tugged at his lips. This spy was sexy as hell.

He shook himself mentally and reined in his hormones. A sexy body was probably the bait. The horny male employees were supposed to spill their guts after a couple flutters of her eyelids.

As she walked off the elevator, he stepped into her path and captured her gaze. "Josie, what a pleasant surprise. You're just the person I was looking for. I'm glad I caught you."

She frowned and wariness clouded her eyes. "Why were you looking for me?"

He chuckled self-deprecatingly. "This doesn't seem to be my day. I think I left my car keys on your desk. I was on my way back up to your office to check."

The elevator doors closed behind her. "I didn't notice them anywhere."

"Would you mind going up with me and taking a look?" He hit the call button quickly before she could answer. The doors opened again.

She glanced around the lobby as if searching for a way to refuse. He watched her think for a second then draw in a deep breath. "I guess so."

He motioned for her to board the elevator first, and she stepped by him. "I'm sorry to delay you. Do you have a husband or boyfriend you're rushing home to?"

"No. I'm not in any hurry. That's okay." Her posture said just the opposite.

The doors opened at the fourth floor. They stepped out,

and he followed her the six paces to her office. She pulled a key out of her purse and unlocked the door. No one else at Emmeline's, except maybe Victor, locked his or her office, and he wondered why she felt it necessary. "Most people leave their offices open."

"Crime is rampant these days. It never hurts to be cautious."

Security was a reasonable explanation, and if she was on the up-and-up, her actions could be considered conscientious and admirable. But he intended to be cautious too. He filed away the info and let the subject drop.

She swung the door open, flicked on the lights, and walked inside.

He spotted his keys sitting where he'd left them. "I was right. There they are," he said, pointing.

She picked the keys up, turned, and handed them over. "Here you go."

Ignoring her why-would-this-fool-set-them-on-my-desk expression, he took the keys and flashed her another smile. "Thanks, you're a lifesaver."

She started toward the door, and he followed. Enjoying the light scent of her perfume, he stood next to her in the hallway and waited while she re-locked the door. The elevator was still at their level, and they stepped aboard.

"So where are you off to now?" he asked.

She stared in the direction of the buttons flashing red as the floors counted down. "Home."

"If you don't have plans, then maybe you'd join me for dinner. I have reservations for two downtown, but my mother called and told me she's tied up and can't make it."

He watched her take a deep breath. Her breast rose and

stretched the material of her jersey top.

"Thank you, but no thanks."

"I owe you something for saving my skin. Without my keys, I'd be stranded in the city hunting for a locksmith. Plus I'd like to get to know you."

Her cheeks turned an adorable shade of pink. "I really should go home."

He put sincerity in his eyes. "I'd enjoy your company. No strings attached."

"Thank you, Kent. But no." She stepped off the elevator in the lobby and spoke to him over her shoulder as she streaked for the exit like a guided missile. "Have a good evening."

He stopped dead in his tracks, watched her walk away, and his jaw dropped. She'd turned him down. She'd actually turned him down. He'd been brushed off, and his great plan to get to know her and uncover her secrets had crashed and burned.

The unfamiliar feeling of rejection caused a strange rolling in his gut as he quickly analyzed her actions. If she actually was a corporate spy, she might turn him down because she was afraid of dropping her guard and blowing her cover. Or because she didn't see a payoff for spending time in his company. He grinned. Of course. He needed to dangle some bait and make her think he'd be a good source of insider information.

Kent squared his shoulders and focused on the sway of her sultry hips until she disappeared out the front door.

Well, Josie darling, this is only round one, and I'm not giving up. I'll get you to talk to me for sure the next time.

Chapter Six

The next afternoon at five fifteen, Kent's wide shoulders and sun-bleached hair appeared in Faith's office doorway again. Her heart knocked in surprise at both the sight and the slightly unsettling hint of pleasure that rushed all the way to her toes.

He was attractive in a way that made women forget about common sense. He had a mesmerizing smile and a lean, athletic body. His dark, almost black, eyes held the confident look of a man who regularly went toe-to-toe with heavyweights and came out the winner, the look of a man who possessed a lion's instincts and a cougar's cunning. He was studying her like a puzzle he'd set his sights on solving, and she sensed letting him get too close would spell trouble.

"Hi," he said with a dazzling smile that lit his eyes and showed his perfect teeth. "Can a hard-working member of the financial department whose brain is muddled from shuffling huge piles of corporate money all day buy you dinner tonight?"

She bit on the inside of her cheek. Mom had warned her about smooth-talking men and the troubles they could cause if you let down your defenses. She didn't want to be a paranoid recluse, but this was no time to be careless.

Her brain clamped onto another reason for refusal. The less time she spent with any of Emmeline's employees, the less chance she'd slip up and say something contradictory.

Then she remembered last night's phone conversation.

"You mean you turned down a dinner date with an attractive man?" Josie had said in an outraged tone. "How could you? You're supposed to be me. Before I met Cal, I never would have eaten home alone if a charming, polite guy invited me out."

Guilt nipped at her wall of reluctance. She'd assumed the incident yesterday was history, never expected him to return and ask her out a second time. But now he was here, and she was trapped. She'd promised Josie she'd act like her, and Josie would wring her neck if she ever found out Faith had turned Kent down again.

Her heart yelled *go ahead, be Josie, take a chance*, but her stomach rolled at the thought of spending the evening telling lies.

Before she had time to finish her mental debate, he said, "I should warn you, I'm very persistent. I'm going to keep asking until you accept."

Devilish mischief sparkled in his eyes, tempting her to say *yes*. The repressed half of her brain warned: *No, he's too gorgeous and enticing. Don't encourage him, it's not safe.* The other half presented a logical argument: *Do it, he works in the financial department. Maybe you can discover some piece of information about Victor Telemann.*

The idea of using him to get information produced a ripple of guilt, but she shook it off. Following the rules would get her nowhere. If she was going to get justice for her mother, she had to look at the bigger picture and do whatever was necessary, investigate any promising trail. "Then maybe I should accept now and save you a lot of trouble."

"That would be the easiest and most logical solution."

Logical, yes. But smart? She knew nothing about him. Did she dare go out with him? The answer came in words her mother had repeated often: only to a very public place where you'll be completely safe.

"Where are you suggesting we go?" she asked.

"Have you ever heard of *The Crimson Spider*?"

She chuckled. "No, and the name doesn't do much for my appetite."

"It's actually a great place for steaks and seafood. The owner celebrates Halloween all year long, hence the name."

Her curiosity piqued by what he might be able to tell her plus a restaurant that celebrated Halloween in the spring, she made her decision. "Can you give me a couple minutes to finish up this module and organize my desk?"

"Sure thing." He stuffed his hands in his pockets, leaned a shoulder against her doorjamb, and crossed his long legs at the ankle.

She dragged her eyes back to the monitor. She'd meant he should leave and come back, but he'd either missed the hint or he was used to controlling situations and acting as he pleased.

His unnerving gaze seemed to drill into the top of her head, and knowing he was watching muddled her thoughts.

After making two typos and writing a line of flawed code that would have started an infinite loop, she saved her work, closed her file, and activated the security routine she'd programmed into her account. If he'd been playing a psychological fishing game aimed at keeping her on his hook, he'd won.

Logging off, she raised her eyes and met his. A tiny shiver of excitement rippled through her frame, and she drew in a sharp breath. Maybe having dinner with any man, and especially this one, would be a bad move. She had enough on her plate right now, and a man could get in the way and cause complications.

"I'll just be another minute," she said, wondering if she could change her mind without seeming rude or hurting his feelings.

"Take your time."

He continued watching her, and she worried he could see her nervousness.

She stuffed a pile of notes into her desk drawer, locked it, and pulled the key. Then she scanned the rest of the office for anything out of place. Satisfied her work would be safe overnight, she slipped her feet into the shoes she'd kicked off under her desk, retrieved her purse from her bottom drawer, stood, and tried to smooth the wrinkles out of her skirt. Unfortunately, it was one of Josie's skirts, so there wasn't much material to smooth. Even if she tugged until her knuckles were raw, the snug material would never get any looser or longer.

She glanced at Kent. Her tugging had caught his attention, and his eyes were focused below her waist. Wishing for a less revealing skirt, Faith raised a hand to toss her hair over her shoulder. Air. No hair. Reminded of her short cut, she huffed out her breath, detoured the flipping motion, and straightened her collar instead. She hung her purse strap on her shoulder and moved away from her chair.

"Okay, Kent. I'm ready anytime you are."

He smiled, stepped toward her, and reached out a hand. "Then we're off to see the spiders."

She hesitated for a second, then placed her hand in his. His warm fingers closed around hers and a rush of adrenaline slipped into her bloodstream and accelerated her heartbeat.

He stepped out the doorway behind her. She stopped short. "Oh, wait. I have to close up."

She took out the key and locked the door. As she slipped her key chain back into her purse and turned back toward him, his large, masculine hand slid around and lightly touched the small of her back. A tingle of sexual electricity shot along her nerve endings. She jerked in surprise, gasped, and pulled away.

He lowered his arm and frowned slightly. "Sorry, I was just…I mean…I really wasn't trying anything."

She felt foolish for acting like a man had never touched her before and ignored the fact that the contact had ignited a bonfire of awareness. Telling herself her nerves were frayed and the intensity of her physical reaction to this virtual stranger had simply caught her off guard, she forced an embarrassed smile. "That's okay. You surprised me, and I overreacted."

The elevator doors opened. He put out a hand and prevented them from closing until they were both aboard the car. She stood inches away from him, held her arms tight at her sides, and stared at the floor numbers lighting up as the car descended. The whir of the motor filled the awkward silence. She caught a whiff of his musky, male cologne and felt a heart-pounding wave of attraction.

When the doors slid open on the first floor, she stepped off the elevator and stopped a few feet away. "Maybe I should just go home."

He held up both hands and turned them for inspection. "I swear I'll only use these to eat. Please come with me."

The innocent, pleading look in his eyes did her in. He seemed like a sweet guy. Maybe she was being ridiculous, and it was time she filled Josie's stilettos. She pulled in a steadying breath. "Okay."

A broad smile and something like relief brightened his face. "We can go out the back way. My car's in the employee lot."

• • •

Buoyed by his success at making contact with his target, Kent directed Josie to the bright red Mustang parked between his Porsche and Ben Kipfer's Lincoln Town Car. Once there, he unlocked the doors with the remote and held open the passenger side door.

As she sat, he watched her shapely legs swing into the car and wondered why she wore provocative clothes if she was so obviously timid. The sexy wardrobe clashed with the shy woman he'd seen so far, and he found the contrast intriguing. Expecting the discovery of Josie's secrets to be a pleasant challenge, he planned the next step of his fact-finding mission: Gain her trust and get her to relax.

He slid behind the steering wheel and scanned the

unfamiliar dashboard, locating the AC fan, stereo controls, wipers, and turn signals. Before anything else, he needed to figure out the peculiarities of driving this car. The shift lever for the standard transmission looked awkwardly located and might require a conscious effort to avoid grinding gears. Confident he could manage, he stuck the key in the ignition and was rewarded with the instant purr of a powerful, eight-cylinder engine.

Josie said, "Your car smells new."

He grinned. Busted. He'd been so focused on hiding his unfamiliarity with the car, he'd overlooked the obvious clue that would give him away. "It is. You're my first passenger."

As he pulled out onto the road, Josie asked, "So how long have you worked in the financial department?"

"A couple years."

"What do you do?"

The question was consistent with Victor's suspicion she was a spy. It was also the obvious thing for any innocent person to ask on a first date. Wanting to give her enough rope to hang herself if she was beginning to pump him for secrets, he kept his answer truthful and vague. "Property acquisitions. I research independent stores in good locations that are having financial difficulty and find the ones ripe for a buyout. Emmeline's expansion philosophy is based on buying quality businesses with established clientele who demand high-end merchandise and appreciate service."

"Are they expanding so quickly that you have a constant supply of work? I mean, that seems like a sort of intermittent job."

The Mustang's steering was looser than his Porsche and every one of his senses were on high alert as he strained to drive the strange car and talk intelligently. "I was busy for a solid year preparing for a deal that closed last week. I'm already narrowing in on another property."

"Does the job in the financial department you wanted me to consider involve research?"

Trying to remember exactly what he'd said about the fictitious job, he scrambled to invent credible details. "Some. Mostly it's organizing our data."

He hit a torn-up patch of blacktop, clenched the wheel tighter, and braced for the bone-jarring lurch that would slam his skull into the headliner. Unlike the tight suspension in his race-ready Porsche, the Mustang's shocks handled the bump in stride and hardly rocked the car at all. Feeling a little foolish at his white knuckled grip, he turned onto Harmony Boulevard and noted Jack's directions were spot on so far.

Testing the depth of her interest in his function at Emmeline's, he veered to a different subject. "Keep an eye out for Maitland Road on the right, would you please?"

"Haven't you been to this restaurant before?"

"No. A good friend recommended it."

"I got the impression you'd eaten there." She pointed. "The next cross-street."

He read the sign, clicked on the turn signal, took the corner, and shot her a sidelong glance. "I've been meaning to get here for a while, but it's no fun going new places alone. I needed someone to share it with."

She looked away. "There's the building."

He noted that she hadn't tried to steer the subject back to Emmeline's acquisitions or pump him for information about upcoming deals. Did that mean she was cagey or uninterested?

"I should have asked before," he said. "You're not dating anyone else are you?"

"No. I…ah…just got into town."

Flashing her his most charming smile, he said, "Good, then I hope we'll see more of each other."

"Maybe."

As he parked, he noticed her smooth her skirt and squirm in her seat. The hint of nervousness in her actions and the uncertainty in her voice were interesting. Other women would be baiting a guy with flirtatious innuendoes by now. Yet Josie was reserved and cautious…and a little bit of an enigma.

He wondered if knowing his identity would change her response to his overtures. If she knew he had a huge trust fund and owned a forty-nine percent share of Emmeline's, would she suddenly be a lot friendlier?

He clenched his teeth. His whole life, ninety-nine percent of everyone he'd ever met had wanted something from him. He'd looked behind the saccharine smiles and seen the requests. Money, influence, social acceptance, there was always something driving the hearty handshake and come-hither gaze.

He glanced over and saw her studying the building through the windshield. She had no come-hither gaze and hadn't even offered him an inviting smile. Why not? Was his money really his major charm or was he just slipping?

Pride stiffened his shoulders. He could walk into any club in town and have a woman at his table in minutes. He could choose who he took home for the night. None of the women he met knew about his money, yet they were attracted and wanted to be with him.

Amazed at the direction of his thoughts, he shook off the ridiculous doubts. His ability to charm women wasn't the problem. Her unexpected responses were. For the first time since he'd discovered the birds and the bees, and decided he liked being a very busy bee, he was facing a woman who seemed downright indifferent. Her reserve was a new experience.

He reminded himself a spy would have to be a convincing actress and a smooth liar. She'd know how to manipulate people to get what she wanted. She might appear demure and sweet, but if she had stabbed him in the back with his last deal, she was far from a playful kitten, more like a coiled viper. A viper he was going to defang.

Walking around toward her door as she got out without waiting, he put a confident bounce back in his step. She might act uninterested now, but eventually he'd charm her and peel away her exterior shell. Based on her hairstyle and makeup and the way she dressed, she was aware of her sexuality. So maybe she was playing hard-to-get. In that case, revealing her true colors was just a matter of being persistent and biding his time.

His lips tugged up into a smile. If it turned out Victor was wrong about her being a corporate spy, he might even enjoy the challenge of chipping away her defenses.

He set his jaw in stony resolve. But if she was a spy, and she was playing him, she'd met her match. He'd crush her pretty shell and take her down.

• • •

Faith's nerves were taut as the hostess led her and Kent through a dimly-lit room with skeletons hanging in the corners and spider webs clinging to the windows. The decor was definitely Halloween, and she realized she fit right in wearing her Josie costume and masquerading as someone else.

Kent held her chair while she sat at the small table with a black tablecloth, orange candle, and orange napkins, then he took the seat across from her. A waitress wearing a black cape over a snug, lace dress and looking like a sexy vampire brought ice water and took their drink orders.

"This place reminds me of a low-budget horror movie," Kent said.

Realizing the decor would provide enough conversation to make pretending to be Josie less stressful, Faith's blood pressure returned to within twenty points of normal. "Or the fun house at a carnival."

She crossed her feet at her ankles, tucked them under her chair, and tried not to think about the attractive man sitting so close she could feel the heat radiating from his legs. She told herself it was only a dinner, she could do this without any problem.

Hoping to conceal her anxiety, she opened the coffin-shaped menu and studied the list of dinner entrees. "I wonder what's good."

Kent stared at his menu then pursed his lips. "I'm thinking of a Dracula's Delight."

"The *tender filet* part sounds tempting, but I'm not sure I want the *cool, bloody interior*."

"They can probably ruin it by cooking if you ask."

She closed her menu. "I'll stick with the blackened grouper. The aroma of the spices has my mouth watering, plus I like my food dead."

He sniffed. "The scent of peppercorns and paprika is tempting, but I'll stick with the steak. Unless it'll bother you watching my food bleed."

"No, please, go right ahead. If you get your fill of blood now, at least I'll know you won't be biting my neck later."

He laughed and leaned closer, his eyebrows raised. "Ah, but, my dear, it is such a lovely neck. Such creamy skin, such a tempting curve. I shall hunger for you regardless."

She smiled and held her hands up in the form of a cross. "Back, wicked one. You'll never taste my corpuscles."

His eyes sparkled in the candlelight. Gorgeous eyes, sensual eyes. "We shall see, my sweet Josie."

"Yes, we shall. Maybe you'll be the one devoured by me."

His mouth quirked with a suggestive smile. "All my dreams might come true."

Her teasing had gone too far. Heat crept up her cheeks.

The waitress appeared with pad poised and saved Faith from a full-fledged blush. "Are you ready to order?"

The waitress scribbled down their orders and left. They kept up the light banter, depleting the subjects of the menu and decor while eating their salads and sharing a loaf of crusty sourdough bread.

After a few minutes, Faith was considering how to bring up the topic of Emmeline's financials when Kent said, "So where are you from?"

"Williamsburg, Virginia."

"Do you have family there?"

"Just cousins, aunts, uncles. I'm—I was—an only child of a single mom. She died of colon cancer a few weeks ago."

"I'm sorry."

"Thank you. I'm starting to get used to the idea, but it still seems unreal."

He was quiet for a minute, then cleared his throat. "I'm an only child too. I asked my mother for a brother once, but she said one of me was more than enough."

"I was lonely and prayed for a brother or sister every night. I guess that's why I've always planned to someday have a big family."

She kicked herself. Talking about how many children she wanted was taboo for a first date. Plus she'd made a more serious mistake: Josie had two brothers and her mother was alive.

"This is pretty good for sourdough," he said. "Most American restaurants do it wrong. The best I've ever tasted in the States was at a little hole-in-the-wall restaurant in Seattle."

Okay, time to get practical and ask some questions about Emmeline's. She steered the subject toward his job. "How often do you have to travel?"

"Maybe one week out of a month."

"It must be fun dealing with huge amounts of someone else's money. How much does a typical acquisition cost?"

"Anywhere from five to fifty million, but the money is mostly on paper and arranged through bank loans. It's not like I'm carrying around barrels of cash."

"I suppose a good credit rating is vital to continued expansion and the security of your job. Is the company's financial condition strong enough to withstand a sudden downturn?"

He placed his knife across his bread and butter plate and sat back. His dark eyes grew darker, until they shone like orbs of ebony. "Emmeline's is as profitable and stable as they come. What kind of downturn are you talking about?"

She chuckled to make her line of questioning sound casual. "Oh, you know, something like what happened to the peanut butter companies when their supplier was closed down for unsanitary conditions or the toy companies when they had the problems with lead paint. A retail store could have a scandal that involved a company officer."

His expression didn't change. A muscle twitched ever so slightly in his jaw. "Any officer in particular?"

Had she hit on a professional sore spot? She waved her hand as if to brush away her offending words. "Oh, no, I just picked a scandal out of the air as an example."

"I wouldn't worry about any big financial storms hitting us too soon," he said, jutting out his chin. The temperature of his tone dropped several degrees. "We have good people watching the money and can handle any challenge. Our competitors shouldn't underestimate our strength."

While she pondered his strange, defensive posture and remark about competitors, their waitress cleared away the salad plates and served the entrees. Faith had the uncomfortable feeling that she and Kent were playing a game of cat and mouse, and she wasn't at all sure who was the cat.

Kent picked up his steak knife and cut into his Dracula's Delight. "I'm not usually bloodthirsty, but I guess the old survival instincts surface once in a while. Me man, kill and protect, enemy lose and die."

"I've never thought of a cow as an enemy."

"A bloody steak is a throwback to our cave-dwelling days." His eyes took on a predatory gleam, and he revealed his perfect white teeth in a razor-sharp smile. "It's a metaphor for a lot of things in life and in business."

Was he talking about the cutthroat nature of acquisition negotiations and his job?

She considered the metaphor for a couple seconds. A connection to her life seemed apropos, too. Her fight to bring Victor to justice would be considered bloodthirsty by some, but unless someone fought against his base instincts and the base instincts of other criminals like him, wouldn't society erode and eventually collapse? Taking violent criminals off the streets was vital to a civilization's survival, and a willingness to look at the symbolic blood was an essential part of becoming a warrior.

Her gaze drifted to the small, crimson puddle forming on Kent's plate. If she was less than bloodthirsty in her pursuit of a rapist, would another woman she could have protected someday suffer?

She picked up her fork and attacked her fish.

Other than *how's your grouper, delicious, how's your steak, perfect*, they ate in silence for a few minutes. A band set up and pumped ear-splitting music into massive speakers. A singer in Goth garb belted out lyrics about spells, and crypts, and the charms of crawling insects.

Kent caught her eye and beamed her a two hundred and twenty watt smile. "Doesn't the idea of a love sonnet to a spider just warm your heart?" He reached across the table, placed his hand on top of hers, and squeezed gently. Then he shifted his hand and softly rubbed her fingers.

Disquieted by the jump in her pulse, she wet her bottom lip. "It's quite touching."

"Have you ever been in love?" he asked in a serious tone.

"I had a crush on my lab partner in college, if that counts."

"What happened?"

"He got arrested for hacking into a military database and stealing the passwords of the Joint Chiefs of Staff. Needless to say, the dean kicked him out of school."

"Interesting, but I meant in regard to your crush. Was he madly in love with you?"

"Not even close. He hardly knew I was alive. His only real love was the Internet."

"It's hard to believe any red-blooded male could choose to spend his time on a computer rather than be with such a beautiful woman."

She choked down a snort. Talk about hard to believe. She was sitting here dressed in Josie's clothes, enjoying the excitement of being someone else, and flirting with a handsome man. The entire situation seemed absurd. "Thank you for the lovely compliment, but when I was in college, I was a lot different from the person you're seeing tonight."

He pulled his hand back and picked up his wine. "I can't believe you were that different. The guy must have been crazy to let you get away."

She watched him swirl the dark liquid in his glass. Was this what the world of romance was like? Enjoying the touch of a warm hand, treasuring a compliment like water in the desert, feeling light-headed and shy, yet at the same time bold and daring? Was this what she'd been missing while she'd cloistered herself in the college library and studied calculus and logic and physics until her brain felt swollen and bruised? Longing pulled her gaze to his face, his mouth, his inviting lips. She imagined the heat of his kiss.

She felt a niggling of fear and shook off the thought. Her reaction to him was purely physiological, the result of traitorous hormones invading her bloodstream and trying to disable her good sense and sound judgment. She was here for one reason—to build a case against Victor. Detouring from her goal could get her into trouble.

She gave him an embarrassed smile and thank-you-for-the-compliment nod then twisted the conversation away from her drab past. "What about you? Any former loves?"

He shrugged and smoothed his beautiful, quilted silk tie. "One or two. Nothing serious." He reached for the dessert menu. "Have you seen this luscious looking death-by-overdose-of-chocolate cheese cake?"

Faith had spent many years sitting and observing others. She'd learned to notice body language clues most people missed. Watching him pretend interest in dessert, she admired his social skills and how smoothly he'd worked in the distraction. But what about his past love life did he want to hide?

The band played the first notes of a slow, romantic tune. He looked up, put down his menu, and asked, "Would you like to dance?"

The thought of being in his arms sent tremors of delight to her toes. The tremors were followed by the voice of logic whispering in her ear. He was out of her league, a man to treat casually and keep at arm's length. Did he charm naive women, manipulate them, and then break their hearts? Was he even more dangerous than she thought?

Despite her reservations, she couldn't resist his invitation. She got to her feet as if in a trance and pushed away the question lingering in her brain. *Instead of standing and*

moving closer to his body like a lamb waltzing into a slaugh-
terhouse, should she be running for her life?

• • •

Kent slowed the Mustang and parallel parked in front of
Faith's apartment building. He got out and started around
the back of the car.

She sighed, disappointed the evening was over. He'd
turned out to be charming, and she hadn't laughed or danced
so much in ages. For the last two hours, images of Victor and
her mother had retreated to the back of her mind, and she'd
simply enjoyed Kent's company and entertaining sense of
humor.

She swung her door open before he reached the passenger side.

"I could get that door for you," he said.

"Thank you, but I'm quite capable."

His tone was teasing. "Are you one of those feminist
who insists on being independent?"

"Not really," she said with a small smile. "I've just always
done it myself."

He stepped closer. "You must not have had the right
man around, one who'll put you on a proper pedestal and
treat you like a queen."

Her cheeks warmed. What could she say to such an
outrageous remark?

"Would you like a ride to the store in the morning to
pick up your car?" he asked.

"Thank you for offering, but I usually walk to work, so
my car is already here."

"Darn. I thought I had a good reason for you to see me again. Can I walk you up to your apartment?"

"No thanks. I'm fine."

He lifted a hand, brushed a few strands of hair off her cheek, and rested his fingers under her chin as he stared into her eyes.

Earlier in the evening he'd rubbed her fingers. He was treating her like fragile china he wasn't sure he should touch, and his restraint gave her a sense of comfort and security. "Thank you for a wonderful evening," she said.

"Thank you for coming with me. You made the food more delicious, the music more hilarious, and the decor more fun." His velvet voice touched her like a caress.

Every atom in her body focused on his masculine scent and dazzling smile.

He urged her chin slightly higher so her face tilted up toward his mouth. She held her breath, unsure if she should pull away or move closer. Did this fabulous man really want to kiss her good night?

He questioned her with his expressive eyes.

She should hold tight to reality and keep her defenses in place, but she swallowed, let her desire show in her gaze, watched him comprehend her message.

He lowered his mouth and pressed it over hers. His lips were soft and sensuous. A strange warmth curled low in her belly. She wanted him to hold her close. She tried to argue against the things her body was suggesting, but her brain had stopped working and no thoughts formed.

He kissed her at his leisure, taking his time, pressing feathery kisses to her slightly parted lips. His arms went around her, his hands burning her back. She leaned against him, enthralled, floating, light-headed with longing.

He stepped back, putting a few inches between them. "Good night, Josie."

Josie. Of course he wanted to kiss her. He didn't know she was plain, mousy Faith.

Her body solidified to a lump of gray lead. She looked at the ground, slumped her shoulders, and imagined telling him the truth. How fast would he dump her once he saw the woman beneath her disguise?

Chapter Seven

At lunchtime on Thursday, her nineteenth day in Palm Beach, Faith slipped onto the local network, managed to get access to Victor's terminal, and looked through the history of his recent Internet searches. He'd visited the websites of several yacht brokerages and two different real estate agencies specializing in Cayman Islands properties. She filed the information away in a corner of her brain. His searches were understandable for a man with the resources to purchase a boat or home in the Caribbean, but inputting criteria, viewing videos, and bookmarking seemed out of character for someone with a reputation for being less than tech savvy.

She wondered if he was pretending to be old-fashioned, but she couldn't fathom a reason for anyone to present that façade to the world.

Shutting down her wormhole into Victor's computer, she Googled *detective agencies New York City*. The search returned over two hundred thousand items. The first ten pages of responses listed over a hundred and fifty names. Overwhelmed, she stared at screen after screen, huffed out her breath, and raked her fingers through her hair. How in the world was anybody supposed to know who would be professional and reliable?

She sat back and chewed the inner edges of her lips. She needed help. Steve Zurich was the logical solution.

After securing her computer and locking her office, she left the building. She strolled past the messenger service with a streaking fox logo on the door and the branch bank on the corner, then around to the far side of the block. Stepping out of the flow of foot traffic in front of an insurance company, she pulled out her cell phone and punched in the number for Steve's office.

"Zurich."

"Hi, Steve, it's Josie. Josie Ashland."

"Hey, Josie. What's up?"

"I was wondering if you can recommend a good investigator in New York City, someone reliable who could go to the Bureau of Public Records and do some research."

"I can put you onto someone. What do you need?"

"Victor Telemann applied for a marriage license up there twenty-three years ago, but I can't find out if he actually got married, or if he did, when he received a divorce decree. The information is too old to be online. I need an investigator who can go to the archives and dig through the microfiche records."

"Interesting." The pitch of his voice dropped and the tempo slowed. "I found something like that myself. What date and names were on the license you found?"

"Ruby Swain, November third, nineteen ninety-one."

"That jives with my info," he said, his voice more confident. "Tell you what. I've got a buddy who lives in Jersey. I'll have him shoot into the city next week and see what he can dig up. He'll be hourly. I'll have him fax the bill to my office."

"Okay. Let me know what he finds."

"I'll email you a report of my recent findings later this morning. Nothing much of interest."

She sighed, beginning to suspect *nothing* would be his perpetual report. Hiring an investigator had seemed like a smart idea at first, but now she was starting to wonder. "Keep trying."

"Will do." He disconnected.

Faith disconnected too, and as she stuffed her smart phone into her purse, she bumped a newspaper box. She glanced down, and her gaze landed on a sidebar headline: *Panda Births Have Zoologists Giddy.*

Finally some good news. Maybe at least one species could be saved from extinction.

Eager to read the full article, she dug for change, and bought a copy of the paper. Then she grabbed a ham and cheese sandwich and a small bag of chips at a nearby deli, and rushed back to her office. She'd only been gone fifteen minutes, and the rest of the floor was still deserted.

Rousing her computer from sleep mode and entering her password, she breathed a sigh of relief. Maybe she could finally get some private time to review Victor's recent emails without worrying about interruptions.

While she waited for her program to execute and download copies of the messages in Victor's inbox, she ripped open her chips, unwrapped her sandwich, and took a bite.

"There you are."

Her heart jumped. She jerked her eyes toward the door.

Ronnie crossed his arms over his chest and shook his head as he stepped inside.

Oh, crap. Victor's emails. Her finger flew to her kill key.

For some reason, the system was sluggish. A second passed. Two.

Three long strides and Ronnie was next to her desk. Fear rippled down her spine. She stared at her monitor. *Change. Come on, damn it, change.* An eternity dragged by with the world in agonizing, stomach-churning slow motion. Then zip, the screen display vanished and a data-entry form appeared.

She made a show of swallowing her bite of sandwich while she searched for her voice and wished her heart would go back to beating normally. "Hey, Ronnie. How are you doing?"

The food crash-landed in her stomach. Had he seen the list of emails in Victor's inbox as big as life on her monitor? Was she in deep doo-doo?

"Good. Hungry," he said. "I was going to drag you out to lunch, but I see you're prepared to barricade the world and keep working."

She chuckled, but it came out too high-pitched. Her cheeks felt like she was standing too close to a roaring fire. "Sorry. I would have waited if I knew you'd be coming by."

"Tomorrow I expect you to be ready and waiting at eleven forty-five. The gang's going to Mertha's."

Her reply was automatic. "I have a lot of work to do. I might be too busy."

He wagged a finger side to side in rhythm with the shake of his head. "No excuses. If I didn't see you wearing different clothes every day, I'd half believe you were living here. Lighten up, girl. It's a job, not your life. Or at least I hope it isn't."

Deciding he hadn't seen Victor's emails or he would have mentioned them by now, she breathed a sigh of relief. This time she was safe.

She smiled, warmed by Ronnie's sense of caring. She needed to be friendly and socialize if she was going to uncover any information. "Okay. Tomorrow. Mertha's."

He leaned over and peered at the data input form on her monitor, then scanned her desk. "What are you working on that's so fascinating?"

All the blood drained from her face. Was she in fact safe? "Ah, nothing much. Just the website design."

"I can do a basic WYSIWYG page, but programming in HTML is above my head. You must really know your way around the bowels of the computer system though."

She shrugged and eyed the doorway. Should she bolt on the pretense of rushing to the ladies' room before he asked about the emails and her world came crashing down? "Pretty much."

"What do you think? Is Emmeline's the kind of place where the boss snoops into our emails and keeps track of how much time we spend online browsing porn sites and Facebook?" He stole a chip from her bag, popped it into his mouth, and gave her a penetrating look as he chewed.

Relief gushed into her chest. He hadn't seen Victor's emails. He was thinking about something else.

She considered the question, and it sparked a flurry of ideas. If a boss could watch employees, why couldn't an employee watch the boss? If she installed a monitoring software package like WorkControl on all Victor's accounts, she could record the sites he visited when he surfed the web, track his keystrokes, and sift through his email for keywords without the risk of detection she was facing now. Once she cracked his cell phone, she could use the kind of position-tracking software employers installed on company cars to download his GPS records and recreate a map of his movements.

A tingle of excitement ran down her spine as she filed the plan away for later and pulled her attention back to Ronnie's original question. "From what I've heard of Victor Telemann, I doubt he's computer savvy enough to monitor anyone."

"He could have someone doing it for him. Someone who knows her way around a computer system."

She met his eyes, saw a question in their depths. Damn, she'd missed the subtext to their conversation! Her curiosity flared. "Okay, Ronnie. Spill it."

He cocked a brow. "Rumor has it you're doing more than building a website in here. I heard you're snooping into everyone's computer use." He gave that a half a second to sink in, than asked, "You're not a spy for Victor, are you?"

A laugh burst from her lungs but caught and twisted in her throat. It formed a hard knot and sank, free-falling toward her stomach. Had someone else detected her hacking? How long did she have before reports of her activities reached Victor?

Struggling to keep her expression neutral, she dismissed the question with a wave of her hand and put a note of disbelief in her voice. "No. Of course not."

He chuckled. "I didn't think so. I imagine the rumor was started by some insecure, jealous bitch trying to turn people against you."

"Who'd be jealous of me?" she said, forcing herself to chuckle along with him. "I'm not anything special."

"Don't kid yourself. Lots of these women would love to have even half your style, looks, brains, and confidence. Some of them probably consider you a threat because they seem so pathetic in contrast."

What? She'd always felt everyone else was self-assured, and she was the only one intimidated by others and wracked by monstrous self-doubts. But if his theory about her co-workers feeling inferior was true, maybe she wasn't so different after all. She felt a momentary sense of comfort. *You're not a spy for Victor, are you?* Yikes. Her mouth went Sahara dry.

"Seriously, Ronnie, who's saying what about me?"

He shrugged and sounded apologetic. "I don't want to name names and cause animosity. It was just something I heard batted around at the water cooler and figured I should mention. Don't let it bother you. I'm sure the person who suggested you were a management mole will realize she's wrong once she knows you better."

"I don't want people distrusting me. I mean, I need to ask a lot of questions to do my job, and if people are afraid to tell me anything, I can't be effective." *And I'll never find out the truth about my father.*

"It's the number of questions that have people wondering. Throttle back for a while."

If her inquiries about Victor and the business had sparked the rumors, then Ronnie was right. She needed to be more subtle and come up with other ways to find information.

"I guess I should. Thanks for the heads up, Ronnie. I appreciate your honesty." She bit on her bottom lip. Too bad she couldn't be honest with him in return.

"Okay then, I'm off in search of sustenance. See you tomorrow."

"Sure." She waved and watched him leave.

Her shoulders slumped under a ton of discouragement as soon as he was out of sight. Damn. First Steve and now this. Every time she thought her information gathering was on the right path, she bumped into another complication.

At home later, she prepared a cheese omelet and a pot of herbal tea, then settled down to read her newspaper. The panda babies were healthy, and their births reminded her of Josie, whose delivery date was drawing ever closer.

Trying to shake off her suffocating sense of loneliness, she searched the newspaper for another interesting story. More deaths in Afghanistan and Iraq. Politicians fighting in Washington. An exposé of corruption on a nearby suburb's city council.

An exposé. She sat up straighter. Bingo. That would be her Plan C.

She would search the local newspapers and TV stations and identify an investigative reporter who might be interested in a story about a rapist who was freely walking the Palm Beach streets.

• • •

The next afternoon, the group lunching at Mertha's seemed infected with a case of TGIF. Twelve forty-five came and went, but the rowdy conversation continued. Faith concentrated on not asking questions and kept one eye on the clock. Trying not to appear aloof or unfriendly, she pushed away her empty plate and ordered an iced tea refill she could sip and use as a prop.

Her gaze traveled around the table following voices from speaker to speaker, analyzing faces, trying to see behind the smiles. How many of these people had been gossiping about her? Was one of them capable of inadvertently scuttling her plan to make Victor face justice? Was there a single person among them whom she could trust?

She remembered Ronnie's remark that whoever had suggested she was a spy would realize she was wrong once she got to know her better. Fat chance. If they got to know her better, they might find out her secrets, discover she was a fraud. Guilt reared its ugly head again, grinding her nose in the reality that she was alone. She couldn't let anyone in this crowd know her better. Not even Ronnie. Anything any one of them discovered could put her at risk, could allow Victor to stay free.

Laughter erupted at a remark from Ronnie, but she'd missed what he'd said and covered her ignorance with a smile. The topic was dating and sex and, reluctant to draw attention to herself, she squirmed and shrank into her chair. She had no funny stories to contribute and felt a keen sense of being an outsider peeking into the lives of happy, normal people. People who could joke about their misfortunes with sex.

The extended lunch finally broke up at one fifteen. As relieved as a felon on parole, she hustled back to her office while half the others were still waiting for their change. Plopping down at her desk, she dove into her program code with a vengeance. Work was simple and logical. Work kept her loneliness and guilt and shame and nagging questions at bay. Work could fill the agonizing gaps in time when she was stalled in finding the answers she desperately wanted but, at the same time, was terrified to hear.

The next time she looked up, Kent was standing in her doorway watching her with a keen, unnerving gaze.

He was wearing a perfectly tailored suit in a gorgeous slate gray. His shirt was one shade lighter, his crimson tie the bright spot. With one hand in his slacks' pocket and an enigmatic smile on his lush lips, he looked like he'd just stepped from a men's fashion magazine, so suave, masculine, and sexy her toes curled. Why was it that every time she saw him her pulse pounded wildly?

She moistened her lips and tried to sound nonchalant. "Hi. How long have you been there?"

"A couple minutes. I was watching those cute frown lines you get when you're concentrating and the way you twist your mouth when you're thinking."

She felt flustered. Was her face turning red? "It's not fair to sneak up on people."

He stepped into the office. "Why? Do you have something to hide?"

The question socked her in the stomach. Had he heard the rumors about her spying too? She picked up a pen and chuckled, then scribbled a couple words of nonsense on a scrap of paper as an excuse to keep her eyes downward. She put down the pen and drew in a deep breath for composure. "Me, something to hide? No, my life is an open book with a boring plot. There's nothing worth hiding."

His eyes sparkled demonically. "Maybe we need to do

something wicked so you'll have a deep, dark secret."

She thought of her parentage. Being conceived during a rape was a dark enough secret, and her genes might already be wicked. "No thanks, I'll stay dull."

"I hardly find you dull. In fact, I'd like to spend more time with you. Would you like to go to the jazz festival in the park tomorrow?"

Her heart fluttered in delight. He seemed like a nice guy and going with him would be fun. As she was about to say *yes*, reality hit her. Going would be too dangerous. They'd be together for several hours. He could discover she was an imposter. Knowing what was at stake and what had to be done didn't make saying *no* any easier. Disappointment weighed heavy on her chest. "I'm sorry. I have other plans."

"What about tonight? Are you doing anything? We could grab a bite to eat then take in a movie."

She knew she was making a mistake, but quickly rationalized accepting the invitation. Spending a little time with him was a logical move. She needed a source she could question without raising suspicion, and at the moment, he was her best prospect. As long as she kept up her guard and remembered to be Josie, a quick dinner then a couple hours in a movie theater where they couldn't talk except in whispers would be safe and useful.

She squashed a twinge of guilt over her despicable motives and let a rush of happiness burst onto her face. "Yes, I'd like that."

· · ·

"What type of food are you hungry for?" Kent asked after

starting the red Mustang.

"I'd love a pizza if that's okay with you."

"Then *Mama Leoni's* it is." He pulled from the parking lot and turned left. After all the nights he'd spent at the poolroom and bar next door to the restaurant in the past, following the familiar route again seemed like a journey home. "They have a fantastic tropical toppings pizza with pineapple and shrimp."

"I'm more traditional. Could we order half with pepperoni, mushrooms, and lots of cheese?"

"No problem. We'll get one of each."

She flashed him a lopsided grin. "I figured you for something spicier than pineapple and shrimp."

"Not tonight. They have a Mexican specialty loaded with hot peppers that scorches the roof of your mouth, but it takes about six pitchers of beer to keep the flames from shooting out your ears. It's great if all you've got planned is a night of shooting pool at the dive next door, but not when you're driving."

The parking lot of the little restaurant hadn't changed. He glanced at the entrance to the poolroom next door where he and Jack had spent many long hours in Jack's bachelor days. As he steered Josie toward the restaurant entrance, Kent wondered if any of the regulars were hanging out by the pool tables betting on crazy shots and if the owner's niece, Gina, with the long, shapely legs, was flashing smoky if-you're-rich-I'm-available looks at a new target.

Josie paused and breathed deeply of the air inside the doors. "It smells wonderful in here."

The waitress led them to a table near the front windows and laid out menus. "What can I get you to drink?"

"A Coke, please," Josie said.

"A pitcher of Heineken, and an extra glass in case the lady decides to switch."

The waitress left and Josie opened her menu. "The glass isn't necessary. I don't drink beer."

"Would you like something stronger? TGIF and all that."

"No thanks. I never developed a taste for liquor."

Amazed at yet another unexpected aspect of her complex personality, he chuckled. "You obviously went to a different college than I did. My fraternity brothers and I had bottles stashed in every nook and cranny. We never had a shortage and partied almost every night."

"What college did you go to?"

He bit back the truth. She might get suspicious about his identity if he admitted to four years studying business at Princeton or his grad work at Harvard. "University of Florida. Go Gators. What about you?"

"Virginia Tech."

"Sorority?"

"No. I shared an apartment with my cousin and two other girls. We all had to work nights and weekends to pay our tuition. Our parties were rare, small, and bring-your-own-everything."

The waitress came back with their drinks and took their orders.

When they were alone again, Kent got to work probing deeper into Josie's background. "Wasn't your family able to help with college expenses?"

He hoped for a clue about her financial condition that would reveal what she'd be willing to do for money. The time until she learned his identity was limited and passing quickly, and so far, he'd discovered very little useful in determining if she was a spy.

She looked down at the tabletop and fiddled with her silverware. "No. I got a small scholarship, but mostly I had to depend on a mountain of student loans. I'm still paying them off, probably will be until I'm ninety."

Paying her student loans sounded admirable and honest. Maybe finances weren't the right trail. "What was your major?"

"Computer Engineering."

"Right. I remember you mentioning your friend getting arrested."

"He was brilliant, probably would have graduated first in our class. But I learned a lot from him before he was expelled." She sipped her Coke. "What was your major?"

"Nothing as challenging as computer systems. Just business."

She gave him an understanding smile. "That's not easy either."

"I hung in there. The curriculum gave me a good background in finance and qualified me for my current job."

"Did you get the job you have now right out of college?"

"No." He spent a few minutes giving her a carefully edited version of his history. The year he'd spent on a grand tour of Europe became a short backpacking adventure. He skipped the lost years of idleness that he now regretted and described the route an average employee would have taken: an entry position then increasing responsibility.

"Emmeline's is an interesting company," she said. "Do you ever deal directly with Victor Telemann?"

His attention had wandered to the provocative curve of her chin, but at her mention of Victor, he snapped his mind back to his role as spy investigator. He was here to figure out her game, not fantasize about nuzzling the soft skin of her neck. His muscles tensed, but he shrugged and worked to keep his expression blank. "Some."

"What do you think of him?" Her tone said the question was mere curiosity, but her blue eyes were stormy and contradicted her cool air.

The waitress hustled up to the table and placed the two steaming pizzas in the center. She arranged plates in front of him and Josie, said "Enjoy," and rushed away.

"I'm starving," he said, surveying the pineapple chucks and selecting a juicy slice. "But I doubt I can eat this whole thing. If you want to sample some, help yourself."

"I may try a slice later." She picked up the server and slid a slice of the supreme pizza onto her plate. Mozarella cheese stretched across the gap, and she twirled the strings to break them free. After she set down the server, her pink tongue licked a wayward strand from her fingertip. His pulse jumped at the provocative little gesture.

She glanced at him and their eyes collided. She grabbed a napkin and scrubbed at the finger she'd licked.

"So," she said, "you were about to tell me what you think of Mr. Telemann."

Stalling, he took a bite of his pizza and put on a thoughtful expression. What to say about Victor? Obviously not the truth. He couldn't rant about the man's overblown ego or the course language he used when alone with his family. Victor's unfaithfulness to his wife was well known, but the fury that sparked in Kent's gut even now was deeply personal and not the reaction of a simple employee. Whatever he said had to be vague and at a professional level or he'd be taking the chance of giving himself away. He swallowed and wiped tomato sauce from his lips.

"He's a reasonably good businessman most of the time. A little too curt with employees. Far from my idea of a perfect CEO, but then he's never asked for my approval."

"What do you mean by curt with employees?"

"His management style is based on power and intimidation. I prefer a more relaxed atmosphere and a team spirit. It leads to better productivity." She had a faraway expression, a cold, harsh look in her eyes that made him believe her questions had a personal connection. "Have you met him?"

She shook herself. "Yes." She crossed her arms over her chest and ran her hands over her bare forearms. "Is it chilly in here, or is it just me?"

Her face had gone three shades paler. Odd, he thought, wishing he could look inside her pretty little head and read her mind.

He debated making a provocative offer to share his body heat. With most women he would. But despite how the idea excited his imagination and quickened his blood, he decided, in Josie's case, chivalry seemed more appropriate. Placing his napkin on the table, he stood. "I'll run out to the car and get you my suit jacket."

"No, please, sit down. That isn't necessary."

"I can't sit by and eat while you're uncomfortable. I insist."

When he returned with his jacket, she leaned forward in her seat, and he draped it over her shoulders. His fingers brushed her hair then slid to her shoulder and smoothed the material. His thoughts drifted to caressing her more intimately. "Better?"

"Yes, thank you. It was probably just the ice in the soda."

He forced his hands to his sides and sat, wondering why this woman seemed to draw him like a moth to a spotlight. What subtle magic made her more attractive and desirable than the beauty queens, party girls, and socialites he usually took home? Was it her lack of availability, the lure of her intelligence, or respect for her work ethic and struggle to support herself while going to school? Or was it her unassuming manner and the fact that she seemed totally unaware of her own beauty?

"I'm sorry I made you get up. Your food will be cold."

He drank the beer in his glass and refilled it from the pitcher. "One more slice and I'm done anyway. I want to save room for popcorn."

She shook her head and gave him an impish smile. "Do you always eat such nutritious meals?"

"Once in a while I go home and let my mother feed me. But when I'm on my own, I don't sweat the whole food pyramid thing. Someday when my arteries are hard and my blood pressure is through the roof, I may regret my 'bad' habits, but I'd rather live for today, today. I'll worry about tomorrow, tomorrow."

She laughed. "You remind me of my cousin —" She stopped abruptly, looked startled, and wet her lips, "Faith, my cousin Faith. That's exactly her philosophy of life."

He puzzled over the strange interruption. She'd acted almost as if she didn't know her cousin's name.

Before he could respond or ask another question, she lifted her arm, glanced at her watch, and picked up a slice of pizza. "We'd better stop talking and finish eating or we'll miss the start of the movie."

Sliding a slice of pizza on his plate, he released a long, slow breath. His instincts told him something about her wasn't right, but hard as he tried, he couldn't pin down what rang sour.

Chapter Eight

The morning sun felt unusually warm and bright, and Kent half whistled, half hummed the tune of *Because I'm Happy* as he sauntered toward the guest cottage. At the door, he told Jack he'd come by to check for any important messages rather than admit he had an irrational urge to play with the baby.

"No messages. What movie did you see?" Jack asked.

"We went to the classics festival at the Strand for a double header. *North by Northwest* and *Gaslight*. Turns out we're both mystery fans. Where's Christian? You sell the kid to pirates already?"

"No, but I have to admit that while he was screaming like a banshee at four a.m. the idea did cross my mind. Carrie's rocking him in the bedroom trying to get him to fall asleep. Sounds like his refusal to conform to normal night and day routines is something that runs in her family. So, should I send the mysterious Miss Ashland the usual roses?"

Kent shrugged off his disappointment that he couldn't make funny faces at Christian. What did he know about babies anyway?

"Yeah, roses are okay. Or on second thought, no, don't bother. I'll pop down to the florist's and pick out something myself. Josie's kind of an enigma. Sweet but sexy. Soft but gutsy. Maybe I'll get an assortment to match all the contrasting facets of her personality."

Jack grinned. "A second date and special flowers? She must be making an impression."

"She's just a challenge, my man. She's bright, and it's actually fun to spar with her. I've dropped a couple hints, I know she's up to something and watched the effect. She acts guilty as hell, squirming in her seat and avoiding my eyes, but for the life of me, I can't picture her doing anything as underhanded and ugly as corporate spying."

"I asked a couple people in her area for their impressions. Her supervisor says she's a hard worker, smart, a computer whiz, and keeps her private life private. Other than constantly asking questions, there's nothing negative."

"She's brought up the subject of how we finance takeovers, but she seems more interested in Victor than the details of the business. She's never asked how we choose our prospects or what companies I'm digging into now. If she was stealing info on where we're going next, those would be the obvious subjects to pursue. Plus, if she was here to ferret out information on acquisitions, she'd have to know who I was."

"Maybe she's a naturally curious person."

Kent found it comforting to hear Jack's impressions of Josie and have his opinions re-enforced. He liked her and distrust sat like a rancid lump in his stomach. "That's my read. I'm convinced either Victor's all wrong, or there's something else entirely going on, and he's working a different angle."

Jack smirked. "Could be he's sizing her up as a replacement for his current mistress?"

Kent pondered the idea. Picturing Josie in bed with Victor made his blood cool, then quickly heat with outrage. "I doubt she's his type. She seems to have morals."

"Or so you think."

"My instincts say she's too smart for him." Little daggers of hatred for Victor flashed red before his eyes. He fisted his hands, then realizing he was starting to act like a jealous fool, quickly stuffed them in his pockets. "He goes for huge breasts. Hers are perfectly proportioned to the rest of her body and would be too refined for his tastes."

"He might spring for double-E implants like he did with that stripper."

Kent found the idea revolting. "My guess is she'd say 'no thanks.'"

"If he's not testing a new mistress to see if she'll cheat on him, and she's not a spy, then what's left?"

"Beats me. Maybe nothing. Could be I'm jousting with windmills."

Jack grinned and arched an eyebrow. "So if you think she's on the up and up, are you going to dump her and get back to your normal whoring routine?"

The remark made him sound shallow, and Kent decided he didn't like the image. Maybe sometime soon he'd work on changing it. "No, you can keep the Carrera a little longer," he said, shifting back to the subject at hand. "It bothers me that she's hiding something. Before I set her adrift, I want to be sure she's not an Oscar winning actress who's conning me completely. I need to dig deeper and get a little closer."

"Closer? Does that mean you haven't gotten close? As in the horizontal tango?"

He shrugged. "Not yet."

Jack whistled and shook his head. "I always knew the day would come when you'd lose it."

Kent bristled at the jibe. He kept his expression neutral and hid behind a façade of nonchalance. "I haven't lost a thing. Up until now I've been holding back, figuring she was the enemy. I'm still not sure it's time to shift gears and make our relationship less about business and more about pleasure."

"When are you going to drop the act and tell her who you are?"

Kent thought about telling her the truth. *By the way, I don't just work at Emmeline's, I own a big chunk of the company.* If she was innocent of all the nasty things he suspected and found out he'd lied, would she be angry and refuse to have anything else to do with him? Or would she keep seeing him with a changed attitude, their relationship tainted by his money?

He didn't want to find out. There was that other puzzling question: What was it about her that occasionally left him feeling uneasy? Uncertainty made him reluctant to let down his guard. His instincts about people were usually good, and in her case, he sensed she was telling him a lot less than the whole truth.

"I'm going to keep up the charade a little longer. She's bound to find out sooner or later, but I'm not ready to spill anything yet."

Better safe than sorry, especially if she was somehow mixed up with Victor.

• • •

Faith rubbed her burning eyes and glanced at the time in the bottom corner of her computer monitor. Six fifty-eight p.m. Yikes. Between her official work and her snooping, she'd been at her desk almost ten hours.

The library closed at eight on Mondays and was five blocks from her apartment. She'd returned her rental car on Saturday, so she'd have to walk. If she wanted to get there and have time to browse and check out a few books, she needed to hurry.

Wishing her search for justice was moving faster, she stretched her neck, rolled her shoulders, and sighed in resignation. The tracking software she'd attached to Victor's computer account was proving useless. The list on the window open in front of her included only twenty sites, his total for two entire days. The only value they held was that some of the pages displayed competitor's merchandise and raised a question: Why had he argued against an Emmeline's website for so long when he must be aware that without one he was losing sales?

She switched to another window and scanned the information. She'd hacked his cell phone GPS to track his movements, but the few places he'd gone in the last twenty-four hours—a restaurant, his home, a bank—seemed normal and innocent.

If she hadn't met him and didn't know his history, she could almost be lulled into believing he was a harmless, upstanding citizen.

She flipped open the file containing what little she knew about Victor and stared at the top sheet: a printout of the latest report from Steve Zurich. Victor had a mistress, the most recent in a string of many. Maybe the fact he was cheating on his wife was valuable to know, maybe not, but it was the only evidence of anything amiss she had so far.

After adding a printout of Victor's driver's license to the file, she closed it and locked it in her drawer. How much longer would it take to find anything incriminating about Victor? Half of her six weeks was gone, and her vacation time was running out.

She pictured Josie's swollen middle and thought about not being by her side to squeeze her hand if she went into early labor. Her heart twisted and distress dragged at her soul. She fought a suffocating urge to pack up and go home.

Her mind reviewed their recent phone conversations. Every time they talked, Josie insisted she was doing fine. Last night, she'd reported the ultrasound at her doctor's appointment had showed everything was normal. She'd even bragged she had only gained five more pounds.

Faith massaged the back of her neck. As long as Josie was okay, there was no need to rush home yet. Besides, tomorrow was another day. She had to believe something would happen soon.

Humming to keep her depression at bay, Faith shut down all her programs, left her office, and boarded the empty elevator.

Riding downward, she smiled inwardly in anticipation of wandering the library and soaking in the comforting smell of thousands of beckoning books. She always felt excited as she rushed home with an armful of new books waiting to be explored. They promised excursions to exotic lands, adventures with larger-than-life characters, information to satisfy her curiosity.

She recalled the nagging curiosity that had caused her to open her mother's diary. Maybe all knowledge wasn't equally good, but regardless, she couldn't stop her mind from seeking stimulation and answers.

In the lobby, a three-woman cleaning crew was waiting to board the elevator.

Faith stepped off, moved aside, smiled and nodded. "Have a good evening."

A gray-haired woman chuckled and quipped, "If I could sit and rest in that cushy chair in the penthouse office instead of cleaning that man's bathroom, my evening would be great."

As Faith watched the elevator doors close behind the women, memories swirled in her mind. She pictured her mother dressed in a worn uniform, leaving the house at six every night, scrubbing and cleaning for eight long hours, returning exhausted and hollow-eyed at dawn. Then she pictured her Mom's modest, wood casket being lowered into the ground, and sadness weighed heavy on her heart. Without warning, raw hurt and loss rushed up behind her in one of their sneak attacks, grabbed her by the throat, and squeezed off her air.

She choked back tears and idly stared at the pointer over the door. It swept toward the second floor, the third, fourth, then the fifth. She imagined the women switching elevators and heading for the penthouse to bend sore backs and strain arthritic knees in the almighty Victor Telemann's office.

Her mind's eye saw his big desk with his appointment calendar, ashtray, and fancy humidor for his cigars. Did he seriously work or simply sit there and put on a show? What had been on the papers spread for his inspection? Privileged company financial information or rubbish assembled to make him appear busy? Cynicism colored her conclusions. Most likely he spent his days figuring out how to hide his true character.

Her brain sprinted in a new direction. Had any of those papers spread on his desktop been personal or contained dark secrets? Did they document anything incriminating? Anything she needed to discover? She sighed and wished she knew.

She gasped as she realized she didn't have to wish or wonder. She could know. If she dared. Cleaning women got to wander all over with no one wondering what they were up to. All her life, her mother had told her stories of empty buildings, janitors who snooped after office-holders went home, the secrets revealed by a person's trash, and desks with valuables or sensitive documents left sitting in plain view.

Did Victor Telemann leave sensitive documents or a journal on his desk? Did he shred or crumple his trash? Could something in his office serve as evidence of past crimes or help her prove he was a rapist?

Her brain took off at breakneck speed. Asking questions and hiring an investigator weren't getting her the information she needed. It was time to get more aggressive.

Searching his office could work. She'd need to know the cleaning crew's schedule and what type of security protected the penthouse. She could buy a worn uniform, soft-soled shoes. A wig. Cleaning props.

Her pulse galloped with hope as she stepped out Emmeline's front entrance and into the early evening's warmth and waning light. As soon as possible, she'd locate a couple thrift stores and do some shopping.

She set off down the sidewalk swinging her arms, smiling broadly, and chirping "Good evening" at passersby.

This could be the breakthrough she needed. In the morning, she'd reconnoiter the building.

• • •

Two hours after she reported for work in the morning, Faith left her office to investigate the difficulties she'd face in getting into Victor's lair. The security office was on the second floor and shared a short hallway with the store employees' break room and rest rooms. A dirt-smudged keypad was mounted on the wall to the left of the office door, and an aged stainless-steel water fountain stood about two feet to the right.

Relieved the hallway was empty, Faith paced near the ladies' room door and waited. The *click-clink* of her heels on the linoleum floor echoed like gunshots at a dawn execution, and she wished she'd worn a pair quieter and more appropriate. She filed away the lesson. Nerves taut, she leaned against the wall and glanced at her watch. Ten thirty-one.

Hearing the squeak of rubber-soled shoes coming closer, she jumped to her feet. A tall, middle-aged man came around the corner and sauntered toward the break room. She rushed into the ladies' room and hovered inside the door, holding her breath, listening for footfalls. When everything outside was quiet, she cracked the door open and checked for foot traffic. Seeing no one, she inched back out.

Her nerves vibrated. A flickering fluorescent ceiling panel snapped incessantly and she ground her teeth. How long could she hang around the hallway without drawing attention to her loitering? She checked her watch again: ten forty-two. Would Gladys notice she was missing from her office and question where she'd gone?

She crossed her arms and drummed her fingertips on her elbows. Another minute. Two. Three. She glanced furtively over her shoulder, wet her lips. Should she leave and come back another day?

The security office door creaked and swung open.

Sucking in a breath, she dashed to the far side of the hallway and launched into step one of her plan: to bend over the water fountain and pretend she was getting a drink.

A potbellied man with a bushy mustache and rumpled blue uniform strode out of the security office and headed toward the men's room.

Time for step two. Whipping a thick slab of duct tape from her pocket, she darted to the left and slapped it over the latch on the office door before it could click shut. Seconds ticked by. The restroom door slammed behind the security officer with a resounding whap.

Step three. She grabbed the handle of the security office door and pulled. The door opened. The tape had done its job. Her skin prickled with fear and excitement.

Piggybacking in the door, as the maneuver was called by hackers, was an old ploy the security officer should have expected. She was surprised it worked, but it had, and the small success raised her hopes that he was equally lax with the electronic systems. If he'd left a computer terminal active without password protection, she could piggyback on his security account. If she could get into the security network, she'd be able to access information at a higher authorization level than if she were assigned an account as a simple user.

She stripped the incriminating duct tape off the door latch and stuffed it into her pocket. Slipping into the office, she scanned the interior for other occupants and breathed a sigh of relief. Empty. He worked alone, just as Gladys had implied the day Faith started her job.

On the wall directly over the guard's desk, she spotted a bank of about three dozen surveillance monitors. The lowest row showed customers shopping on the bottom floors and cashiers working at registers. Above those, another row showed corridors and employees she recognized. The upper floors. One monitor showed an attractive oriental woman walking in the building's front entrance, another the lifeless back parking lot. A separate monitor was focused on the closed doors of the penthouse elevator. There was no indication surveillance cameras were mounted inside any offices.

She sprinted across the room, perched on the edge of the chair in front of an active computer terminal, and checked the prompt. A pound sign. *Yes!* A pound sign prompt meant the account holder had root privileges at the highest authorization level. He was a superuser who could go anywhere, read any file, execute any program. And she was sitting in his seat.

Foot tapping *agitato* and fingers flying over the keys, she typed a quick command and established another root account she could use from her office. She ran a quick check for an intruder detection system. If IDS software was installed, it would alert security someone was trying to penetrate the network and complicate her task.

The system found no IDS, which meant no one would know what terminal she was working from when she accessed the system remotely. Everything would be available without any trail. She could alter the modification times of the account creation files and snip out the evidence of her visit from the logs, adjust the angle of surveillance cameras, and if necessary, even edit tapes.

She heard the echo of a door slamming closed in the hallway, pecked at a couple keys to quickly clear the screen, stood, and scurried away from the chair.

A buzzer sounded, and a split-second later the door creaked opened. The security officer stepped back inside. When he saw her, a scowl creased his pudgy face. "Huh? How did you get in here?"

Pasting on a welcoming smile, she stuck out her hand and strode toward him. "Hi, I'm Josie Ashland. I'm developing a new website and online store for Emmeline's. I wanted to ask you a couple questions about security."

His eyebrows went up interrogatively. "The door was locked."

She tilted her head, frowned, and feigned innocence. "No, it was ajar."

He shook her hand, then glanced at the door and back to her. He scratched the nape of his neck as his lips pursed then disappeared back under the thick mustache. "I'd better have maintenance check that out." Looking satisfied with her explanation, he hooked his thumbs in his belt. "Okay, so if you got questions, shoot."

"I was wondering if you have control of computer

security and how good the firewall is for the current computer network."

The guard pushed out his chin. "We don't do none of that here."

"Is there a separate electronic security department?"

He shook his head. "Nope. Everything's here. But I don't know nothing about computer security. I'm building security. Burglar alarms. Shoplifters. We gotta keep a sharp eye peeled every minute. Professional gangs steal stuff worth millions every year. Can suck a company dry."

She nodded and tried to look sympathetic. "I noticed all your monitors. Staring at them all day must be a thankless job."

"It's gotta be done. Thieves are sneaky. But we catch 'em."

"What about at night?" She motioned toward the monitors. "Does someone watch then, too? Or should I be locking my door?"

"The watchman makes rounds of the perimeter. Checks the hallways hourly. After closing, there's nothing much to see inside. Your office is safe."

"I suppose." She chuckled and waved a hand to indicate the irrelevance of her position. "I guess it's not like I'm the CEO in the penthouse with big company secrets. I bet his office gets locked, right?"

"Yeah." He narrowed his eyes, asked, "What did you say your name was again?"

"Josie." She scrambled to divert him from any suspicions. "You know, hackers are just like shoplifters, except they steal online. They can suck the store dry too. I hope you don't mind if I come back and ask your advice if I run into any tough problems. Security isn't my strong point, but you seem to have a good grasp on the dangers."

His chest puffed out. "Come back any time you need help."

She hustled toward the door. "I will. Thanks." She had one more thought, stopped half out the doorway, and turned. "By the way, I like to stay and work late. Should I use any particular door after the retail floors close?"

"Only way in or out after eight at night is the employee door to the back parking lot. Don't touch the front, or you'll set off a zillion alarms. But be gone by ten. After that, even the back needs the watchman's code."

Triumph gave her heart a joyous jolt and she flashed him a wide grin. "That's good to know. I wouldn't want police cruisers surrounding the building just because I was trying to go home."

. . .

A few minutes before five that afternoon, Faith chewed her bottom lip and shuffled documents on and off the Xerox machine at the fifth floor copy center. She watched the penthouse elevator through the glass partition between the copier and the hallway, hoping to see Victor Telemann come down and switch elevators as he left for the day. She guessed his secretary would also leave within a few minutes of his departure. If that happened, she'd only have a narrow slice of time to get up to the penthouse floor and make an excuse to get inside Victor's office.

She glanced at the surveillance camera mounted in the hall corner, imagining the picture being transmitted to the security office.

The down arrow next to the penthouse elevator lit up. Victor stepped off the private elevator at five ten, sauntering with a regal bearing. He strolled to the other set of doors, punched the down button, and boarded the elevator to the street level at five eleven.

Faith hurried into the hallway and onto the penthouse elevator. She pressed the up button. When the doors slid open, Victor's secretary, Peg, had her purse on her chair and stood straightening papers on her desk. The door to Victor's office was shut.

Faith smiled and waved as she approached the desk. "Hi, do you remember me? Josie Ashland."

Peg smiled back. "Yes, of course. Is there something I can do for you?"

"I need to check Mr. Telemann's computer terminal id number and match it to his node assignment. Would you ask him if it would be all right if I came in for a minute?"

"He's gone for the day."

"Oh. Phooey. Just my luck. I wanted to stay late and load the database table tonight." She sighed for effect and put a sad plea in her eyes. "Could I just go in for a second? The number I need is on the back of his monitor."

Peg frowned. "He dislikes anyone going into his office, but as long as I'm with you, it should be okay."

"Thank you so much." Faith let the joy bubbling inside her chest pull her lips into a grin. "I really appreciate this."

Peg opened the center drawer in her desk and removed a ring of keys. She shuffled through them reading the little tags, then said, "Here it is."

Faith followed her to the door and waited while she

turned the key in the lock. The little tag said *V.T.* printed in red ink. When Peg opened the door and motioned her inside, Faith walked directly to Victor's desk. She bent and squinted at the back of his monitor. "I'll need the lights on to make out the numbers."

She watched Peg hit three of the light switches on the right-hand side of the doorway. Taking out the small notebook she'd brought along to make her mission look legitimate, she copied the serial number from Victor's monitor. Trembling slightly inside, she sucked in a deep breath and turned toward Peg. "That's all I need. Thanks."

"How is progress coming on the website?" Peg asked as she turned off the lights and they walked out the door.

"Good, but there are quite a few security issues I need to work out. I wouldn't want to have customers' personal information compromised by a hacker. That's a serious problem these days."

Peg pulled the door shut behind them, put the key ring back in her desk, and slid the drawer shut. "I think it's going to be a wonderful addition to the business, though. When people can shop twenty-four hours a day from anywhere, they're bound to love the convenience."

Faith lingered. "Are you heading home? We can share the elevator."

Peg grabbed her purse and slung the strap over her shoulder. "Sure."

Noticing Peg didn't lock her desk, Faith moistened her lips and suppressed a surge of relief. Tonight's unlocked drawer might be a mere oversight because of distraction, but for her it was a godsend and gave her the opportunity she needed.

As they walked to the elevator, Peg said, "You're not at all like the stereotypical computer nerd. I guess things have changed since skinny boys in thick, horn-rimmed glasses sat around chewing pencils and watching all these big computer drives whirl."

Faith chuckled. "Computing used to be a man's world, but women are quickly taking over. Most of my engineering classes at Virginia Tech were at least fifty-percent girls."

"Yes, but pretty girls usually aren't given credit for having brains. Bravo to you for making the most of your brains and not depending on your looks to get by."

Faith felt her cheeks warm. "Thank you."

Guilt stabbed at her, and she averted her eyes. Peg was a friendly and likable person, and tricking her was horrid and underhanded. For the millionth time since leaving Williamsburg and starting her life of lie piled on lie, she wished there were some other way to balance the scales of justice.

The words in the diary flashed before her mind's eye.

She raised her chin marginally and set her jaw in stony resolve. Time and circumstances had left her no choice. She'd just have to be doubly sure not to get caught in Victor's office and drag Peg, Josie, the night watchman, or anyone else into trouble. And if she did get caught… She shivered at the thought of the consequences and all that could go wrong.

The penthouse elevator stopped on the fifth floor. Faith carefully slipped the little notebook from her pocket and dropped it by her feet. She followed Peg as they switched to the other elevator. At the fourth floor, she waved and said, "Goodnight," as she got off.

She chewed on the inside of her cheek as she waited in her office. The seconds flashed by on her watch. After three minutes, she took the elevator back up to five. Using her best acting skills, she made a show of scanning the area. If the security officer happened to be looking at the monitor, she wanted him to believe she'd lost something and returned to find it.

Pulse racing, she pressed the button for the penthouse elevator and the door slid open. Still making a show of searching, she hit the up button, and the door closed.

When the doors slid back open at the penthouse, she raced to Peg's desk, grabbed the key chain, removed the key with the proper tag, and hurried back to the elevator. She hit the down button and kicked her notebook to a position where it would be visible on the monitor when the doors opened onto the fifth floor. For the sake of the surveillance camera, she made a show of bending over to pick up the notebook before exiting the elevator.

As she went to the copy center and claimed the papers she'd left earlier, her heart pounded so furiously she thought it would burst from her chest. Step one was complete. She had the key. Now all she had to do was copy it, return the original to Peg's desk, and get in and out of Victor's office without getting caught.

She wiped her moist palms on the sides of her skirt. The cleaning crew wouldn't start work for another hour and a half. She needed to get a key copy made, stash her change of clothing and wig in the ladies room, and rush back to her office as if she'd gone out to grab a quick dinner. She'd established a routine of working late so a nighttime guard wouldn't think her presence was odd. But she wanted to be in her office when he made his first round at seven.

Once she'd demonstrated nothing was unusual, she'd

log onto her security account, angle the fourth-floor and fifth-floor surveillance cameras a few degrees lower, don her disguise, go back up to the penthouse, and find out if Victor's office held any secrets.

Chapter Nine

The cheap wig itched. The rubber-soled work shoes weighed a ton. The smock-style dress hung like a burlap sack.

As Faith tucked the case holding her blue contact lenses into her pocket, her fingers bumped against her Virginia driver's license. She ran her fingertips over the plastic card, taking slight comfort from its presence. If she got caught, she'd be Faith Rochambeau with dyed hair, not Josie Ashland. She'd be in big trouble, but at least Josie wouldn't get blamed and the damage would be contained.

She took a deep breath in through her nose and let it leak out slowly. She'd taken every precaution she could. Now the trick was to stay calm and pull this off.

After tying a bandana around her head, she carefully folded the clothing she'd worn all day, lifted her dress, and stuffed the packet between her waist and the loose cummerbund she'd bought for the purpose. Smoothing the dress back down, she examined the outfit and her new matronly shape in the ladies room mirror. Drab. Nondescript. Perfect.

She left the ladies room, keeping her head angled downward so her face was hidden from the cameras as she walked to the stairway. She carried the roll of paper towels and bottle of glass cleaner she'd smuggled into the building inside her briefcase, but wished she'd figured out a way to smuggle in a mop or bucket. Either would be a better prop.

Careful to keep her back toward the fifth floor surveillance camera, she boarded the penthouse elevator. Nervous perspiration soaked her underarms and trickled between her breasts. Her stomach churned in trepidation.

She stepped off the elevator and scanned the outer office area to be sure she was alone. Seeing no one, she slipped on a pair of latex gloves and replaced the stolen key on the ring in Peg's desk. Her key copy clutched in her hand, she stared at Victor's office door. There was still time to abort her plan and leave.

Faith hesitated. She'd come this far, and something had to be done or Victor would never be brought to justice. Hands-off research wasn't yielding any useful information. Logic demanded a bolder approach. She'd just have to get in and out as quickly as possible. Sucking in her breath, she unlocked the door, slipped inside Victor's inner sanctum, and pulled the door shut behind her by the cold metal handle.

Darkness and a heavy scent of stale cigar smoke blanketed the room. The only sound was air rushing in and out of her chest. She stood frozen for a second, staring through the huge window at the collage of eerie building shadows, lonely lighted windows, and gaudy flashing signs on the West Palm Beach skyline, trying to catch her breath. She was in, but the door behind her was the only exit.

Shivering and no longer able to endure the darkness, she moistened her lips and flipped on the same light switches she'd watched Peg choose. The surface of the huge desk and the wall of windows reflected the bright overhead lights and hit her like a spotlight aimed at her eyes. Feeling exposed and vulnerable, she flattened her hand over her abdomen to calm the rolling waves of nausea. *Get a grip!*

She squared her shoulders and crossed the room. Blood roared in her ears, but her footsteps were silent on the thick carpet. She read the label on a file folder resting in one corner of the desk. *Fiscal Projections – 2011 Winter Season.* Ignoring the folder concerned with the future, she flipped back through the recent pages of an appointment calendar. A page from two weeks ago had the notation: *Gardener's Emporium Acquisition Results – Kent and Ben.*

She pictured Kent, handsome and composed, sitting in this room meeting with Victor. He hadn't mentioned anything about a meeting at dinner. Maybe if she'd pressed him harder, she could have found out some useful details.

Faith flipped backward through several more pages, unsure why she was here and what she was looking for. Some of the notes were in an almost illegible scrawl. Most, like the note about Kent, were in a neat, feminine looking cursive, but nothing on the calendar looked interesting or pertinent. She glanced over her shoulder at the closed outer door, caught her bottom lip between her teeth, and walked around the side of the desk.

She passed the trashcan and paused, studying the contents. She bent, removed a couple of the crumpled sheets on the top, and smoothed them out enough to read the print. A memo from someone in the marketing department about a fashion show in Paris. An ad for a slick eight-passenger corporate jet. She re-crumpled the papers, placed them on the edge of his desk, and glanced back at his trash.

A pair of latex gloves? Why would he need those?

He certainly wasn't changing the toner in his copier or the cartridges in a printer. She couldn't picture the self-important man who'd strutted around this office doing anything that might soil his hands. He'd leave the dirty work for others.

She glanced at the gloves on her hands. Picturing a crime technician dusting the desk for fingerprints, her heart fluttered in fear.

Storing the knowledge of gloves in Victor's trash away to ponder later when she was safe at home and time wasn't as precious, she examined more discarded papers. Several donation requests from charities. A nasty letter from a disgruntled customer. Nothing revealed a clue about the gloves or anything significant about his business. Releasing a sigh of disappointment, she swept the pile of trash off the edge of his desktop and back into the trashcan.

Continuing around to behind the desk, she eyed the shiny brass drawer handles. The idea of snooping inside Victor's desk was more intimidating than inspecting things sitting in plain sight. But she suspected his darkest secrets would be hidden deep, and if she was ever going to see him pay for his crimes, searching his private documents was a necessity.

She pulled in a fortifying breath, steadied her hand, and reached for the handle on the top right, expecting it to be locked.

A muffled male voice. A high-pitched giggle.

Her eyes widened. Her heart stopped. Someone was

coming.

Was there some kind of a motion-detecting system in here that had set off an alarm? Why hadn't she thought of that earlier?

Another giggle. Whoever was coming probably wasn't the police.

She scanned around her. A doorway on the left side of the office seemed her only hope for a place to hide. She remembered the cleaning woman's remark about a private bathroom and said a silent prayer as she dashed toward the inlaid mahogany door.

The voices were louder and bumped her blood pressure higher. She whipped open the heavy mahogany door, pushing it to the left. Yes, a bathroom. The louvered door of a linen closet was on the right.

Metal slid on metal as a key slipped into the outer door lock.

Grasping the gold-plated handle and ripping open the linen closet door, her heart sank. Shelves. The bottom one was less than two feet off the floor. Could she squeeze under it?

No time. No choice.

She pushed four multi-packs of toilet paper to the left and scooted onto the closet floor with her knees tight against her chest and her head bent painfully to the side. Her fingernails caught the lower louver on the door and pulled it shut with a small click. She prayed the closure was magnetic, so she'd be able to get back out. And she prayed the crack where the door didn't meet the frame was too thin for anyone to see her inside.

Victor's voice was now in the office. "Damn cleaning

crew left the lights on."

A woman's voice. "Lights are good. I can watch you get turned on."

Faith noticed an elaborate spider web near her right foot. She cringed and scanned around her for any sign of its owner.

"Let me grab my stuff first," Victor said. "Once you distract me, I might forget."

"You're such a tease."

The sound of a drawer sliding open. A pause. The sound of the drawer closing. A click, like the clasp on a briefcase. Another click, like the case closing. The sound of a zipper.

"You've got me hard, baby. Now do something about it."

The blood drained from her face. They were going to… She pulled in a huge breath. Her nostrils filled with the stink of toilet bowl cleaner.

The woman laughed then made a purring sound. "You're always so ready, and so big."

"You talk too much. Take it. Suck it."

Why couldn't the floor open and let her drop through? She didn't want to listen to this man, whose sperm had impregnated her mother, have sex.

She squeezed her eyes shut. *Focus on something else.* The heavy breathing and grunts from the other room assaulted her ears. The words in her mother's diary flooded into her mind. The sex of her rape had been violent, cruel, painful. No laughter, no teasing, no giggling.

"Oh, baby. That's good. Take it deeper. Harder. Take it." A low groan.

Faith clenched her teeth and pressed her hands over her ears. The sounds penetrated, regardless. Second after second ticked by, one thunderous heart thump at a time.

"That's it, baby. Suck me dry."

A growl of satisfaction. Bile rose in Faith's throat.

A pause, then the woman's voice. "You gonna do me too, sweetpants? Just a quickie to get me off. I'm drenched and ready."

"Not now. You'll make me late for dinner."

"Can you come by later?"

"Not tonight. Use that big plastic dick and the vibrator I got you. Videotape it, and I'll watch tomorrow. Come on, I gotta go."

"Just give me a sec."

The bathroom light flashed on and Faith started. Her skull thunked against the underside of the closet shelf. Her heart beat so furiously she was sure the person on the other side of the closet door would hear the racket and investigate.

A woman's voice muttered something like, "...a stinking animal."

High heels clicked on the floor. Through the spaces between the door's louvers and the narrow crack by the frame, Faith saw red shoes, shapely calves, knees and a swath of skin-tight, bright-pink silk move toward the sink. Water came on and splashed. The woman gargled and spit.

What if she came to the closet looking for mouthwash?

Faith held her breath. Was she going to be caught and thrown into jail?

The woman ripped off a length of toilet paper, tossed the wad of paper in the trashcan, then her heels clicked back toward the mahogany door.

Perspiration trickled between Faith's breasts.

The bathroom light went out.

"Okay, sweetpants. I'm ready. But don't forget my present."

A pause then faint, rapid clicking. A clunk that sounded like a heavy door latch. "Same arrangement as always," Victor said. "Use this to buy a diamond bracelet. Return it in two days and put the bucks in the usual account. I'll bring the bracelet on Friday."

A second clunk. The door shutting?

"This is so complicated. Why can't I just keep the one I buy?"

"Do as you're told and write down the style number. Don't I always bring it back to you?"

"Yes."

"Then shut up and quit complaining. Your jabbering is going to make me late."

A couple small noises. A door opened. Everything went dark. The door shut. Metal on metal as a key turned.

Darkness. Goosebumps erupted on her arms.

Eerie silence.

Faith's pulse accelerated to breakneck speed as she fought her fear of the dark. She imagined a huge spider creeping near her feet. Tried to draw them closer. Waited. Her pulse pounded in her temples, rushed in her ears. The blackness closed in and tried to suffocate her.

Too soon to leave. She couldn't move, not yet.

Victor's muffled voice came from somewhere far away. "Don't touch the window. And if you're the last crew, shut off the lights."

"Yes, sir," a woman's voice said.

The cleaning crew.

Despair weighed on Faith's chest. Now she'd have to stay hidden even longer.

A vacuum started and rumbled in the outer office. The office door opened, lights switched on, and the vacuum's roar grew louder. The light flashed back on in the bathroom. The rubber soles of battered running shoes squeaked across the tiles.

Faith bit on her bottom lip. She had light again, at last, but what if the cleaning crew needed supplies and opened the linen closet?

Her neck ached from being twisted over at the extreme angle. Her lower legs were numb. She shifted deeper into the closet, pressing her side against the back wall. Using her feet and legs as best she could, she slid the toilet paper multi-packs toward the door. The sound of the plastic wrapping scraping on the floor seemed deafening, and she chewed her lip, worried that despite the cleaning noises someone would hear. As soon as the packages were close enough to reach, she stretched a hand down beside her and positioned them strategically along the bottom of the door where they would be handy.

The cleaning lady ran water in the sink then wiped down the tank and pedestal of the toilet. She sloshed a brush around the toilet bowl, flushed, and put down the lid. Picking up the wastebasket, she disappeared outside. A few seconds later, she brought the empty basket back. As she folded the end of the toilet paper roll over neatly to form a little point, Faith breathed a sigh of relief. No need for a toilet paper refill.

The cleaning lady pulled the hand towel from the rack.

Faith gulped. Towels.

The woman walked toward the linen closet. Faith pressed against the wall and held her breath as the door swung open.

Chapter Ten

The cleaning woman's feet were only inches away. Faith saw dirt ridges in the folds of the white sport socks and double knots securing the laces. The wet spots under her arms grew cold in the rush of outside air.

The door shut. She squeezed her eyes closed. *Thank you, God.*

The shoes squeaked as the woman walked away. She shook out the clean towel with a snap.

The vacuum noise stopped. The woman in the bathroom called out, "The floor is okay here. Leave it be until tomorrow." She walked to the door and the light went out.

Spanish chatter came from the office. The scent of lemony furniture polish.

Minutes passed that seemed like an eternity. Wheels squeaked, maybe on the vacuum. The office lights went out, and the outer door clicked closed.

Faith's heart hammered, and her blood roared in her

ears. Her buttocks hurt from the hard floor. The darkness closed in, and her hands trembled. She counted off thirty seconds. The cleaning crew should be gone.

She shifted her weight, freed an arm, reached between the toilet paper packs and pushed against the door. It swung open. She dropped onto the floor on her side and pushed her body from the closet by levering her feet against the back wall.

Pins and needles prickled her legs and arms. She lay on the floor and rubbed her extremities, gritting her teeth against the painful surge of blood as her circulation returned.

When the numbness and pain lessened, she stood, flicked on the light, kicked the toilet paper back into the closet and shut the door. She turned out the light and stood silent for ten more seconds. The only sound was the whir of the air conditioning fan. Torrents of cold blew over the perspiration-soaked dress plastered to her back and goose flesh prickled her arms. She shivered, extended her fingers, and felt her way out of the bathroom.

The office was dark. Scary dark. She ran her hand over the wall, groping for a light switch. Nothing. Hands in front of her like a blind woman, she crept in the direction of the exterior door. Her fingertips scraped a wall. She bumped a piece of furniture. Something heavy slammed onto her foot. Pain exploded in her arch, and she bit her lip to keep from crying out.

The intense pain radiated up her leg. She couldn't move. Tears stung her eyes. She sank cross-legged onto the floor and rubbed her bruised bones. Was anything broken?

Please beam me up and get me out of this nightmare. Or at the very least, let the sun rise and take away the darkness.

The thought of sunrise jolted her brain. Her time in the closet had seemed like an eternity but probably wasn't. Oh, crap, how long had she been in the office? She sucked in a breath and lit up her watch display. Nine forty-six. She pictured a night watchman locking the back door and trapping her inside the store, and quickly pushed to her feet. She had no time to feel sorry for herself or lick her wounds. She had to get the hell out of here.

Running a hand along the smooth wall and gingerly stepping on her throbbing foot, she felt her way toward the exit. Her fingers touched a door casing, and she slid them lower. Switches. She flicked the lights on and huffed out a sigh of relief as the demons of darkness retreated.

Her heartbeat a little steadier, she turned and scanned the carpet behind her. A bronze statue of a horse lay on its side. She hobbled over and set it on the nearby table. Then reluctantly turning off the lights again, she pressed her ear to the door. Quiet.

Faith cracked the door open and scanned the outer office. Empty. She wiped her sweaty forehead with her sleeve, pulled the door shut behind her, and limped away.

After the penthouse elevator doors whooshed shut and the car started to descend, Faith slipped off her gloves and stuffed them into her pockets. Her hands still shook and she clutched them together. One more elevator then she'd be out of the building and safe. She was close to getting away with breaking and entering.

Shame rolled through her in massive waves.

The elevator stopped. Head down, she scanned the corridor. Empty. She switched elevators and held her breath until the cab stopped in the lobby. Rushing to the back door that was the only unalarmed exit, she retraced her actions of the last couple hours and shivered in shock.

She'd become a criminal. After twenty-five years of her mother trying to raise her to be a good person, she'd met Victor, and in less than two weeks, given in to her tainted genes.

. . .

She hurried home, staying in the bright circles cast by the streetlights and watching every shadowed entryway and alley for any hint of danger. She wanted to run like a sinner stalked by the devil. *No, control your pace, don't attract attention.*

Once she'd secured the locks on her apartment door, adrenaline stopped spurting into her veins. Her legs felt rubbery, her body drained of energy. She wanted to sink to the floor and cry. She'd been through a hellish night, all for naught.

She looked down at her outfit. The spider web. The closet floor. Eyeing her bed longingly, she kept herself upright, stripped off her cleaning woman disguise, shuffled into the bathroom, and turned on the shower.

Faith stepped under the steaming spray. The cleansing water soaked her hair, cascaded off her shoulders, and rolled down her back. She closed her eyes, raised her face to the pounding spray. The sounds she'd heard from the bathroom closet echoed in her skull. Images of the sex in Victor's office assaulted her brain.

A chill rippled up her back, and she adjusted the water temperature until it threatened to singe her skin. Steam enveloped her. She grabbed the soap and washcloth and scrubbed, wishing she could eradicate the foul sounds and images, dislodge every trace, and rinse them down the drain.

Refusing to rerun the mental sex tape again, she shoved back the memories and concentrated on the conversation afterward. Why would Victor instruct the woman to buy something then return it?

She pondered the question while she shampooed her hair, but found no logical answer. She rinsed her hair and banished the incident from her mind. Gifts to a mistress were part of a sleazy, but legal, lifestyle. What she needed was a confession to the rape he'd committed or concrete proof of another crime.

Feeling marginally cleaner, she turned off the water and stepped from the shower. A rapping noise. Someone knocking on her door?

Her skin prickled. She didn't know anyone who would visit this late. Maybe the building was on fire!

She grabbed a towel and turbaned it around her dripping hair. "Coming."

As she rushed toward the door, she slipped on a long fluffy robe, and cinched the belt around her waist. Her heart pounded. If not a fire, what other emergency?

The police.

She froze, staring at the closed door. Her heart seized up and refused to beat. Her chin trembled. Had they recognized her on the security tapes and come to drag her off to jail? She hadn't checked the office for surveillance equipment. Was there a separate system that had caught her every move?

Too late to worry about it now. One door to her apartment. No way to escape.

Faith tiptoed to the door and peered through the peephole.

Kent.

Her breath whooshed out. Tears of relief rushed to her eyes. She stood gulping oxygen. When she'd regained her composure, she cracked the door on the security chain. "What in the world are you doing here?"

He leaned and looked in through the crack. "Hi, can I come in?"

"Ah…" Questions zinged through her mind. Why had he come here and how did he get past the security gate in the lobby? Did he know where she'd been tonight? Were the police on their way?

"I stopped by your office earlier, but you were nowhere around," he said, looking sheepish. "Your phone went to voicemail. I was worried when you didn't answer. You said you weren't dating, and it's not safe for a woman to be out wandering the streets alone at night."

Her mind flashed on a young girl who'd been out alone. Been raped. Swallowing hard, she came back to the present and searched for something reasonable to say. She grabbed the first excuse for her absence that popped into her mind.

"I walked to the library. Turned off my phone so it wouldn't make noise."

A library visit was believable. She had books stacked on every flat surface in the room. But instantly she regretted her choice. Faith would go to the library and be happy browsing the stacks for hours, but Kent knew her as social-butterfly Josie.

He seemed unfazed. "That's a relief. The only other explanation I had for your disappearance was that you were at the store looking for company secrets in the corporate offices." He gave her a penetrating look, paused, and then chuckled. "Well, now that I'm here and you're safe, could I come in?"

She gulped. He'd made the remark about corporate offices as if he were joking, but it was too close to the truth for comfort.

When she didn't move or speak, he frowned. "May I?"

The question was more daunting than it should be. Having dinner with him was a far cry than inviting him into her apartment late at night, especially when she was naked under her robe and had just finished breaking the law.

But worrying about her was a sweet gesture. She'd be rude to send him away.

Her instinctive response as Faith warred with what she should probably do as Josie. He wasn't a complete stranger. Turning him away might make him suspicious. "Just a second, I need to get dressed."

She shut the door and glanced toward her closet. Her gaze landed on the pile of discarded cleaning woman clothing with the gray wig conspicuously on top. *Yikes!*

Biting down on her bottom lip, she ran to the pile, gathered the evidence of her clandestine activities, and stuffed them into the farthest corner of the closet. She scanned the room. Was anything else incriminating? The rubber-soled shoes. She tossed them into the closet, too, and slammed the door. Anything else? No, the room looked clean.

Her pulse pounded in her veins. She'd already kept Kent standing in the hallway too long. He'd wonder what was taking her so long. No time now to dress. She'd thank him for his concern and send him home quickly.

She stepped into pajama bottoms, cinched the robe tighter around her waist, slipped the security chain, and opened the door.

He flashed her a smile and stepped inside. "I could have driven you to the library if you'd said something."

She left the door open. Better safe than sorry.

"Thank you for offering, but it's not that far. I'm sure you would have been bored."

"Actually not. I read quite a bit."

His gaze seemed overly intent, and she wrapped her arms across her chest.

He cocked his head to one side and looked puzzled. "Your eyes are brown."

Her blue contact lenses! She'd taken them out.

"I wear tinted contact lenses once in a while," she said, tamping down panic and forcing a laugh. "It's fun to change your eye or hair color occasionally. Tonight I decided brown eyes fit my mood."

"I like the color, it goes with your skin tones. Your natural blue is beautiful, but the brown is soft and warm."

She swallowed hard. *Get him off my eye color.* "What do you like to read?"

His gaze slipped from her face and wandered around the room, stopped at a pile of books. An expression of something like relief came over his face. "Mysteries, adventure, sci-fi. A lot of nonfiction. What about you?"

"You'd probably call it woman's fiction. Family sagas, stories of life, love, friendships. Once in a while, I enjoy sci-fi or a techno-thriller."

She realized she should ask him to sit, but resisted the impulse. Her nerves were too raw for small talk or banter, and his presence in her living room was discomforting. He was dressed casually in neatly pressed slacks, boat shoes, and a maroon Izod shirt. But as usual, he oozed sex appeal. She'd be smartest to keep a distance between them and give him the bum's rush out her door.

When he swung his gaze back to her face, she blurted, "I don't understand, Kent. Why are you here?"

His expression turned serious. He shook his head. "In all honesty, I don't know."

He held her gaze for a long minute, then raised his hands, and removed the towel from her head.

She froze. Her breath caught in her throat. What in the world was he doing?

He worked his fingers into her hair and his face softened. "On second thought, maybe I do."

His fingertips smoothed the tangles in her hair and caressed her scalp. Awareness curled low in her belly. She instinctively knew what he would do next.

He lowered his mouth to hers. Warm. Soft.

A quiver shook her frame. She raised her palms to his chest to push him away, but her arms seemed to move of their own accord, circling his neck. She stretched onto her tiptoes and pressed their bodies closer. Parted her lips.

His tongue found hers. Her knees went to jelly. Erotic sensations spiraled through her torso.

He slipped his hands down to her neck, around to the opening of her robe. His thumbs rubbed across her collarbone, setting her insides aflame.

She struggled for air and control. Longing warred with reason. Some primal instinct sent blood rushing through her veins, made her skin sensitive, sparked a physical craving like none she'd known before.

He broke their kiss and captured her eyes. His raspy voice seemed to caress her entire being. "You've become important to me. I came here tonight because I want to be with you, Josie."

Josie.

The name slapped her in the face. She jerked back to reality and schooled her expression. He'd kissed her, but he didn't even know who she was. He didn't want her. He wanted a mirage, someone who didn't exist. A woman who was half Faith, half Josie. 100 percent phony.

Little daggers jabbed her heart. She backed away from him and clutched her robe at her neck, raising the collar and closing it tight. "I'm sorry, Kent. I think you'd better go."

He nodded and then smiled sadly. "I'm the one who's sorry. I value your friendship. I was foolish to come here uninvited this late at night and put our relationship at risk. Forgive me?"

He looked so contrite that she wanted to take him into her arms and soothe him. She gulped and nodded. "Forgiven." She stepped to the door and held it open, fighting back the urge to cry. "Good night."

He huffed out his breath. "Good night. Pleasant dreams." Then he walked out the door leaving his masculine scent perfuming the air, his taste lingering in her mouth, and a terrible loneliness in her soul.

• • •

At the end of the hallway, Kent punched the call button for the elevator and tapped his foot until it arrived. After making a fool of yourself, it was always best to make a quick exit.

When the doors were shut and the cab started down, he balled his hands into fists and tapped them on his thighs. What the hell had he been thinking? She hadn't been out playing Mata Hari. She'd gone to the library. For heaven's sakes, why had he shown up here at her apartment at this hour of the night?

He stabbed his hand through his hair. His suspicions were a handy excuse. And yes, he'd been a little concerned because she was new in town and might not be familiar with which neighborhoods should be avoided at night, but there was really no contest about his true motive. He'd just plain wanted to see her.

Damn it! The woman turned him inside out. Less than five minutes with her and he was a disaster. With one kiss, she'd managed to shake loose emotions he didn't know he had. What the hell was she, some kind of mythical siren trying to lure him onto the rocks?

The elevator reached the lobby. He stomped off and out the building's front door, stepped off the sidewalk and into the traffic. A horn blasted. A man yelled an obscenity out his window. Staring straight ahead, Kent stepped onto the curb on the far side of the road and headed for the Mustang.

For Christ's sake. He was supposed to be the one in control. He was supposed to be the one throwing *her* off balance. Every other woman he'd known had always fawned over him.

He got in his car and slammed the door. If he didn't know better, he'd think he was falling in love. Well, he did know better. He wasn't crazy enough to fall in love. All this acting like an idiot teenager with raging hormones had to end here and now. He had to regain his sanity.

Jamming the key into the ignition, he started the engine, peeled out of the parking spot, and rammed the gas pedal to the floor.

Teeth grinding, he vowed he would get a grip. There would be no more asinine visits to her apartment like a pathetic puppy.

• • •

In the morning, Faith sat behind her desk feeling jumpy as hell and regretting last night's excursion into Victor's office. She thought of the duplicate key sitting on her kitchen counter at home and resolved never to use it again.

Footsteps approached her office door and her pulse spiked. A man walked by without even glancing inside. She breathed a sigh of relief.

Something dropped with a loud noise. She jerked backward. Her elbow hit her morning coffee. It spilled and soaked her muffin. She dropped the soggy mess into her trashcan, clenched her jaw, and tried to bury herself in work.

Her feet jiggled, and she couldn't sit still. Her brain seemed short-circuited, and her fingers kept striking the wrong keys. The minutes ticked by. Nine o'clock. Ten o'clock. Eleven o'clock. Lunchtime came and went. No one came to drag her away to jail.

By the time the second hand swept up to the twelve and made it officially five o'clock, she felt like she'd run a triathlon. She straightened up her office and went home, looking forward to changing into pajamas, slipping into bed, and cuddling up with a book.

She remembered Kent's words about liking to read and imagined him, head propped on a pile of pillows, chest bare, stretched out beside her. A smile tugged at the corners of her mouth. If Kent were lying in bed beside her, she doubted they would be reading.

A tiny pang of sorrow squeezed her heart. She hadn't seen him all day. Maybe after she'd sent him away last night he'd never come back. Her mind was a frenzy of confusion. Suddenly, her fatigue seemed overwhelming.

The walk home seemed twice its usual length. She yearned for the solitude and sanctuary. Her cell phone rang shortly after she bolted her door and slid the security chain into place.

Maybe it's Kent.

Her heart raced as she dug in her purse, grabbed the phone, and swiped the screen to answer. "Hello."

Steve Zurich's voice. "Hey, Josie. My buddy combed through the NYC records. There's nothing there about a marriage or divorce."

Disappointment pushed down on her shoulders, but then Steve's words registered, and her blood heated. Since she sent his investigator friend to New York, her Internet searches had turned up the record of a marriage between Victor and the woman in question. It took place in another city borough, but a sharp investigator would have been thorough enough to find the record. All Steve's reports had been sketchy. Now he'd missed something even an amateur could uncover. Obviously neither Mr. Zurich, nor his friend, were up to the job. She was wasting her money.

"Did you get the recording device I need, yet?" she

asked.

"Yeah, you want me to Fed-Ex it over?"

She tossed her purse on a chair and started to pace. "No, I'll stop by your office so you can show me how it works. You might as well prepare your final bill after that. I don't think I need your services any longer."

"I've set up an appointment to talk to an old friend who's real close to Telemann now and could know some valuable dirt."

She considered the remark. It was probably meant to be a teaser and keep her sending checks, but could she afford to ignore it? She clenched her teeth. Damn him. He had her hooked.

"Go ahead and follow that one lead, then, but afterward, the job is over."

• • •

Twenty-four hours later, Kent popped in her office door wearing an expensive-looking pinstriped suit and a pearl white silk tie. His appearance was always impeccable, and she wondered how he afforded his designer wardrobe on a mid-level management salary. Did he shop at Emmeline's and get an employee discount?

He smiled ear to ear. "TGIF. How about coming sailing with me tomorrow?"

He radiated masculinity and sex appeal. The scent of his aftershave made her heart contract with longing. "Sailing?"

"Yes, you know, water, boats, sunshine, those big white things catching the wind."

She chuckled. "I know what a boat is, but I don't know

how to sail."

Her eyes went to the pale streaks in his hair. If he was a sailor, that explained the wonderful, sun-bleached look. She pictured him tousled, tanned, and bare-chested in his swimsuit. Awareness curled in the pit of her stomach.

"You don't have to know how to sail. All you need to do is lie on the deck looking gorgeous. I'll do the rest. I'll even supply lunch."

Excitement shivered up her spine. "I'd love to go, thanks."

"Okay then. Wear a bathing suit, bring something dry to change into later, and I'll pick you up in the morning at nine."

• • •

She rushed home after work and checked Josie's wardrobe for a swimsuit. She lifted the two tiny scraps of spandex and the blood drained from her face. No way.

Her phone rang, and she dropped the bikini parts back into the suitcase.

"Hey, babe, how's it going?" Josie asked.

"Do you actually wear those miniscule scraps of spandex at the beach?"

"Of course. The horizontal print emphasizes my boobs. It will look great on you. When and where are you going?"

"I have a date to go sailing tomorrow."

"That same guy Kent who you've been going to dinner with?"

"Yes. I can't wear that bikini in front of him. I'll feel naked."

"Then wear the one-piece tiger print with the halter top and plunging neckline. You can show a bunch of sexy cleavage without worrying about falling out. The legs are high-cut and will show off your butt. And the back is real low so he'll have to help spread sunblock where you can't reach."

Her pulse did a happy little jig at the image of Kent's hands sliding over her back. She felt her cheeks warm and shut down that inappropriate line of thought. "Maybe I'll shoot out to a store tonight and buy something more modest."

"Oh no you don't. You promised."

Faith sighed. "I'll try on the other suit. It better not be indecent."

"You want this guy to spill his guts, don't you? Then dazzle him. Once he starts drooling, he'll tell you every company secret he knows."

"He's a nice guy. I'm not trying to trick him with false expectations of sex."

"Are you finding anything out otherwise?"

"Not much. The detective I hired contacted a friend in New York to do some digging into that marriage license. He blew it, so I'm firing him. Otherwise I'm spinning my wheels. I've had to lay off on asking questions because people are getting suspicious. Trying to find new sources of information is driving me crazy."

"Well, then play this angle for all it's worth. Wear the bikini. Live dangerously."

"You're impossible."

"Maybe. But remember, you're me, so that means you have to be impossible too."

She remembered Kent's provocative kiss, and her pulse

accelerated. "I'm not very good at it."

"Practice makes perfect. Listen, I called because I have something to tell you."

"Are you okay?"

"Fine, this concerns you. I went to the library today."

"You're supposed to be taking it easy. Buy mail order or download e-books on the Internet."

"I have been, but I also have to get out from inside these walls once in a while if I'm going to keep my sanity. Anyway, I took a cab so I didn't have to drive and only stayed an hour. You need to hear what I found."

"Found where?"

"In the newspaper archives. That's why I went. I've been doing some searching for information about your father too. And I found a reference to his family I wanted to check out."

"Something about his brothers?"

"No, his father. He was a Norfolk cop who got fired for taking a bribe."

Faith sat down hard on the floor. "When was this?"

"Back when Victor was in high school. His father and several other cops were suspected of extensive corruption, but only one charge could be proven."

"I hope you're not hinting he has an excuse because he grew up in a household where he didn't learn right from wrong."

"No. Not at all. But it does give us a little insight into what formed his personality. Having a bad cop for a father probably gave him a warped sense of morality. Plus, the shame of your father being arrested has to be hard on any teenager. Something like that could cause a kid to rebel or act out."

"I don't care about his psychology. Nobody forced him to commit rape."

"Agreed. I just thought you might want to know."

Faith wondered: Did she want to know? Her grandfather was a corrupt cop on top of her father being a rapist. Half her family tree was rotten to the core.

She shook off the veil of hopelessness that was threatening to fall. "Thank you for helping. It's not good news, but might be useful to know." She shifted her focus to Josie. "Please don't go out on my behalf again. The last thing we need is you giving birth in a cab."

Josie laughed. "I'll try not to. Listen, I gotta run and start dinner. My mom is coming over in half an hour. Have fun tomorrow."

"I'll try."

"Promise you'll wear the tiger print?"

Faith laughed, feeling grateful for Josie's support but longing for her company. "Okay. Promise."

Chapter Eleven

Kent double-parked the red Mustang in front of Josie's building at exactly nine. She dashed out the doorway, whipped open the passenger side door, and jumped in. The driver in the car behind him laid on his horn.

"Sorry to make you run for it," he said. "I've circled the block three times without finding a spot."

"Most people have guest spots in the building parking lot, but reserving one was an extra fifty a month. I didn't plan on visitors, so I passed."

Wondering why such a beautiful woman wouldn't expect a parade of male visitors, he ran his eyes over the curves in the tiger print bathing suit cover-up cinched beneath her rounded breasts. It ended mid-thigh and revealed smooth, shapely legs. He tried to ignore a familiar tightening in his groin and forced his eyes back to the road.

She twisted around and dumped her tote bag into the back seat. He turned toward her and gazed at the exposed curve of her breast. Her cheeks turned pink as she settled back into the bucket of the seat and crossed her arms over her chest.

Concentrating on his driving, he maneuvered the Mustang through the stop-and-go Saturday morning traffic and, a few minutes later, turned onto Route One north.

"Where do you keep your boat?" she asked.

He'd decided to claim his house and boat, and the Porsche, were Jack's. Building the bigger web of lies seemed like the only way to keep up his story. "The boat's not mine. It belongs to a friend from college who lives on the Intracoastal Waterway and has a dock in his back yard. I help him with maintenance in exchange for using it every other weekend."

"Will he be going with us?"

"No. He and his wife had a baby a couple months ago, so they've been staying in lately."

He crossed the bridge to Hutchinson Island. "His place is about five miles from here."

She pointed to the right. "That's the ocean right there."

"Yes, all these houses front on the beach. They own a strip from the ocean to the Intracoastal. The road runs behind the houses, and all the owners have to do is walk across it to get to their docks."

"Wow. What a fabulous place to live."

He nodded and flashed her a I'm-a-working-stiff-too smile. "I guess it's nice to be rich."

Kent pulled into his driveway and parked beside his Porsche. He noticed Jack had folded down the rear jump seats and installed an infant car seat. He and Carrie must be getting ready to go out. He hoped Jack had seen him drive up and would stay out of sight for a few minutes. Carrie might not know the situation with Josie and say the wrong thing.

He pulled the car key and reached to open his door. "Here we are."

"It's beautiful, almost like a palace. What does your friend do for a living?"

Kent was amazed to find it easier to talk about himself when he was attributing the history to Jack. "He works in his family business. His father died when he was eight, and he inherited a large trust fund and a big block of stock in a major retailing company."

"And he went to the University of Florida instead of some posh Ivy League college?"

Busted! His brain raced to find a logical explanation. "Ah, his Dad was a U of F alumnus, and he wanted to go to the same school."

"Oh. I suppose that makes sense."

He got out, rushed around to open her door, and jumped at the chance to change the subject. "I forgot to ask before. Can you swim?"

"Yes. My high school had a team. I raced freestyle and relays my junior and senior year."

"Good. Then you can save me if I go over." He popped the trunk and removed their lunch and his change of clothes. He grinned and motioned with his head. "Only kidding. I'm a good swimmer. The dock is this way."

She stepped away from the car and paused. "The lawn is so thick it's like a plush carpet."

Surprised, he stopped and looked down at his feet. "I guess I never noticed."

Her appreciation for little things like the spicy smells in

a restaurant or the feel of soft grass made him realize he'd spent too many years in the fast lane. He'd taken much for granted that he should appreciate, and most of his life had been superficial. He studied her as she bent to sniff a yellow hibiscus blossom. The women he usually dated were superficial too, as superficial as mannequins, but Josie was different. She was sweet and innocent, honest and real.

At the dock, she paused and craned her neck to gaze up at the masthead. "How high is that?" She shaded her eyes with her hand, and a gold bangle at her wrist glimmered in the sunlight.

"Sixty-three feet."

Her eyes wandered from bow to stern. "It's a beautiful boat. So sleek."

"That's why sailors refer to boats as if they were women. She has a shape that can set a man's heart on fire."

Her lips twitched in a smile. "I would have thought you'd prefer a woman with a slimmer waist."

He wiggled his eyebrows and made a slow scan from her beautiful head to her crimson-painted toenails. "I do."

Cheeks tinged with pink, she dropped her gaze and shrugged her tote bag strap off her shoulder. "What can I do to help with the boat?"

"Just make yourself comfortable. I take her out alone all the time and have the procedure for getting underway down to a science."

After showing Josie where to stow her gear, Kent started the auxiliary engine, slipped the dock lines, and backed the boat out into the Intracoastal Waterway channel. He turned the bow toward Jupiter Inlet, then radioed the bridge-tender and requested she open the drawbridge.

The horns sounded, traffic stopped, and the two halves of the bridge slowly lifted and parted. He steered through the open bridge on the swift current and navigated between the red and green inlet channel buoys. The bow rose to the ocean swells as he motored the boat out into the Atlantic.

The fresh breeze cooled his face and tugged at his hair. Sunshine sparkled on the shimmering blue horizon. He engaged the autopilot and unfurled the mainsail, then shifted the engine into neutral and set the Genoa jib on the bow. On his way back to the cockpit after opening the hatches, he told Josie, "It's a perfect day for sailing."

The boat tipped gently to starboard and settled in for a brisk cruise out to sea. Shutting off the engine, he soaked in the sounds of wind sweeping over the water and their wake gurgling happily at the stern. His muscles relaxed. He sucked in the salty air and felt as if he hadn't really breathed since he'd last done it at sea.

He watched Josie close her eyes and lift her face to the sun and the breeze. Her long lashes lay against her creamy skin. Her sensual mouth curved into a satisfied smile. His heart did an odd gallop.

He pondered his decision to invite her sailing. He never brought women out on the boat. This was his special place where he felt free, where he could find a deep joy he couldn't explain. He'd always avoided tarnishing his time on the water by letting phony relationships intrude. He wondered why he desperately wanted to share the air, and water, and sunshine with Josie. Was it because, unlike most women he knew, she seemed to have a keen appreciation for the details of life? Might she appreciate the beauty and contentment? Was she someone who might share his deepest emotions?

He clenched his jaw and shut off that thought. She may be someone who could enjoy boating, but finding any deeper meaning in his invitation was a road he refused to travel.

She opened her eyes and turned toward him as if she'd sensed she was the subject of scrutiny. "The sky is such a gorgeous blue down here, even in the city," she said while the wind ruffled her hair. "I was pleasantly surprised to see it when I walked out of the airport. I half expected dingy, industrial-gray skies and smelly clouds of pollution."

"That's one of the nice things about the east coast of Florida. The sea breezes keep the air clean."

The sun's rays were hot on his shoulders. He stripped off his shirt and tossed it onto the port cockpit seat. His gaze was drawn to the cover-up hiding her swimsuit. He was anxious to view the body underneath, but held back from inviting her to sunbathe. Slow and easy, like with their magical kiss. She'd obviously been hesitant. The next move had to be hers.

He held a course offshore, making the best use of the easterly wind. Boat speed was a secondary consideration, but his racing instincts kept his hand on the wheel, constantly making minor adjustments to squeeze out every tenth of a knot.

Farther offshore, a flock of brown pelicans dive-bombed a school of fish about twenty yards from the bow. Josie stood and pointed. "Look at those crazy birds. They slam into the water and then come up looking dazed, like they're trying to figure out what happened."

She ran onto the foredeck and gawked wide-eyed at the pelicans' crazy aerobatics. Her joyous abandon made him throw back his head and laugh. He couldn't remember the last time he'd felt so bubbly inside.

A rogue wave rolled under the bow and tilted the deck precariously. She grabbed the rail on the cabin top to stop herself from falling. "Maybe you'd better sit," he called.

Sliding her hands along the lifelines, she made her way back to the cockpit. "You're probably right."

A few minutes later, Josie slipped off her cover-up. He feasted his eyes on the curves in her tiger-striped swimsuit and fought down an urge to engage the autopilot and sit by her side. The swell of her breasts tantalized him at the bottom of the deep V, and his blood heated.

"Care to try a few minutes at the wheel?" he asked, hoping she'd accept and come closer.

She stood. "Sure, but you'll have to show me how."

"Stand here in front of me."

He positioned her with her hands on the wheel, spread his legs, and stood behind her. He leaned so his chest brushed the warm skin of her back. His cheek touched her silky hair, and he breathed in her sweet scent. Tamping down his runaway imagination, he swallowed and rested his hands on top of hers.

"The idea is to keep the sails full and pulling. Right now we're beating, that means sailing into the wind at a close enough angle to create a slightly rounded shape on the front side of the sails."

His mind focused on rounded shapes other than the sails, specifically the ones on her body. And as for what he really wanted to fill…

His fingers itched as she nodded her understanding and the sunshine sparkled in her hair.

He lifted his eyes back to the bow. "The leading edge of

the Genoa, the big sail in the bow, will luff, or flutter, if you steer too close to the wind. Turn a couple degrees to the left and you'll see what I mean."

Her soft buttocks shifted against him as she rotated the wheel slightly. The Genoa fluttered as predicted. So did his pulse.

Kent tightened his grip on her hands and eased the boat back onto their original heading. "The sail's luffing stops when your angle is back to a point where the wind is hitting at a proper angle."

He moistened his lips. His reaction to her nearness wasn't about to stop that quickly.

"That seems easy enough," she said, her breath coming in short, nervous puffs. "So, how does the boat move ahead when the wind is blowing against us?"

He smiled at her wonderful, innate curiosity. Her engineering background meant he didn't have to simplify the explanation, and he plunged in. "The airfoil over the outside of the sail creates lift and pulls the sail into the resulting low pressure area. If you think of it as a vertical airplane wing, the aerodynamics are easy to visualize."

He visualized pulling her into the pressure area of his arms and getting horizontal.

She nodded. Her fingers clenched and unclenched on the wheel. "I guess the bigger the sails, the faster a boat can go, right?"

"For the most part. Distribution and the boat's displacement matter, too. And more sail area requires a higher mast to support the load. The whole rig plays into the equation."

"Is your mast considered big?" She leaned back slightly as she glanced upward.

The mast growing hard in his swim trunks twitched, and he suppressed a groan. "As far as I know."

She shivered slightly. "This is wonderful, but a little scary. It's like we're slicing through the waves, out of control. I never realized a boat could sail so fast. I mean, I've seen pictures of America's Cup races, but I didn't have any concept of how the real thing could feel."

"It's what boats are designed to do. If she's handled with care and properly prepared, creating blood-pounding moments comes naturally."

"Do you do this often?"

He slid his thumb over her knuckles. A grin tugged at his lips. *Not as often as he'd like.* "Every chance I get."

A speeding sport fisherman overtook them and roared by close on their starboard side, pulling up a huge wake.

"Hang on," he said.

The wave slammed the sailboat and rocked the hull. Josie fell into him. He wrapped one arm around her waist and clutched the wheel with the other.

She fit against him perfectly. Her soft hair blew into his face. The bare skin of her back caused heat and tension to spread over his chest. Blood rushed to his extremities, and he felt himself strain against the layers of cloth separating him from her firm buttocks. A longing to make slow passionate love to her skated through him. He slipped his hand upward from her waist and tiptoed his fingers over her ribs.

She regained her footing, pulled in a deep breath, and leaned slightly away. He thought he felt her trembling as he nuzzled her hair, kissed the crown of her head, then reluctantly let go.

• • •

An hour later, the wind diminished and Kent changed course and set a different sail. Faith stretched out on the deck, staring up at the red, blue, yellow, and white striped spinnaker billowing above her head. She wanted to roll over and let the sun warm her back, but hesitated. If she did, she'd have to ask Kent to smear sunscreen on her, and she wasn't sure she could stand having him touch her that intimately without melting into a puddle at his feet. She glanced at her cover-up. Maybe she should put it on and sit in the cockpit in the shade of the little awning.

"I think your thighs are getting pink," he said from where he stood at the helm. "Roll over, and I'll put some lotion on your back."

Her pulse accelerated. He was looking at her thighs.

She wondered if he could read her mind and sensed her tension. Her brain searched for an excuse not to accept his offer. "Who's going to steer?"

"Autopilot."

He engaged a lever, let go of the wheel, and walked up the side deck. He sat beside her and casually laid a hand on her shoulder. "You're getting hot. The Florida sun is much stronger than you're used to, and with your fair skin, unless you're careful, you'll burn to a crisp."

His touch seared her skin and her insides were already aflame.

"I'm enjoying the heat," she said, dragging her eyes away from his toned body. "It feels wonderful."

"Roll over and change your exposure then."

She did as he said, flipping over, raising her arms, and piling her hands to cushion her chin.

He picked up her tube of sunscreen. "Want some on your back?"

"Yes, please." Her heart beat wildly in anticipation.

His palms made contact with her shoulders. She sucked in a fortifying breath.

He slid his hands downward, past her waist, to the patch of skin in the dip of her swimsuit, then up again to her shoulders. Outward. Toward her sides.

She closed her eyes, waiting, wanting. She wasn't sure what she wanted, but the longing inside swelled and grew as he massaged her muscles. His fingertips brushed lightly down her sides and a shiver of awareness curled her toes.

His hands left her back. Disappointment surged through her body. She glanced at him, her breathing slightly too fast.

A smile touching his lips, he squeezed out more lotion and rested his palms on the backs of her thighs. She almost moaned with pleasure.

"Your legs can get burned, too," he said with an intimate note in his voice. "People ignore the backs of their knees, but the skin there is super sensitive."

Oh, so sensitive. She couldn't speak. Fabulous sensations rippled in her lower abdomen. She closed her eyes as his magical fingers rubbed and caressed. They did something to her that had nothing to do with sunburn or sailing or reality. She felt limp and pliable, the proverbial putty in his hands. A huge sigh escaped her lips, and her face heated in embarrassment.

He kissed the back of her knee. Her pulse danced. He kissed the other. Warmth licked at her insides. She wanted to purr like a kitten.

His fingers caressed her ankles. His hands slid slowly back up her calves. An inch onto her thigh. Another inch. They stilled.

He shifted and lay down beside her.

She swallowed and opened her eyes. He was on his back, arms raised, hands piled beneath his head. His chest rose and fell rapidly, and below his waist his bathing suit bulged. Waves of masculinity radiated from his body. She had the urge to kiss him, draw him to her, and ask him to teach her what to do next.

Her heart seized up.

She thought of Josie's frequent urgings. *Don't let your mother's fear of men make you into an iceberg. You've got to give in to your physical needs and lose your virginity sooner or later. Why wait until later and miss out on all the fun?*

Her body ached to reach out to him, but the voice of reason crept out and whispered, *No. He doesn't even know who you are. Having sex with him would be stupid. In a couple weeks, you'll be going home.*

She squeezed her eyes shut, listened to the wind slip by the sails and the water rush by the boat hull, and concentrated on calming the need clawing at every cell in her body.

• • •

After a full day on the ocean, they were both famished. They changed into street clothes. Kent steered the boat to a sea-food restaurant with docks for boating customers, and they enjoyed a delicious meal. The rose garden patio was bathed with slanting rays of afternoon sunlight, and he hated to see the day end, but several boats were circling in the waterway, their crews waiting for someone to leave the restaurant so they could take a turn to dock and dine.

"Ready to go?" he asked.

Josie nodded. "Yes, but I hate to leave. It's such a beautiful spot."

"Come out sailing with me again next Saturday. We'll reserve the same table."

"I thought you only got to use the boat every other weekend?"

Damn it! If he didn't want to get caught in the tangled web he'd woven, he needed to do better at remembering his lies. "Jack is going out of town next week. So I'm in luck."

An impish smile spread across her face. "Then I guess it's a date."

He slipped an arm around her waist and steadied her as she re-boarded the boat. After he had the engine running and the attendants shoved the hull off from the restaurant dock, he steered toward home.

Ten minutes later, he pulled alongside his own dock and killed the engine. When the lines were cleated, he said, "Unless you're in a hurry, I'd like to sit in the cockpit and watch the sunset."

She turned toward the blazing sun sinking behind the tall Hawaiian palms on the far side of the waterway. "I'm not in any hurry. It's gorgeous, isn't it?"

"I'm not sure which part of the day I like best. Being out there on the water, or watching the sun set and listening to the peep frogs and cicadas singing love songs at dusk."

Her eyes were lit with mirth. "Is that what they're doing?"

Kent shrugged. "That's the story my fifth grade science

teacher told me."

He grabbed two cushions and placed them side by side on the small aft deck. He kneeled on one and patted the cushion next to him. "Come sit."

She lowered herself, drew her knees up toward her chest, and wrapped her arms around her legs. "This has been a wonderful day. Thank you."

He reached out and pushed a stray lock of hair off her forehead. "Thank *you*."

Her eyes met his. With Herculean effort, he resisted the urge to kiss her. This time he'd play it cool and let it be her move, but he wasn't going to sit by and wait without letting her know how he wanted the day to end. Holding her gaze, he took her hand, rubbing his thumb over her slender fingers. "I always enjoy sailing, but you made today very special."

Desire flickered across her face. She swallowed and leaned toward him, parted her lips.

He met her half way. Their lips touched with a spark that made his desire explode. He took her into his arms, nudged her mouth open farther, slipped his tongue into her warmth, felt her slide her knees to the deck and melt against him.

Her breasts pressed against his chest. Her tongue tangled with his, and he deepened the kiss, no longer hiding his desperate desire.

He curved his hand around the back of her neck and drew her even closer. His hands moved upward into her hair, fingers raking the silky strands. His pulse tripped and sped. Heat spread through him like a wildfire, blazed in his loins.

He slid his hands down her back, exploring the landscape of her spine.

She sighed, pressed closer to him. Her arms held him

tight.

Dumping his caution, he moved his hands to the sides of her breasts, ran his fingers along the edge of their gentle swell.

Her breathing grew raged. Her caresses more ardent.

He cupped one soft breast and waited, teasing her with his stillness, giving her the opportunity to pull away. Seconds ticked by. He gently rubbed the pad of his thumb over her nipple, found it taut, straining against the fabric of her blouse.

She fisted her hand in the fabric of his shirt, pulled her mouth from his, and whispered, "I want you to make love to me, but…I've never…you'll have to show me how."

I've never. The realization of what she was confessing jolted his brain, and he blinked. Josie was a virgin.

The impact of the responsibility and trust Josie was bestowing on him caused a slight quivering in his stomach. He'd been with hundreds of women over the years, but couldn't remember one who hadn't known the ropes and had a few prior lovers. When he had sex with an experienced woman, they both knew the score. He always tried to be sure to give his partners a satisfying experience. He didn't think he'd ever let a woman down.

But a virgin was a different story. Any woman's first time should be special, and Josie was even more special than other women. She was sensitive, sweet. He'd have to hurt her, and that would hurt him too. Could he make her experience special enough to make the pain of first penetration worthwhile? Should he be honorable for a change, suggest she wait for a man she loved, a man capable of loving her?

She drew back slightly, maybe sensing his hesitation. Her intake of breath caused her breasts to rub against him.

Decision made. Only a fool was *that* honorable. And maybe he *was* capable of love.

He captured her luscious mouth. It opened eagerly beneath his, and she went pliant in his arms. His blood hummed. His body was hard, and ready, and hungry.

He took her hand. "Let's go below to the master cabin."

Chapter Twelve

She was trembling but couldn't seem to stop. The soft, silk pillows and intoxicating scent of maleness flooded her senses. Her skin tingled, sandwiched between the cool sheets and Kent's blazing body. She wanted to stay, but at the same time wanted to run away. She felt awkward and sweaty, yet knew this was right.

His hands cupped her face, and his mouth molded to hers. A rush of desire and adrenaline pushed her to the verge of collapse.

His mouth slid to her neck, his warm breath tantalizing, searing. His hands roamed over her breasts, her rib cage, slid lower. His mouth covered her nipple and sucked gently. Wonderful electric impulses skittered through her lower abdomen.

Her brain couldn't work, couldn't analyze. She arched toward him, struggling to feed tingling nerves hungry for sensation. Shy and unsure, her fingers explored his back, sensitive to the wonderful texture of his moist skin, feeling his muscles tighten and relax, amazed by the perfection of his body.

His hands slid to her inner thigh, and he gently spread her legs.

She held her breath in anticipation and wonder.

His palm cupped the pulsing center of her heat. He rubbed, caressed, made her ache for him to be closer, then his mouth followed the path seared by his hands. His tongue, oh, his tongue…teasing…licking.

A low sound like whimpering or pleading rose from the back of her throat. Shocked, confused, caring about neither, she bent her knees and raised her hips. Need stripped her mind of thought. Her body and soul yearned for nothing but to be his.

He knelt between her legs, his fingers exploring and arousing. She bit on her bottom lip. Embarrassed by her wanton eagerness, she writhed in longing and frustration.

His breath was hot next to her ear. "I might hurt you."

"I know." But she trusted him like no man before. "It's okay."

He rustled something at the bedside. The wrapper on a condom? She blushed. At least one of them was smart enough to be prepared.

A few seconds later, he pressed at her entry. When he hesitated for a split second, she thought she would die from want. She raised her hips, whispered, "I'm sure, Kent. I want you."

He kissed her, his tongue dancing in a sensuous, age-old rhythm. Then he suddenly rocked his hips and plunged himself inside her body. Her mind stopped working as he stretched her. A nanosecond of sheer, pristine pleasure gave way to a ripping pain.

She gasped.

His hips stilled, but his lips continued to nuzzle her ear, his fingertips gently caressed her neck and stroked the underside of her jaw.

She contrasted the caring and tenderness of the man with her, inside her, to the brutality of the animal who'd raped her mother. A million raw emotions that she couldn't sort out or separate squeezed her heart in a vise. Hot tears flooded her eyes and rolled down her cheeks.

Kent's fingertips brushed away her tears. "I promise," he said in a voice like dark honey, "it's all uphill from here."

She smiled as their gazes met and locked. His eyes, only inches away, were glossy with desire. The raw emotion in their depths heated every bone in her body.

Reveling in the sweetness of their intimacy, she brushed a fingertip over his cheek and subtly rolled her hips. "I think this is going to be worth it."

He curved his hand behind her neck and drew her mouth to his. His tongue probed symbolically as he moved inside her. Slow, easy, with tantalizing leisure, gentle thrusts that tortured her with pleasure and erased any remnants of discomfort.

Her blood roared in her ears. A hard knot of reckless need tightened in her belly. Expanses of bare, moist skin slid against each other overloading her senses. She rocked her hips faster, held her breath, then found herself saying, "Please, Kent, please."

The world slipped away. She felt bare and vulnerable, but complete and safe in his arms. He thrust deeper, stroke after stroke claiming her with an ever-increasing tempo.

Her inner muscles clenched, quivered. She clung to him as electricity shot through her. She pushed against him, raised her hips and strained to take him deeper. She exploded, leaving this world for a glowing state of nirvana.

"Oh, Kent," she whispered, her voice filled with awe.

"You're perfect," he said, his hot breath next to the sensitive skin of her ear.

He kissed her again, his tongue caressing her mouth. She lost herself in him, following his lead, matching his determined thrusts. His rhythm accelerated, he pushed harder and deeper, filling her beyond full.

His breathing grew ragged. He groaned. Buried himself. Pulsed.

Her inner muscles responded to the wonder of his orgasm, and she soared to a new peak. Heat melted their bodies into one liquid being. Her heart swelled and joyful tears flooded her eyes. In Kent's arms she'd been reborn as a woman, and if she lived to be two hundred, she'd always treasure this man and these perfect moments of passion.

• • •

Daylight. Morning. The sound of a motor grew progressively louder, then the pitch changed and became more distant. Waves lapped against the outside of the boat hull, and the bed under her swayed. "What was that?"

"Probably a fisherman going to dangle the early worm."

Her body hummed with pleasure as Kent's tongue flicked over the warm skin of her throat. "You're insatiable," she whispered.

"Are you tired of me already?"

She ran her fingers through the tousled cloud of his hair. "No, just tired. I don't think I can move a muscle. I doubt I'll be able to walk for a week."

He chuckled. "Then I'll have to keep you lying in bed."

"That probably won't help."

"True." His devilish smile promised a palace of delights. "But I'm willing to try."

"Your friend will want his boat back. Are you sure he won't be upset we're still here? The sky's light outside. It must be almost sunrise."

"He'll understand. Making love once is just the hor d'oerve. The second and third times are the main course."

"We must be on dessert."

"Close."

His hand slipped to her breast, and his thumb drew tiny, tantalizing circles around her nipple. She sighed and closed her eyes as renewed desire coiled in the pit of her stomach. Her mouth twitched.

His voice stroked her with slow syllables. "You have a fabulous Mona Lisa smile."

She focused on the ever so slight pressure of his fingertips grazing her skin. So this was what ecstasy felt like. This was the promised pot of gold at the end of the childhood rainbow.

After spending this night with Kent, she would never think of her body the same again. Now she'd be aware that passion lay beneath the surface, understand what it meant to be flesh and blood and have sexual needs. And Kent. Kent would no longer be just an exciting companion, he'd be the gentle lover who played her body like a delicate instrument and taught her wonderful things about life. He'd be the man who showed her how to truly be a woman.

His warm mouth rested on hers. His tongue slid between her parted lips, probed deep and sensuously.

Her world shrank to the movements of his slow hands, the taste of his tender kisses, his whispered endearments as he touched and teased. Her hips undulated against his strong hand, and she forgot to breathe.

She tasted the saltiness of his skin, ran her fingertips over his chest, scraped a nail gently across his nipple. Sliding her hand to the flesh of his inner thigh and upward to the essence of his maleness, she cupped him, caressed him, and smiled at his groan of pleasure.

Languid heat simmered through her veins. Her passion burned until every limb was shuddering in anticipation. She moaned with hot reckless need and fierce arousal.

The dark, wonderful hunger returned. He rolled and raised himself over her, filled the emptiness in her body, and fed her soul once more.

She lacked the strength to open her eyes, but reveled in the wonderful exhaustion. Certain her muscles would never move again, she nuzzled her face against his neck, cuddled next to his firm, moist body, and drifted off to sleep.

A warm hand brushing her hair from her forehead woke her. She opened her eyes. *Kent.* Memories flooded back. A smile tugged up the corners of her mouth.

"Sorry to wake you, but we have to get up," he said, as his hand took a long, lazy trip over her body. "I need to get you home, pack a bag, and catch a plane in four hours."

She blinked, fully awake. "A plane? Where are you going?"

"To the West Coast to check out a possible acquisition.

Then I fly to New Orleans and meet with the management of the last store we acquired. We're still working out details of the transition. I won't be back until Friday night."

Disappointment settled on her chest, followed quickly by a slight sense of relief. She didn't know how to act the morning after spending all night making love to a man, but his need to get up and start moving would help cover her awkwardness.

She sat, clutching the covers to her chest, feeling exposed and embarrassed to stand naked before him. "Where are my clothes?"

He tugged the light blanket from her grasp. "Forget them for a few minutes. Let's hit the shower."

She felt the blood drain from her face at the level of intimacy he was suggesting. Yes, they'd made love, several times, completely shared bodies, and slept in the same bed side by side. But now it was the harsh light of day and they were back to reality. She was plain old Faith, not exciting Josie. Faith didn't shower with her lover.

"Maybe I should just…"

He took her hand and smiled wickedly as he pulled her toward the bathroom. His eyes crinkled above a sexy scruff of whiskers. "Oh, no. You're not scampering away. I want to soap your back, slip my hands all over that wonderful skin."

She felt herself blush. "I suppose I could do your back."

"As long as you do the front too."

The tiny shower stall barely accommodated two bodies. The hot water cascaded over her shoulders as she stood stiff as a mannequin, eyes closed, her bare back against his bare front. One of his arms nestled around her waist. His other, soapy, hand slipped over her breasts creating wonderful, erotic sensations. Her blood heated. She relaxed her muscles and surrendered to the marvelous massage.

His hand slid over her stomach and hips, moved between her legs. She gasped as his fingers parted her and slipped inside. He probed and stroked. Her body responded with mind-numbing speed. She wondered if in the course of one night a person could be sucked into the quicksand of addiction.

She rested her head back on his shoulder as he reduced her to a quivering mass of heat and need. The water seemed to sizzle on her skin. Steam billowed around them in a magical fog. When he brought her to a searing climax, she clung to him, panting, her legs rubbery.

Ohmigod. I could shower like this every morning for the rest of my life.

As he supported her weight, he whispered in her ear, "You're beautiful inside and out, Josie. And a very sensual woman. There's no need to hide behind blankets or be embarrassed about anything we do."

She hardly heard his words. Her brain had stumbled over her last thoughts, and her emotions were swirling in chaos. Being here with him was heaven, but she might not shower like this ever again. Kent was a fantasy prince and part of an elaborate charade. She'd been lying to him all along, and her time with him might already be over.

Her chest ached with a crushing sense of loss. He'd irrevocably changed her life, but she could make a false move, do or say something before she saw him again, and in a blink of an eye her subterfuge would be revealed. When he found out who she was and the shameful things she was capable of doing, he would shun her forever.

She drew in a shaky breath. If her moments with him were limited, she might as well enjoy every one.

Craning her neck to reach his mouth, she kissed him with a sense of urgency and impending separation. "Pass the soap and turn around," she said, her fingers itching to caress his skin. "Let me do your back."

Chapter Thirteen

Monday morning, Faith resisted the urge to sit daydreaming about her weekend with Kent and focused all her attention on her goal. She phoned The Palm Beach Examiner and asked to speak with Leesa St. James.

"St. James."

"Good morning, Ms. St. James. I have an explosive story I believe you'll be interested in hearing. Is there a possibility you could meet me for lunch?"

At the stroke of noon, Leesa St. James walked into the restaurant. Faith signaled her, and the reporter sat.

"Sorry, but I can't stay long enough to eat. You said you wanted to discuss an explosive story."

Her spirit buoyed by hope, Faith crossed her fingers in her lap and pulled in a deep breath. "Would you be interested in writing an article about a prominent Palm Beach businessman who is actually a rapist and has gotten away with his crime?"

"That depends. Who is he? And do you have proof?"

"Victor Telemann, CEO of Emmeline's Department Store chain. Yes, I have proof."

Leesa pulled a pen and notebook from her shoulder bag, placed them on the table, and sat forward. "Telemann. Rape. Hm…what kind of proof do you have?"

"My mother's diary, and the page from the night that he raped her."

"Will your mother swear an affidavit that her claim of rape is true?"

"She can't, she's dead."

Leesa twisted her mouth and shook her head. "Then you don't even have proof a rape occurred?"

"I'm sitting here. I was conceived that night."

"It's an interesting angle, but I can't print an unsubstantiated accusation. I'd need DNA to prove he's your father, and an expert's opinion that the diary is—how old are you?"

"Twenty-five."

"— at least twenty-five years and nine months old and not in your handwriting. Were there any witnesses? Police reports? Any proof you're not being spiteful and making this up?"

Faith's hope began to fizzle. "No."

Leesa sighed and put away her notebook. "I hate to see criminals escape punishment. If you can get me something with more teeth in it, I'll be happy to write the story, but I can't do much with the little that you've told me. I'd be slapped with a libel suit, and my editor would kill me."

"I understand. I've been trying to find more proof, and I'm not giving up until I do."

Leesa handed Faith her business card. "That's the spirit.

You never know when you'll find the key piece of information and the situation will burst wide open. That's my private cell number and email. If you get anything else, call me right away."

"I will."

Faith sighed and watched the reporter walk away. Plan C wasn't a complete bust yet, but neither was it looking good.

. . .

On Wednesday, Faith reviewed her latest download of Victor's emails. The first two were the online equivalent of phone sex, pornographic invitations from his mistress that she closed quickly after reading the first sentences.

She thought of making love to Kent and how much she wanted his hands on her body again. Desire quivered low in her abdomen and her cheeks burned hotter. How pathetic could she get? Her inexperience had probably killed his interest. He wouldn't want a repeat performance.

She considered wandering over to the financial department and locating Kent's desk. He wouldn't be there because he'd said he'd be out of town until Friday, but she could see where he sat, touch his chair, find out what personal items he treasured and kept close at hand.

A smile curved her lips, and she rolled her eyes. *Don't be ridiculous. You can't go around acting like a love-struck schoolgirl.*

The yearnings that hovered beneath her exterior barricades were bad enough. She ached to hear his voice, was starved for his smile, could barely keep from grinning like an idiot every time she remember the wonder of lying in his arms. She needed to pull herself together, stop daydreaming and wishing her phone would ring.

Reminding herself she had to concentrate on finding evidence against Victor, she shifted her focus back to the list of emails. The next one was from Quick Fox Messenger Service. The subject line read *delivery appointment*. The text of the message was cryptic and confusing. It was signed by someone named Brody.

She closed that email and opened six more in succession. Most were business related, mundane, and boring. To her disappointment, nothing seemed incriminating or pertinent to her cause.

She closed the email program and double-clicked the icon for the Work Control monitoring software. The list of Internet sites Victor had visited was short. He'd browsed luxury cars and checked out a resort in the Cayman Islands.

She cleared the incriminating records from her monitor screen. Exasperation forced her breath to huff out of her lungs. If only she could dig into his bank account and credit card records. Any illegal activity would surely leave a money trail. She gritted her teeth. As tempting as the idea of searching his finances was, she had to draw a line somewhere. Hacking into a bank was probably a federal offense and could land her in jail.

A shiver rippled up her spine. He was supposed to be the one who ended up in jail, not her. She'd already bumped the border between right and wrong far enough.

Her brain was still churning through facts about Victor, but she appeared to be diligently working when Ronnie popped into her office doorway.

"Are you going Friday night?"

"Going where?"

"The opening of the dinner theater."

She remembered the notice and envelope she'd found in her office mailbox. "No, do you want my tickets?"

He frowned and shook his head. "It's a royal summons, woman. Not at all smart to refuse."

She shrugged. "Is there something more to this than I know about?"

"Definitely. This dinner theater is partly financed by Victor Telemann, and his girlfriend just happens to be starring in the lead. Reading between the lines, I'd say we've been sent tickets to make sure the place is sold out the first night. And the boss isn't going to look kindly on any corporate employee who dares not to go."

Her mind went back to the day in his office when he'd treated her like a peasant. "I'm just a lowly temp. He won't care."

"Maybe so, but come anyway. It's free and could be fun."

She dreaded an evening pretending to be light-hearted and outgoing while actually feeling like a wallflower, and the prospect of seeing Victor's mistress on stage after the scene she'd heard in his office made her stomach roll with nausea.

Maybe she could bear going if she'd be with Kent.

Doubt crept out and poked her in the chest. Even if he was here, what right did she have to assume he'd want to go with her? She'd slept with him, and weren't all men simply after sex? Once they scored, the game was won. If he cared about more than a one-night stand, wouldn't he at least have thought about her, wanted to hear her voice, found a minute to call?

The silence of her phone took on a new, devastating

meaning.

Ronnie tapped on the corner of her desk. "Hey, snap out of it, woman. Earth to Josie."

Shifting her attention back to him, she stalled. "Are you taking a date?"

"No. A bunch of us are going stag. We'll share a table and have some laughs."

She didn't want to sit home alone mooning over Kent. She didn't want to sit in her apartment depressed that her fourth week of seeking evidence had been as fruitless as the first three, but she was even less anxious to go out in public and bump into Victor. Logic told her to go. The theater opening might be a good opportunity to observe him from a safe distance. Maybe she could learn some useful bit of information.

She drew in a deep breath. "Okay, count me in."

. . .

Friday afternoon at three, Kent glanced out the window at the familiar turf as Emmeline's corporate jet taxied onto the ramp outside their private hangar at Palm Beach International. He thought about Josie's sense of fascination when she was on the boat and wondered if she liked to fly. Picturing her sitting beside him as he kicked the rudder in his little acrobatic-rated Pitts over hard and snapped through a four-point roll, a smile tugged at his lips. His pulse rate sped up, and he realized he was unusually excited about coming home.

He glanced across the aisle at Jack. Carrie would be waiting for him, excited to welcome him and hear about his trip. If Jack could settle down and find happiness with one special woman, maybe it was possible for him to find a soul mate too. Maybe Josie was his chance at a different, more meaningful life.

He let the thought spread and grow while the jet rolled to a stop. Then the pilot announced, "Welcome home to West Palm Beach."

Kent erased the idea of finding wedded bliss from his mind. That kind of life might be right for Jack, but it wasn't right for him. He wouldn't get sucked into believing in anything as stupid as love.

He quickly scrolled through the last messages on his smartphone, decided the rest could wait, turned the unit off, and stuffed it into his briefcase.

As he and Jack prepared to disembark, he nodded at the perky flight attendant. "Thanks, Angie. Everything was perfect."

She flashed him her usual I'd-love-to-have-you-call-me smile. "You're welcome, sir. Have a good day."

Kent descended the steps from the cool interior and slammed into a wall of ninety-degree afternoon heat. The suffocating stench of baking tarmac and jet exhaust depressed his mood and reminded him of his next destination. He hung the strap of his laptop bag over his shoulder and turned to Jack. "Carrie will probably be glad we got home early. After we grab the bags, you can bolt. I have to go by the offices and see Victor."

"No argument. I'll take Carrie and Christian over Victor any day. What's he want?"

"I don't know. I just got an email from Peg asking me to stop by."

Daydreaming about taking Josie sailing tomorrow, and then making love to her all night tomorrow night, he drove the Mustang to Emmeline's. Careful not to have a sappy grin on his face, he rode the elevators up to Victor's penthouse office.

"How'd it go?" Victor asked.

Kent sunk into a chair, crossed his legs, and smoothed down his tie. Annoyance warmed his blood. Was he here for some kind of inquisition about his current project that was motivated by the problems with his last deal? Or did Victor have a new game? "Good. The operation looks promising."

Victor nodded. "Keep following up on it then."

"I intend to."

"Good. Good."

Kent sensed his trip wasn't the reason he was here. "You didn't want me to stop by to talk about Bob Brandt."

"No." Victor picked up a remote on his desk, pushed a button, and the wall panels slid back to reveal his fifty-inch video screen. "We're placing a couple new ads on channel twelve. This is the late night."

The screen lit up and trumpets vibrated from the speakers. The thirty-second commercial featured a long-legged woman sprawled on a satin-sheeted circular bed and draped only in furs and diamonds.

"This is for the dinner hour slot."

Another thirty-second bit rolled by, this time featuring a fake celebrity exiting a limo and strutting down a red carpet in a Jacques Bouchard gown and glistening Whiteside diamonds. The closing scene showed her dragging a fur casually behind, then casting a come-hither look over her left shoulder.

Kent shrugged. "Pretty good stuff. The new agency?"

Victor nodded. "They're proposing something similar for every market where we acquired in the last couple years. Meyerson will be calling you for input."

"Right."

The image on the screen flicked to the living room of Emmeline's corporate-owned beach house, then went to a split display of four rooms.

Kent frowned. "What in the hell is that?"

Victor grunted and the screen zoomed in on the bedroom image. A woman Kent recognized as Victor's mistress was parading around the room naked.

"I'm sure you've seen tits and cunt before."

"I thought the beach house was leased out for the season."

"A slight fib to prevent your mother from stumbling into an embarrassing situation."

The woman pulled a blue dress from the closet and held it front of her while studying herself in the mirror.

Kent glared at Victor. "Since when is that place for you to have a sleazy rendezvous or stash other women? And who put in the cameras?"

"You wanted me to be discrete. I am." Victor gave him a smug grin. "I had a video surveillance system installed for security and to keep an eye on my property while I'm not there. I don't like to share."

"Does she know she's being watched?"

"Not at the moment. Once in a while she tapes some hot stuff for me to view later, but right now she thinks she's shut the recorder off. Actually, it's sound and motion activated. I know everything that goes on inside and outside that house.

Pretty neat, huh?"

Kent's stomach rolled over in disgust. He stood. "It's been a long day, and I'm not going to sit here watching like a peeping Tom. You want anything else?"

Victor shrugged, hit a button on the remote, and the video screen went black. "I understand you're stopping over for a cocktail with your mother later?"

"That's the plan. Should I mention your guest at the beach house?"

"You won't do that."

He clenched his jaw. True. He wouldn't. Telling her about Victor's bimbos would only cause her pain and humiliate her more than she'd been humiliated already. As much as he wanted her to divorce Victor, he wouldn't be the one to rub his stepfather's infidelity in her face.

"I'm busy elsewhere tonight," Victor said. "Tell her I got tied up and won't make it home for dinner."

Kent narrowed his eyes. "I heard about the dinner theater opening and the free tickets you spread around to all the employees. I won't be your lackey. Make your own excuses."

"I'm only thinking of your mother's feelings. The explanation will be better coming from you."

"Bullshit."

"I'm part owner of the club. This opening is strictly business."

"Right, and I'm Santa Claus."

The intercom buzzed. Victor leaned across his desk and hit a button.

"Your masseuse is here, Mr. Telemann," Peg said.

"Good. Send him in." Victor released the button and looked up at Kent. "You should try this guy's Swedish treatment. In half an hour, he works out every one of my kinks. His foot and calf massages are the best. If you go to his shop, he's got a seven towel hot lather shave and cleansing with caviar balm."

Kent fisted his hands, turned, and stormed from Victor's office, almost colliding with the masseuse who was pushing a portable cart toward Victor's door.

He boarded the penthouse elevator and switched cars on the fifth floor. Being with Victor had left a sour taste in his mouth. Contact with a good person might wash it away, but in this situation, a few minutes with his mother wasn't the solution. He got off the second elevator on Josie's floor. Just for a few minutes he needed to be with someone who could help restore his hope for mankind.

At her doorway, he stopped short and huffed out his breath. Her office was closed and locked.

He raked his fingers through his hair. Maybe he should have called during the week. He could have at least called this morning, let her know he'd be home tonight, and made arrangements to see her. Assuming she'd be available had been stupid.

Now it was too late to call and expect her to jump at a moment's notice. Maybe she had other plans, like going to the dinner theater opening.

Confusion battered his brain. He hadn't called because he didn't want to admit he cared, but this feeling of disappointment at not seeing her was evidence he did care, and it scared him to his core. He was definitely getting attached.

• • •

Faith handed the doorman her ticket and stepped into the ornate, dinner theater lobby. She licked her lips and clutched her purse. Her dress was cut too low for comfort, and she felt as if every male eye was glued to her cleavage. Darn it. Why had she ever promised Josie she'd dress the part?

The lobby was crowded with people chatting and laughing. Voices of every tone and pitch echoed off the floors and walls and merged into one ambient roar. Anxious to join a group where she could blend into the background and stop feeling so conspicuous, she searched the crowd for Ronnie or any of the women who worked in her office area.

She spotted the back of a head with dark, wavy hair on the far side of the lobby. Hoping it was Ronnie's, she shuffled through the crowd stretching onto her tiptoes occasionally to keep the familiar locks in sight.

Ronnie turned, their eyes met, and he smiled as she approached. "Just in time. We were getting ready to go in."

She nodded to the women standing with him. "Hi, Rose, Bev."

Bev raised her eyebrows and fanned her face with her fingers as if suddenly hit with blazing heat. "Hey, Josie. Wow, that's some sizzling dress."

Faith adjusted the spaghetti strap of Josie's crimson mini and wished she'd had the choice of wearing her navy blue shirtwaist. "I think I should have brought a sweater. It's freezing in here." She scanned the clothing of her companions and smiled at Rose. "You better watch out. I might steal that beautiful, warm-looking jacket."

Now that she was with people she knew and could feel relatively safe, she noticed individuals in the crowd. Many people held cocktails. Women were dressed in tight revealing dresses and flirted openly with ogling men. Nearby, a burly man who looked out of place in an expensive black suit had his hand resting low on his date's hip. Few of the people fit her image of patrons of the arts. They looked more like gangsters or the audience she'd expect at a wrestling match.

She swallowed her uneasiness. The crowd and atmosphere were out of her comfort zone, but Josie would probably feel right at home. At parties, she loved to wander from group to group, and she'd be laughing and joking with people in a matter of minutes. She may have met new friends, but no one remained a stranger.

Faith released a pent-up breath. Josie could blend in anywhere. And she was supposed to be Josie.

As she scanned the room, she met the eyes of a gray-haired man about ten feet away. She gave him her best Josie smile. He smiled back, then turned away. The fleeting contact felt good and gave her courage to try friendliness with someone else.

"Come on, our table's ready. The rest of the group can find their own way," Ronnie said, taking Faith's arm.

The gesture seemed odd, not at all fitting with his normal behavior, but she shook off the thought and walked with him. A huge poster on the wall beside the entrance to the dining room caught her eye. The image of a beautiful woman was sandwiched between the words *Opening Night: **Temptation** starring **Melinda Hart**.*

Her brain put the woman's face with the dress, legs, and feet she'd seen from her hiding place in Victor's bathroom closet. A drop of disdain trickled down her spine.

Faith pulled her gaze away from the poster and focused her attention back on following the waiter.

"Faith, honey!"

A woman's voice calling her name. Who? She turned to look behind her. Then froze.

No. Don't.

Mortification stabbed at her throat. She couldn't look. She was Josie to the people she was with. She had to ignore the woman and keep walking.

"Faith. Yoo-hoo, over here."

She held her breath, put one foot in front of the other. How could anyone who knew her be here tonight? Mouth suddenly dry and palms suddenly moist, she scanned around her searching for an exit. Maybe she could escape before she was cornered in front of Ronnie.

No exits. She contemplated ducking under a table, but threw out the idea. She might evade the person who recognized her, but she'd never be able to explain her actions to the group from Emmeline's. Feeling like a rabbit watching a trap spring shut on her leg, she eyed a red fire alarm lever on the wall two feet away. Was keeping her identity a secret worth causing a stampede for the doors and the risk of someone getting hurt?

Squeals of delight rose behind her. "Suzie-Q! It's been ages."

"I thought that was you, girlfriend. Wow, you look so fab."

She recognized the original woman's voice.

The breath whooshed out of her lungs. The woman had been calling to someone else who just happened to share her name.

Still beside Ronnie, she maneuvered through a maze of furniture before the waiter stopped beside a table for ten located about fifteen feet from the stage.

Ronnie held her chair, while the waiter held chairs for Rose and Bev. Then Ronnie sat at her right.

"May I take drink orders?" the waiter asked.

Ronnie ordered a draft beer, Rose asked for the house wine, Bev got a margarita, and Faith ordered a large Coke hoping to moisten her dry throat.

After the waiter left, Ronnie craned his neck, looked around the room, and said, "Just about everyone from the corporate offices is here."

Faith scanned the faces at the tables, looking for one in particular. Just about everyone, yes. But no Kent. She sighed and disappointment weighed on her shoulders.

• • •

Their drinks came. Five more colleagues arrived and took seats at the table. Faith slipped off her pointy-toed shoes and wiggled her feet under the table as she listened to Ronnie and Bev debate the qualifications of the candidates in the upcoming mayoral election. The room slowly filled with the smells of perfume and beer. Dozens of loud voices competed with the sounds of clinking glasses, laughter, and background music.

Her Coke was two-thirds gone when the lights dimmed, the band drowned out the room noises with a flourish of drums and trumpets, and a master of ceremonies in a blue tuxedo took center stage. The room grew quiet. He welcomed the crowd and introduced the pre-dinner entertainment.

Applause filled the room as lively music blared from the orchestra pit and four scantily clad women pranced onto the stage. Sequins adorned their outfits and glitter sparkled on their stunning bodies and long shapely legs. Suddenly conscious of her own imperfections, Faith slunk lower in her chair.

For the first few minutes, the dancers' routine seemed artistic, then the tone subtly changed. Faith had never been to a strip club, but she guessed the dancers there would be similarly dressed and have similar moves. When the dancers spread their legs wide and undulated in a sexual pantomime, she felt her face heating and wished she could slip out of sight.

She wondered about the play scheduled to start after dinner. Was it equally risqué? If so, could she manage to leave without drawing attention to her departure?

Ronnie whispered, "Wow, they're really pushing the envelope with this stuff. I hope the place doesn't get raided."

Keeping her eyes low to avoid seeing the lurid dance moves, she glanced his way.

She blinked. The napkin spread in Ronnie's lap was tented in the middle. Ronnie was sexually aroused from watching the women on the stage, but how could that be? He was gay, he was supposed to be attracted to men.

Faith swallowed and averted her eyes. Who was she to question why a gay man became aroused. Maybe his imagination had substituted a friend he found attractive.

After what seemed like an eternity, the music exploded in a grand finale. As the dancers slinked off the stage, the audience applauded with much more enthusiasm than she could muster. As waiters began weaving between the tables serving salads, she breathed a sigh of relief. Thank God that embarrassing episode was over.

Sitting up straight, she looked around and searched for Victor in the crowd. If she wanted to slip out early, she should gather any information now.

She located him holding court at the head of a long table next to the stage. The huge cigar stuffed in his mouth belched beastly smoke. As she studied his face, he turned and their eyes collided. Her stomach somersaulted. Cold sweat slicked her hands. She jerked her gaze away.

For several seconds she sat torn between an urge not to look and an equally strong urge to stare. The man was her father, yet all she knew about him was what she had seen in Steve's reports or read on the Internet. She'd formed a horrible impression based on her summons to his office. But he was sitting right across the room. Maybe tonight he'd show a better side, be relaxed and different. If so, this might be the only chance she'd ever get to glimpse his true colors.

Unable to resist, she looked back. He wore a suit that probably cost several thousand dollars. The people seated around him at the table seemed to hang on his every word, and his chest was puffed out and his chin held high as he lapped up the attention.

She studied him, searching for any tiny clue that would indicate he was a good man. Grinding her teeth, she watched his eyes, his expressions, his body language. Inside her head, she muttered a prayer.

Please let him do something admirable, something virtuous. It doesn't have to be anything magnanimous. I'll settle for something merely polite.

He snapped his fingers at a waiter, spit out a few words he punctuated with a sneer and an eye roll.

Faith swallowed and dropped her gaze to her hands

clutched tightly together on the tabletop. Fighting against a smothering wave of dejection, she wished she'd never read her mother's diary, wished she could still believe the fairy tale that her father was a decent person who died a hero. Wished that she didn't have to wonder how many of her genes came from a man who reminded her of the Devil.

• • •

When the entrée dishes were cleared away, Rose said, "I can't wait to see Melinda Hart. I hear she's even more gorgeous in person. I'll tell you one thing, if I was Mrs. Telemann, I'd be livid. I'd kill my husband for doing something like this tonight."

Faith thought of the night in Victor's office. A mental tape replayed the sordid sounds of clandestine oral sex. She wrapped her arms around her midsection and forced the memories away. Her mind's eye pictured her safe little apartment, and she desperately wished she was there, curled up in bed, reading a good book, alone and free to be herself.

Bev said, "Maybe Mrs. Telemann doesn't know. You know what they say about the wife."

Ronnie added, "She must. He's been running around with other women for years. I heard a rumor he paid for Melinda's breast implants and that hers aren't the first set of boobs he's financed."

Faith leaned back and filed away the information, suddenly glad she'd come. Gossip wasn't necessarily reliable, but might give her some clues about where to continue her research.

Rose said, "I wish some of his generosity extended to his

employees. I don't need boobs, but I could sure use a raise."

Ronnie wiggled his eyebrows. "Melinda got free boobs, plus he's paying for this extravaganza. I guess she's doing something you're not."

"Well, I got rid of my ex quick when he started paying too much attention to his secretary," Bev said. "Mrs. Telemann would be smart to give old Victor the heave-ho. He's nothing but a skirt chaser."

Ronnie inclined his head toward the doorway. "Speaking of skirt chasers, here comes the prodigal son."

Victor had a son? How could Steve Zurich's reports have been so useless and incomplete they'd left out that fact?

Curious, Faith strained to see who Ronnie was talking about.

Bev said, "Don't pick on him, he's a sweet guy."

"I'll give him that, but he's still following in the old man's footsteps. His charm just makes him more successful."

"You're just jealous because Kent isn't gay, and you don't have a chance."

Kent? The name hit like a sucker punch.

She didn't know his last name.

The blood gushed from her face. She forced her cold lips to move. "K…Kent?"

Ronnie pointed. "Over there in the expensive-looking gray suit and signature Hermes tie. Kent Telemann. Haven't you met him yet?"

Chapter Fourteen

Faith's breath was trapped in her lungs. Her heart was paralyzed with fear. Her mind was a frenzy of confusion. *No. No. No. No!*

She looked in the direction Ronnie pointed and caught a glimpse of the man's face before he turned away.

His back was to her. His suit jacket stretched between wide shoulders as he raised his arms. He hugged Peg then drew back, holding her hand and nodding as they talked.

She wanted to deny the identification, insist there must be some mistake, but the hair was the hair she'd run her fingers through only days before. The body was the body she'd touched and caressed. He moved with the same masculine grace. She saw his profile and his chiseled features erased all doubt. He was the same man she'd made love to, laid with in his bed.

A howl of protest rose inside her head, swelled and enveloped her mind, erupted in a world-ending sonic boom.

Her heart lurched, staggered, stopped. She'd let herself be used for sex by a sweet-talking womanizer!

Victor Telemann's prodigal son. She gasped as the words bashed her brain like a volley of grenades. Her blood pressure shot off the charts. Kent was her half-brother? She'd slept with her half-brother!

She felt light-headed and nauseous. Fearing her voice or expression would betray her utter shock, she jumped up from her chair and grabbed her purse. "I have to go. I'm going to be sick."

Ronnie pushed his chair back to stand. "Do you want me to take you home?"

"No. Stay."

She dashed for the door, eyes focused on the portal of escape, heart thumping frantically against her ribs. Pushing outside, she bolted for the bushes along the far side of the U-shaped drive. She had to run. Escape. Hide from the horrifying images darting through her mind.

She gulped huge quantities of air that pained her lungs. Horror burned the sweat from her skin.

A voice inside her head screamed, *don't go into the darkness.*

The light from the theater building had faded. She gazed at the darkness beyond, and commanded her feet to stop. Her legs felt wobbly. She collapsed onto her knees with tears streaming down her cheeks. Her chest ached.

Conflicting thoughts pounded at her temples like her skull was about to explode. She pressed her hand to her stomach, bit down hard on her bottom lip.

Stop this. Now! Think. Something's wrong here. Figure out what.

She fisted her hand over her mouth and pictured the meager reports from Steve Zurich. They'd said nothing of a son, but they had listed the date of Victor's marriage to Emmeline. Victor married his current wife twenty years ago. Kent would have to be younger than her to be her half-brother.

Use your brain. Do the math.

Her breath roared in and out of her lungs and sweat ran down the side of her face as she struggled to concentrate.

If Kent was Victor's son, he'd have to be…nineteen? Even stretching conception to before the wedding would only make Kent twenty or twenty-one.

She shook her head. No. That was impossible. He looked closer to thirty. He'd talked about graduating college and said he'd worked for Emmeline's for a couple years.

Could he be the child of Victor's previous marriage to the woman she found records of in the New York City archives?

She calculated. If that were the case, Kent would be no more than twenty-four, a minimum of a year younger than she was. The numbers might be feasible but still didn't make complete sense. He was too mature and sophisticated to be under twenty-four.

He could be illegitimate, conceived while Victor was in high school and before her mother was raped, but then why would he have Victor's last name? Her brain grasped the explanation she liked best. Maybe he was adopted, not Victor's biological son at all.

She felt raw and exposed, dirty inside. Kent might not be Victor's son, but he was a member of Victor's family, had grown up in the same house.

Her mind swirled and recalled Ronnie's words. *Following in the old man's footsteps.* How alike were Victor and Kent?

A noise. A real footstep. She jerked back to reality.

More footsteps. A branch swished off to her right.

Fear squeezed her chest like a steel band. Someone else was out here in the semi-darkness.

Faith's breath caught. She looked around, taking in her surroundings. She was kneeling on wet grass behind a thick shrub emitting a sickeningly sweet odor. She was cold, barefoot, vulnerable.

The tiny hairs on her nape stood on end. Goose flesh prickled her arms. She'd been stupid to leave the brightly-lit area by the theater.

She jumped to her feet and spun toward another, closer sound. A flashlight beam hit her face.

"Are you all right, Miss?"

She gasped and blinked. Raising her hand to shield her eyes, she squinted at a security company logo on the pocket of the man's uniform.

Trying not to hyperventilate, she jerked her chin up. "I'm fine." The words wobbled and came out sounding like the lie of the century.

Still wary of the man's intent, she stepped out from behind the shrub and scanned the area to her right. Several taxis were lined up at the edge of the road waiting for fares.

Mumbling, "I'm just leaving," she squeezed her purse tightly against her waist and, the dewy grass slick under her bare feet, ran for the safety of the first vehicle.

• • •

A few minutes after he'd spotted a woman who might have been Josie bolting from the theater, Kent walked along the edge of the thick underbrush and raked his fingers through his hair. There was no sign of anyone here. If Josie had been here earlier, she was gone.

What had upset her enough to send her running from the theater? Concern nibbled at his gut. The doorman's description might have been wrong and the woman might have been someone else, but what if it were Josie and she was in trouble?

He handed his valet parking ticket to the attendant and waited for the Mustang. Seconds ticked by and he wished he'd skipped the second drink with his mother. If he'd come a few minutes earlier, he might have found Josie before she'd fled.

He pulled out his cell phone and speed-dialed her number. No answer. It switched to her voice mail. He put the phone away and slid behind the wheel of Jack's car.

Traffic on the boulevard was light, and he let his foot press hard on the accelerator. He covered the miles like a grand prix driver speeding toward a checkered flag.

In the lobby of her building, he buzzed her apartment. No answer. He buzzed another apartment claiming, "Pizza delivery." Eleven apartments later, someone punched him through.

Grinding his teeth, he knocked on Josie's door.

No answer.

He knocked again. "Josie? If you're in there, open the door."

Silence.

He banged harder. "I'm not leaving until I know you're

all right."

"Go away."

His soul jumped with relief at the sound of her voice. "Are you okay? Why did you run from the theater?"

"Leave me alone."

He debated his next move. Had he done something to anger her? Damn, he should have called. He'd treated her like one of his disposable dates and hurt her feelings.

Determined to explain, he rapped on the door again. "Please let me in and tell me what's going on."

Silence. Then the rattle of a chain and slide of a deadbolt. The door opened.

Her expression was cold. "No, why don't you tell *me* what's going on, Mr. Kent Telemann."

• • •

He blinked then winced. "I can explain."

She swallowed and crossed her arms over her chest. The pounding of her heart reverberated through her bones. She didn't want to hear his explanation, but she had to know. "Make it quick."

He shrugged, smoothed his damn designer tie, and offered her a smile that didn't quite reach his eyes. "I don't like to tell women too much about my background. It changes the relationship." He stepped inside.

She opened her mouth to protest he wasn't welcome inside her apartment but thought of the alternative: a nasty hallway scene played out in front of her neighbors. She reconsidered, backed up one step, and let him close the door. "In other words, lying insures against the sex becoming personal."

"No, Josie. That's not what this is about."

His selfish motives painfully squeezed her heart, but she fought against her whirlpool of feelings. What did his motives matter? They had no relationship, could have no relationship, and their past had no place in the future, especially if he was her half-brother.

She steeled herself and forced out her most important question. "You're Victor Telemann's son. Yes or no?"

"Yes…"

Her stomach somersaulted.

"…and no."

How could he torture her with illogical, glib answers? She fisted her hands and spit out, "You can't be both. Pick one."

He frowned and looked perplexed, but didn't address her acrimony. "I can be both. Legally I'm his son. He adopted me a year after he married my mother, but he's not my father and never will be."

She closed her eyes, faint with relief. Not a blood relation. Not her half-brother. Her shame could be for sins lesser than incest.

"What does it matter whether I'm related to him or not?" he asked.

"What does it matter?" Memories of lying in his arms swamped her brain. Then her thoughts shifted to the man who was his adoptive father, ricocheted to her mother's rape. Her blood heated. "You never told me. You've been lying to me all along."

His hands rested on her shoulders. Heady sensations churned through her, then disgust at her weakness. How could she want his touch now that she knew who he was?

"My last name is irrelevant." He sucked in a deep breath. "Open your eyes and look at me, please."

Refusing to let her swirling emotions show, she clenched her teeth, schooled her face, and met his gaze.

He cleared his throat, dropped his arms to his sides, and hooked his thumbs in his belt. "Listen, apologizing is new to me, but here goes. I'm sorry, Josie. I was wrong not to be open with you up front."

She wanted to put aside his identity, let herself forgive and forget, but the hurt of his deception and the memories of her mother's ordeal kept her defenses on high alert. "I want you to leave now."

"Let's start over."

"I can't do that. You're part of Victor Telemann's family."

He huffed out his breath and shook his head. "Okay, I take it you don't like the guy. I don't like him either, but be reasonable. We're not *family*. Living with him was never my choice."

"But you're just like him. You use women."

"No, you're wrong." A muscle worked in his jaw. "I could never sink to treating any woman the way he treats my mother. He's a low-life cheater. He tricked my mother, he didn't let her see how despicable he is until after she married him."

"Yet you follow his example. Trick women. Lie about your identity. Sleep around. Hurrah for me. To hell with anybody else."

His expression grew dark, and a dangerous look passed through his eyes. "I respect women. I like women. I saw the pain my mother suffered after my father's death, and it showed me how love can cut out someone's heart. I made a vow to myself back then. I never intend to do that to anyone."

Tears rushed to her eyes. What about her? Didn't she count?

Her throat clogged with the effort not to cry. Frantically trying to shore up her composure, she raised her chin and sucked in a lungful of air. She was attracted to him and even cared about him, but her heart wasn't really involved. She hadn't done anything stupid like fall in love.

The muscle worked in his jaw again. "Damn it, Josie, think whatever else you want of me, but please don't ever think I'm like Victor. That's the worse insult anyone could ever throw my way."

Her own fears that she might be like Victor surfaced and some of her animosity leaked away. "If you dislike him so much, why do you work with him? Why not get as far away as you can?"

"I did, for years, but things finally got so bad I couldn't keep my head buried in the sand. I'm here because of what he's doing to my mother, because I'm trying my damnedest to convince her to divorce him, and because she and I are the majority stockholders in Emmeline's. Victor's up to something that's adversely affecting the company. If it's the last thing I ever do, I'm going to find out what and stop him."

She blinked. "Up to something? What has he done?"

He hesitated, stared for a long, silent moment, then he crossed his arms over his chest and gave her a skeptical frown. "Why is my name so important? And why are you so interested in Victor?"

"Ah, I … I work for Emmeline's too."

Something between them shifted. His eyes overflowed with doubt. "That's a lie and you know it. Since I'm spilling my guts here, try this on for size. Victor thinks *you're* up to something. Care to tell me what that could be?"

Faith cringed. In her shock, pain, and righteous anger, she'd forgotten she was lying about her identity too.

Fear rippled down her spine. What did Victor suspect? She spun away from Kent and stalked to the far side of the room. How much, if anything, should she reveal to him? Was he an ally or an enemy?

She stalled. "When did he tell you that?"

"When he asked me to get to know you and find out if you were a corporate spy."

Her mouth dropped open. She turned, needing to see his face. His eyes were doubting and wary. Once they'd been dark, sexy, and teasing.

Humiliation made her throat go dry and her words erupted in a croak. "You mean you asked me out because of him?"

His expression was stoic. "Originally."

Sadness crept into her bones. Nothing about him had been real. "And that was the real reason for neglecting to tell me your name."

He watched her keenly. Nodded.

"Did he tell you to sleep with me too?" Her chest ached with a desperate need to dissolve into tears. He'd used her, and she'd been too naïve to recognize his smooth talk as the come-on of a playboy. "Did you give him a full report? Did you both have a good laugh?"

"My reasons for seeing you changed long before we slept together. I told Victor I didn't think you were a corporate spy. That's the only subject we discussed."

It was all she could do to keep from bolting for the bathroom and barricading the door. She'd been a fool in so many ways. Using him had been part of her plan, but she'd never suspected he might be playing the same game.

Her world deflated. Kent was only the visible symbol of her naïveté. All her efforts to be covert were laughable. If Victor suspected her of subterfuge, she'd never accomplish what she'd come here to do. She might as well pack up Josie's clothes and go home.

"You didn't answer my question," he said. "Are you up to something?"

Under his calmly spoken words, she sensed bubbling anger. Unable to gauge how long she could equivocate without causing a blowup, she wrapped her arms around her midsection and felt her way carefully. "What if I am, but it's something unrelated to Emmeline's? Something personal between me and Victor."

Hurt flickered in his eyes before he quickly masked his emotions and gave her a stiff smile. "I didn't think you were his type."

Her chest tightened. She caught her bottom lip between her teeth. Everything was getting twisted and out-of-hand. She didn't want him to think she was attracted to Victor, and he didn't seem like a bad person. Maybe she should stop assuming the worst about him and cut him some slack. She'd misled him too, pretended to be Josie for good reason, but now, if Victor suspected her, continuing to lie to Kent might serve no purpose.

Could she tell him the truth, believe he was no friend of Victor's, and trust him to keep her secret? She'd be taking a big risk. He'd deceived her and fooled her before. Not completely happy with her options, she fought down the urge to bare her soul. She'd compromise.

"Victor's right, I am up to something, but it's not what either of you think. I'm here to get Victor to admit he has a daughter."

He frowned. "You?"

"Faith."

"Your cousin?"

She nodded, ashamed that lying was becoming easier all the time. "She believes Victor is her biological father, and I came here to either find proof or, better still, get him to admit it."

"Why didn't she come herself?"

"It's a long story, but it boils down to... she needs a kidney transplant." As soon as she said the words she wanted to snatch them back. How cliché. Idiotic.

He snorted. "Victor's not the kind of person who'd donate a kidney to anyone."

"She doesn't want his organs. She wants to prove paternity and convince him to help pay her medical expenses. She has no insurance. The bills for doctors and dialysis are piling up."

"So why not just walk up to Victor and say 'you're my father, pay up'? If you want to do it for her, I'll go with you. It should be interesting to watch the big bug squirm."

"No. We can't get confrontational until I have more ammunition. I have to go slow, get a sample of his DNA, have it tested and compared to hers."

He reached out and took her hand. "Next time I go by the house to visit my mother, I could slip up to his bedroom and see if there's hair in his brush."

She winced inside at all her lies. But the lies were necessary, and maybe the situation wasn't as bleak as it first seemed. "Thank you. It's been a bit of an ordeal tracking him down and looking into his background. I've been playing it by ear so far. I hadn't really thought about how to get his DNA."

"I've never known much of his history. I'd be interested in hearing what you've turned up about his background."

Relief at being able to share something truthful hastened her reply. "He grew up in Williamsburg. Was always a bit of a troublemaker. He left for New York City about a year after graduating from high school. I probably wouldn't have found him as quickly if not for an older brother who still lives in town." She slipped into her new role as supposed defender of her cousin. "Victor impregnated my aunt while she was in high school. He left town before the baby was born."

"Why didn't your aunt ask for child support back then?"

Faith lifted a shoulder and let it drop. "Going to court would have meant revealing she'd had his child. I don't think he knew. And I guess she never wanted anything to do with him."

"That's understandable. If I had a choice, I'd probably try to forget he existed too." He pushed his suit jacket open and hooked his thumbs on his belt. "Have you discovered anything suspicious about him? Anything that might explain why he gives me the feeling he's up to something sleazy and no good?"

Rape is sleazy and no good. She shook off an impulse to tell him about the events in the diary. *Go somewhere else. Anywhere else.*

The conversation between Victor and his mistress popped into her mind. "I overheard something puzzling, something about buying and returning jewelry then buying the same piece back a couple days later. He said to do it 'like always.'"

"Why?"

"I have no clue."

Kent frowned. "Who was he talking to?"

"I'd rather not say."

"When was this?"

"About ten days ago."

"Where?"

"Somewhere I shouldn't have been."

A million more questions showed on his face.

She felt her cheeks heating and resisted the urge to turn away.

Concern flickered in his gaze. "Maybe there's something going on I should know about, especially if this is going on in our stores. I'll dig around in accounting and see if an inquiry into returns leads anywhere."

Her blood still surged in her veins, but she started to think more clearly. She caught a glimpse of the future and fought down a sudden urge to cry. Kent was Victor's stepson. He had a reputation as a playboy, and she'd be foolish to sleep with him again. Now that she knew his true identity, she had to step back from their relationship, restore a safe distance between them, and more vigorously protect her heart.

Sadness tightened a painful knot in her chest as she tried to console herself with logic. Their relationship had been based on deception. She'd always known it was temporary. The end had simply come in an unexpected manner. She had to accept reality and focus only on her original goal.

Kent's dislike for his stepfather could work to her advantage, and maybe she could trust him not to expose her as a fraud. Maybe he'd even be able to help her prove something against Victor.

She pulled in a fortifying breath. "Promise me you won't tell Victor anything about my cousin until I'm ready? You'll let me keep working and won't give me away."

He took her hand and gently squeezed her fingers. "Don't worry, your secret is safe with me."

He leaned closer. She saw a kiss forming in his eyes.

Every fiber of her being wanted to lean into him and melt into his arms, recapture the magic of their moments on the boat. But she knew what she had to do, and a heavy shroud of melancholy fell over her shoulders.

She dropped her chin to her chest and sighed. "Thank you. Now if you don't mind, I'm really exhausted. I think we should say good-night."

Chapter Fifteen

Jack came into Kent's office shortly after lunchtime on Monday. "I've gone over every detail three times and still haven't found any reason for the snag in the Gardener deal," he said.

Kent sighed. "Well, Josie's not a corporate spy, and neither of us have found anything out of the ordinary in our debriefing notes. I guess we'll have to chalk it up to a run of bad luck and make sure we're better prepared for surprises next time."

"What did Gardener say when you asked him?"

"He claims he simply had a change of heart, and I believe him." Kent leaned back in his chair. "Table the analysis of that deal for now. What else is on today's agenda?"

Jack plopped a folder onto Kent's desk. "Caldwell in accounting found some interesting return-related data."

Curiosity piqued, Kent sat up straighter, flipped open the folder, and scanned the top page. "Like what?"

"Several of our stores, including this one, have an unusually high merchandise return rate. The spreadsheet is on page three."

A flicker of excitement quickened his pulse. This might be the information he needed to prove Victor was mismanaging Emmeline's. He turned to the appropriate page and focused on the *Percent of Gross Sales* column. "These percentages are high for the retail industry in general and way above what we should strive for as a company."

"Exactly. Everything Emmeline's sells is high-end, quality merchandise. Our return rate should be lower than the industry average, not higher."

Kent read down the *Store Location* column.

New York City, Boston, Chicago, Dallas, Fairfield, LA, Miami, Philadelphia, here in West Palm. Discomfort gnawing at his gut, he pondered the list and tried to figure out why these particular locations jingled little bells in his head. None were stores he'd acquired. In fact, most were opened way before his time.

He saw the pattern and lowered the page. "Most of these are older stores. At least half are part of the original chain from when my Dad was alive. None of them have been opened more recently than the last eight or nine years."

Jack leaned over the desk, was silent for a few seconds, then nodded. "You're right. I didn't notice that."

Jack's cell phone emitted a cavalry charge ring tone.

"That must be Carrie," he said, scrambling to pull the phone from its holder. "She took Christian to the pediatrician for his check-up this morning."

Kent gave him an understanding smile. "Go ahead, take it."

He tapped his cell and answered. "Hi sweetheart. How did everything go?"

His face glowed as he listened. "Hang on," he said, then turned to Kent. "Christian rolled over one way."

Deciding the feat must be good news, Kent gave him a thumbs up.

Pride bright on his face, Jack went back to his conversation. After a few seconds, he nodded. "Great, then I'll see you later." He lowered his voice a notch. "I love you too. Give Christian a hug for me."

Kent felt a pang of envy for his friend's happiness, but he stiffened his spine and ruthlessly pushed it away. He did his best to convince himself the solitary life of a bachelor was the only life for him. Thinking about any relationship longer than a one-month affair was nothing but foolish masochism.

He envisioned Josie last night in her apartment. She hadn't elaborated on her plans for after she cornered Victor and made him pay her cousin's medical bills, but her intentions seemed fairly obvious. Once she succeeded she'd leave, and anything between them would be over. He'd be back where he started, whether he wanted anything more or not. So why kid himself about other possibilities?

He needed to stay loose and go with the flow. Help her out, enjoy her company, and wave fondly when another episode in his long string of episodes was over. She might be special and hard to forget, but they were destined to part, sooner rather than later.

Shuffling the papers on his desk and trying to focus on the numbers, he told himself he wasn't going to dwell on her inevitable departure.

Jack disconnected and put his phone away. A silly grin

lingered on his face. "The little guy put on two and a half pounds and grew an inch and a quarter. Doctor says he's in the ninety-fifth percentile and healthy as a horse."

Kent pretended to understand the statistics and nodded. "Good. Glad to hear it."

Unaccustomed to discussing the foreign world of babies and wanting to shake the strange longing nibbling at his gut, he cleared his throat and dragged his attention back to business and the report.

He studied the last column on the spreadsheet and tapped his fingers on his desktop. "Some of these locations are only borderline profitable despite high-volume sales. The unusually high return rate would explain a lot about their bottom line."

"They stock the same quality of merchandise as every other store. I wonder why so much of it comes back."

Suspicion settled in his midsection. "That makes two of us. Let's look closer at this situation and see if we can find out. Have Caldwell do some more digging. Tell him to go back as far as he can and get us all the details."

• • •

The restaurant where Kent had made dinner reservations was so quiet Faith could hear the bartender in his waistcoat measuring out rose water and grapefruit bitters behind the early 1930s era bar. The hushed atmosphere did little to calm her nerves. If anything, it made her more aware of the tension that hung between her and Kent.

She chewed the inside of her cheek and wished they'd gone somewhere with lively music or playful entertainment where she could forget Victor, her mother's rape, and the mountain of lies and deception she was building. What she really wanted to do tonight was to savor the sound of Kent's laughter, listen to his warm voice, hold his hand, and simply enjoy his company.

She shifted in her high-backed leather seat and whispered to him, "Did they call them speakeasies because it was taboo to talk loud?"

"Maybe it was because the word outside the doors was *mum*."

"If they don't advertise and the number is unlisted, how did you know to come in through that phone booth?"

"A friend's friend told my friend."

She smiled. "I feel like we stepped into a time machine."

"Wait until you taste the raspberry crumble dessert. Your taste buds will think you're in heaven."

She looked at him over the rim of her glass and remembered the night on his friend's boat. By comparison, raspberry crumble didn't stand a chance. That night and this man would forevermore be her standard for reaching heaven.

She dropped her gaze. Thoughts like that would only lead her into quicksand. She had to keep one foot on solid ground and maintain a safe distance between them. She was playing a role and, if she weren't posing as Josie, he would have no interest in her at all. Kent Telemann was rich and lived in a world she could only imagine. He was too suave and sexy to want drab Faith Rochambeau by his side.

A little voice inside murmured there might be hope, she wasn't really her old self anymore. Since coming here, she'd done dozens of things that were not quite Josie but unlike Faith. She was changing, becoming something or someone new.

For a few seconds excitement buoyed her mood, then a louder voice drowned out the whispers of optimism and extinguished her spark of brightness. Being somewhere in the middle between drab Faith and flamboyant Josie wasn't good enough. Kent was still a fantasy.

A few grains of nutmeg floated on his creamed bourbon and clung to his lips when he drank. He ran his tongue along his upper lip. The muscles tightened low in her belly. She ruthlessly pushed away the sensation.

Enough. She had to stop melting every time she looked at him. She had to be practical and use him to do what she'd set out to do, get information about Victor. Then she had to forget her silly emotions and walk away.

Images from her latest Google searches ran through her mind. Kent out on the town with a former Miss Universe. Kent hugging a starlet. Kent with a gorgeous society girl to whom he'd been engaged. Not one picture of Kent with a mousy computer geek whose father was a rapist.

His mellow voice broke her reverie. "Ready for that dessert?"

"No thank you. I overdid the rotisserie duck. It was delicious, but filling. I couldn't eat another bite."

He dabbed his napkin at his lips and cleared his throat. "Josie…"

Faith. I'm Faith.

"…let's talk about the elephant in the middle of the room."

She sighed. "You mean Victor."

"I need to know exactly what you overheard about store returns and anything else you've uncovered that might be related."

"I told you everything."

She shifted, re-crossing her legs with a whisper of black nylon. This was the reason they were together. They each wanted information from the other. They were playing a ghastly game. But there's another game, her mind rushed to add. There's the strange mutual physical attraction and the explosive sex. *The mating game where he's the champion and I'm the novice. The dangerous game I need to stop playing because I'm destined to lose.*

"Who was Victor talking to and where did this conversation take place?" he asked.

Guilt nagged at her. She hesitated, toyed with her bracelet, and finally mumbled, "I really can't tell you where, but I'm sure that has no relevance anyway. The conversation was between Victor and his mistress."

He studied her for a minute, head cocked. "That explains how jewelry came into the equation. A gift for her?"

"Yes."

"He gave her a piece of jewelry, but she was supposed to return it?"

"No. He gave her the money to buy it, then return it. Then he would buy it for her again a few days later."

His face scrunched into a puzzled frown. "I wish I could figure out exactly what he's up to."

Hope fluttered in her chest. "Do you think he's doing something illegal?"

"Hard to say. Giving gifts to your mistress isn't a crime, at least not in the eyes of the law."

"You lived with him for years. Couldn't you tell if he was doing something illegal? Wouldn't he act guilty?"

"Drinking in a speakeasy like this was a crime in the days of prohibition, but no one cared." He leaned back in his chair and steepled his fingers. "The patrons didn't get tied in knots by guilt. In fact, they liked the feeling of risk. That's probably why this kind of place is so popular today. The vicarious thrill of subterfuge. Victor might enjoy that feeling too. He wouldn't feel or act guilty if he doesn't see what he's doing as wrong."

Looking around the dimly lit room, she said, "This place does give you the feeling you're breaking the law."

She swallowed and considered how that thrill of subterfuge had rippled through her veins when Kent whispered the password and they'd been allowed through the entryway-disguised-as-phone-booth. Was the excitement of breaking the law something passed down in her genes?

No, breaking into Victor's office had been terrifying. Nauseating. Anything but a source of kicks.

Shaking herself mentally, she said, "Maybe he's trying to cover his tracks to keep your mother from finding out he cheats."

Kent snorted in disgust. "He leaves a trail any idiot could follow. My mother's friends don't mention his cheating to her, but the whole world knows. And she probably does too."

"Why doesn't she divorce him?"

"My mom's a true southern lady in every sense of the word. Her outfit and hairdo are always perfect. Her upper lip is always stiff. She'd rather deny Victor's philandering forever than sit in divorce court and face the embarrassment of having her private life exposed and ripped to shreds."

"The prison of pride."

Kent nodded. "And resignation. I think she knows she

made a terrible mistake marrying Victor."

"How so?"

He got a faraway look in his eye. "My father was the love of her life, and vice versa. He named the business after her, treated her like a queen. I was only a kid when he died, but I can still remember how her face lit up whenever he walked into a room."

Love and pain merged on his face as he continued. "Their marriage was a fairy tale. Then Dad had a fatal heart attack. Mom never recovered. She became an empty shell for a couple years. She closed her heart to everyone and everything, even sent me off to boarding school claiming her company was depressing and bad for my mental health."

She could tell he was remembering painful days by the way he stared toward the middle of the room, eyes glazed, lips a thin, sad line. It struck her that he was hiding a vulnerable heart behind his playboy exterior, that deep inside he was empty and aching for a special connection like the one his mother had shared with his father.

An echoing ache spread in her chest. She prayed that someday the void in his life would be filled.

He pulled in a deep breath, and his expression hardened. "To make a short story shorter, Victor came along. He discovered her need for a shoulder to lean on in running the business and took advantage of her grief. Before she woke up to who he really was, she'd been rushed into a miserable marriage with someone crude and mean."

"How old were you when all this happened?"

"I was nine when she married him. I was summoned back from boarding school to attend the ceremony and then informed my new stepfather was adopting me. I've never forgiven her for letting him take away my father's last name."

She heard the raw emotion in his voice and let the words hang for a few seconds. "It seems strange that he would adopt you."

"Not when you consider the way Emmeline's stock is divided and the provisions of my father's will. My mother and I each own substantial blocks, but her share has to pass to me. If something happened to her while I was a minor, and I wasn't legally under his thumb, Victor could have lost control of the business."

"How does he have control now that you're an adult?"

He downed the last of his drink and a flicker of something like disgust passed through his eyes. "For a few years after my twenty-first birthday and college, I stayed as far away from here, and Victor, as I could. London, Malibu, New York, Rio. I'd spend a few months here, a few months there, partying and basically wasting my life. I ignored Emmeline's and let Victor vote my shares by proxy."

"But you came back, you're here now."

"I finally woke up. I stopped home to visit my mother at Christmas three years ago. Victor couldn't wait to get rid of me. He was so over-anxious for me to leave, that I decided to stay and find out why he didn't want me around." Pure satisfaction lit his face and curved his lips. "I thought he'd have a stroke when I told him I was taking back my proxy and planned to get involved in running the business."

"But isn't he still in control anyway?"

"We've reached a sort of Mexican standoff. My mother has a fifty-one percent voting share. He's bullied her into letting him act on her behalf."

"Couldn't she demote him if she wanted to?"

"Legally, yes." His hand fisted on the edge of the table. "I've often wondered what would happen if she did. I hate to think about it, but I believe he'd arrange an accident for her and then go to court and try to use community property laws to fight me for her estate. I wouldn't be surprised if she believed that too. Sometimes I get the impression she's extremely afraid of him."

Her heart jumped in alarm. "You think he's capable of murder?"

"There's not an iota of doubt in my mind. I've seen him kill."

"My God, who?"

"Not a person, but a friend of mine. When I was twelve, he owned a racehorse named Chocolate Fever. She was a sweet three-year-old, with huge eyes and an insatiable love of apples." He paused and pushed his fingers through his hair. "I loved those trips to the stables with Victor."

She pictured a man and a child walking toward a barn. Only the child wasn't Kent but a blonde-haired girl. Pricked by a sudden jab of jealousy, she blurted, "You mean he was a good father, took you places, cared about you, acted like a dad?"

"Hell no," he said with a scowl that morphed to a sneer. "He put on an act, pretended to be a family man to score points with business associates. I let him use me because I wanted to see Fever and, once in a while, her trainer would let me ride."

Shocked that jealousy lurked in her heart, confused by the discovery of the illogical emotion, and mortified that she'd interrupted his story to ask such a ridiculous question, she pressed her lips together and waited for the rest.

He took a deep breath through his nose and his chest rose slowly. Then anger flared in his eyes. "It was the day after a race with a big purse. Fever didn't even place. Victor was furious. He stomped to her stall and let go a torrent of curses. Then he pulled out a pistol, grabbed her nose in his left hand, and shot her between the eyes."

She gasped and searched his face, hoping she'd heard him wrong. "In front of you?"

His pained expression and slight nod confirmed what she'd heard and brought hot tears flooding into her eyes. She swallowed and blinked them away, reached out and gently touched his arm. "And you were devastated."

"Fever suffered and took a long time to die. I was twelve. To me she was more than an investment or a possession, she was a friend and a pet. It was the second time in my life that I lost someone I loved and cried."

Her throat clogged with the effort not to dissolve into tears. She recognized how difficult it was for him to let down his defenses and reveal the sensitive man who lived behind the stoic mask. Her voice shook. "You were a normal, feeling human being. Caring is nothing to be ashamed of."

His eyes darkened, and his mouth became a thin, tight line. "Up until that day, I'd always disliked Victor. When he pulled the trigger on that gun, when the barn filled with the horrible stench of Fever's blood and fear, when she collapsed with a gut-wrenching squeal, at that moment, Victor taught me to hate."

She closed her eyes and bit on her bottom lip, trying to block the grisly image forming in her mind's eye. She wished someone had put Victor in jail years ago and prevented his act of cruelty.

"I'm sorry," Kent said, huffing out a sigh. He took her hand and rubbed his thumb lightly across her knuckles. "I don't know why I told you all the gory details. Fever's murder isn't polite dinner conversation."

She opened her eyes and met his gaze. He'd shared a painful event with her and given her a glimpse inside his soul. Her heart squeezed, and she felt his pain. "I don't care about the timing. I'm just sorry a twelve-year-old boy ever had to go through something so terrible."

"I'm sorry my mother ever met Victor."

A shiver rippled up her arms. To a man who'd committed a violent rape and shot an innocent horse, harming his wife probably wasn't out of the question.

"I wish there was something we could do to help her."

He gave a tired sigh. "That's a big part of why I'm keeping my eyes open for anything suspicious. I intend to get rid of him. Plus, if I think she's in any kind of danger, I want to be close by and ready to come to her defense."

Faith pictured Victor handcuffed and being led off to jail to serve a sentence for rape. So far, she hadn't met anyone who would miss him.

She considered Kent's mother and his concern for her safety. What would he think if he knew she was in another type of jeopardy? If Victor went on trial for rape, his wife's world would probably be shattered. Every ounce of her pride would be crushed beneath the heels of tabloid reporters. Her husband's history would be public knowledge, her privacy non-existent. She'd be dragged into his quicksand, sucked into the mire, and pay an unfair price for his crime.

Kent downed the rest of his drink, wiped his lips, and then tossed his napkin on the table. "Nothing would make me happier than to have Victor gone from her life."

Faith's chest grew heavy as she thought of the other implications of her quest for justice. Kent's business could be ruined too. She recalled being parked in front of Emmeline's, staring at the building and wondering what Victor Telemann's exclusive clientele would think if they knew he was a rapist. Hatred flowing in her veins, she'd wondered if they would shun his stores and cause him to go bankrupt. Back then she'd wanted to stand in the middle of the street screaming the truth to the world.

She gazed at Kent and the images of her triumph over Victor didn't seem as sweet. Emmeline's was Kent's business. He'd suffer financially, and she was the person who threatened to destroy his legacy. He'd sat here and given her a glimpse into his private world, trusted her to know the deep emotions he'd felt as a child. In return, she would hit him with betrayal.

Could she continue her crusade to bring Victor to justice, knowing she'd hurt Kent, and his mother, and the friends she'd made at Emmeline's? Guilt grabbed her by the throat and squeezed mercilessly. Justice for Victor's victims and potential victims was important, but so were the lives of the people around him. Good people who didn't deserve the pain.

She wished there were another way. Some way she could get Victor's confession and see him sent to jail with a minimum of collateral damage. The duck sat heavy and sour in her stomach. Another way wasn't to be.

Her heart thudded. She couldn't give up. And when the truth about Victor came out, Kent would hate her for the damage she would do to his mother and his company. Would he one day forgive her for what she had to do?

Cold, lonely emptiness seeped into her soul. No hope existed. The fragile bond they'd formed would be broken. Their relationship was doomed.

Chapter Sixteen

Monday at ten, Victor's intercom buzzed and he answered.

Peg said, "You have a call from a Ms. St. James. She's a reporter with a local paper. Shall I put her through?"

"Go ahead." He held the line.

"Good morning, Mr. Telemann. I'm Leeza St. James, Palm Beach Examiner. I'm working on an article on the reasons why some of our well-qualified citizens decline to run for elected office. I understand you've been asked to run for the state senate and declined. Would it be possible to schedule an interview and discuss your feelings on the subject?"

He only needed one second to decide he didn't want to talk to a nosy reporter. "Sorry. I'm very busy at this time of year. Perhaps in a few months."

"I only have a few questions. Can you spare fifteen minutes?"

"I'm sorry. No."

He hung up, and the intercom buzzed again almost

immediately.

"There's a Quick Fox messenger here with a delivery," Peg said.

"Send him in."

Victor puffed on his Havana while he waited for Peg to shut the door behind Brody and leave them alone. When she was gone, he asked, "What's this? You back to running the route yourself?"

"The messenger business is booming. I'm making legit money hand over fist. When I have customers backed up, I send out everybody I can on deliveries. That leaves me short on people I can trust with a hand-off."

"Just remember where the big money comes from and keep your priorities straight."

Brody grinned. "No need to remind me. I'm here."

"How much have you got?"

Brody stretched out a tattooed forearm and handed the black satchel across the desk. "Thirty."

Victor set his cigar in the ashtray and accepted the delivery. He weighed the satchel in his hand, considering the need for a count. He pictured a filthy, crack-snorting addict making a buy and cringed at the idea of touching the wrinkled bills. His gaze wandered to the handle on his bottom drawer. Every time he slipped on a pair of the latex gloves, the creepy-feeling powder lining the insides got all over his skin.

Too much effort. Brody and he went way back. They'd had each other's backs in a lot of dicey situations. Another messenger might try to skim some off the top, but Brody wouldn't cheat him, couldn't without cheating himself.

He stood, walked across the office to the left side of the

minibar, opened the fake cabinet door, exposed the safe's combination lock, and spun the dial to forty-four then twenty-four then thirty-six. An image of Melinda's nude body ran through his brain, and his fingers inched to squeeze the firm forty-fours.

Pulling his mind back to business, he swung open the safe door. He unzipped the satchel, shook it upside down until three bundles of bills fell out and landed in a heap.

His gaze went to the partition dividing the safe in half. No one knew about his emergency running kit, not even Brody. The secret compartment in the safe held two separate IDs with matching passports and credit cards, plenty of cash in green backs and half that amount in EUROs. Plus a clean weapon. If he got a whiff of trouble, he could walk out of his office, follow the precise plan he'd worked out to the tiniest detail, and disappear in the blink of an eye.

As he slammed the door shut and rotated the lock, he grinned to himself. As a kid competing with his older brothers to make a few bucks on the street, he'd dreamed of his own safe full of money, secure from his brothers' stealing hands. For years, they'd been able to find his stash and take it for themselves. When he got older and smarter, they'd beat on him until he gave it up. Now, every time he locked away his loot, he remembered the vow he'd made at thirteen to someday be bigger, and better, and richer than all of those thieving bastards combined and enjoyed knowing he could buy and sell them several times over with just the amount in his safe.

"The street's dead quiet," Brody said. "I got nothin' on who might be snooping around."

Victor shrugged and handed back the empty satchel.

"I've got it covered. It's a new employee here using the name of Josie Ashland. No doubt about it. She's a cop."

"How come you didn't let me know so I could take care of her?"

Victor waved his hand to sweep away the suggestion. "I've got everything under control. If she disappears, the cops will get upset and step up their efforts. If we play her along and make sure she finds out squat, we can beat them at their own game."

"I'd rather grab her, persuade her to tell us how much they know."

"And then what? Every other cop in the city would be on our doorstep. Stop thinking like the same dumb thug you were twenty years ago. We've covered our asses well, and we can shut down at a minute's notice," he said in a tone meant to brook no disagreement. "Relax."

"My skin is at risk here, too. How sure are you she's contained?"

Victor sat, leaned back in his chair, steepled his fingers, and gave Brody a stern look. "One-hundred percent." The lie rolled easily off his tongue, but he was starting to have doubts. She was a loose end, and he was uncomfortable when things weren't tied up neatly. What if he was wrong about her being the mole? He remembered the lesson he'd learned from his father's arrest—never get smug and think you're safe. "But just as extra insurance, I'm going to let you do something you should enjoy."

"Say the word and she's history."

He shook his head. "No, I want her alive. Here's what I want done."

When Victor finished with his instructions, Brody

touched two fingers to his cap in a mock salute. "Quick Fox guarantees fast service. We'll get right on it."

. . .

Faith slipped out at lunchtime and took a cab to the building that housed Zurich Investigations. As she leaned forward to hand her fare to the driver, she noticed Steve walking out of a restaurant across the street.

She did a double take. His arm was around a woman's waist.

Her breath caught. *Melinda Hart?*

She blinked, finished paying the driver, and slipped out of the cab on the passenger side. She ducked onto the sidewalk behind a parked car and stared at the couple not a dozen yards away. Melinda was just as beautiful as on the posters at the theater. Her mane of blonde hair shown like spun gold in the sunlight.

His arm still possessively around her, Steve walked Melinda to a bumblebee-yellow Corvette convertible with a black top. They stopped and turned to face one another, embraced, and kissed. It was a kiss overflowing with promise of more, one that shouted we-know-each-other-very-well.

Faith gulped and her mind filled with questions. What was Steve doing with Victor's mistress? Where exactly did his loyalties lie? Her feet were stuck in place. Her eyes remained riveted on Melinda until after she got into the Corvette, pulled it from the parking spot, and the car roared off down the street.

"Hey, Josie. How's it going?"

She jerked her gaze to Steve as he strolled across the street and stepped up onto the curb with his hand outstretched.

Studying his face for a clue to what she'd just witnessed, she shook his hand half-heartedly. "I'm not sure. That was Melinda Hart you were with."

"Yeah, Melly and I are old friends. We go way back to the old neighborhood. We were both born about six blocks from where you're standing."

"You kissed her."

He grinned, and his chest puffed out with masculine pride. His tone was suggestive and boasting. "We're old, very close friends."

"But she's Victor's mistress."

"Yeah." He nodded. "And therefore, she's an excellent source of information about him. I haven't seen her in a couple years, but I thought I'd buy her brunch, rehash old times, and see what she could tell me."

Faith eyed him suspiciously. His local roots had been her main reason for hiring him. So it shouldn't be a surprise he knew people, especially another Palm Beach native. Maybe it was perfectly logical for him to interview Melinda Hart as part of his investigation, but she totally didn't like the development. "So she's the new lead you told me about?"

Steve nodded, then inclined his head toward the building entryway. "I've got your bug upstairs."

She fell in step with him, he swung the door open for her to enter, and they went into the lobby. As they waited for the elevator, she said, "So did she tell you anything useful?"

"Not much. He's a pig and a prick." The elevator arrived, they stepped aboard and the doors slid shut. "He treats her like dirt and has a jealous streak a mile wide."

Faith wondered, if that was true, then why would

Melinda agree to meet Steve and kiss him so lustfully on the street in plain site? But she asked, "Why doesn't she break up with him?"

The elevator stopped on the third floor, and they stepped off.

"That's easy," Steve said. "Money. He's loaded, and she likes nice things."

Faith's mind jumped back to Victor's office. *Things like diamond bracelets.*

He unlocked his office door and ushered her inside.

She silently questioned how a woman could trade pride and respect for money. The answer, a twisted sense of morality and overwhelming greed, caused an alarm to jangle in her head. "Do you think she'll go back and tell Victor you were asking questions in order to stay in his good graces? I don't want him to know we're investigating him."

"Not to worry," Steve said with a chuckle. "I told you. Melly and I are friends. She won't rat us out. She taught me how to kiss in kindergarten. I refined her technique in sixth grade. Back in high school, we taught each other a bunch of other things and almost got married."

"Married? Really? Why didn't you?"

"She got an audition to dance in a chorus line. Dancing center stage was always her big dream, so she chose to shoot for fame and fortune. She wasn't ready to settle down and have babies. She wanted excitement, know what I mean?"

Faith nodded.

He shrugged. "She's making her way the best she knows how. If screwing Victor gets her what she wants, then who am I to stop her?"

A strange look that could have been jealousy, regret, or

smug satisfaction flickered in his eyes, but it was gone before Faith could decide which. The slump of his shoulders, however, spoke volumes. "Something tells me you'd like to have a say in the company she keeps. Your body language screams you're in love with her."

He motioned for her to sit and made a lame attempt to feign nonchalance. "Ever since I was ten."

She was tempted to probe deeper into their relationship, but Steve walked to his desk and slid open the top drawer. "You ever worn one of these things before?"

The device in his hand was as foreign to Faith as an ocean to a camel. She shook her head.

"The best place to put it is inside your bra between your breasts." He put his finger on a small, side-mounted switch. "You activate it with this, down is On. It will only record for about twenty-five minutes, so wait until the last minute to start it."

"It's bigger than I expected." She took the inch and a half square, half-inch thick box from his hand, stared at the switch, then turned it over and checked out the back.

Steve flopped into his chair and the pivot mechanism groaned.

"Sony makes the most reliable recorders out there. And the easiest to use. I figured since you're an amateur, I didn't want to get anything too sophisticated or complex. No sense in taking a chance on lapel mics or wires. This will be a snap to conceal, and you won't have to worry about messing up any sensitivity settings."

"How much do I owe you for it?"

"Fifty."

Thinking the price sounded padded, but resigned to

paying regardless, she stuffed the recorder in her purse and pulled out her checkbook. "Why don't I pay for everything you've done up until now, including the bill for your friend in New Jersey, and then we call off the investigation? Other than reuniting you and Miss Hart, it's not accomplishing anything."

· · ·

The work day ended, and Faith stopped at a nearby market on her way home. She juggled her grocery bags in her left hand and, with her right, dug her apartment keys from her purse. She smiled in anticipation of a quiet dinner with Kent as she slid the key into her door lock. Before she even turned the key, the door moved a few inches and cracked open.

Her chest tightened. Had she forgotten to lock it? Her brain raced back to that morning. She'd been in a hurry to leave for work, but she always kept the lock set to engage behind her. Had she been thinking about Kent and been distracted? She gave a short, nervous laugh. Damn it, she was letting the man turn her brain to mush.

She leaned slightly and stared through the open crack. Darkness, but that was expected. She'd left the balcony drapes drawn to block out the hot rays of the afternoon sun. Her lamp was on a timer and should be lit, but the bulb could have burned out. Feeling foolish, she told herself she was worrying needlessly. Forgetfulness and coincidence was the only logical explanation.

Her pulse kicked into a higher gear despite her self-assurances. For years, her mother had poured warnings and cautions into her head. The voice of common sense told her to move slow and take some of them to heart, be smart and minimize the risk.

She reached one hand inside the doorway and felt for the light switch. Sucking in her breath, she flicked it up and quickly pushed the door open wide.

The sight struck her like a punch below the belt.

She gasped, dropped her grocery bags, stood stone still. Stared. A can of soup rolled toward a toppled chair and hit the wooden leg with a clunk. Her stomach somersaulted, and her brain whirred numbly.

Her eyes darted over the chaos and destruction. Her few pieces of furniture were upset or broken. Books lay open on the floor. Josie's clothes had been ripped from the drawers and closets and scattered like discarded rags.

Who could have done this? Was the culprit still here?

She stole a glance to the right, then left. The elevator doors were closed and the cab was gone. The hallway was empty. Her too-rapid breathing echoed off the stark walls. She debated whether to step inside or run for help.

Eyes scanning for any movement in the apartment, she dug out her cell phone to call the police and hit *nine, one*. She jerked her finger back before hitting the other *one*.

No. She couldn't report a burglary. They'd ask her name, ask questions she didn't want to answer. Filing a false police report could drag her into big trouble. But what if the intruder was still here?

Caught in a whirlpool of indecision, she debated leaving, waiting an hour, and returning later, giving the intruder time to flee. Would that do any good? She wondered how long ago the apartment had been trashed.

No sound came from inside. She told herself that, most

likely, the culprit had come and gone much earlier in the day. He'd left once he'd discovered she had nothing of value to steal.

She corralled the fears, speculations, and questions running wild in her mind and made the decision to go in. Just in case, she clutched the phone tightly in her hand, finger hovering over the square that would send the final *one*. Her breath rushing in and out hard and fast, she slipped off her high-heeled shoes. They'd only slow her down if she had to run back out the door and dash down the emergency stairs.

Cold sweat soaked her body as she took one step in the doorway and stretched her neck to peer into the U-shaped kitchen. *Please let him be gone.*

Cabinet doors stood open. Pots, dishes, and foodstuffs littered the floor. Nothing moved. No one was there. *Thank you, God.*

Logic said that if anyone was in the apartment they would have to be hiding in the shower stall or closet. There was no place else large enough to hold a person.

The closet doors gaped open. Other than two dresses drooping off their hangers, the space was empty.

That left the bathroom.

Nerves stretched like a tightrope, pulse pounding in her ears, on high alert and ready to bolt at any second, she crept inside. One small step at a time, bare feet silent on the thick carpet, she crossed to the bathroom door. Once she had a clear view inside, she held her breath and studied the frosted shower stall glass for any hint of a silhouette.

Nothing.

A buzzer sounded.

Her heart jumped into her throat. She gasped and her

hand flew to cover her mouth. She spun around, hyperventilating, searching for her attacker.

The buzzer sounded again. Recognition dawned. Someone was calling from the lobby.

She rushed to the far wall, and hit the intercom button to respond. Her words came out between gulps for air. "Kent? Is that you?"

"Yes."

She pressed the door release button and rasped, "Come up, please. Hurry."

Her lower lip started to tremble in a gush of relief. Kent was here. Now she'd be safe, at least physically.

Some of her terror retreated, but her heart still pounded like a bass drum and the queasy feeling in her stomach remained. Her peace of mind was damaged and wouldn't be easily repaired. Her apartment had been ravaged. She'd been violated.

She had a sudden urge to go home. Run, flee, hide. Crawl into the bed she'd slept in as a child, pull the covers over her head, cry. She closed her eyes and struggled to pull herself together.

Don't become a quivering mass of Jell-O. Get a grip. Think. Be logical.

Faith pictured her mother's diary, secure in her safe deposit box, along with most of her cash. She breathed a huge sigh of relief. Nothing she'd had here was irreplaceable. Except her sense of security.

Footfalls pounded out in the hallway. Her eyes popped open. Who?

Kent burst in the door, chest heaving as he sucked in a breath. "What…?" He skidded to a halt. His head swiveled as he scanned the scene. He rushed to her and gathered her into his arms. "Are you okay?"

She clung to him. Tears puddled in her eyes. She nodded rubbing the side of her face along his firm chin.

His hand cradled the back of her head. "What happened?"

"I don't know. I stopped to pick up a couple groceries. When I got here, the door was unlocked and ajar."

"Have you called the police?"

"No. I just got here a minute ago."

He gently kissed her forehead, removed one hand from her back, then reached into his pocket. "I'll call 911. The person responsible may still be in the neighborhood."

"No!" She grabbed for his phone. "Don't call them. It's not necessary."

He shook his head. "Of course it is. You can't ignore something like this. They have to catch the guy."

"But I have no idea who it was. I didn't see anyone."

"Maybe someone else in the building did."

"I didn't have anything of value for anyone to steal. My credit card is in my wallet, along with my ID. My cash is in the bank. Other than the mess, there's probably no harm done."

He frowned. "A crime has been committed. We should report it."

She squeezed his hand, pleaded with her eyes, said a little too heartily, "Let it go, Kent. It's nothing. Calling the police makes no sense. I'll get new locks and be fine."

Faith watched him think for a few seconds, impatience clear on his face. She expected him to protest her decision and insist she dial 911.

Instead concern softened his gaze and he said, "Okay,

if you're sure that's how you want to handle it, but grab whatever you need. You're not staying in this apartment tonight."

"I don't have anywhere else to go."

He walked to the door and examined her locks. "They look operable, like they were picked, not broken. But if someone got in before, they can do it again. I won't have you here alone when that happens."

A chill ran down her spine. Would the culprit return? "Why would they, he, whoever, come back if they know there's nothing here of value?"

He gave her a determined look. "I don't know, but you're not staying to find out."

She glanced around the room. "I have to clean up this mess." Then she pictured someone sneaking toward her while she lay asleep in her bed. Her knees felt rubbery and fear crawled beneath her skin. She hurried toward the door, but stopped when she caught sight of her groceries scattered on the floor. "Wait just one minute. Before I leave, I have to put away the meat and cheese."

He crossed his arms tightly over his chest. There was a core of steel in his voice. "I still think you should call the police. Let them investigate."

Faith gathered the perishable food items and stuffed them into the refrigerator. "Clothes. I'll need a change of clothes."

She plucked a bra and panties from the pile dumped in front of now-empty chest of drawers, then she rushed into the bathroom for her toothbrush. After stepping over a broken lamp to get to the closet, she picked up a mound of Josie's suits that were still on hangers and hung them back on the rod. A red dress was heaped on a half-empty laundry bag. Noticing the laundry bag still held her cleaning woman outfit and wig, she snatched it up and tossed it out of sight in the back corner of the closet. Then she draped the red dress over her arm and walked back to Kent.

Feeling disengaged, like she was moving in a surreal dream, she slipped on her shoes, grabbed her purse, and said, "Okay, I guess I'm ready. Let's go."

Chapter Seventeen

Kent allowed Josie to ride in silence while he drove to his house. Anger at the thugs who'd brought fear into her life sizzled just under his skin. But he clenched his teeth and held it in check. He couldn't vent his fury and act all Neanderthal and ballistic. She needed him to be calm and reassuring. Making her peace of mind his priority, at every stoplight he reached over and squeezed her hand to remind her he was by her side and she was out of danger.

The sun slipped below the horizon and the shadows merged into dusk as he pulled into his driveway. When he opened her door and helped her out of the Mustang, she stopped short next to the car, staring.

"Of course. This was part of the lie," she said, a stricken expression marring her beautiful face. "The palatial house doesn't belong to a college friend."

"No."

He considered coming clean about everything, telling

her the boat was his and the car she'd been riding in belonged to Jack. Reason told him to wait. She'd figure out the boat was his soon enough on her own. If he sparked her anger about his deception again now, she was likely to stomp away from him and head right back to her unsafe apartment or somewhere else where he wouldn't be able to protect her.

"Maybe you should take me to a hotel."

He took her arm, mentally editing his next words as he tugged her gently toward the front door. "This is a better place for you to be tonight. I have the best security system money can buy. And brandy. You need a stiff drink to steady your nerves."

Her body stopped moving as if frozen in place. Her eyes widened, and her face went white. "Does Victor live here?" she said in a tremulous voice.

"No." Kent wanted to protect her from any more unsettling thoughts, and the subject of Victor seemed perpetually unsettling. He lifted her chin, pushed a stray lock of hair off her cheek, and brushed a soft kiss over her lips. "Victor's never been inside this house. And never will be. It's my home, and he's not welcome."

Her breath whooshed out.

He pondered her intense reaction to anything connected with Victor. Hesitation and avoidance he could understand, but the way she'd completely unraveled at the prospect of running into him was bothersome. Kent felt a prickle of suspicion, but quickly fought down his niggling doubt. Maybe he was imagining things. Maybe her emotions were jumbled and raw because she was upset about the break-in.

After unlocking the door and ushering her through the foyer and into the den, he headed for the bar. "Brandy will settle your nerves. When you feel calm enough to eat, I'll call out and order dinner."

She shook her head. "I'll just have ginger ale."

He removed two snifters from the bar rack and selected a carafe of brandy. "Tonight, you need something stronger."

Josie sank into an armchair by the fireplace, dropped her head back, and closed her eyes. "I'm alright now. It was just such a shock to open that door. My mother always warned me about the dangers of living in a big city, but I never expected anything to happen to me, that I'd be the one whose apartment was broken into or robbed." She wrapped her arms across her chest. "I had an extra lock with a steel rod installed when I moved in, but it wasn't engaged. It can only be operated when I'm inside the apartment."

"At least you weren't inside when they broke in," he said while he poured. Images of the destruction in her apartment flashed in his brain and a fresh wave of alarm at what could have happened if she'd been home caused a slight tremor in his hand.

Her voice shook. "Yes, there's that."

He slipped his fingers under the bowls of the snifters, crossed the room, and held one out to her. "Here, try some of this."

She opened her eyes, hesitated, and then took the glass. "I wonder what they wanted."

"Probably looking for money to buy drugs or merchandise they can hock for cash." His suspicions got the better of him. "Unless you had something they were looking for. Did you have anything in particular of value?"

Shock flickered across her face then her expression became unreadable. She took a delicate sip of the brandy, swallowed, and winced. The reaction seemed exaggerated and struck him as a stalling tactic. He let the question hang.

After a few seconds, her chin jerked up. "What could I possibly have that a thief would want?"

He rubbed his jaw, unsettled by his nagging doubts about her truthfulness. Unwilling to let her off the hook, he kept his voice neutral as he sat across from her and voiced a sudden realization. "I don't know much about your private life. You tell me."

Her gaze skittered away. For a moment, she stared at the floor, seemingly lost in thought. She swirled the brandy remaining in the bottom of her snifter. She slowly shook her head. "There's nothing to tell. Nothing at all."

She raised her eyes and met his gaze. Her sadness was palpable. Then her breath whooshed out in a sigh and the corners of her mouth turned up in a weak smile. "You were right. The brandy did the trick. I'm feeling much better now. Are you going to feed me or simply try to get me drunk?"

Every bone in his body told Kent she was hiding something from him, and the fact that she wouldn't trust him with her secrets gnawed painfully at his soul. Knowing this wasn't the time to press her and exacerbate her emotional turmoil, he decided to drop the subject. For now.

He set his glass on the side table and reached for his phone.

· · ·

Faith nibbled a bit of pizza, eating more out of politeness than hunger.

Kent's remark echoed in her brain. *Unless you had*

something they were looking for.

Victor couldn't possible know about the diary. Could he? Even if he did, why would he suddenly care it existed? Unless...she shivered. Could he know who she was and be worried about the bad publicity of exposure?

Fighting to calm her waves of anxiety before they built into a tsunami of panic, she focused her thoughts on a slightly more positive explanation. The break-in probably was a fluke. Her apartment had been chosen at random. The diary, her money, and the recording device in her purse were all safe. Her cleaning-woman disguise was still in its bag. Victor had no part in this. He didn't know she was anyone other than Josie Ashland, employee, website developer. Kent had told him she wasn't a spy.

The pepperoni tasted like cardboard. Unable to force another bite, she set her paper plate on the coffee table and glanced at Kent. A little rush of pure sexual awareness skated over her skin. Knowing exactly what would happen if she stayed the night, she shivered in anticipation.

Her brain interrupted the yearnings of her body and injected a dose of reality. She liked him on a deeper level, one that made her want him to care about her, even like her—love her—as Faith. But hoping an exciting man like him could ever want the bland woman beneath Josie's exterior was plain foolishness. He was doing a male mating dance with the goal of obtaining sex. Letting her emotions get involved would only sour the notes of the music. She had to ignore her hormones, deny the chemistry.

Faith released a long, slow breath and chewed on her bottom lip. Being so attracted to Kent was an unforeseen complication, but she couldn't just wait for the relationship to blow up. She needed to extinguish the fuse, disarm the bomb that would shatter her heart. Coming here with him had been a mistake and figuring out what to do next was the most immediate problem.

She considered returning to her apartment. An image of the chaos jumped into her mind's eye, and her insides went cold. No. Tomorrow, after she'd had time to rebuild her courage. Options bombarded her brain. Should she call a cab and go to a hotel? Stay the night with Kent and risk exposing her deception?

Her stupid heart wanted to pour out everything, the truth about her mother and Victor, the truth about who she was, the truth about her growing feelings. She yearned to be snug in Kent's arms while she divulged every secret she'd been holding back and shared all her worries and fears. Her conscience weighed a ton and frantically screamed for relief, but her brain kept reminding her of the dangers of revealing too much and all she had at risk.

He met her gaze and smiled, and she felt a distinctive clutch in her lower abdomen. No doubt about it, her body wanted to stay. Damn, she had it bad.

She ached to hold him and make love to him. Recalling the heavenly night on his boat, desire danced in her veins. She struggled against an urge to be wanton, drag him onto the carpet, and forget the rest of the world.

Faith released a pent-up breath. She had to stop wanting him, had to stop dreaming about things that could never be. They couldn't have a future.

His eyes darkened to the color of rich cocoa. Recognizing his desire matched her own, her body heated until she could have melted into a puddle.

He placed his plate on the coffee table, rose, and came to sit close beside her. His face and mouth only inches from hers, his thumb gently stroked the underside of her jaw. Her pulse tripped and sped.

An odd look brightened his eyes. "I like having you here, Josie."

The rich timbre of his voice spread warmth through her limbs. She whimpered a low sound in the back of her throat. She struggled for air as much as control.

His mouth touched hers. Soft but firm.

As if by their own accord, her fingers ran through his silky, sun-bleached hair.

His tongue grazed the seam of her lips. She opened to him, and he lazily explored her mouth. The brandy tasted much sweeter on his lips. He deepened the kiss, and ripples of pleasure spread all the way to her toes. Her breasts felt heavy and ached for his caress. Her heart beat double time.

Twining his fingers with hers, he whispered, "Would you care to see more of the house, perhaps my bedroom?"

Her hormones did a happy little dance, and a faint humming started in her ears. Unaccustomed to reacting so strongly to a man, she gave up on any hopes of rational thought and answered the only way she could—with a hungry kiss.

His tongue met hers in a bone-melting, intimate promise of more.

Continuing a relationship with him was insanity, but right now she didn't care. She ruthlessly pushed away worries about the future and grabbed for the pleasure of tonight.

• • •

Kent woke holding Josie in his arms and bathed in a sense of contentment. He grinned at the irony. After all the nights he'd avoided cuddling with a woman after making love, here he was curled next to Josie and totally enjoying the sensation. He felt her warmth and his skin tingled. He buried his face in her hair, breathed in the subtle, soft, female fragrance, and wondered if he'd found nirvana.

A twinge of discomfort intruded on his pleasure. Was enjoying her company so completely a sign he was caring too much, moving dangerously near the edge of falling in love? He shook off the idea. Sure, he cared about Josie, but he knew better than to fall in love. Nothing that serious would happen.

He recalled his mother's inconsolable grief after his father's death and felt a wave of sadness. An open heart could be wounded beyond repair. He'd steadfastly protect himself from that fate until he took his final breath.

Josie stirred.

"Morning beautiful," he whispered in her ear.

A smile brightened her face, and she opened her eyes. He noticed a slight arc near her iris, like she was wearing a contact lens, and felt oddly pleased to have discovered the intimate secret that her eyesight was less than perfect.

"Good morning," she murmured. "What time is it?"

"About eight."

Her body stiffened. "Oh, no. I'll be late for work."

He pulled her closer and playfully nuzzled her neck. "Forget work. Let's stay in bed all day."

"I probably should take the day off, but not to spend in bed." Her expression sobered. "I have to get a locksmith over to my apartment and then clean up that awful mess."

His mind conjured up an image of the upended furniture and clothing strewn in every direction. He felt an overwhelming urge to take care of her. "Stay here with me for a few days."

She rolled on her back, gazed into his eyes, then ran her fingers through his hair as she gave him a tender kiss. "You're sweet to offer, but I can't. I have to go back to my own place today and get back on the horse, so to speak. If I let myself postpone it for too long, I may never get the courage to face that apartment again."

He caressed her soft cheek. "Do you want me to go with you?"

"No. Thank you for offering, but I'm sure it will be safe now. Putting everything back in drawers and closets will be tedious work, but I can handle it alone."

She briefly nuzzled against his palm, then tossed back the comforter and climbed from the bed. "I'd better call Gladys before I get dressed. I guess my purse and cell are still in your den."

Disappointed, he lay there for a few seconds watching her walk toward the doorway, noticing the smooth lines of her back, the smooth roll of her hips, and the sexy stretch of her legs. A rush of heat overtook him, and his groin tightened. Everything from her smoky gaze to her whimpers of satisfaction turned him on.

Down boy. You've had all you're getting for now, he told himself with a sigh.

He reached out and turned off the bedside lamp. Josie's discomfort in the dark meant making love with the lights on. He grinned. One more thing about her that was perfect.

A minute later, she came back into the bedroom, shyly

holding his suit jacket up to block his view of her torso. "Which way to your shower?"

She looked so enticing he wanted to lock all the doors and keep her with him forever, but he decided to settle for the promise of a date. Plucking the bracelet she'd removed in the middle of the night from the bedside table, he stood and delivered it to her hand. "My mother's club is having a charity ball Friday night. I hate going to those things alone. I'll tell you where the shower is if you'll you go with me to the ball and make it fun?"

A flicker of hesitation. "I'd love to meet your mother, but do you really think we should be seen together at an event like that?"

"Why not?"

"Does Victor know we've been together," her gaze dropped to her bare legs and she moistened her lips, "like this?"

The muscles tightened in his jaw. "I don't give a damn what Victor knows. It's none of his business who I see or make love to."

Her voice was suddenly small and vulnerable. "He told you to date me."

"That's ancient history." His nerves started jumping. A tiny ripple of doubt chilled his skin. Why the hell was she so obsessed with Victor if she was here for the sake of her cousin? He pulled in a breath and fought down a wave of confused feelings. "Forget him. Do we have a date for the charity ball?"

He watched her think for a moment before she smiled. "Yes, I'd love to go."

A burst of exuberance filled his chest. He gave her a

half-hug and nuzzled her cheek. "Okay, lady, then let's grab a shower, and before I let you go face your apartment, I'm making you a nutritious breakfast."

Chapter Eighteen

By six p.m. Faith was out of energy. After a day spent sorting, folding, and re-organizing, she dragged herself to the kitchen looking for a pick-me-up. She filled the whistling teakettle and set it on the stove. Then she got out a teabag, set it in her cup, and grabbed a sleeve of Ritz crackers.

She flopped onto her bed and stretched out. She glanced at her baggy sweats and bare feet and pushed her stringy hair from her face. Not quite ready for a charity ball. Thankfully, she had two days to make herself presentable.

She stifled a yawn and closed her eyes. Her arms ached after hours of bending and lifting and sweeping. Although last night with Kent was heavenly, she'd missed out on several hours of sleep. A snack, a shower, then she was more than ready to hit the sheets.

Images of Kent floated before her. His hair blowing in the sea breezes. His tantalizing smile. His electrifying touch.

In her mind's eye, Kent appeared beside her, planted his

fists on his hips, glared at her and said, "Who are you?"

She stammered, couldn't find the words to tell him the truth. He looked at her with disgust, turned and got on his boat, started to sail away. The wind in the boat's rigging began to whistle. The whistle became a shrill, sharp sound like the scream of a banshee.

She bolted awake. Looked around for attackers. No one. Whistling. The teakettle.

A nightmare.

She jumped from the bed, raced to the kitchen, and shut off the stove. The banshee scream faded. She sagged against the breakfast bar and wrapped her arms around her midsection to keep from shivering.

She was alone and safe. Kent turning his back on her was only a dream, but the message sent by her conscience was undeniable. She couldn't lie to him any longer. When he picked her up for the charity ball Friday, she had to trust him and tell him the truth.

• • •

A few minutes before ten, Kent poured himself a third cup of morning coffee. He raised the pot toward Jack, "Refill?"

"No thanks. I thought you promised your mother you'd cut down."

"She won't know unless you tell her." He sat back in his chair and stretched his long legs out under his desk. "Speaking of my mother, I stopped over at the house to see her and pick up a little something I promised I'd get for a friend. While I was there, I told her I'd go to that charity thing tomorrow night. You and Carrie want to come along? Don't let her use the old 'I don't have anything to wear' excuse. She can come pick out a dress from the store and charge it to my account."

Jack grinned. "You need protection from the matchmaking members of the Women's Club?"

"No, I'm safe on that front. I'm bringing a date."

"Ah. The plot thickens. Josie by any chance?"

Kent nodded and felt a silly smile tug the corners of his mouth.

Jack burst out laughing. "Well, I'll be damned. You've got it bad." His eyes sparkled with amusement. "I'll talk to Carrie and see if she can get her mother to babysit. A ballroom full of boring stiffs or not, I'd love to be there and watch this gal twirl you around her finger."

Kent scowled. He didn't have anything bad. He liked Josie. He enjoyed being with her. But there was no reason for anyone to think he was love-struck.

Refusing to give Jack the satisfaction of a protest, he flashed him an indulgent look. "By the way, smart ass, when you get a chance, run the Mustang over to the Ford dealer and have it detailed. Once they get it cleaned up, it's all yours."

"Are you done pretending to be a working stiff?"

"Josie knows who I am, so the car swap doesn't serve a purpose any longer."

"Okay, I'll run it over this afternoon." He tossed Kent a set of keys. "Thanks for the new wheels and the use of the Carerra. It was fun while it lasted."

Kent stuffed the Porsche keys in his pocket, then he gathered the transaction reports spread on his desk and shoved them into their folder. He picked up his mug, took a sip of hot black coffee, and let the warmth ooze down his chest and spread in his midsection. "Going over these reports hasn't answered many questions. If anything, they've made me more suspicious. What jumped out at you?"

Jack pursed his lips and scratched his head. "Ninety percent are big-ticket items, mostly jewelry and a few furs. The same customer names pop up over and over."

Kent nodded as his mind jumped to one name in particular, Melinda Hart, Victor's mistress. His blood heated at the exorbitant price Victor paid for extramarital sex. No woman, even the most talented call girl in the country, could be worth over half-a-million a year. And what the hell was a no-talent dancer doing with all that bling? Wearing it would get her mugged. *She must have a safety deposit box that weighs a ton.*

The dinner conversation he and Josie had at the speakeasy swirled through his head. Melinda bought expensive items and returned them, then Victor bought them back again. Why didn't he have her keep the stuff in the first place? Were the two separate sales the objective? Was he trying to artificially pump up sales volume numbers so the company financials looked better on paper? Emmeline's credit rating was already triple-A. So what purpose did the repeat sales serve?

As much to himself as Jack, he muttered, "The big questions are: What is Victor's game, and what can we do about the return situation?"

"What's Victor got to do with this?"

Kent told him about Melinda and the jewelry returns, carefully leaving out any reference to Josie.

"Victor's game is always anyone's guess," Jack said,

shaking his head. "As far as the number of returns are concerned, it seems like we need a new refund policy. Maybe we should think about return ceilings. Some of the big retailers are setting a dollar limit on how much any one customer can return in a year."

"The chain department stores have tried that with some success, but we've built a reputation on guaranteed customer satisfaction, plus our customers have different buying patterns. A lot of wealthy women shop as entertainment. They keep a much larger percentage of merchandise than they return, and if we restrict the dollar value of what they can bring back, they might feel insulted and take a lot of lucrative business elsewhere."

"We could stop giving cash refunds, give store credit instead."

Kent set down his coffee and stood. He shook his head as he walked to the dartboard and chose his weapons. "I like that option, but bookkeeping will probably balk. Store credit would add another level of complexity, like with gift cards. Credits would need to be carried on the books for months or even years."

He stepped back even with his desk, aimed, and threw the first dart. The point lodged in the green bull's ring a half-inch from dead center. "Twenty-five."

Jack walked to the whiteboard, started a column for each of their scores, then picked up three darts with red tails. "But if we gave out cards, inflation and lost cards would work to our advantage. Sixteen percent of gift cards are never redeemed. A card with a store credit would be just as likely to be lost or forgotten."

Jack stood by the desk, threw, and hit black for sixteen.

Kent took a turn and hit red on the thin inner ring. "Triple seven. At the very least, we should look closer at what's happening and consider a policy change. Get someone you can trust to keep their mouth shut to help you work up a white paper on the pros and cons of our options and the potential profit of credits. We'll bring it up at the next management meeting."

Jack subtracted their scores. His next throw speared the bull's eye and he grinned. "Victor will be pissed if you don't run the ideas past him first."

"Probably, but let him be pissed. I learned a little something from our fiasco with Gardener. Total surprise can catch your adversary off guard and give you a leg up."

"I'll get on it this afternoon."

Kent heard the glee in Jack's voice and smiled.

He aimed his last dart, hit white twelve. His mind was preoccupied with questions about Victor and Emmeline's finances, and his game was suffering. He shook his head in frustration. "I'm going to get someone in accounting to do a statistical analysis and see if we can pin down why some stores are seeing drastic differences in return levels. If we can correlate returns to geography or demographics, it might be something to consider when we're investigating acquisitions."

His secretary stuck her head in the door. "Peg is on the line. Mr. Telemann wants to know if you can stop by his office at about three."

Kent glanced at Jack, who always had a complete schedule of appointments for the next month stored in his head. Jack said, "You're free all afternoon."

"Tell Peg I'll be there."

Jack threw and scored a double eighteen, then said with

a heavy dose of sarcasm, "I'm sure you can hardly wait."

Kent had an idea and called, "Wait a second, Mandi."

His secretary leaned back around the corner. "Yes?"

"Put Peg through, please."

He walked back to his desk and picked up the phone. "Peg, Kent. How are you this morning sweetheart?"

"Good, thank you. Are you coming in answer to the summons?"

"I'll be there. But listen, will you do me a favor?"

"Of course."

"The next time Melinda Hart shows up to see Victor, will you give me a buzz and let me know? I want to talk to her when she's leaving, but don't mention anything about it to her or Victor."

"If she comes by, it's usually around eleven. I'll let you know if today is one of the days."

"Thanks, Peg. I'll owe you."

She chucked. "You'd better be careful. Someday I'm going to collect."

He hung up and met Jack's questioning gaze. "If we want information about Melinda and Victor, I might as well ask at the source."

"Victor will be double pissed if he finds out you're crossing into his well-marked territory."

"If I play the game smart, and Melinda turns out to be as greedy as I think she is, he will never know."

. . .

Within minutes of Peg's eleven-fifteen call, Kent was in the lobby waiting for Melinda Hart to step off the elevator.

When the doors opened, he flashed a big smile. No Melinda. He smoothed his tie and resumed pacing.

Half a dozen openings later, his target arrived. Her red Capri pants hugged smooth, portioned hips and legs toned to perfection by hours of dancing. She wore a low-cut white jersey top that clung to her breasts and nipples and left little to a man's imagination. The chain around her neck dripped a teardrop diamond he estimated at more than a carat. The expression on her perfectly made-up face shouted boredom.

"Melinda Hart! What a wonderful surprise," he said rushing forward and holding out his hand. "I enjoyed your performance at the dinner theater last week immensely."

She looked him up and down, smiled, and asked, "Do we know each other?"

He feigned embarrassment. "I'm sorry. I'm Kent Telemann. I've heard so much about you, I feel as if we've met."

She tilted her head and appraised him through a coy flutter of eyelashes. "Well, of course. That's why you look familiar. You're Victor's stepson."

"And a great admirer of your talent." He casually touched her elbow and steered her out of the flow of foot traffic. "Would I be too forward if I asked to buy you lunch, or a least a cup of coffee? There's no reason we should be strangers."

"Well, I was on my way to a rehearsal, but I suppose I can spare a few minutes for a handsome fan." She pushed her hair off her shoulder and trailed her fingers seductively across the swell of her ample breasts. "Do you know a quiet place we can get acquainted over a cup of coffee?"

He suppressed a grin. She was good. Her body language and the tone of her voice oozed flirtatious promises. A few more minutes of this treatment, and ninety percent of all red-blooded males would be hard and twitching.

Letting her see him ogle her cleavage, he continued to the next step of his plan. "There's an intimate club right around the corner." He slipped a hand to the small of her back. "Shall we?"

She nodded and fell in step beside him. Once they were on the sidewalk outside the store, he said, "How's the show going? Are ticket sales what the promoters expected?"

"No, and if things don't pick up, we may be closing in a couple weeks max."

"I'm sorry to hear that," he said with a shake of his head. "You have a great talent, but you can't carry the show alone. I noticed several members of the supporting cast don't measure up."

His flattery hit its mark. She smiled warmly at him. "It's too bad the critics don't see things as clearly. If the director would dump Brian Butler, I know I could make the show a hit."

He nodded sympathetically. "So, are you out shopping today, or visiting Victor?"

"Visiting."

"That's a stunning diamond pendant. Is it one of ours?"

She smiled. "Of course. Emmeline's has the best jewelry in town."

"But it can only show off its brilliance when showcased by the proper beauty."

She sucked in the compliment like a drop of rain hitting desert sands. "I love diamonds, and I firmly believe in the adage that they're a girl's best friend."

"And I firmly believe that special women deserve to be

showered in extravagant gifts."

He watched her lips quirk from the corner of his eye and knew his message was getting across loud and clear. He moved in. "So tell me, what does a fabulous woman like you see in a dirty old man like Victor?"

"You don't beat around the bush, do you?"

"Why waste time when we could be doing all sorts of exciting things in luxurious places?"

She tossed her head and mischief danced in her eyes. "Victor is the jealous type, you know?"

"Forget Victor. Run away with me. We'll jump on the corporate jet and be in Paris for dinner, get a suite with a balcony, toast the lights of the city with vintage champagne, and romp in a bathtub filled with caviar." He turned and captured her eyes. "We'll make love until you're drained of orgasms and scream for mercy. Then we'll rest on a bed of mink and start over again."

She smiled and licked her lips. "You're proposition is tempting, of course, but a girl has to think of the future."

"There are other men, better men, who have the means to offer you everything Victor is giving you now. And more."

"But you don't know what Victor is giving me. How can you be sure?"

He stopped walking and turned her to face him. He raised his hand and lightly ran his fingers over the bare skin above her blouse then slipped his hand behind her neck, pulled her toward him, and claimed her mouth.

She opened to him, welcomed his tongue, pressed her breasts to his chest and her belly against the front of his slacks. It was a practiced move guaranteed to make most men hungry for more.

He raked his fingers through her hair, dragged his mouth to her neck, then up to nip at her earlobe. "Tell me what your arrangement is with Victor and I'll match it dollar for dollar. Plus I'll give you real sex. The kind of sex a vibrant woman like you needs. Hot satisfying sex that will melt your bones and last all night. No little blue pills necessary."

She sighed. "It all sounds delicious, but as much as I'd like to tell the self-centered creep he turns my stomach, breaking off with Victor isn't going to be that easy."

"What does he give you?"

"Jewelry."

"I'll give you more jewelry and plenty of spending money."

"I have money. I return some of his gifts for cash. A girl has to save for retirement."

He pulled away slightly, took her hand, and caressed her fingers. Trying to establish she was well off without him showed she was a reasonably good negotiator. But he was better. Now that he'd made her believe she had the upper hand, he could veer off subject for a while and get her to supply some information. "Doesn't he get suspicious when you don't wear the pieces he's given you?"

Her chuckle hinted at contempt. "He's so focused on having me buy new pieces, he forgets about the last one instantly."

"Doesn't he see the return on the store records?"

"I'm careful. I take care of those particular returns in Miami."

He filed away the exact wording of that interesting tidbit and tried a slightly different tack. Running a fingertip over the diamond at her neck, he said, "This is a gorgeous piece that belongs against your fabulous skin, but I don't see Victor having enough class to select anything this exquisite. You must pick out your own gifts."

"He specifies what to get. And they have to come from Emmeline's."

"Why?"

She stiffened and pulled her hand away. "It doesn't matter."

"No, it doesn't." He flashed her a meaningful smile. "I simply want you to know I'll treat you better and let you shop wherever, and for whatever, your heart desires."

Her eyes sparkled, and he sensed she was ready to seriously deal.

She said, "Victor is terribly jealous. We'd have to be careful. If he ever found out I cheated on him…"

He had her, but he didn't want her and things had moved a little quicker than he'd planned. He decided she was even greedier than he anticipated, and if he went any farther with this charade, permanent damage would result. It was time to drop in a deal breaker so he could back off with the information he'd obtained and she could walk away with her pride.

"I'll give you everything you could ever want." He paused and shook his head to emphasize his next point. "But I don't share. If you come to me, his hands never touch you again."

Fear flickered in her gaze.

He wondered if she'd been subjected to threats or violence and felt a stab of sympathy. He'd witnessed Victor's disrespectful and crude behavior with his wife. When he pictured how much worse the man must act while with a mistress, disgust churned in his stomach.

"Fat chance," she said, wrapping her arms across her chest. "He's not going to just let me go to be with you. So unless you have a magic bullet up your sleeve, this whole discussion is pointless." She swallowed and pulled in a long breath. "I think I'd better skip the coffee and go straight to rehearsal after all."

He backed down slowly. Too quick a reversal might hurt her feelings or make her suspicious. "What are you doing after the show tonight? Can I at least buy you dinner and try to change your mind?"

Her laugh was bitter. "No. I'm at Victor's beck and call. No dinner. No hot affair."

He put a hint of desperation in his gaze, hoping for a chance to find out something else. "I could help you leave him."

Melinda shook her head. "You're sweet to offer, but I'll be fine. I know how to play just as dirty as he does, and I'm working on my freedom from another direction." With that, she raised her chin, turned, and walked away.

. . .

The air conditioner fans kept up a steady drone, but Victor's office still stank of stale cigar smoke. The butter-soft, chair leather crinkled as Kent sat and smoothed his silk tie.

"What did you want to see me about?" he asked.

Victor pulled a manila folder from his top desk drawer. "I want to give you this."

"What is it?" he said, leaning forward and taking the proffered folder.

"A background report on our corporate spy."

The idea that Victor was chasing shadows gave Kent a warm bolt of satisfaction. He was looking forward to having Josie bring Victor down a notch, proud of her strength, and proud of her commitment to proving her cousin's claim. He pictured the plastic bag stashed in his desk drawer. How long would it take to get the results of a DNA analysis on the dandruff-flecked hairs he'd collected from Victor's brush when he'd visited his mother last night?

Carefully schooling his face to mask his affection for Josie and disdain for the man in front of him, he said, "I don't believe she's spying."

"So you've said. Well, see if you still think that way after you've read the report. There's something fishy about her. I'm not sure what, but you should know her pretty good by now and be able to figure it out." He leaned back in his chair, flicked on a lighter, and held it to the tip of a cigar. He huffed and he puffed, and white smoke billowed toward the ceiling.

Kent's vindication of Josie would be more convincing if he played along. He flipped the folder open and stared at a copy of her employment application. Guilt washed over him. He shouldn't be snooping into her background this way. He should get to know her by asking and answering questions, letting her volunteer information at her own speed.

He looked up and glared at Victor. "Where did this come from?"

"A security firm we outsource to occasionally. All prospective employees are told they're subject to verification of references and a background check. Once in a while we pursue that option."

"Using the information on her application and résumé to dig into her life is a violation of her privacy."

Victor's face turned mottled red and a vein bulged in his temple. He pointed with his cigar for emphasis. "To hell with her privacy. I'm running a business here, and she's a threat. I'll investigate her or do whatever else I need to do."

Torn between stoic refusal to look at the report and the need to put on a good show so Victor would believe his assessment and leave Josie alone, Kent turned a page, then another. Slowly leafing through the pages, his gaze stalled on a doctor's report. He felt a prickle of unease. Medical records weren't in the realm of a normal background check.

He glanced down the page. How had Victor's security firm accessed the information? The word *pregnancy* caught this eye, brought his scan to an abrupt halt, and kicked his curiosity into high gear. He focused on the beginning of the paragraph containing the word and read the rest of the text.

Last trimester. High stress job. Risk of premature labor.

Josie had quit her last job on doctor's orders two months ago. Because she was six months pregnant with twins!

The report slammed him in the gut. She'd been pregnant? Faked her reluctance and shyness? Taken him for a fool? He clenched is teeth. Damn her.

A little voice argued she'd ripped and bled like a virgin. A good actress could pretend inexperience, but the physical proof was impossible to fake.

His blood ran cold. The woman he'd made love to wasn't Josie Ashland. Her story about a cousin and a kidney transplant was a bald-faced lie. She was a complete imposter, she'd scammed him, and most likely Victor was right—she was a corporate spy.

A massive jolt of adrenaline gushed into his veins. He slammed the folder shut and hissed, "She's a lying bitch."

"What'd you see?" Victor asked with a predatory glint in his eye.

Kent gritted his teeth, and a muscle jumped in his jaw. Pain, anger, disgust, and devastation whipped through him, battered his heart and brain, and flooded his chest making it difficult to breath.

She'd conned him, used him, and he'd fallen for her lies like a naïve schoolboy. He'd taken her sailing, made love to her without holding anything back. He'd even let himself care and get attached, the worse mistake of all.

"I don't know who the woman on the fourth floor is," he said through clenched teeth, "but I'm sure she isn't this Josie Ashland. She's a fraud."

Victor narrowed his eyes to dark slits. "Then you need to push harder and find out what she's up to."

Kent tossed the folder onto Victor's desk and shook his head. "No. I'm done. Fire her."

"Her employer will send in someone else."

"Don't hire a replacement unless it's someone we're sure we can trust."

Victor sucked on his cigar then slowly blew out a stream of smoke. It settled around his head and ears and made his hair look like a smoldering heap of coal. A smirk curled his lips. "That means killing the website you were so hot to get up and running."

Kent's anger seeped from every pore and vibrated around him in an almost palpable energy field. Nothing was as important as booting Josie, or whoever the hell she was, out of his life. "The website can wait. I'm firing her, damn it."

Chapter Nineteen

Faith set her morning coffee on the corner of her desk, dropped her purse in the bottom desk drawer, and plopped down behind her monitor. Another Friday. The end of her fourth week working at Emmeline's and the fifth week since she'd arrived in Palm Beach. In one more week, she'd have to grit her teeth and write a letter of resignation from her real job, give up the career she'd worked hard to build. Plus Josie's due date was getter closer every day. She might miss being with Josie when the babies were born.

Damn. If only she could find something about Victor that would put him behind bars and let her go home.

The overhead light glinting on the gold bracelet on her wrist sparked vivid memories of two nights ago and the amazing, bone melting sex with Kent. She recalled his mock yelp of protest when the bracelet clasp tangled in his hair, and the playful nips at her shoulder that he'd joked were his way to get even. The memories provided her only ray of sunshine.

Anticipating seeing him again, she pulled herself out of her depression and considered what to wear to the charity ball tonight. Black tie, he'd said, meaning formal. As the computer flashed through its series of boot-up screens, her mind sorted through Josie's wardrobe.

Should she tantalize Kent with her thighs sliding in and out of the side slits on Josie's white lamé? Could she get and keep his attention with the curve of her breasts peeking over the neckline of the naughty, skin-tight red satin? Should she splurge and go shopping for something new that would be hers to keep, along with the memories of Kent taking it off before they made love again?

Realizing what she was doing, she gave a soft laugh. Not that long ago she would have been weighing the pros and cons of her plain black sheath versus her gray silk suit. But she was actually starting to enjoy dressing bold and wearing fun clothes. Picturing Josie's reaction when she told her of this change, Faith's lips twitched in a smile.

A tingle of apprehension intruded. What would Kent say when she told him the truth about her masquerade and quest to bring Victor to justice? Should she tell him before or after the ball? How should she bring up the subject and what words should she use?

She stared blankly at the computer screen and asked herself the most important question. Would her confession drive him away and tonight be their last night together?

I'm sorry Kent, but I'm going to ruin your company... About your mother, I'm going to devastate her pride...By the way, your step-father is a rapist.

Like a cat who'd crept up on silent feet, Gladys suddenly

appeared in her doorway. "Josie, we have to talk."

Faith started and blinked. The clipped tone of Gladys's voice made the hairs on her nape stand on end. No *good morning*. No *how are you today*. Not a good sign. Had someone detected her hacking?

She swallowed heavily. "Sure, what's up?"

"Mr. Telemann, Mr. *Kent* Telemann, left specific orders that you were to be fired as soon as you came in. He said you were to be escorted out of the building immediately."

She caught her breath in a gasp and grabbed the desk edge for support. *Fired?*

Kent…specific orders…

The words slammed through her brain maiming neuron after neuron like freight cars twisting in a train wreck. Her stomach lurched.

Kent's orders.

She had a strange out-of-body sensation. This couldn't really be true. She'd wake up and discover she'd dozed off and had another nightmare.

"Please get your personal belongings together," Gladys said in a tight voice.

Faith's tongue felt numb, her brain frozen. She gulped air.

I trusted him, loved him. Love? Yes, I loved him. Do love him. And yet he betrayed me like this. Why? What's changed?

She wanted to curl into a ball and disappear in a deep pit. Her chest ached with a desperate need to cry. Her insides went heavy and raw, as if every organ was scraping against bone and bleeding into her muscles.

No, please, God. Don't let him really be doing this, intentionally trying to hurt me. Don't let it end like this.

The raw, cold pain she'd felt after her mother's death returned and wrapped around her like a shroud. Then, she'd assumed no pain could be worse. Now she struggled to bear a pain twice as raw, twice as cold, twice as suffocating. Another person she loved ripped away. Gone.

The memories of her mother roused sharp thoughts that launched another assault on her brain. Her pulse rate doubled; her heart wasn't the only thing shattered.

Without this job, I'll never get a confession from Victor.

Straining for composure and rationally, Faith yanked her mind from Kent to the information on the memory board of the computer in front of her.

She couldn't fall to pieces. She needed to maintain a tight rein on her emotions. Her tangled feelings would have to wait. She would have plenty of time to cry and stem the bleeding from her heart. Later.

Squeezing her fingers around the edge of the desk, she forced words from her dry throat. "Please, I'll need a few minutes."

Gladys studied her for a couple seconds. Then her lips pursed in disapproval and her expression softened. "I don't like the idea of kicking an employee out on a minute's notice. It's unfair. I'll be back in five. Sorry, but that's all I can do."

"Thank you," Faith said, trying to put normalcy into her voice.

Gladys turned then disappeared from the doorway.

Think. Think.

Her brain took inventory and screamed out a plan. The superuser account was secure. She could access it from her laptop at her apartment. But she'd need to work fast to copy all her data. As soon as she got home, she'd have to dump everything onto her laptop. The security firm Emmeline's contracted with would probably have her account blocked within twenty-four hours, and anything not downloaded by then would be lost.

Lost like Kent. An image of him, hair tousled, eyes bright with desire, a sultry smile on his lips, flashed in her mind. Her chin quivered. She pressed her lips together tightly and fought off the paralysis of visceral pain.

She opened her bottom drawer, grabbed the folders holding the information she and Steve Zurich had collected about Victor, and stuffed them into her briefcase. She scanned her desk for any stray printouts of emails or evidence of her covert activities.

Would the maintenance technician brought in to delete her account be able to find any evidence of her hacking? Her mind's eye raced over the code of the firewalls she'd erected. He might find her macros and wonder at their purpose, but everything that constituted proof of her unauthorized accesses would stay hidden.

She pictured Kent standing in her apartment doorway looking like he'd just stepped from the pages of a menswear magazine and smelled the scent of his English Leather cologne. Her mouth went dry and tears stung her eyes. Her heart felt empty and hollow, her chest ready to cave in.

The energy drained from her body. She propped her elbows on the edge of her desk and dropped her head into her hands. What did it matter if she had access to the information on the office computer or copies of useless emails? She didn't have evidence of any illegal activities or any proof Victor had raped her mother. Everything she'd been trying to do was in ashes now. And Kent had betrayed her. He was tossing her out, and she'd never see him again, never touch him again.

Gladys's voice came from the doorway. "Ready?"

Faith raised her head, took a deep fortifying breath, removed her purse from the desk drawer, nodded, and stood on shaky legs. "I think so."

"Personally, I think the parts of the website you've designed so far are great, and I'd be happy to give you a reference, but I have strict orders not to." Curiosity filled Gladys's eyes. "Mr. Telemann didn't mention what you did to make him so mad. All I can say is, if I were you, I wouldn't have a prospective employer call anyone here. You'll be blackballed for sure. Your best bet is to not even list Emmeline's on an application."

"Thank you for the warning."

She'd damaged Josie's reputation. Could things get any worse? Sadness seeped deeper into her bones.

"Do you know what this is all about?" Gladys asked.

Breaking and entering? Hacking Victor's emails? Lying to Kent? She hung her head and sighed. The lies were the worst crime. At least, the one she regretted most.

"I can think of a couple possibilities." She stepped toward the door, removed the office keys from her purse, and handed them to Gladys. "But it doesn't matter. It's too late now."

• • •

"You look very handsome tonight, dear," Emmeline whispered in Kent's ear. "I'm going to bring Sarah over so you can meet her."

He bit back a sharp remark and settled for, "I'm not in the right frame of mind for small talk with a stranger, Mother. I'm not even sure why I'm here."

She hesitated then her expression grew serious, and she squeezed his hand. "Is it something you want to talk about?"

He clenched his teeth. The last thing he wanted was to spill his guts to his mother. She'd go all feminine on him. His rage over Josie's deception needed to be buried deep, not dragged out into the open for dissection and analysis. "I'm fine."

She patted his arm and smiled reassuringly. "You're probably just upset because Jack canceled, and you're wandering around without a buddy. Once you have Sarah to talk to, I'm sure you'll perk up. Stay right here for a few minutes while I go find her."

He squelched the urge to protest. He might as well get it over with. He'd meet his mother's "perfect match," then duck out of the damn ball and go home. He'd written a ten thousand-dollar check for the Women's Club charities, so his obligations had been met.

After watching her regally weave through the crowd and disappear from view, he snagged two glasses of champagne from a waiter's tray. His black mood had nothing to do with Jack and everything to do with Josie.

He pictured her lying on his bed, her hair spread on his pillow, her lips swollen from his kisses. Maybe he wouldn't go home. He'd be reminded of making love to her.

He drained the champagne from one glass. Sleep probably wasn't going to come, and even if it did, Josie would probably haunt his dreams. He'd be best to find an all-night bar. Maybe if he got drunk enough, he could annihilate his memories and then pass out for the night in the Carrera.

Out on the dance floor, a dozen couples swayed to a waltz. The women held perfectly coifed heads high. Their elegant gowns swirled like silk flowers in a windstorm. Their rubies, diamonds, and emeralds sparkled in the light cast by the huge chandelier.

The men wore crisp tuxedoes. Mostly, they were here with their wives. Like Victor, they would drink and be boisterous, flaunt their wealth, play one-upmanship games, treat their wives with decorum.

Kent snorted in disgust and drained the champagne from the second glass. What a farce. Ninety-five percent of them were cheaters and liars. The first chance they got, the men would be back in bed with their mistresses, and the women would be sneaking out to meet lovers while playing the long-suffering martyr. Even his own mother was a liar. She wouldn't admit her feeling toward Victor, but he'd often seen daggers of hate slashing out in her eyes.

What the hell am I doing here?

He banged his empty glasses down on a sideboard and turned to leave.

"Kent, dear." His mother's voice. "Wait."

He blew out his breath in a heavy sigh and stopped in his tracks.

Her gown rustled as she approached. A petite blonde in shimmering silver that hugged her curves in all the right places walked at her side. He met the blonde's green eyes, and she flashed him a radiant smile.

A woman I would have wanted if I'd met her before Josie.

The thought punched him in the solar plexus and took his breath away.

"Dear, this is Sarah Davis. Sarah, my son Kent."

Sarah tilted her head beguilingly. Her hair brushed across a bare shoulder as she held out her hand. "I'm very pleased to meet you. Emmeline has told me so much about you I feel like we've been friends for years."

His feet inched to run out the door. Shit, he might as well stay and get it over with. Here or in some bar, what did it matter which hell he was in?

He took Sarah's hand. Warm, slender fingers. *But not as warm as Josie's*. He forced his gaze to meet Sarah's and nodded. "My mother has told me a lot about you too."

Holding Sarah's hand, his heart raced. His mind wandered in a maze of memories. His body recalled every sensation. The wonderful electricity that surged through him when he touched Josie. The tickle of her marvelous laugh. The bubbly feeling that filled his chest whenever she smiled.

His mother cleared her throat.

He snapped back to the moment. Refocused on Sarah. Squared his shoulders. He would not let Josie haunt him another second.

He put on a socially acceptable face and asked Sarah, "Would you like to dance?"

"I'd love to."

"Will you excuse us, Mother?"

Her eyes flashed a mischievous grin. "Of course."

Guilt jabbed his gut. She loved him and wanted the best for him, and once again he was raising her hopes that he'd someday settle down. He remembered the conversation a year ago when in a pensive moment she'd said, "Every day, I dream about playing with my grandchildren. It's the only hope I have left."

If that was her only hope, then he was leaving her with no hope at all.

Shrugging off the dismal truth, he rested a hand at the back of Sarah's waist and guided her onto the dance floor.

She walked into his arms, then said, "You don't have to feel obligated to do this. I know Emmeline is only trying to help, but matchmaking rarely works."

"A dance with a beautiful woman is just what I need to brighten my night." He managed a polite smile. "If everything she said about you is accurate, you're highly intelligent, compassionate, generous, and would be the perfect mother for her grandchildren." He thought of Josie's childlike wonder at the dolphins. Shut off his reminisces. "Why wouldn't a man want to get to know a woman who comes with such a glowing recommendation?"

She gave him a mocking look. "I don't know. Maybe because he realizes my virtues have been vastly exaggerated by his hopeful mother or because he's thinking of someone else."

He hesitated, searching for words. "That's a strange thing to say."

"When you shook my hand, you were definitely somewhere else. Maybe with someone else."

He held her a little closer and noticed her sweet perfume. His mind jumped to the softness of Josie's hair and the fresh scent of her orange blossom shampoo.

Sarah must have taken his silence for an admission of guilt. "My guess is that Emmeline introduced us a little too late. You've already fallen for another woman. But it's not going smoothly, is it?"

He gave up on the phony banter and let his anger bubble

to the surface. "It's over. She turned out to be a liar."

"What's her name?"

"I don't know."

She leaned away, met his eyes, and her mouth twitched. "That's a strange thing to say."

Her attempt at levity was no match for his mood, and he let it pass.

Staring at a spot off in space, he pictured the woman he'd thought he knew sitting behind her desk. "She said her name was Josie, but that was the first of a long string of lies." He allowed more steam to escape. "She seemed so honest and real that it hit me like a ton of bricks to find out she was a fraud." He decided his remarks sounded too personal and steered his rant in a new direction. "The final kick was when I discovered she was working for Emmeline's under false pretenses. I'm an experienced negotiator and usually spot-on when it comes to reading people."

"Why did she impersonate someone else?"

He shrugged as if the same question wasn't gnawing at his heart like a hungry hyena. "I never got an answer to that. I'm guessing she was a corporate spy."

"Did Emmeline tell you I'm a criminal defense attorney?"

"She mentioned you were a lawyer but left out the details."

Sarah smiled. "She probably wanted to soften my image so you wouldn't think I had claws and fangs and be scared away. Anyhow, I deal with human dramas every day, and one thing I've learned is that looking at the surface of a situation is rarely enough. It's always worth the effort to dig until you find motive and unearth the truth. Even if you don't like what turns up."

He instantly saw the wisdom of her words. Knowing

Josie's actual motive was probably better than making assumptions or letting his imagination run wild. He might not like her motive, but ignorance was a galaxy away from bliss. His conscience prickled with a twinge of regret. Yes, Josie had lied, but maybe she had a compelling reason. He'd been wrong to react with raw anger and assume the worst without giving her a chance to explain.

He looked more closely at the woman in his arms. "My mother was right about you. You are smart."

Sarah smiled up at him. "Thank you, kind sir."

He smiled back, liking her keen mind and unique wit. She would be a good person to have as a friend.

A strobe-like flash went off. Kent blinked and saw a man with a camera to his left.

The photographer said, "For tomorrow's edition of the Post, folks." Then he rushed away.

Sarah rolled her eyes and shook her head. "I hope tomorrow's a busy news day and they don't have room to print that. If my mother sees a picture of us dancing, she'll be phoning your mother to make wedding arrangements. I can't seem to hammer it through her head that I'm not interested in long-term commitments."

Kent heard a subliminal message of availability without complications, the kind of message he would have acted on in a heartbeat just a few weeks ago. But he swept her in a circle and dipped her low to the last notes of the song, letting her invitation pass. A night in bed with Sarah wouldn't cure his problem. Now that he knew the difference between making love and having sex, he didn't want to settle for any available woman. Heaven help him, he only wanted to make love to Josie.

• • •

Faith clicked the icon on her laptop to send the email she'd composed to Leeza St. James. Maybe the reporter would be interested in exposing Victor's bigamous marriage.

She stared at the screen and considered reviewing her data, but clenched her teeth and shut down the computer. Why even try to lose herself in the files? She didn't remember one piece of data she'd downloaded or one word from the reports she'd reread. Her head was filled with disconnected thoughts of Kent; her heart was empty.

Was there any way to stop the memories and regrets? Any way to keep her sanity?

Start packing your stuff. The activity will be a distraction.

Faith knelt and slid her suitcases out from under the bed. She opened the biggest case on the bed and transferred her underwear from the chest of drawers. Then she walked to the closet and grabbed an armload of clothes, still on the hangers. She laid them on the bed to be folded. The dress she'd planned to wear to the charity ball was spread on top.

A dagger pierced her heart. Kent was at the ball without her. Who would he touch and hold? Who would he kiss and caress? Who would he take home and love?

Her throat constricted, and she fought to draw a breath. She couldn't stay here and think about him or she'd suffocate. She had to pack faster.

She grabbed the dress, stuffed it in the suitcase, and quickly covered it with others. She returned to the closet for another load. Her hands flew. Remove the hangar, fold, pack. She worked like a woman possessed. When the closet was empty, she paused and looked around, her blood roaring in her ears.

What next? Could she go now?

Her gaze fell on a stack of library books that had to be returned. She glanced from the bookcase to her bed and then to her small table and chairs. The furniture had to be donated to charity.

Oh, God. The cash and Mom's diary. They're in the safe deposit box.

Dread spread through her veins. The bank was closed. Her valuables were unreachable. She wasn't going to escape tonight. The false life she'd created had her trapped.

Faith closed her eyes and choked back tears. She couldn't stay in this apartment. She had to get away.

Just go. Come back and face everything later.

She dug in her purse for her phone and called a car rental company. "I need a car right now. Can someone come pick me up?"

She texted Josie, *I'm taking a day to settle my mind. Don't worry.*

The rental car was due in ten minutes. She threw a change of underwear into a tote bag, grabbed her laptop, locked her door, and rushed down to the curb to wait. A half-hour later, with the rental paperwork complete, she turned off her phone, slid behind the wheel, and drove.

The road was dark. She followed the center lines with an odd sense of detachment and no concern for where the pavement led. Time passed. Miles passed.

Somewhere on a lonely stretch of highway, she glanced down and blinked. Her fuel supply was low.

She took the next exit. Her headlights pierced the

darkness, seeking a destination. A large neon sign said *Twin Palms Days Inn*. The words *Vacancy* and *Free Wi-Fi* were lit up under the name. Rubbing her blurry eyes to see the road more clearly, she knew she was too drained to go on. She turned into the parking lot and stopped at the office.

After taking the last room, she locked the motel door securely behind her, turned on every light, then flopped on the bed. The desk clerk had welcomed her to Islamorada, but she barely knew where that was. Somewhere in the Florida Keys, more than five hours of mindless driving from West Palm Beach. A trillion miles from Kent.

The air conditioning unit rumbled. She pulled the bedspread and blanket tightly around her, chilled to the bone. What now? Physically leaving her apartment hadn't wiped out the memories of the last few weeks. Driving aimlessly hadn't led her to answers. Staring at the white line in the road hadn't dulled the raw pain in her heart. Locking herself in a different room hadn't stopped her from imagining Kent dancing at the ball, his arms around someone else.

A warm tear ran down the side of her face. Emptiness closed around her, and her heart felt too burdened to beat.

She wished she'd never found her Mom's diary.

She wished she'd never read about the rape.

She wished she'd never lied to anyone. Especially Kent.

A sob grabbed her by the throat, and she squeezed her eyes shut. Oh dear God, how she wanted to go home. Home. She sniffled, swallowed, made a decision. Keeping the blanket snug around her shoulders, she sat, opened her laptop, and went to United.com. The next available seat to Norfolk was Tuesday morning, departing at 11:07.

Pulling her bottom lip between her teeth to still her

quivering chin, she purchased a ticket. She'd return to her apartment Sunday night. Monday she could straighten out her affairs, and Tuesday morning she'd return to her old life. Changed forever, but at least back where she belonged.

Chapter Twenty

Josie hadn't answered her phone or her door for over thirty-six hours.

Kent listened to his breathing echo in the empty hall outside her apartment, fisted his hands, and swore in frustration. "Damn it. Damn it. Damn it." He knocked again. "Come on, please, answer. Where the hell are you?"

More silence. A ton of loneliness pressed on his shoulders, and he clenched his teeth. The utter despair he felt without Josie ate at his gut, and he fought to push it away. No use. He was swamped by a sense of loss.

Was she gone? If she was gone, how would he ever find her? What if every trace of the woman he knew as Josie vanished, and he never got a chance to clear the air?

He headed for the elevator, pushed the call button, and tapped his foot while he waited. Maybe he'd hurt her with his knee-jerk reaction to learning she was an imposter. Or maybe she'd shrugged it all off, and he was the world's biggest idiot. He had to know the truth.

The elevator arrived. The doors slid open. He scanned the empty interior and felt a prick of disappointment that she hadn't appeared. It was followed by a stab of grief. Would he spend the rest of his life wishing for her to step out of every elevator, looking for her in every crowd?

He boarded the elevator and hit the button for the lobby. The sinking of the cab mirrored the sinking in his stomach. Maybe he was too late.

He recalled the contentment he'd felt holding her in his arms, the joy that came with seeing her smile. The bubbly feeling she caused in his chest.

Determination stiffened his spine. He wasn't about to give up. He'd go home and grab a meal tonight, but he'd be back again tomorrow. She might be his only shot at love. Now that he'd found the one woman who made him happy and completed his life, he was going to see her again and know the reason for her charade.

• • •

Faith woke from a nightmare. Her face and pillow were wet with tears, her heart thudding and heavy. She was back in her apartment. It was morning and she needed to call Josie. She ran her fingers through her damp, tangled hair as she dragged herself out of bed, located her phone, turned it on, and made the call.

Josie answered, "Hi, babes. Okay, where did you go that you wanted to be incommunicado? I'm picturing some hot, romantic weekend. Come on, tell me, I'm dying to know what's happening."

"Hi, Josie." She squeezed her eyes shut and tried to summon up a few scraps of courage, but the cupboard was bare. "No romantic weekend. I needed to be alone. Everything is terrible."

"Why? What's wrong?"

"Oh, Josie, I'm so sorry." She moistened her lips. How could she have been thoughtless enough to drag Josie into this? "I got fired, and now it's going to show as a black spot on your work record. I can't believe I did this to you."

"What happened? Did your father find out who you are or why you're there?"

"I'm not sure what Victor knows. He didn't have me fired. Kent did."

The line was silent for a few long seconds. "Oh." Her voice was suddenly soft with sympathy. "Are you okay? I know how much he meant to you."

She paused to take a deep breath so she wouldn't fall apart. Legs weak, she sunk into a chair. "I'll get over it," she said lying. "It wasn't like we could ever have…lasted. Not after the way I used him and lied to him. I should have been more prepared for the end."

"I don't think there's ever a good way to prepare for losing someone you love."

"I didn't love…Oh, God, Josie. I do." Cold pain stabbed through her chest. Even though she had no right, she'd wanted him to love her, wanted him to want her the way she wanted him.

"I know."

Faith pressed a fist to her mouth, closed her eyes. How had she let this happen? Why hadn't she been smart enough to see the train of despair speeding down the track? Why hadn't she run away before it ran her over and annihilated her heart?

Josie said, "Are you still there?"

"Yes. When my mother died, I thought nothing could be worse, but this is. It's like there's a massive hole in my life that's going to suck me in. It's like I'm trapped in the dark, alone."

She remembered the nightmare. Kent stood in a bright light by her bed, but he wouldn't reach out, wouldn't let her touch him. He turned his back and stepped onto his sailboat. Darkness closed in behind him as he got farther and farther away then disappeared over the horizon. He took the last rays of light with him and left her in total blackness.

"You're not alone. I'm here. I'll always be here." Josie's voice hitched as if she was trying not to cry. "Are you coming home now?"

"I booked a flight for tomorrow." Faith thought of Victor and the plan she'd formulated during yesterday's long drive north from the Keys. A chill crept over her skin. "But I have some unfinished business to take care of today before I leave."

"I don't like the cold tone of your voice. What are going to do?"

The only things that would brighten her life now would be hearing Victor confess, and then watching him dragged off to jail.

"I'm going to get it over with, confront my father."

• • •

Shortly after lunch, Victor's intercom buzzed.

"What is it Peg?"

"There's a messenger here to see you."

He pursed his lips. Nothing was due today. What was up?

"Send him in."

He didn't recognize the skinny, pimply-faced kid who walked into his office, but the awed look on the guy's face gave him a smug sense of pleasure. Before the guy could drool on his expensive carpet, Victor said, "What have you got?"

The guy snapped to attention. "I have a message for you, sir. Personal and confidential." He held out an envelope in his right hand.

"Did Brody send you?"

"No sir. I mean, yes, sir. I work for Mr. Brody, sir. But this message came through regular channels, not from him directly." The guy shifted his weight from foot to foot.

Victor took the envelope, and ripped it open.

Be at your beach house at seven tonight, alone.
I know your secret, and I'm prepared to tell the world.

He read the message a second time then turned the sheet of paper over and scanned the back. Nothing indicated the identity of the sender. His blood heated. Narrowing his eyes for effect, he spit out, "Who gave you this?"

The guy looked ready to pee his pants. "I told you, sir. It came through our office. Someone who walked up to the counter, sir. I didn't see them."

Victor pulled out his wallet and handed over a fifty-dollar tip. "Forget you were ever here. Now get out."

"Yes, sir." The messenger turned and practically ran for

the office door.

As soon as the door clicked shut, Victor tossed the note on his desktop, picked up the phone, and punched in Brody's private number.

"Quick Fox Messengers. Dan Brody speaking."

"What's with this message?" Victor growled.

"What message?"

"One of your guys just delivered a threatening message. You know anything about it?"

"Which guy?"

"Some pimply faced stick figure. Never seen him before."

"Sounds like Berkinski. He's new. Only his second day. We're only sending him out on legit, outside deliveries. Whatever he brought you must have come from a walk-in or online customer."

Victor fisted his free hand. His pulse pounded at his temples. "Check into it. I want to know who sent it."

"Sure. I'll call you back."

"I'll hold. Go find out, now."

He heard a clunk, then footfalls, then muffled voices. He clenched his teeth and rapped his fingers on the desktop. He'd teach the son-of-a-bitch who dared fuck with him.

Another clunk, then Brody's voice. "Some woman dressed like a cleaning lady came in about two hours ago and dropped off the envelope. Paid cash. Said it had to be delivered before three. My clerk says she had gray hair, but her face looked young. We were busy, so that's all he can remember."

"Didn't he get a name?"

"I pulled the slip. Mary Jones."

"Shit." Victor slammed the phone into its cradle. He

picked up the note and read it again.

You'll see, bitch. Nobody screws with Victor Telemann.

He crumpled the paper and tossed it into the wastebasket. Then deciding not to leave evidence lying around, he retrieved the note and stuffed it into his pocket.

His brain raced ahead. Making sure the note disappeared was only step one. He needed to plan the rest of this out. Next order of business was to get rid of potential witnesses.

He called Melinda at the beach house.

"Hey, doll, I want to be alone tonight. Take off for the theater early and spend the night at your own place. Understand?"

"Yeah, I guess. But do you mean you're coming out here later? And you're going to spend the night alone?"

"That's what I said. So beat it. And don't show up back there until I tell you."

"Okay, okay, I'll go. Don't get pissed."

He scowled. "Don't question me, you hear? Just shut up and do what you're told."

She purred into the phone. "I'm going to miss you, Sugar. That's all."

He hung up, blood rushing in his veins. The dumb slut was starting to be a pain in the ass and needed to be replaced.

Stashing the thought and steering his mind back to the business at hand, he walked to the wall safe, spun the combination lock, and yanked open the door. He reached for the derringer sitting between the stacks of greenbacks and closed his fingers around the handle. Picturing a tiny hole trickling blood from a woman's chest, he stuffed the little gun in his pocket.

The derringer would do for backup, but the right stopping

power and penetration called for a more persuasive piece, something that could push an expanded hollow-point slug three or four inches into tissue.

Something like the piece he kept at the beach house, the Bersa three-eighty.

Chapter Twenty-One

Faith tapped her fingers against the steering wheel as she cruised Worth Avenue in her rental car for the third time, searching for a parking space. She checked her watch again. Four forty-six. She'd failed to plan for the hellish traffic, and she had to find an empty space soon, or she'd be too late.

Two blocks from Emmeline's, she spotted a car pulling out from the roadside. She sped to the vacated space and quickly parallel parked. Ignoring the violation warning on the meter, she jumped from the car and hurried down the sidewalk toward the store.

A siren sounded nearby. A driver frazzled by the afternoon rush hour yelled out his window in frustration. The moan of a ship's horn came from the direction of the harbor.

As she cut through an alleyway that led to the rear of the building, a vicious wind whipped down the narrow canyon and blasted her face and bare legs with sand. She lowered her head and drew her thin raincoat tighter around her then broke into a jog, heading toward Emmeline's employee parking lot.

She glanced up at the low black clouds rolling in off the ocean, breathed in the sharp scent of rain, and hoped the thunderstorm would hold off a few more minutes. She had to catch Kent when he left for the day. Her mission would be over later tonight, and before she went home she had to see him and at least try to explain.

Her chest squeezed painfully. She'd lied to him repeatedly, and he had every right to be angry, but somehow she had to make him see that she'd never meant for the deception to go this far.

Anxiety rippled through her. If she wanted to earn back his trust, she had to tell him everything: her name, why she was here, the name of her mother's rapist. She had to divulge her deep, dark secret and reveal the ugly truth.

As she rounded the last corner, the familiar red Mustang backed out from between a Lincoln Town Car and a shiny Porsche.

Her heart leaped into her throat, and she sprinted the remaining ten yards. The car stopped backing. The front end swung toward the exit. She couldn't see the driver past the headrest. *Please glance in the mirror.* Waving her arms as she ran, she called, "Kent, stop, please."

The Mustang reached the exit on the far side of the lot, and the brake lights lit. One second, two seconds, then either not noticing her or choosing to ignore her, the driver pulled out into the line of traffic.

She froze and stared as the taillights got farther and farther away.

Her stomach flopped and fell like she'd just stepped off

a second floor landing and realized there were no stairs. Her last chance was gone.

She'd been harboring the hope they could clear the air between them and go back to being lovers and friends. She wasn't here solely because of a guilty conscience. She wanted to be close to him, have him smile at her just once more. But he was gone.

The front-page, newspaper photo of Kent smiling at a beautiful blonde at the charity ball filled her mind's eye. Knowing he'd never look at her with desire again made her heart feel too heavy to beat.

Thunder rumbled and a chill wind swirled around her ankles and calves, tugging at the hem of her raincoat. The sky turned grim and dark, as if Kent's departure had stolen the sunlight.

"Hey, Josie." Ronnie's voice came from behind, and he stepped up next to her. "What are you doing here? I heard you got fired."

"Oh, Ron, hi." She drew her coat tighter around her waist and swallowed the lump in her throat. "It's a long story, but, yeah, you heard right. I got fired."

"I expected as much."

She blinked. Why would he expect her to be fired? Her pulse accelerated. "What do you mean?"

"The week before last a report came across my desk that indicated someone might be hacking into Victor Telemann's emails."

She schooled her face and tried not to show her alarm. "What report? From who?"

"An incident report from our Internet provider. Our corporate system is linked to all the stores, so as liaison, they notified me instead of the individual user, in this case Victor."

"Did the report say who did it? Did you tell Victor?"

"I guessed it was you." His gaze was hard, telling her denial would be useless. "But no, I didn't tell Victor. I *lost* the report."

Her breath whooshed out. She covered her mouth with her fingers and closed her eyes. "Thank you."

He cleared his throat. "In exchange for covering for you, I think you owe me an explanation."

Her eyes flew open. She felt like a deer caught in headlights and grabbed at the first plausible excuse. "It was a mistake. I wanted to link him to the website."

"Right, and I'm Batman." For a few seconds, he looked at her with one eyebrow raised and she could visualize neurons firing in his brain. Then the lines around his eyes crinkled, and he broke into a grin.

"Your secret's safe with me. I'm not going to protect that holier-than-thou stuffed shirt. But you have to tell me, what exactly was in his emails?"

Assuming his interest stemmed from voyeurism, she searched her brain. What could she disclose without admitting to the extent of her spying? She shrugged. "I really don't know. I only saw his inbox once."

He winked. "Come on, Josie. You're a rotten liar. You're holding out." He motioned with his fingers like he was a beckoning a misbehaving child. "Tell Ronnie all."

He'd never seemed this hungry for gossip before. Bewildered by his sudden keen curiosity, she decided to give him a tidbit and then make an excuse to leave. "There was one message from his mistress. I didn't open it, of course, but the subject was: *How soon can I earn another gift?* I think he gives her jewelry."

She shut her mouth. Any more would be too much. A normal person wouldn't know the gifts were jewelry, only someone who'd hidden in Victor's closet.

He huffed out his breath and dismissed her revelation with a shake of his head. "I could have guessed that. Come on, tell me something about dark business secrets, suspicious friends, or bank accounts buried in Switzerland?"

His persistence was unsettling. She wet her lips and tried another tack. "How would I know anything like that? I told you, I only saw his inbox once. There were about a dozen new emails, but I don't know what was in them, because I didn't open them. If I had, the text color would have changed. That would have been a dead giveaway that someone had been snooping."

When she'd opened the copied messages in her mirror account on another server, the owner never knew. But she wasn't about to explain her methods to Ronnie, and hopefully, he didn't know enough about hacking to guess.

He studied her for several seconds with disbelief evident on his face.

"Listen, I have to go," she said. "It was nice seeing you again. Thanks for being my friend. I'm leaving town soon, so this is good-bye."

Good-bye to everyone.

Memories of Kent struck her like a sudden tornado and ripped a swath of destruction all the way to her heart.

"Where are you going?" Ronnie asked.

She huffed out her breath. Did where she went really matter? A few days ago she'd been alive, energized, had hope that someday her life would be happy and full. But now, she had nothing to look forward to. When she'd fabricated the story about a cousin who needed a liver transplant, she'd smashed any chance that Kent would ever trust her or want her in his life.

All I have left now is myself.

A little voice inside scolded her for allowing defeatist thoughts. Having herself was enough. She'd survived quite well without a man in her life for the last twenty-five years, and she'd do just as well for the next fifty.

Refusing to dwell on all she'd lost, she crossed her arms tightly over her chest and shook back her hair. "I grew up in Williamsburg, Virginia, and I'm going home."

"When are you leaving?"

"In the morning." She thought about meeting Victor and a chill crawled under her skin. "That's why I have to rush off. I have some important business to wrap up tonight."

He stuck out his hand. "Good-bye and good luck." Thunder echoed off the tall concrete buildings nearby, and he looked up toward the storm clouds. "Looks like the world's about to come to an end. Are you walking? Can I give you a lift somewhere before it starts to pour?"

She shook his hand. "Thank you, no. I have a rental car parked on Worth Avenue."

"Okay, then. Well, take care." He saluted, turned away, and rushed toward his car.

She watched him go. He'd seemed strange. She'd always felt comfortable with Ronnie, but somehow today had been awkward and different.

I'm a nervous wreck about meeting Victor and upset about Kent. Of course everything seems different.

She took one long, last look at the spot where the Mustang had disappeared, then ignoring the cold raindrops pelting her face and head, she forced her feet from the parking lot. The moisture on her cheeks was just rain. Only rain.

Back in the rental car and driving away from Emmeline's with the wipers waging an ineffective battle, Faith scrubbed away the drops running from her eyes and glanced at the dashboard clock. Five twenty-two. The Internet map site had said the drive to Victor's beach house was fourteen miles and should take thirty-three minutes. She had plenty of time to get back to her apartment, conceal the mini-recorder she'd purchased through Steve Zurich in her bra, and drive to Jupiter Island.

She pictured Route 95 gridlock and then four lanes of traffic backed up solid for half a mile waiting for Jupiter's Federal Highway drawbridge to complete an opening.

Victor would be there at seven. Rather than be late and take the chance of missing him, she'd allow herself an hour.

• • •

Wastewater ran in the gutters, and the rental car's wheels splashed through puddles leftover from the retreating storm. The exits and overpasses on the first several miles of the drive to Victor's beach house were familiar from her trips with Kent to his boat and house. Faith fought the urge to change course, detour south, and go knock on his door. She set her jaw and clenched the steering wheel until her knuckles were as white as her slacks and her hands shook.

Give it up. Face the facts. There are too many lies and too much deceit tainting what we shared. We can never be together. He doesn't want to see you again.

She'd send him an email and hope he'd read it. Saying her piece would be easier that way. There'd be no need to look into his eyes and see animosity or disgust, no need to hear his voice and be hurt by his hostility. She'd be spared the need to keep up a brave front while daggers slashed her heart.

It was all a fantasy, she reminded herself. He had a relationship with Josie. *If he'd originally met you as your bland self, he never would have given you a second thought.*

Except, of course, when Victor told him to date you.

Her chest tightened as if caught in the claws of a vice. Fresh tears blurred her vision.

Outside the city limits, the road was dry. She merged left as the highway narrowed to two lanes. She kept a sharp eye on traffic while wondering if she should bring up the subject of Kent with Victor. Maybe she could learn the true depth of their relationship. Kent must be more loyal to Victor than she'd believed. Why else would he have betrayed her and had her fired?

If she knew Kent was despicable, maybe she could hate him and her pain would lessen.

She took the off ramp at the Jupiter exit and headed east.

The Federal Highway drawbridge was down, and the car wheels whined on the metal grating as she crossed to the north side of the river. As the miles ticked away, and the car GPS announced she was approaching the right turn onto Hibiscus Boulevard, her palms grew clammy. She wiped them on her pant legs. Six-thirty-five.

After a lifetime of wondering about her father and

yearning for the presence of a loving dad, in a few more minutes she'd confront the man who shared her DNA.

• • •

Kent steered the Porsche across the slippery surface of the drawbridge grating with his eyes glued to the traffic ahead. In the center lane, three cars in front of him, Josie's blue rental sedan braked for a yellow light and came to a stop. He breathed a sigh of relief. If she'd sped through the light, he would have been trapped in his lane by the cars around him and most likely lost her.

His foot poised to spring from the brake pedal to the accelerator, he drummed his fingers on the steering wheel and considered her location. For the first time in days, he felt a wave of optimism. Could she be driving to his house? Why else would she come to Jupiter? When he'd seen her get in the car outside her apartment building, he'd been panicked by the fear that he really would never see her again.

But maybe following her in hopes of catching up to her was unnecessary. Maybe, if he'd gone home, he would have had the chance to talk to her anyway. Maybe she was on her way to see him and explain everything, prove the medical report was a simple mistake or a fake Victor had given him as part of some sleazy plot.

Yeah. Sure. Get real.

His optimism dimmed. Doubt nibbled at his brain as he adjusted the setting of the air conditioner fan. She'd slid into the car wearing trim white slacks and a long-sleeve, quilted, burgundy jacket, buttoned-up tight at her neck. A light sweater would compensate for extreme air conditioning in the coolest restaurant or store. Why in the world was she dressed like an Eskimo when the temperature outside was eighty-eight degrees? How could he believe she was innocent of corporate espionage when she'd lied about her identity and acted so suspiciously?

He remembered the pizza restaurant where he'd wrapped his suit jacket around her shoulders, recalled how her eyes sparkled when she laughed at his dumb jokes, felt the warmth of her soft hand and the silkiness of her hair. Loneliness squeezed his soul.

The traffic light turned green, and the car in front of him started forward. He ruthlessly shook off his reverie and tromped on the Carrera's accelerator. At the same instant, a battered Jeep changed lanes abruptly and cut into the fifteen-foot space in front of him. He slammed his foot on the brake and swerved left to avoid colliding with the vehicle's rear bumper. The irate driver in the left lane made space but laid on his horn.

Kent gritted his teeth and scanned ahead for the blue sedan. Josie had shifted from the center to the right hand lane. Dammit. Now he was two lanes to the left, blocked in by solid traffic, and the distance between him and her rental car was increasing.

He flipped on his turn signal and glanced over his shoulder. "Come on, you idiots," he growled at the line of cars in the adjacent lane. "Let me in. I can't lose her."

• • •

Victor dropped the single-stack magazine from the deadly thirty-eight and checked for empty spaces. Full. Good.

Not that he'd need seven rounds of ammo. In a straight-on, frontal shot, he'd probably drop her with one bullet, but it never hurt to be prepared. If she made a sudden move, she could put an arm in the bullet's path, reduce penetration, and necessitate a second slug. Plus there was always the chance she would be armed and he'd have to defend against return fire.

Satisfied the gun was ready, he slid the magazine upward until it clicked back into place. Then walking to the octagonal teak table sitting at the juncture of the room's two eight-foot leather couches, he opened the top drawer, disengaged the weapon's safety, and positioned it at the drawer front.

He hesitated before closing the drawer, running his fingers over the dull black, checkered-plastic grip and savoring the idea that he could control life and death. A surge of power flooded his chest. His pulse accelerated in anticipation. A smile tugging at his lips, he shut the drawer and wiggled his ankle. The derringer's metal bumped against his leg. The solid feel of the emergency weapon intensified his excitement.

Energized by visions of a lifeless, female visitor, Victor focused on the beach house living room, analyzing its future as a crime scene. Hiring out the cleaning would create a loose end and leave him vulnerable. He'd be smartest to sanitize the place himself.

He looked around. Blood splatter could be wiped from the leather furniture. He glanced at the floor picturing a pool of red around a body. If need be, he could scrub the tiles with bleach. His gaze went to the blue, green, and white flowered print in the expensive, oriental throw rugs. The damn rugs would be difficult to clean. Replacing them soon after a dead body was found in the neighborhood could raise suspicions.

He tugged on his bottom lip with his thumb and index finger. They'd have to go now. He'd put them somewhere out of spray range and replace them after any clean up. The less clutter in the room, the less chance of trace evidence.

The light grew dim as thunderstorm clouds moving west toward the Everglades blocked the sun's slanting rays. He switched on the table lamp, bent, and folded the first rug.

His odds of avoiding suspicion would be better somewhere else, in a location where the scene could be more easily sanitized. The best scenario was to shoot her on the beach at the water's edge. From there, he could push the body directly into the surf. The currents of the falling tide would suck it out to sea. Then, before dawn brought the infernal supply of beach joggers, the tide would rise and wash away any residual blood or tissue.

He sighed. Taking care of her outside was dangerous. None of the oceanfront houses in the area had more than three hundred feet of water frontage and, even in the cover of the quickening darkness, a beach shooting risked the possibility of a witness. He could stall for a while, maybe tie her up for a couple hours and wait for more darkness, but the gunshot noise would still present a problem.

What he needed was a silencer. He glanced at the throw pillows heaped on the couches. He could use one outside, but not in here where the stuffing would fly around and be a bitch to vacuum. He shook his head in frustration. Nothing was ever easy. Either way, he'd have to find someplace to dispose of a pillow stained with gunshot residue, another fucking pain in the ass.

He carried two throw rugs to the kitchen, went back for a second load, then gathered all but one pillow from the couches. No point in leaving a dozen of them so close when they might get blood splattered too.

After piling the pillows in the kitchen, he dragged a dinette chair to the foyer and stepped outside the front door. If he was lucky enough to get her outside and down to the beach, he didn't need the damn motion-sensing, security lights activated by their movements. A lit spotlight would call attention to the house and possibly expose him to the neighbors.

He climbed onto the chair, unscrewed the bulbs in the two spotlights in front of the house, then went around to the beach side and unscrewed the three near the deck. Back inside, he threw the breaker for the patio and garage to *off*, so the complete yard would remain dark.

He checked his gold Rolex. Only six-forty. Plenty of time for a drink.

The ice cubes clinked against the glass and crackled when he poured in the golden rum. His stomach growled. Grabbing a jar of Russian caviar from the refrigerator and a spoon from the drawer, he settled into a chair with a driveway view and put his feet up on the ottoman. He glanced at his five-hundred-dollar shoes and decided there was no need to ruin them with blood. After removing both his shoes and his socks and stashing them in the bedroom, he fetched a pair of flip-flops. Skin he could clean, cheap flip-flops he could toss in a dumpster.

He settled back into his chair. The rum burned down his throat, but as he envisioned his bullet piercing flesh and the life draining out of his victim's eyes, anticipation was an even stronger stimulant.

Chapter Twenty-Two

Six forty-five on the dashboard clock. An eerie orange glow backlit the low clouds to the west.

Faith slowed the car, straining to read house numbers on the ornate mailboxes in the fading light. The GPS announced the beach house was on the right and fifty yards ahead. Rather than go past and be seen before she was ready, she pulled the car onto the apron of the road one driveway before her destination.

Was Victor already there waiting?

She shifted into park and turned off the ignition. Her heart pounded in a staccato rhythm, and her fingers trembled. Studying the mailbox ahead, she fisted her hands and crossed her arms tightly over her chest. The recorder felt huge between her breasts. She chewed her bottom lip and slid her right hand over the unit, tracing the sharp outline through the thick fabric of her quilted jacket.

Despite her attempt to conceal it under layers of cloth,

would he realize the bug was there? What would he do if he guessed she was recording their conversation?

Too late now to worry about that.

She stuffed her purse under the seat, pulled the key from the ignition, and swung open the car door. Stepping into the hot air heavy with post-storm humidity was like walking into a sauna. Within seconds, her forehead and upper lip were peppered with beads of sweat. She prayed the recorder wouldn't short circuit in the drops running between her breasts.

Cicadas screeched in the thick landscaping along the road. Although the ocean was hidden by the privacy fences and shrubs shielding the exclusive homes, surf thumped, thumped, thumped close by, and the sharp smell of salt and sand hung in the air.

Along with the scent of her fear.

She touched the recorder at her chest for reassurance one more time. Then squaring her shoulders, she wiped her moist palms down her sides, stuffed the car key in her pocket, and headed for the end of Victor's driveway and her moment of truth.

. . .

When Kent suddenly realized Josie was heading to the beach house, his stomach did a sickening somersault. A sense of impending doom weighed heavy on his chest. Why would she be on this road if not to meet Victor?

The blue rental car stopped on the side of the road a short distance before the beach house driveway. Wanting to stay far enough away that he could watch undetected, he braked the Carrera hard and pulled onto the apron too.

What the hell? Victor was the only one using the house. *For playing around with his mistress.*

Bile rose in his throat as he watched her get out of the car and walk along the edge of the road. Her hair seemed on fire in the harsh sunlight. Her movements were slow and stiff like a prisoner being led to the gallows.

She turned into the beach house driveway and disappeared behind a clump of fan palms. He swallowed the lump of dread in his throat. Yanking his keys from the ignition, he swung open the car door and hustled to follow. He seemed to have arrived at the moment of truth.

• • •

There was no one in sight, but the hairs on her nape stood on end and she knew Victor was there. Her intuition whispered eyes were watching her every move.

The garish crimson clouds and the sun setting behind her reflected off the windows and gave the house a foreboding look. Combined with the suffocating heat, the color brought to mind the fires of hell.

Just where he belongs.

Her heavy jacket was soggy in her armpits, but her skin prickled with fear. Sand crunched under her feet, and the pounding of the surf seemed to grow in intensity and echo inside her skull. She turned from the driveway onto the stone sidewalk, and stepped up onto the granite stoop. Her mouth went dry. Fighting off an urge to flee, she swallowed and depressed the glowing, mother-of-pearl button next to the front door.

Muted chimes sounded inside the house. The gay little tune mocked her tension. The last notes died as the door swung open. Victor's one-eyed gaze slammed into hers.

He returned her stare in silence for a second, then smirked, and said, "Come in."

As he stepped aside, his teeth gleamed red in the afternoon light like a hyena's fangs discolored with blood. Faith ordered her legs to move and took two steps into a dimly lit foyer.

The door bumped shut. Without a word, Victor slipped past her and walked away.

She followed him into a huge living room with a cathedral ceiling. A wall of windows looked out over a barren beach and an angry ocean. The drastic cold of the air-conditioning turned the sweat on her neck to ice and sent shivers up her arms. Her pulse throbbed in her throat.

He stopped on the far side of a leather sofa. Turned to face her. "What do you want?"

The sudden blast of venomous words hit like a physical blow and made her jump. She caught her breath and studied his hostile expression and rigid posture. *Not the look of a man who would want to do the moral thing, clear his conscience, or confess to a crime.*

Her heart sank. Her plan was going to fail.

Tears threatened, but she ruthlessly pushed them away. Whether her mission was doomed or not, she had to try. What did she have to lose?

She pried her dry tongue free from the roof of her mouth and plunged ahead. "I came here for justice."

• • •

From his vantage point behind a cluster of Formosa palms, Kent watched the door open, Victor say something he couldn't hear, and Josie step inside.

Drained and disheartened, he considered going back to his car and leaving. There was probably only one reason for their rendezvous. Did he want to know the details?

Waves crashed on the beach, ticking away the seconds, pounding an ugly picture of Josie and Victor into his mind. Disgust whispered *forget her and go*. But the questions swirling in his brain rooted his feet in place. He couldn't leave. Regardless of what he discovered, he needed answers about Josie. About her fixation on Victor. His blood heated. Damn it, he was here and he was going to get those answers.

He set his jaw with iron-willed intent. Staying hidden in the landscaping, he moved closer to the house. He'd try observing through the windows first. The sun was sinking below the horizon and darkness was falling quickly. Any lights on inside the house would help his cause. A lot would be explained by a kiss, physical contact, or two silhouettes moving into a bedroom.

He tasted bile and wanted to crash through the door, grab Josie by the arm, and drag her away. Maybe he could stand her being with any other man, but not with Victor. Despite her lies, he yearned to believe Josie was pure and good, ached for proof she didn't belong in Victor's sordid world.

Behind a drooping clump of pampas grass, he paused to think. All the top executives had been issued a set of keys so they could use the house to entertain. Maybe he could use his to sneak in through the back patio door and hear what was going on. He stuck his hand into his pocket, pulled out his key chain, and took inventory. Carrera, his own house

— front and back —his desk at home, the boat. No beach house key. Memories flared in his brain. Damn it, he'd been sick of carrying the extra weight and tossed the keys into his office desk drawer months ago.

He huffed out his breath, squashed a mosquito biting his sweaty neck, and stuffed the keys back into his pocket. He needed to get a grip, make a plan, and act rationally. His best shot was to figure out which room they were in, sneak in near a likely window, and try to eavesdrop. Hearing their voices over the *thump-swish* of the surf and the chirping of the insects would be difficult, maybe impossible. So to have any chance, he had to get close.

No jumping to conclusions, he warned himself. Maybe she's not here for sex.

· · ·

"What kind of justice?" Victor asked.

Faith hesitated, debating whether to proceed slowly or call his hand right away with an outright accusation. Impatience rushed to the surface. After all these years when he'd been living free while her mother had been imprisoned by fear, the moment for confrontation had come. "You committed a crime. I think it's time you admit what you've done and get it off your conscience."

He twisted his mouth in disdain and challenge. "What crime is that supposed to be?"

"Rape." Her stomach flip-flopped, and she wanted to vomit the filthy residue the word left in her mouth onto his spotless tile floor.

His eyes widened. Beneath his three-hundred-dollar

shirt, the muscles stiffened in his shoulders. His voice was tight and menacing. "Listen bitch, I can guess what kind of game you're playing, and I can tell you this, you won't win. I don't shake down. I do the shaking. Now get the hell out of here and don't come back."

She shook her head. Her knees felt boneless. She gripped the back of the leather sofa that separated her from Victor and leaned toward him. "You must remember."

"If you leave in the next ten seconds, I might forget you ever cooked up this scam."

His lips were thin and bloodless, his eyes colder than a glacier.

A shiver ran the length of her spine. Her mouth was parched, her tongue numb. "It's not a scam. I'm talking about a rape you committed in Williamsburg. Twenty-six years ago."

She saw a nanosecond of hesitation, then a spark of knowledge flickered in his eyes, but his expression remained unchanged, void of remorse or conscience.

He snorted. "What do you think you know?"

"You viciously raped a seventeen-year-old girl named Suzanne Rochambeau. And you left her lying on the side of a dark road, bruised and bleeding."

His crossed his arms over his chest, jutted out his chin, silently studied her for a few seconds. "Why would you want to concoct that story?"

Her heart thumped hard, surging against her breastbone. Her pulse pounded in her ears, and her stomach twisted into a hard knot. This was the moment when her father would know the damage wrought by his sperm.

Dread, fear, anger, and hatred fought for control of her

body. She wanted to run screaming back out the door, or maybe lunge at him and slap the smirk from his face.

"It's a fact, not a story. I know because Suzanne Rochambeau was my mother. My real name is Faith Rochambeau, and I was born nine months to the day after that night."

Understanding crept into his eyes. He looked her up and down. Then a grin split his face, and he laughed. Chuckles swelled to fill the room. He stuck out a hand, pointed at her, and laughed some more. His face grew red. His mirth expanded into a belly laugh, and he pressed his hands to his bouncing sides.

Her blood froze in her veins. How could he laugh?

"Stop it," she shouted. "You hurt her. You ruined her life. Why is that funny?"

He squeezed his lips into a thin line and squelched the laughter as quickly as it had appeared. Then he glared at her. "You really expect me to believe this crap, that you're my kid? That's the scam?"

"It's true. You're my biological father." She swallowed hard. "Believe me, I don't like it either. I'd much rather never have known about my connection to you than have to spend the rest of my life hating my own genes."

He snorted. "So what if you are my kid? Am I supposed to give you a payoff and you'll go away?"

"I told you what I want. Justice. I want you to admit your guilt."

"I'm not admitting anything. Maybe she was less than enthusiastic, but you can't prove rape." A vein pulsed in his temple. His look was pure malevolence. "I have power and the money to hire an army of lawyers. I'll crush you like a roach, drag your mother's name through so much mud she'll regret the day she cooked this up every minute of the rest of her life. Drop it, bitch. Go home to your pathetic mama."

Faith fought down tremors of panic and pulled out the only ammunition she had left. "Even if you won't admit to rape, I can punish you another way, show the world your true colors. I know you were married in New York before you ever met your rich wife. You're a bigamist. And when your wife finds out, you'll go to jail. At the very least, she'll kick you out. You'll end up broke and out on the street."

His cheeks turned scarlet, and his eyes narrowed to black slits. He leaned toward the end table under the only circle of light in the room, opened a small drawer, reached inside. "We'll see about that."

His hand came back into sight holding a gun.

Visceral fear grabbed her by the throat and strangled her breath. Her stomach did a roller coaster dip downward, flipped up and over, went into a spiraling free-fall. Paralysis seized every muscle until she feared she'd collapse in a heap.

She stared at his finger on the trigger of the ominous weapon, trying to calm her screaming nerves. Was the gun real? Loaded? Maybe it was a toy. Maybe it was just for intimidation.

"You don't have to worry about living with my genes much longer," he said in an icy tone. "Nobody gets away with coming in here and threatening to blow up my life."

Hysterical laughter wanted to burst from the clog in her throat. How could she have been so naïve? Kent had told her Victor had killed. Why didn't she foresee a gun?

He laughed again, this time it sounded more like a snarl. "Yeah, I took what I wanted from your mother, some people would call it rape. She fought like a wildcat, but she was no match for me. I was young and strong and determined, and her resistance made my cock even harder. I got my rocks off good." He touched the black patch over his eye. "She scratched me good. So I'll never forget the bitch." He bared his teeth and chortled. "To be safe and make sure this ends once and for all, I suppose I'll have to find her and take care of her, too. Teach the both of you a lesson."

Tears flooded her eyes. He'd confessed. Really confessed. But all her efforts could be for naught. If he killed her, who would ever know? She stalled. "You can't kill her, she's already dead."

An evil grin tugged at the edge of his mouth. His face was lit from the bottom by the dim lamplight and the shadows around his eye sockets made him look like an effigy of the devil. "Good. That saves me the trouble."

A noise came from outside, like something falling through the bushes. His gaze jerked toward the sound.

Her brain registered his distraction. With no time to spare, she lurched and slammed her arm against the table lamp. As if in slow motion, it took flight then crashed to the floor. The bulb shattered and went out, plunging the room into darkness.

Darkness.

The setting of evil.

The setting of nightmares.

She bit her lip to keep from crying out. This nightmare was real.

She needed to escape. Praying he wouldn't shoot blindly, she bolted in what she hoped was the direction of the foyer. He swore. Over the roar of her breathing, she heard footsteps following behind.

He knew what direction she'd go. He was familiar with the layout of the house; she wasn't. He'd catch her while she fumbled around in the dark, or he'd get to the door first and block her exit.

She needed a different plan.

Reaching out to her side, her fingertips banged the curved, raised surface of a door molding then found open space. The entrance to a dining room or kitchen? She swerved, lurched through the doorway, and flattened herself against a nearby wall.

His heavy breathing was only a few feet away. She held her breath and tried to think. There had to be another exit. Which way to go? She searched her brain for the image of the wall of windows looking out over the beach. Had there been a door to a patio?

No, going backward and searching blindly for a patio door was too big a risk. If she couldn't make it out the front door, her only chance was to somehow get the gun.

Yeah, sure. Good luck with that.

Her heart beat so frantically she was sure he would hear the racket. Her eyes were starting to adjust to the lack of light, and gray shadows appeared scattered in the black. But her deep-seated fear of darkness kept her from welcoming the cover of night.

He'd find her in a minute. No time to delay.

A ceiling fixture flashed on in the foyer and light spilled through the doorway. Her time was up.

He chuckled. "You can't get away. Come on back out. We'll talk. I won't shoot."

Right. He must think she was a moron. Sick with dread, she scanned around her and spotted a dining room sideboard topped with a tall vase of flowers. She tiptoed the three steps to the sideboard, thankful for a plush area rug that reached almost to the wall and muffled any sound. She needed two hands to lift the heavy crystal vase.

Footfalls behind her.

She spun around, caught sight of Victor's leering face, tossed the vase at his head.

He raised his left forearm to shield his face and jumped to the side. "Shit, white fucking wallpaper."

Frozen in fear, Faith stared as the gun barrel swung in her direction.

Chapter Twenty-Three

Victor's shoulder and elbow slammed the wall when he twisted to avoid the vase, and the sudden impact knocked the gun from his hand.

Gaze glued to the weapon, Faith jumped for it. Arm outstretched, she dived toward the floor. Pain ripped through her elbow when she hit, and the skin on her arm burned as her body skidded on the rug. The weapon came to rest several inches from her fingertips.

Before she could fight off the sickening haze of pain and scramble forward to grab the gun, Victor stepped on her arm, his weight crushing her bone. She clenched her jaw and squelched a scream. She twisted closer to him and sunk her teeth into the tender, bare flesh on the top of his foot.

He roared and lifted his other leg to kick.

She tried to roll away, but a sharp pain exploded in the middle of her chest. She gasped and grabbed at his leg to block the momentum of a second blow.

His swing interrupted, he teetered, flailed his arms, and crashed to the floor.

She sprang at him and jammed a knuckle into his good eye.

A fist struck her stomach and took away her breath. A yank on her hair snapped her head back. Her breath whooshed out as his body landed on her, heavy, crushing her ribs.

Tears of frustration stung her eyes. She thought of her mother fighting against her rapist, knowing he was bigger and stronger and would eventually win.

Ignore the pain or you'll die. Faith drew in a fortifying breath, spit in his face, and drove a knee up into his groin.

He recoiled and fell back, breathing hard and fast. His mouth tightened. Before she could sit or scramble away, he recovered, crouched, and lunged like a cobra. Strong hands lifted her half off the floor like a limp sack of rags.

Her skull and shoulder blades slammed against the wall, throbbed as she slid and fell. Her buttocks landed on the rock hard, uncarpeted edge of the floor. She gasped for a lungful of air, her last shred of energy gone and her head spinning.

Her body couldn't endure much more of this punishment. But she couldn't give up.

Blinking to clear her vision, she saw the surreal image of her hand lying limp on the floor, a foot away from the black grip of the gun.

A jolt of adrenaline spurted into her bloodstream. Faith sprang at the weapon, seized it, lifted it. Surprised at the unwieldy weight, she gritted her teeth and summoned the strength to aim it at his chest. "Back off, or you're dead."

He froze where he knelt.

His eye patch had fallen off. She watched him glance from the gun to her face, probably analyzing the possibilities, questioning whether she would shoot.

Breathing heavy, she clutched the gun in two hands and slowly, painfully stood.

He glared at her, said with a sneer, "You think you've got the balls to pull the trigger?"

She grappled with the question. Could she shoot him? If she didn't know, how could he?

She jerked her chin up. "I'm your daughter. Same blood, same genes. Maybe the bad apples don't fall far from the tree. Do you want to find out?"

His expression grew wary, his eyes revealed doubt.

She considered what to do now. She could use the gun in her hand to rid the world of a piece of scum. An eye for an eye. Her mother's chance for a happy life taken by a rapist. His life taken by the product of that rape. Poetic justice.

But murder was wrong.

Chaos and raw emotion caused gridlock in her brain.

He moved his hand a fraction of an inch.

Her finger tensed on the trigger.

"You should shoot," Victor said.

She blinked in confusion.

"But you won't." He laughed, an evil cackle that sent chills down her spine. His expression showed he was enjoying her discomfort. "You won't shoot because your mother probably filled your head with asinine ideas of right and wrong. She thought she was better than me. She was so self-righteous. The goody-two-shoes who cringed when I as much as touched her hand. Did she tell you that the day I raped her, I tried to talk to her in math class, but she ignored me, turned up her nose?"

He curled his lips in disdain, didn't wait for an answer. "I wiped the look that said I was nothing off her face. She begged. But I showed her who was better, who was nothing but a sniveling cunt covered in dirt."

Temper snapped up her spine. "Stop! Don't talk about her like that."

His smile was razor sharp. "You won't shoot, and that means I'll live to kill you. I'm not sure I'll do it right away, though. Maybe I'll make sure you suffer. I'll find everyone you care about, brothers, sister, grandparents, aunts, uncles, cousins. I'll see to it that every one of them has a fatal accident."

Why was he threatening her family and giving her more reason to shoot? Was he hoping to confuse her and create a diversion? Get her so rattled she'd do something stupid?

The cold metal of the trigger tempted her finger. Her breath roared in and out of her lungs. The description of the rape she'd read in her mother's diary echoed in her skull and her revulsion grew. Her body vibrated with outrage.

She couldn't let him live to harm her family. She couldn't let him win. If he wanted her to shoot, then she should oblige. It would be self-defense, and she'd be ridding the world of a predator.

Trying to think logically, she searched her brain for facts about guns. If she missed him with one shot, would she get a chance for a second? An automatic weapon could fire several shots in succession. How could she tell if this one was an automatic?

Maybe he was counting on her to be a neophyte with

guns, be upset, lack focus, and miss. Maybe he knew the characteristics of this gun model, planned to roll or jump away, and anticipated an interval between shots. Maybe he believed the split-second of recoil and confusion immediately after she pulled the trigger would present an opportunity for him to lunge.

Her heart sank. Maybe he was right.

His eyes bored into her, studying her, probably watching for any sign of weakness.

His eyes are the same color as mine. We have the same genes. He's my father.

Words her mom had said often, but had little meaning until now, swirled in her mind. *You have choices in life. You can choose your own destiny.*

Faith weighed the gun in her hand and recognized the difference between justice and revenge. She clearly saw her choice. A knot tightened in her belly. Shooting him would be choosing to let his genes take control. If she opted for vengeance, she'd be choosing to be no better than him.

Was this the ultimate choice Mom had foreseen and been referring to all along?

She blinked. Being like him wasn't what she wanted for her life, violence wasn't how she wanted to win. She couldn't let her evil father seduce her to the dark side.

Victor shifted slightly to his right.

Her antennae went up. "Don't move. Not one muscle."

"My ankle hurts. It might be broken. I just want to check the bone," he said with a plea in his voice.

If he's in pain, suffering...

She shook off the urge to feel sympathy. He was her father in DNA only. Her intuition told her he was hatching some plot, playing on her mercy to try some kind of trick.

Pulling out her last shreds of bravado, she shook her head and said, "Dead men don't have to concern themselves with broken bones. Lie down flat on the floor, real slow. Get on your stomach, arms up, fingers linked behind your head."

He glared at her with those eyes so similar to her own. They held hatred and evil and the worst of the human spectrum.

In that instant, she knew their resemblance to hers ended at the color. Everything behind them was foreign. She was the person she chose to be. She'd been conceived during an act of violence and pain, but those things didn't define her.

Clenching her teeth, holding her breath, trying to ignore the throbbing bruises on her arms and chest, she counted the seconds until he followed her command and laid flat on the floor.

What now?

She remembered her only ammunition.

"Hear this," she said, hoping her voice sounded steady. "Don't even think of coming after me or any of my family. I still know your secret about your marriage."

"Dead women tell no tales."

"Killing me won't stop the truth from getting out," she said. "I'm a computer geek. Every shred of information I know about you is stored in a data warehouse online. If I don't access my account every forty-eight hours, the files automatically get forwarded to the police."

Inching toward the doorway, she clutched the grip of the heavy gun tighter and hoped he couldn't see her hands trembling. He remained still, watching like a hungry vulture that expected an opportunity to swoop in and attack.

She backed from the room praying her counter-threat would buy her time to—what? Escape, get to the police, get home with the recording? She pushed away the problem. She'd worry about what was next after she got away.

The instant the dining room wall blocked him from her line of sight, she pivoted and dashed through the foyer. She heard scuffling and pictured him getting to his feet. She yanked the front door open, and with adrenaline holding her upright and together, ran toward the road as fast as her weary legs would flee.

She spotted a circle of bushes and bordering flowers a few yards from the door and tossed away the cumbersome gun. Sprinting toward the end of the driveway, new fear twisting in her gut at the thought that Victor might chase after her, she skirted around a large shrub by a streetlight and burst out onto the road.

She collided with a gray-haired man, almost tripping over his big black poodle.

Her heart pounded frantically. Grabbing the man's arm to keep her balance, she leaned back around the shrub and glanced toward the house. Light from the foyer spilled out the front doorway. Victor was nowhere in sight.

"Sorry," she stammered, releasing the man and jumping away. "Are you okay?"

He looked her up and down closely as if deciding whether she was dangerous. "Yes, I think so."

Not sure what she would have done if he had been hurt and needed help, she bolted for her rental car. Four seconds to unlock the door, three seconds to get the key in the ignition. The engine roared to life. The rear tires spun and then screamed against the pavement as she cranked the steering wheel over hard, stomped on the accelerator, executed a U-turn that squashed a long strip a manicured grass, and sped away.

Just before the first turn in the road, she glanced in her rearview mirror. No sign of Victor.

She caught sight of her face and understood why the dog-walking man had stared. Even to her own eyes, she looked like a wild woman.

Chapter Twenty-Four

Disgusted at his lack of stealth, and wondering about the strange noises that had come from inside the house, Kent brushed the mulch, twigs, and dry grass off his arm and side. The debris stuck to his sweat-soaked shirt like iron-filings to a magnet. He stretched the arm he'd landed on when he'd fallen off the lawn chair in and out a few times, checking for sprains or bruised muscles as he worked his way back to the cover in the front yard. He moved slowly, watching for tree roots, toads, and snakes. A thin moon had risen, but its meager light was stolen by tree shadows and scudding clouds.

As he approached the corner of the house, he heard the pounding of footfalls on asphalt over the rumble of the surf. He caught a glimpse of Josie dashing toward the street then turning and disappearing at the end of the driveway. He guessed the loud voices he'd heard had been an argument and now she was making a hasty retreat.

He scanned the yard for Victor. The front door stood

open, but no one was in sight.

Determined to talk to Josie and find out what was going on, Kent sprinted across the yard. He took a sharp left, vaulted over a hedge, and cut through the adjoining yard, hoping to intercept her before she reached her car. Too late. He heard the sound of an over-revved engine just as he burst from the shrubbery. Down the street, taillights flashed on as her rental car sped away.

He needed answers. Now. He jogged to his own car, fired up the engine, slammed the transmission into gear, made a K-turn in the narrow strip of blacktop, and raced to catch up. In his present frame of mind, he didn't care if he had to cut in front of her and force her to pull over or collide.

The maze of residential streets wound back toward the main road. The Porsche's engine roared and the tack needle jumped to above six thousand rpm. He clutched the steering wheel like a NASCAR driver and asked for more power. The taillights on Josie's car grew larger as he slowly closed the gap. He lost sight of her car on the blind side of a sharp curve.

Reaching the next straightaway, he saw three cars spaced out in front of him. In the darkness, each set of taillights looked the same. He slammed a fist against the steering wheel. *Shit!*

The first car passed under a streetlight at an intersection. He strained to see if it was blue. Damn, it was the right size and shape, but too far ahead for him to be sure of the color. He snorted in disgust.

The second was a possibility. Definitely not the third.

The first car turned right, the second left. He approached the intersection, downshifted, had to choose. *She'll probably go in the direction of town. Left.*

Screeching around the corner on two wheels, he stomped on the Carrera's accelerator. He shot forward and gained fifty yards on the taillights.

The car passed under another streetlight. It was green.

He swore, sighed, and pulled to the side of the road while he reviewed his options. Go home and try to forget he'd ever met and fallen in love with Josie? Turn around, go back, and try to get the truth out of Victor? Drive to Josie's apartment and hope she was speeding home?

He seemed to have only one choice.

· · ·

Faith clutched the steering wheel for support and checked her rear view mirror. The car she'd suspected of chasing her was nowhere in sight.

She huffed out a sigh of relief, let up on the gas pedal, and reduced her speed to the posted limit. If she got pulled over for speeding, Victor might catch up to her.

Icy sweat trickled down the side of her face. Her extremities ached. She'd lost him for now, but was he gone for good? Did he know where she lived? Did she dare go back to her apartment? Maybe he had another gun. Until she boarded her plane tomorrow, she could still be in danger.

Her brain seemed to have a blown fuse. She raked her fingers through her hair, frantically trying to think past the physical pain throbbing through her body, make sense of the situation, and figure out what to do.

Over the roar of her pounding pulse, a little voice kept shouting: *Stay away from the apartment, at least for a while.*

If he checks and you're not there, he'll leave.

She spotted a well-lit, movie theater parking lot. Maybe the safest thing to do was to lay low for the rest of the night. She braked, drove in, and parked in the middle of the gathering crowd. The theater would be packed until at least midnight. If the lot started to empty, she'd find someplace else to hide in the denser middle of the city.

After dousing the car lights, she locked all the doors. Wanting to be ready if she needed to make a hasty escape, she left the key in the ignition. Nerves taut, she scanned the people walking toward the theater entrance and hoped Victor wasn't lurking in the crowd searching for her face.

The evening was warm and, with the windows shut tight, the inside of the car should have been stifling, but her teeth chattered and her fingers felt like icicles. She pictured black bruises swelling on her arms and legs. A dull, steady ache grew toward epic proportions inside her head. Tears of fear and confusion stung her eyes. Swallowing back an urge to sob, she slid low in the seat and wrapped her arms tightly across her chest.

Her breasts pressed on the corners of the recorder, and she remembered she hadn't turned it off. Working his fingers inside her jacket and bra, she felt for the little switch. Her fingernail caught on a jagged edge of plastic.

The recorder had been damaged in the scuffle with Victor.

Panic spurted into her blood. Was the recording destroyed or intact? She'd failed at everything she'd done so far. Without a recording she had nothing.

She considered playing it back to reassure herself that it was okay. No, the car was dimly lit and cramped. She could do more damage if she bumped or tugged on the recorder removing it from her bra.

Her gaze went to the theater entrance. She could buy a ticket and go into the ladies room, but she'd have to leave the safety of the car.

She reran the events of the last hour through her mind and shivered at the thought of listening to Victor's voice again.

No, she wouldn't listen now. Not yet.

She found the little switch, flicked it to Off, and said a silent prayer.

A group of boisterous teenagers walked past her car. One looked directly at her and met her eyes. After his gaze flicked away, she felt inconsequential and alone. She told herself that sometimes being ignored was good.

· · ·

Kent parked outside Josie's apartment and waited for almost two hours, studying every car, watching every person who went into her building. No sign of her.

He drummed his fingers on his steering wheel then punched his fist into his other palm. Unable to bear sitting helplessly any longer, he got out of his car, slammed the door, and stomped around the block, checking again for any sign of the blue rental car. Nada. He went to the lobby and buzzed her apartment. No answer. Ready to admit defeat and go home, he called her cell again. No answer. Voicemail. He tried to leave another message, but her mailbox was full.

His stomach was a mass of tangled nerves. What the hell was going on and why hadn't she come home?

He waited for another hour before his phone rang.

Suddenly filled with hope, he scrambled to pull it from his pocket.

"Josie, is that you?"

"It's me Kent, Jack."

His heart sank. "Oh."

"Hey, man, you need to get over to St. Mary's Hospital in a hurry."

A chill raced down his spine at Jack's tone of voice. Was Josie hurt? He shook off the idea. No, Jack wouldn't be calling about Josie.

"Is it my mother?"

"It's Victor. He's been shot, and they don't expect him to pull through."

"Victor? Shot?" An image of Josie running away from the beach house and speeding off in her rental car flashed through his mind. He forced it away. *No, it couldn't be.* "When? Who shot him? How did you hear?"

"The police called the landline at your house. You must have had the answering machine set on Forward, because the call came to me. I'll fill you in at the hospital. Your Mom's on her way there too."

· · ·

The street was quiet and completely deserted when Faith drove slowly by her apartment building. She searched the parked cars for any sign of Victor. Nothing looked suspicious. To be extra careful, she passed up a parking spot on the corner and chose one on a side street a block away. Luckily, she only had to retrieve the couple suitcases packed with Josie's clothes, and they had wheels.

She walked in the shadows, watching for anyone moving toward her as she hustled down the street. She rushed into the lobby of her building and took the elevator up to her floor. Still no one around. Quickly unlocking her door, she heard the elevator ding and the doors start to open behind her just as she slipped inside.

Her suitcases stood packed and waiting. Rushing to the dishwasher, she slipped the package with her mother's diary, her cash, and her boarding pass out of their hiding place and stuffed them into her purse. Finding a bottle of aspirin, she washed two down, hoping they'd dull some of her muscle pain. Then she ran through a mental checklist as she made a last scan of the apartment for anything important. The Salvation Army would come tomorrow to pick up her furniture. Her mail would be forwarded. Her library books had been returned. Her bank account was closed.

She stood in silence for a minute, then opened the curtains and walked out onto her tiny balcony. She hugged her arms around her middle and took one last look at the panoramic view of the Intracoastal Waterway. A lone sailboat navigated between the blinking red and green channel lights and headed for the inlet. An overwhelming sense of loss and grief formed a steel strap around her chest, tightening until her ribs threatened to snap.

Her life here was at an end, except for memories of Kent.

Her throat clogged with the effort not to dissolve into tears. How ironic that she'd met the man who could have made her life complete, the man she knew she'd love forever, as a result of her quest to bring down her father. How ironic that she'd lost the man who'd brought light into her life because she hadn't seen the soul-sucking darkness of that same quest. How ironic that her quest for *right* had turned out so *wrong*.

How sad that happy endings only happened in fairy tales.

She clenched her teeth, turned away from view, and unbuttoned her jacket, pondering where to put the recorder. Would airport scanners damage it? Should she put it in carry-on or checked luggage?

A *knock, knock, knock* on her door. Her heart slammed against her ribcage in panic. Her breath caught. Her fingers froze on the top button of her blouse.

Another knock. Harder. "Josie Ashland. Open up. West Palm Beach Police."

. . .

The sky had lightened to gray by the time Kent rushed in through the emergency room entrance and scanned the waiting room for his mother. She stood at the far end near a nurses' desk, talking with a tall man in a white lab coat. She was dressed impeccably in a mint green Dior suit and had her hair swept into a perfect chignon. He noticed she looked calm, almost serene, as he jogged to her side. He hadn't expected a quivering mass of nerves or a public display of overwrought emotion. Melodrama wasn't part of her make-up, but he felt a wave of relief seeing with his own eyes that she was coping.

He gathered her in his arms, hugged her tightly, and kissed her temple. "How are you doing? Are you okay?"

She pulled back slightly, brushed an errant lock of hair from his forehead, and gave him a brave, reassuring smile. "I'm fine, dear. Thank you for coming." Then she turned and said to her companion, "Doctor, this is my son, Kent."

The man stuck out his hand. His face centered around a ski-jump nose and competent eyes. "I'm Doctor Brisben. I was just explaining to your mother that your father's condition is touch-and-go. The bullet entered on an angle and punctured his lung. Our best guess is it ricocheted off a rib, and then went back and hit his heart. He's lost a lot of blood, but we're doing our best to get him stabilized. As soon as possible, we'll be taking him up to the OR for surgery."

"When and where did all this happen?" Kent asked.

"He was brought in by ambulance almost two hours ago. I'll let the police and your mother explain the details. Right now, I need to get back to my patients."

"Of course, Doctor," Emmeline said in the same voice she'd use if she were entertaining friends at a luncheon. "Don't let us detain you. We'll be right here in the waiting room if there's any news."

The doctor nodded and hustled away.

Kent turned back and studied his mother's face. "What in the hell happened?"

Her voice was level, calm. She could have been a CNBC news anchor reading from a script. "According to the police officer who told me the news, a neighbor was out jogging near the beach house and heard a noise like a shot. From what I understand, he shrugged it off as nothing at first, just finished his run and went home. But he couldn't get it out of his mind and called the police to report it a couple hours later. They sent a cruiser out to investigate and found Victor lying on the floor in the foyer."

"When was he shot?"

"I'm not exactly sure."

Kent's mind grabbed at facts as he digested the information. He pictured the open front door and Josie running, but he was outside the house. He would have heard a shot.

It couldn't have been her.

But who else had the opportunity? He hadn't seen anyone else around. Who hated Victor enough to want him dead?

Me. But that doesn't count.

His mother slipped her arm through his. "Would you like coffee, dear? There are machines of course, but you know how bitter that stuff usually is. If it's open, we'd be best going to the cafeteria."

Her nonchalance brought him up short. Was her politeness and lack of distress a mask for panic, or did Victor's condition leave her cold? Did she hate Victor as much as he did? Enough to go to the beach house and shoot him?

The hairs on his nape prickled. Dread seeped into the marrow of his bones. He wouldn't blame her after how deeply she must have been hurt by Victor's cheating. Even a normally nonviolent person had a breaking point.

Kent took both her hands in his, captured her eyes, kept his voice low. "Do you know anything about who did this?"

A man walked up beside them and flashed a badge. "Mrs. Telemann? Mr. Kent Telemann?"

Kent stiffened and slipped a protective arm around his mother. "Yes."

"I'm Detective Rodriguez, West Palm Beach Police. May I speak with you for a few minutes?"

His blood ran cold. Was the wronged wife the obvious suspect? Trying to keep his imagination under control, he answered, "Of course, Detective. My mother and I will do everything possible to help you catch Victor's attacker."

"We already have a suspect. That's where you can help. I have a few questions."

They had another suspect. Relief gushed into his bloodstream. "Go ahead…"

"Do you know a Faith Rochambeau? She also goes by Josie Ashland."

Fear and shock stabbed his gut. His stomach dropped to his knees. "Josie?"

"You know her then?"

He swallowed and tried to think, blinked and decided a denial would be pointless. "Yes, she worked for our company, Emmeline's. But you must be mistaken, she couldn't have done this."

"Why do you say that?"

An alarm went off inside his head and a little voice told him to step carefully. Right now, he would be smartest not to bring up their relationship or mention he'd been at the beach house earlier. He wanted to help clear Josie if she was innocent, but not by throwing the investigation in a new direction and pointing a finger at his own mother.

His thoughts twisted into a knot. Torn between protecting the cherished woman who'd borne and raised him and defending the woman he'd started to love, he called on all his negotiating skills, schooled his face, and offered an impersonal answer. "She's just not the type. She's quiet and was a good worker."

He started to say she was honest and trustworthy, but then the second name the detective mentioned registered, and his brain was bombarded with memories of all her lies. She wasn't honest.

A seed of stomach-rolling nausea germinated and grew. Maybe she *was* the type to go back after an argument and shoot Victor. Did he really know anything about her?

Pulling in a deep breath, he clung to an image of Josie, joy and innocence lighting her face, her hair blowing freely in the wind. He kept his voice poker neutral and tried to extract a few answers of his own. "What did you mean when you said she *goes by* Josie Ashland?"

"We suspect it's a stolen identity. Her real name is Faith Rochambeau."

"How do you know that?"

"I can't divulge that information, sir. All I can say is we've had her under surveillance for a while in connection with another crime."

His world spun into a dizzying whirlpool. Josie? Involved in a crime? Had Victor actually been right about her corporate spying? Or had perpetrating a crime together been her connection to Victor?

The detective turned. "I'm sorry to have to bring this up now Mrs. Telemann, but I need to know if your husband was having an affair with Miss Rochambeau."

Her chin rose a fraction of an inch, so subtly a stranger probably wouldn't notice. But to Kent, the tiny defensive motion revealed the extent of the pain she kept hidden inside and exacerbated his fears concerning her innocence. "Not that I know of."

"Do you know why he was at that house tonight?"

"The beach house is corporate owned. He often entertains business associates there. But, no, I don't know why in particular he went there tonight."

The detective pulled a paper enclosed in a plastic bag

from his inside jacket pocket. "Do you know when or from who your husband got this note?"

The bag was labeled *Evidence*. A date, location, and case number were scrawled in black marker. Kent leaned over to see around the markings and read the note.

Be at your beach house at seven tonight, alone.

I know your secret, and I'm prepared to tell the world.

No signature. The handwriting was neat. Feminine.

Emmeline shook her head and frowned. "No. I've never seen it before. Was this woman trying to blackmail Victor, do you think?"

"That's one theory, ma'am. Do you know what secret he might have wanted to hide?"

"Victor probably has secrets," she said. "But I doubt there was anything he'd pay to keep hidden." Kent marveled at the polite smile on his mother's lips and the cool composure in her voice.

"Does your husband own a gun?"

"Not that I'm aware of."

"What about you, sir? Know of any dark secrets or anything about a gun?"

"I'm afraid I can't help you with any secrets. I know he owned a gun in the past. A small caliber pistol, but I haven't seen it for about eighteen years." Kent needed to think, needed to absorb what he'd heard, and he needed time to talk to his mother alone. "If you'll excuse us, Detective, my mother is upset and I'd like to get her some coffee."

"Sure. I can hold off with some of my other questions. I'll catch up with you later."

Chapter Twenty-Five

Faith clutched her hands together tightly to stop them from shaking.

The detective glared at her across the interrogation room table. "How do you know Victor Telemann?"

"I worked for his company, Emmeline's."

"In what capacity?"

She wet her lips and shifted on the hard chair. "I was a website developer."

"That was your cover, you mean. What were you really doing there?"

Tears flooded her eyes. Her brain seemed unable to function. Should she tell them about her plan to get Victor to confess? She wished she knew why she was here. "I told you. I was a website developer."

"Why were you wearing a wire when you were picked up?"

Her mind bounced wildly from option to option. Keep

lying, tell the truth. Keep lying, tell the truth. Fear stole her voice. Her conscience screamed inside her head, ordering her to explain. Her tongue was dry and numb.

The door clicked and opened. She blinked as another man stepped inside the ugly, cell-like room. Ronnie? What had he done that he was here too?

A tight muscle jerked in his jaw. His eyes, filled with something hard and unfriendly, settled on her. She shivered, suddenly wary.

He slapped his palms onto the tabletop and leaned across it toward her, closing the gap. "Did you shoot Victor tonight?"

She gasped. "Shoot Victor? What do you mean? Has Victor been shot? My God, Ronnie, what's going on?"

Averting her eyes and biting her lip, she fought off pinpricks of guilt. Her mind's eye struggled to shove back an image of Victor's gun in her hand. Her finger had been on the trigger. She'd aimed at his chest. She'd wanted revenge.

They think I pulled the trigger.

She swallowed the lump of panic blocking her throat and frowned. They couldn't think she'd shot him. Victor had been fine when she left.

Schooling her face to hide her building panic, she looked at her friend and tried to make sense of what was happening. "I don't understand, Ronnie. Why are you here?"

He slipped a black, credit-card-sized folder from his pocket and flipped it open to reveal a silver and black badge.

She read the words on the ID card. *Detective Ronald Rickowski. West Palm Beach Police.* Her gaze shot back to his face. He was a police officer and had a different name? Why had he been working at Emmeline's?

Her brain supplied answers. Undercover. Investigating Victor or someone else. He'd pumped her for information. He'd only been pretending to be gay. He'd known about her hacking.

"Tell us what happened, Josie. Or should I say Faith? Come clean and it will go easier on you."

Faith? He knew her name. A massive, cold lump settled in her stomach. How?

He gave her a knowing look and went on as if she spoken the question aloud. "We ran your fingerprints. I've had you under surveillance since a couple days after you showed up at Emmeline's. You're not a very good liar."

"Josie doesn't have anything to do with this."

"We'll decide that. The Virginia State Police are checking her out."

Fear snaked through her bloodstream, and her chin quivered. What if they hassled Josie and caused her to go into early labor? What if the stress harmed her babies? "Please, don't bother her. She's pregnant with twins. She's supposed to rest."

"Why did you steal her identity?"

"I didn't steal it. She's my cousin. She told me I could pretend to be her. She knew about it all along. Please, keep her out of this."

He gave her a sympathetic sigh and an understanding shrug that oozed with sincerity. Then he pulled out a chair, sat, and leaned back negligently. "If you want to keep your cousin out of this, Faith, you have to start talking. Come on, tell me the whole truth."

Now his tone said I'm-your-good-friend-Ronnie, I'm-on-your-side. Was he playing both the bad cop and the good cop? Trying to confuse her or trick her?

Her heart squeezed and struggled to pump. It didn't matter what tactics he used. She had to make them believe her and leave Josie alone before she did any more damage.

She pulled in a fortifying breath. "I borrowed Josie's identity and came here from Virginia because Victor Telemann is my biological father."

• • •

Kent handed his mother a mug of steaming coffee, set his down on the worn cafeteria table, and sat in the plastic chair across from her.

"Thank you, dear," she said.

He scanned the area around them again, checking for anyone close enough to overhear. The only other couple in this section was at least five yards away.

Satisfied their conversation would stay confidential, he whispered, "Tell me what happened."

She looked at him with questioning eyes. "I told you everything I know."

He sucked in a breath, reached for her hand, squeezed and held it firm. "Mom, I need to know. I won't judge you. I'll help you. I just need a clear picture of where we stand. Did you shoot Victor?"

She closed her eyes. A barely perceivable quiver shook her chin.

His pulse raced, and his mind jumped to an image of this fragile, elegant woman, hands cuffed behind her, being led off to a cruel, dirty jail. His world stood still.

After what seemed like a lifetime, she opened her eyes

and met his gaze. "No, dear. I didn't shoot him. I won't deny having been tempted a few times in the last several years. But I've been too much of a coward to act on the impulse. Maybe all along I've been hoping someone would do it for me." She squeezed his hand tightly, tears sparkled in her eyes. "Then it wasn't you, was it?"

Overwhelmed by a need to comfort her, he jumped up from his chair, dropped to one knee on the floor beside her, and gathered her into his arms. "No, Mom. It wasn't me."

She clung to him, and he could feel her trembling, her heart pounding fearfully against his chest. "Thank God. I didn't believe my little boy, my sweet baby, could do such a thing. But still, we all have rage inside. I was so worried."

He wiped away a tear rolling down her cheek. "I've hated him for how he's treated you, but shooting is too good for him. He needs to suffer humiliation."

She smiled weakly. "What a terrible conversation to be having while a man's in intensive care fighting for his life."

"I'm sure he'd do the same for us."

Her composure slipped back into place. She nodded and straightened her spine. "Who do you think shot him? Do you think someone was trying to blackmail him, like that detective said? Maybe someone threatened to tell me about Melinda Hart."

He let the reference to Melinda slide. The fact that she knew the name of Victor's mistress said volumes by itself. "Your guess is as good as mine. Victor wasn't exactly Mr. Popularity."

"What about this woman, Josie or Faith? What do you know about her?"

He hesitated, decided *what the hell*. "Josie, Faith,

whatever her real name is…we've been dating. I know she didn't shoot Victor, because I followed her to the beach house tonight."

She studied his face as if a message had suddenly appeared on his forehead. "You care about her."

"Yes, but she lied to me. I let anger cloud my thinking and turned my back on her."

Kent thought of Josie—Faith? Now that he knew his mom was innocent, his path was clear. He wouldn't turn his back on Josie again. No matter what else she might have done, he refused to sit idly by and let her be falsely accused.

He stood and planted his fists on his hips. "I have to go to the police station and find out what's going on. Jack is on his way here and will stay with you. Will you be all right?"

"Yes, of course. I'm mostly here out of misplaced loyalty and hypocrisy. I haven't even decided yet whether I want Victor to live or die. You go. Do what you have to do, but please, be careful. Don't get yourself into any trouble."

• • •

Ronnie's hard eyes fixed on Faith. "So you went there to make him pay for his crime, and you had a gun in your hand, but you didn't shoot him? It that what you'd like us to believe?"

"Yes. It's the God's honest truth." She moistened her lips, wishing she sounded less pathetic.

"You fought with him, you hated him, you were angry. You had motive, means, and opportunity." He lifted his hands in a gesture of frustration. "Don't take me for a fool."

"I swear on my grandmother's family bible. He was fine

when I left."

Ronnie shook his head. "He's in intensive care now with your bullet in his lung. If I were you, I'd be praying on your family bible that he doesn't die."

An idea jumped into her brain. Hope sparked. "I have our conversation on the recorder I was wearing. Listen to it. It'll prove everything I'm saying."

He shook his head. "No good. The memory card was cracked and ruined."

She glanced up in alarm. Her chest, her shoulders, her spine, her pelvis, every part of her body collapsed into a hopeless mass of defeated flesh. Victor had admitted the rape, but no one would ever know. He'd never be brought to justice.

He'd go free. If he lived. She'd go to jail if he died.

"Your fingerprints are on the gun he was shot with," Ronnie said with crisp logic. "A man walking his dog saw you running away from the scene. The hairs we found in the dining room are going to give us DNA and place you inside the house. Even if Telemann ends up in a coma and can't point a finger at you, we've got enough to put you away for attempted murder. If he dies, you're facing a charge of murder one."

First degree murder! She could spend the rest of her life in prison. She bit on her bottom lip. Oh God, did Florida have the death penalty?

Cold sweat soaked her body. Her voice shook. "Please, you have to believe me. I never shot him."

Ronnie spread his palms on the table and pushed to his feet. "You're going to be our guest here for a while. Get comfy." He stepped away and knocked twice on the door.

Tears stung her eyes. She felt a visceral punch of fear. Did she get to make a phone call and speak to a lawyer? Or did she have to wait until she was officially arrested or charged with a crime? Defeat pressed heavy on her chest. What did it matter? She'd already answered all their questions and told them her side of the story.

And she had no one she could call for help.

A loud buzz shattered the silence and made her jump. Ronnie pulled open the door, and he and the other detective left. The door clicked shut.

She pictured him disappearing down the long, echo-filled corridor the officers had led her through when they brought her in. Terror gripped her throat at the thought of being in this barren room for hours imagining the worst. Was giving her time to wait and worry part of a plan to coerce a confession?

The chair seat was hard as a slab of granite. The flesh bruised from her battle with Victor felt like it was being smashed between rock and her pelvic bones. She shifted her weight trying to relieve the ache. She wanted to pace, but her legs were too much like Jell-O. The room was ominously quiet and smelled of sweat and urine, and she wondered if prior occupants might have lost bodily control in the grip of raw devastation and fear.

Her gaze went to the big section of glass. Was someone on the other side watching her, waiting for her veneer of bravery to crumble?

The walls seemed to be closing in. She squeezed her eyes shut and refused to look. This was temporary. They'd realize their mistake and release her. Soon. Right this minute, someone was probably on the way to open the lock.

She listened for approaching footsteps. The only sound was the loud ticking of an institutional clock.

The hateful room seemed devoid of oxygen. Her chin trembled as she said a silent prayer. *Please God, let Victor live so he can tell the police the truth.*

A terrifying thought made her open her eyes wide. Her chest tightened. Even if he lived, she still could be in trouble. Victor was evil. If he wanted her out of the way in jail, he might not clear her. He might choose to lie and say she fired the gun.

She rested her elbows on the table and dropped her head into her hands.

Seeing herself functioning as an outgoing, social person and finding acceptance by other people, she'd glimpsed what her life would be like if she stayed Josie. Over the last couple weeks, she'd built a deep yearning to be the woman she'd pretended to be. With Kent's help, she'd found the courage to be that woman for real.

Facing Victor, she'd realized she didn't have to be ashamed of her birth.

The temperature in the room seemed to plunge twenty degrees as she waited for something to happen and listened to the lonely ticking of the clock. All the lessons she'd learned could be for naught, because all she'd gained could swirl away like a cloud of cigar smoke rising above an evil man's head. Heaven help her, her future depended on Victor.

· · ·

Kent's footsteps were loud in the hallway, but as he hurried across the squad room toward the man sitting at the desk in the far corner, they became lost in the noise of ringing phones, scraping chair legs, and the babble of multiple conversations. The detective he'd been directed to see looked vaguely familiar. Had he been at the hospital?

He stuck out his hand. "Detective Rickowski? I'm Kent Telemann. They told me at the desk that you're in charge of the investigation of my stepfather's shooting."

The man glanced up and met his eyes. He completed a perfunctory shake of Kent's hand then indicated a chair. "Have a seat. What can I do for you?"

Kent was sure he knew him. "Have we met?"

The detective's mouth twitched. "I've been undercover at your corporate offices for three months. You may not remember me, but I know you quite well."

An undercover operation at the store? "What were you investigating?"

"I'm not at liberty to divulge that." The man leaned back in his chair and laced his fingers behind his head. "What can I do for you? Have you had any word on your stepfather's condition?"

He placed the face. Ronnie something. Inter-store communications. Efficient. Smart. Damn, the guy must be good at what he did. No one at the offices had suspected a thing.

Kent wiped thoughts of the man's past investigations from his mind and focused on what was important. "He's still in intensive care. I'm here about Josie."

"Miss Rochambeau? What about her?"

"She couldn't have shot Victor." He set his jaw. "I saw her go into and come out of the beach house earlier tonight. I was there the whole time and would have heard a shot. There wasn't any."

The detective sat forward, pinched the bridge of his nose, and shook his head slowly. "We're aware of your relationship with the suspect. I understand why you might give false testimony on her behalf, but it's not going to work. We have all the evidence we need to get a conviction. If your stepfather dies, the charge against her will be first degree murder. It won't do any good for you to perjure yourself."

"I'm telling you the truth. I followed her from her apartment because I wanted to talk. When she went to the beach house, I was curious why she'd be meeting Victor. I saw her go in then leave a few minutes later. I never heard a gunshot."

"You'll have to do better than that." The detective gave a tired sigh. "If you don't mind, I'm busy, and you're wasting my time."

"I'm not making this up."

"Are you confessing to being an accomplice?"

"No." Kent's frustration surged, and he banged his fist on the desktop. "Damn it. Will you listen? Neither of us did anything to Victor."

"Please go, Mr. Telemann." He turned away, then swiveled his head back and said with a cold smile. "But in case we find evidence you were there, don't leave town."

Kent stood. They had to believe him. He had to do something.

Call Sarah. She's a defense lawyer.

"I'm going, but I'll be back with the best attorney in town. Your case won't hold up. Too many other people hated Victor. Have you looked at his mistress? He might have been getting ready to dump her."

The detective gave him a hostile glare. "I can assure you

we're conducting a very thorough investigation."

Ken took two steps away from the desk. Maybe Melinda Hart had shot Victor. *He treated her as bad or worse than Mom. She said she had a plan to get away from him.*

A series of rapid-fire thoughts and images slammed into his brain. A jolt of adrenaline flooded his veins. There might be proof.

Fear slithered down his spine. Should he say anything? If he did, he could clear Josie once and for all. But what if Josie was guilty? He'd seal her fate, put her in jail for life.

His gut instinct said she was innocent and worthy of his trust. He spun back around. "One more thing, detective. Have you looked at the videos?"

Chapter Twenty-Six

"You've been cleared, and you're free to go," Ronnie said.

Faith said a silent prayer of thanks. "Then you believe my story?"

"Telemann had surveillance cameras hidden in every room so he could spy on his mistress," Ronnie said. "They recorded audio and video of last night's whole sequence of events. Your argument with him, his threats, the works."

Faith listened, too stunned to breathe. The noise and bustle around his desk was a dull hum in her mind as she prayed this discovery meant her nightmare was over and Victor could be charged with rape.

"But who shot Victor?"

"Your private investigator, Zurich."

"Steve? But why?"

"He thought Telemann would be at the beach house alone. He went there to blackmail him with the bigamy information. Zurich must have seen you throw away the gun.

Then as soon as the coast was clear, he approached the house and retrieved the weapon with your prints on it."

She pictured how outraged Victor had been when she'd threatened him and imagined his response to Steve's arrival.

Ronnie was still talking. "There was a shootout, and he hit Telemann. But Zurich took one to the abdomen. He was hurt bad, but somehow managed to get away from the house. From the size of the blood trail we found leading down the beach, I'm not sure how he made it to his car before he bled out."

"He's dead?" She envisioned Steve Zurich alive and vibrant, sitting in his office.

"His body's in the morgue. Lucky for us, his wife wants revenge. The DA gave her immunity on the accessory charges she would have faced and, in exchange, she's spilling everything she knows, naming the names of store managers and employees who were involved in Telemann's schemes and showing us where the evidence is hidden."

"His wife? I didn't know he was married."

"Three days ago he tied the knot with Melinda Hart."

Her mouth dropped open. "Melinda...? He married Victor's mistress?"

"None other. She had a big cache of jewelry and gifts from various boyfriends. They figured her stash, added to a million-dollar payoff from blackmailing Telemann, would give them a comfortable nest egg. When Telemann called and told her to make herself scarce last night, she saw the perfect opportunity for Zurich to approach him. They were packed and ready to fly the coop. When we searched his place, we found a receipt for two first class tickets on tomorrow's red-eye to Barcelona."

Faith remembered Melinda and Steve kissing passionately on the street in front of his office. Her heart twisted in sympathy for the misguided couple. How sad that a crime Victor committed years ago would bring the high school sweethearts back together, rekindle their romance, then tragically tear them apart.

She sighed. "Assuming Victor lives, what happens now?"

"Latest word is he's going to pull through. So we'll charge him with second degree murder. If he gets a good lawyer, the charge might not stick. He shot first, but he'll claim he was defending himself against Zurich."

"You mean he'll go free?"

Ronnie shook his head. "Far from it. A jury may let him walk on the second-degree murder charge, but he won't beat the rest. Thanks to the info Ms. Hart has given us, the DA should be able to build a strong case and charge him with at least a dozen counts of money laundering and racketeering."

"Did the jewelry Melinda bought and returned have something to do with that?"

He eyed her with curiosity, obviously surprised she knew some of the details. "Yeah. The stuff was paid for with drug money, in small denominations. The dirty money got deposited in a bank with the rest of the store's receipts. When the item was returned, the refund was in larger denomination bills that could be spent without suspicion."

"Why is he being charged with racketeering?"

"The same kind of thing has been happening at Emmeline's stores across the country for years. All told, we're talking about the laundering of hundreds of millions of dollars."

"You mean Melinda Hart was only one of the people buying and returning?"

"Exactly. We're rounding up everyone she named and hoping the dominos start to fall. If we can get a couple store managers to make deals and turn state's evidence, we may snag several dozen conspirators in our net."

She stared into near space, letting Ronnie's words sink in. "So Victor will go to jail for those crimes?"

"Right. Plus we have him on video pulling a gun on you, so we can add a count of attempted murder. And if by some slim chance he beats all those charges, bigamy is a slam dunk."

A slurry of questions churned in her brain. "How long will he get?"

"I'd guess a minimum of twenty-five to thirty years. And if Virginia decides to extradite him and try him for felony rape, he could be away for the rest of his life."

Faith caught her bottom lip between her teeth. A bewildering rush of emotions tangled in her chest. Joy because justice would be done, and Victor would pay for everything he'd done. Regret because innocent people like Kent and his mother were bound to suffer.

Ronnie interrupted her musings. "Anyhow, you're free to go. Sorry for the misunderstanding."

She blinked, wondering how much he knew about her activities at Emmeline's. Fear told her to keep her secrets and walk away. Her conscience screamed *no, Victor couldn't escape his past crimes and neither can you.*

Guilt grabbed her by the throat and forced her to say, "I broke into Victor's office and hacked his email account. Don't you need to arrest me for that?"

He shook his head. "Emmeline's has decided not to press charges. We have no evidence or report of a break-in and are too busy chasing real criminals to waste time investigating incidents that we don't even know occurred."

She swallowed and gave him a weak smile. "Thank you."

"It wasn't my decision. I just gave my recommendation. But I figured it was the least I could do for a friend."

"I still can't get used to the idea you're a detective."

He laughed. "My fiancée still isn't used to the idea I'm back on regular duty and we can have a normal life."

"Was she the one you wanted the pendant for?"

He nodded. "I couldn't break my cover to deliver it in person, but I sent it for her birthday."

"Josie was the one who made it."

"You can tell your cousin Sandi loves it." He stuck out his hand. "Keep in touch, Faith. Let me know if your address changes after you get back to Virginia. The prosecuting attorney may need you to testify somewhere along the line."

. . .

Faith stepped from the police headquarters building and squinted into the bright afternoon sunlight. The welcome ninety-degree heat thawed her chilled bones, and she started down the cement steps. She breathed deeply. The effort hurt her bruised chest, but she relished the refreshing air of freedom.

Freedom.

She stopped on a landing, raised her face to the sun, and celebrated more than the freedom from suspicion. This afternoon, she was truly free. Free from her past insecurities and self-doubts. Free from questions about whom Faith Rochambeau really was. Since leaving home, she'd discovered new strengths. By facing the world as someone else, she'd grown into the person she'd always wanted to be.

Pain welled inside. She'd wished for a happier ending in some respects, but no matter what happened from this day forward, she'd always be thankful for meeting Kent and discovering what it felt like to be in love.

She raised her chin and resumed walking. She'd missed her morning flight home. Should she call the airline and make a new reservation?

First things first. She pulled out her phone and turned it on. Her mailbox was full of messages, but she ignored them and called Josie. When she heard the familiar voice say, "Faith! Are you okay?" tears rushed to her eyes.

"I'm fine. I just walked out of the police station. Free."

"I was so worried."

Faith's chin quivered. "What about you and the babies? Are you okay? I was afraid the stress of being questioned about our identity swap would bring on premature labor."

"I'm not in labor. Yet. I'm waiting for you to come home and be here when the girls are born."

"The girls?"

"Yes. Bridget and Bonnie. The doctor says they'll be making an appearance any day now."

Tears of happiness rolled down Faith's cheeks and salted the corner of her mouth. "I'll get the next available flight and be there as fast as I can."

"Hurry. Cal's unit is on a secret mission somewhere in Afghanistan, and there's no hope he'll get leave. My Mom's got the flu and can't be anywhere near me or the babies. Please come quick. I need your hand to squeeze, now more than ever."

Faith thought of two infants starting life without their father. He might not be in the delivery room, but at least they'd have the promise of knowing him in the future. And when they did meet him, they could be proud. No lies necessary. Their father was a real hero.

"Hang in there. I'm on my way."

• • •

Kent stepped from Emmeline's corporate jet at the Williamsburg airport and told the crew, "Take the rest of the day off and see the sights. Check with Jack in the morning."

Jack grabbed their bags, stuffed them in the trunk of the rental car, then plopped behind the wheel. "I had the rep program the GPS to get us to the hospital. The guy from the florist shop will meet you in the lobby."

Twenty minutes later, Kent jumped from the car in front of Mercy General Hospital. He spotted the florist's deliveryman and took possession of the two huge bouquets. On the third floor, he followed the numbers to room 319.

Halfway down the corridor, he paused for a second and watched a nurse wheel a bassinet back toward the nursery. The tiny infant in the blue cap was tucked in tightly and blissfully asleep, but the sight of his innocent face stirred strange emotions in Kent's chest. He thought of his mother's desire for grandchildren, and his lips curved into a smile.

He heard feminine laughter coming from room 319 and stepped into the doorway. All sounds stopped abruptly.

She was sitting by the bed, staring wide-eyed. Her mouth gaped open. His pulse rate doubled as he made a quick scan. Blonde hair. Brown eyes. A luscious raspberry dress that clung to her breasts and accentuated her perfect curves.

He looked back to her face. Although he wouldn't have thought it possible, she was even more beautiful as a blonde with gold-flecked brown eyes.

She blinked and drew in a shaky breath. Joy flickered in her gaze and exhilaration flooded his chest.

The woman in the bed said, "Hi. Something tells me I should know you."

Kent shifted his gaze to her hair, her eyes, her face. The resemblance was striking. She could only be Josie. The real Josie.

"Hello. I'm Kent Telemann. And you must be the proud mother." He walked to her bedside and held out one of the bouquets. "Congratulations."

"They're gorgeous, Kent. Thank you."

Faith's voice was breathy and uncertain. "Kent? Why? What are you doing here?"

He turned to her and held out the other bouquet. "I came to meet the real Josie Ashland, and of course, see you."

• • •

She couldn't believe her eyes. Kent was here? She must be hallucinating.

The scent of his cologne filled her nostrils and was sweeter than any flowers. Her pulse sped and tripped. Her heart told her *yes*, this was him in the flesh.

Was there really a chance for a love rooted in deception on both their parts?

She took the flowers. Maybe she was jumping to a false conclusion. Maybe he didn't know the truth. The frenzy of her homecoming, Josie's labor, and the twins' birth had given her an excuse. She'd put off writing the email to explain and say good-bye.

She sucked in a deep breath. "Did the police tell you what happened?"

"Detective Rickowski told me what was on the surveillance videos and about your relationship to Victor. Plus I read the article and your interview with Leeza St. James."

Her mind flew back to the night she'd discovered his last name. She'd wanted nothing to do with him because he'd lived in the same house with Victor. But she had Victor's blood in her veins. Their relationship was even closer and could never be changed. Did Kent think less of her because of it? Her mind swirled in confusion. If he knew she was Victor's biological daughter, why had he come to Virginia?

She swallowed. "I'm sorry for all this has done to your family and business."

"Victor is the one to blame."

"If I hadn't dug into the past, none of his crimes would be front page news."

"And he'd still be getting away with everything he's done."

Her chin quivered. "I'm sorry I lied to you."

"I understand why you felt it was necessary, and I admire your courage for coming after Victor."

She thought of her mother, Kent's mother, Kent, Melinda Hart, and Steve Zurich. Victor had damaged so many lives. When would it all stop? "Have they set a date for his trial?"

"It'll be months away, but his lawyers are trying to plea bargain. He's going to do a lot of years, but he wants to trade information for leniency and do them in medium security." He sighed and clouds of helplessness floated in his eyes. "I don't want to see him get off easy, but in a way, I hope they're successful. A lengthy trial will only keep the media agitated and cause my mother more embarrassment."

"How is she taking all this?"

His expression softened. "Like a trooper. She's seen a lawyer about dissolving their marriage."

"Has Emmeline's been too badly damaged? I hate to think of a lot of innocent employees losing their jobs. They're good people with lives and families."

"Business is off, but less than I expected. No one's been laid off and no one will be. I can cover payroll and operating expenses until we go back to making a profit. I've taken over as CEO and started a public relations campaign to rebuild our image."

A picture of cigar smoke swirling around the head of the devil flickered in her brain. "How can you stomach sitting at Victor's desk in that disgusting office?"

"I'm not. We're converting the penthouse to a café where customers can look out over the city as they have brunch."

Josie cleared her throat. "Enough of this chit-chat. Get to the good part. Come on, Kent. Tell us why you're really here."

Kent threw back his head and laughed. The marvelous sound lit a bonfire in Faith's chest.

"Good idea." He turned back to her and captured her eyes. Then he got down on one knee and took her hand.

"Marry me, Faith. I love you. I don't care if your eyes are blue, brown, or green. I don't care if your hair is black, brown, or blonde. I want the wonderful person you are inside to be my wife, share my life, make my world complete."

Tears of joy flooded her eyes. Her dream was coming

true.

Images of their future flashed in her mind. Her chin quivered with one uncomfortable thought: if she married Kent, her last name would be Telemann and she'd constantly be reminded of Victor.

Kent lifted her hand to his lips and lightly kissed her fingers. "Ever since my mother married Victor and he adopted me, I've wanted to legally change my last name back to Morris. So I thought we might assume new identities together. I'll become Kent Morris again, and you can become Mrs. Kent Morris. What do you say?"

Her heart missed a beat.

He flashed her a grin that showed his nervousness at being on unfamiliar ground and completely melted her heart.

Josie applauded. "Come on, Faith. Spit it out. Say yes."

Faith smiled. "Yes. Yes. A million times, yes!"

In a heartbeat, she was in Kent's embrace. His mouth found hers, and her world was bathed in sunshine. She threw her arms around his neck and held him tight, not caring what his name was now or what it would become. The past was a closed book that never needed to be opened again. The future held infinite possibilities. She loved this man with all her heart, and now that she had him back in her arms, she'd treasure him always and never let him go.

• • •

They spent the night in Kent's hotel suite, and after a room service breakfast in bed, Kent ushered Faith into his rental car. He kissed her lightly. "I want to show you something," he said, then started the engine.

She gave him a puzzled look. "Animal, mineral, or vegetable? Bigger than a laptop? Faster than Superman?"

"Bigger than a laptop. Some vegetable, some mineral."

"How many guesses do I get?"

"None. Just relax and enjoy the ride. You'll find out where we're going when we get there."

He drove for about twenty minutes, gazing over at her frequently, unable to get his fill of looking at her. Finally recognizing the road where he should turn, he slowed the car, and pulled off onto the shoulder, and parked. "We walk from here."

She gazed around them. "Nice trees. You never told me you were into hiking."

He opened her door, took her hand, and led her down a narrow path shaded by maples and oaks. "I don't normally hike, but this destination is worth the effort."

They came out into a wildflower studded meadow on a knoll, and he heard her sharp intake of breath. "My God, what a fantastic view. I can see halfway across Chesapeake Bay." She pointed to their right. "And look over there, that must be the skyline of Norfolk."

He squeezed her hand. "Do you think you'd like to live here?"

She chuckled. "It's a fabulous spot, but a little Spartan. Did you bring a tent?"

"No, but we can build whatever kind of house you'd like. The site is twelve acres, it's ten minutes from the highway and twenty-two minutes from your job. When I move our corporate headquarters to Williamsburg, we'll both have an easy commute."

"You're moving the headquarters?"

"Most of the departments, yes. You said you love your job, and I won't ask you to give it up. Josie is here, and you'll want to see her and your nieces often. I can work from anywhere, and I might even open another store in the area." He captured her gaze. "What do you think? Can I build you a castle with enough bedrooms for a dozen children and a master suite where we can make love every day until we're too old to see the view?"

"I'd live in that tent if you'd live there with me."

He reached into his pocket, pulled out a ring box, and opened the lid. "Would you do me the honor of turning me into a Virginian, helping me teach our sons and daughters to sail, making the house we build on this patch of land into a true home?"

She nodded. "It sounds like a fabulous plan."

He took her hand and slipped the ring onto her finger.

When he looked up, tears were sparkling in her eyes. "I can't believe I'm so lucky to have found you," she said with a sigh. She glanced at the ring then leaned forward for a kiss. "I love you, Kent, with all my heart and every fiber of my being. Yes, I'd love to live here, fill our house with children and laughter. How soon can we start?"

He pulled a sheet of paper from his pocket and handed it to her. "As soon as you like. I already bought the acreage, and it's my engagement present to you."

She blinked. "What if I hadn't liked it?"

He grinned. "Then I'd buy you the rest of the state, maybe even the moon. My new goal in life is to spend every minute finding ways to make you happy."

"I have everything I need to be happy. I have a future

with you."

He kissed her long and deeply. Then he slipped his arm around her waist, she rested her head on his shoulder, and they stood contentedly gazing out at the sunlight sparkling on the waves in the bay.

After a moment, she raised up on tiptoes and whispered in his ear. "I wonder if it's too early to christen the master bedroom."

Acknowledgments

My thanks to:

The members of my Central Virginia Sisters in Crime critique group for reading and commenting on portions of this work.

My agent, Michelle Johnson, for doing her job well and having a sense of humor at the right moments.

The talented publishing team at Entangled who helped this manuscript travel the final miles of the road from idea to book.

About the Author

Kathleen Mix is a multi-published author of romance and romantic suspense. A degreed computer engineer, she has developed software ranging from submarine combat control systems to a database devoted to storks. But as an avid sailor and licensed charter boat captain, she eventually sailed off into the sunset and began her second career penning nonfiction sailing and travel articles. One day, while anchored in the Virgin Islands, she turned to writing fiction and found her true love. Kathleen now lives in Virginia with her husband and a spoiled Sheltie. For book excerpts and boat pictures visit www.kathleenmix.com.